T...
IN THE
DEUCE COURT

Frank Deford

Central Book Exchange
2017 South 1100 East
Salt Lake City, Utah 84106
485-3913

IVY BOOKS • NEW YORK

Ivy Books
Published by Ballantine Books
Copyright © 1986 by Frank Deford

Library of Congress Catalog Card Number: 85-28200

ISBN: 0-8041-0138-8

This edition published by arrangement with G.P. Putnam's Sons, a division
of The Putnam Publishing Group, Inc.

Manufactured in the United States of America

First Ivy Books Edition: July 1987

Miss Tantamount's
tennis outfit
has been designed
exclusively for
The Spy in the Deuce Court
by
Ted Tinling

For
Patsey Stephens
and
Bobby Roberts
and for
all the gang
down at
The Bethany Club Tennis

CONTENTS

THE BEGINNING

PUNTA DEL ESTE

Ronnie's mouth wandered away from Luisa Isabel's lips and found its way to one of her lollipop breasts, which he kissed. His hand moved to one of her thighs, softly, rubbing, probing . . . well, teasing really.

"Can we swim afterward?" he asked.

"Mmmm," she said, sort of. Despite all the men she had teased in her life, she didn't understand that, if only for a moment, Ronnie was doing that to her. But then, it was a natural enough question, for even above her heartbeat and the heavy breaths he took (for effect), they could both hear the Atlantic waves tumbling rhythmically, in threes, onto the shores below them. Probably, in fact, even if it had not been a time of such high ardor, probably the waves would have been enough by themselves to mute the sounds of the car pulling into the driveway, the door slamming shut, and the shoes of Luisa Isabel's husband, Gianni, crunching the gravel beneath them as he moved toward the patio door.

On an elbow now, Ronnie drew back from her. *"Qué pasa?"* she asked, sort of.

"I just wanted to look at you," he said. Now, the klieglight school of love, desire under the mazdas, was not for Ronnie Ratajczak, but there was always the journalist in him that needed a certain amount of revelation—even in life's most idyllic moments. And besides, all that aside, there was the specific: Ronnie adored women's bodies. Well, don't all men? No, no, no. That was his point. It amazed Ronnie how few men bothered to look anymore. A lifetime of stylized adult magazines—*adult*, for God's sake—and, eventually, all the swelling breasts, all the tilted chins and tilted nipples, all the navels and dimples, and the rococo pink parts, left an adult man viewing it all as merely some arctic tundra of skin.

When Felicity Tantamount had stunned him by posing in the altogether in *Playboy*, Ronnie had studiously avoided even glancing at the pictures—and for a man so naturally curious, that was all the more difficult. But no, if ever he were going to win Felicity, if ever he were to take her and undress her and drink in her every inch, he was not going to have that sullied by the posed memories of what had been arranged and glossed and brushed and tinted for the lascivious millions.

But never mind Felicity. For goodness' sake, he was in Luisa Isabel's bed, in her embrace, and she was herself beautiful, certifiably so. "You're absolutely beautiful," Ronnie said, "certifiably so." He ran a finger over her, down her. She was as dark as her name suggested, with silky raven hair, ebony eyes, and naturally tawny skin that had turned two shades to the chestnut under the January summer sun of the South Atlantic.

She sighed a special sigh back at him, and neither of them heard the door open downstairs, and Gianni, the big man—Gianni Grande, the cowboys at the ranch called him behind his back—enter the house and pad across the tile to the staircase. That was when he saw Ronnie's jacket, thrown over the arm of a chair, his billfold peeking out the breast pocket like a taxicab flag thrown up on a meter.

What an irony. What a dopey development. For the fact was that this really wasn't Ronnie's scene. Oh, now, to be sure, there had, through the years, been the odd other man's wife. For instance, these days he and Doreen, Mrs. Herbert Whitridge, the effusive executive director of IWOOTP, the International Women's Organization of Tennis Professionals, got it on regularly at widely distant venues about the globe. But cuckolding dictated safe surroundings, and Ronnie had agreed to come with Luisa Isabel to Punta only because she had promised him that her husband would be far away, unbeknownst, at their ranch in the Pampas. So, all right; Ronnie agreed. Otherwise, since there were enough unattached women all over the world who, to coin a phrase, flung themselves at him, there simply was no percentage in risking life and limb with a Mrs., a Señora, a Madame, a Frau.

Through the years, then, almost all his dalliances with the married were more in the line of business. No, Ronnie never thought of himself as a gigolo, but there were these moonlight(ing) excursions into escort professionalism. Always, though, it was Ronnie's own choice of company, and never anything so common as simple cash on the barrelhead. After all, there is nowadays a blurring of what exactly distinguishes paid personal services—something that Ronnie had learned all too well from the tennis players he wrote about.

It is, for example, against the rules to pay a tennis star any money to guarantee an appearance at a tournament. The player must show up and sing for supper, earning only on the court. However, if a promoter calls up a big star's agent and works a deal whereby the star will agree to show up at a department store for two hours for $100,000, there autographing posters for a face lotion the star endorses, said star has not been paid appearance money, has she? People would wonder why Felicity Tantamount, say, would suddenly fly halfway around the world to Nagoya to compete in a $50,000 tournament, when she could slip into her little Mercedes convertible and pop down to the Royal Albert Hall for a $200,000 tournament. "For the good of the game," Felicity would explain.

Same sort of thing with Ronnie's appearances here and there. He had stories to write, a living to earn. And when he met Luisa Isabel at the United States-Argentina Davis Cup matches over in Buenos Aires, and she offered to lend him her car and driver and provide him with all sorts of contacts to help him write some travel stories about Punta del Este—now, that wasn't just a gigolo's guarantee, was it?

He lined up three stories right away. There was "Inside Punta del Este—The Malibu of South America," for an American magazine. "Sexy Punta del Este—The Riviera of South America," for a European magazine. And "The Punta del Este No One Knows," for a South American airline magazine.

When Ronnie wrote about tennis, it was always under his own byline, but he used pen names for his travel pieces. Usually for American audiences he preferred the sophisticated Jean Louis Toulouse, while for British audiences he went with the casual Yankee moniker Randy Frazier. Now and again, if a British byline might add some requisite stuffiness (stories on old hotels, botanical gardens and/or estates and mansions), he turned to T. K. Forester Jr.; and occasionally the safe and bland Scandinavian Ian Lindstrom surfaced. When Ronnie thought that a travel story would be best served by a female appellation, he used either the all-business Audrey Levy-Tydings (if he had enough material left over, he was already considering "What the Single Woman Can Find in Punta del Este" for Audrey) or, for the racier audiences, Karen Winsome—which always included, in tandem with the byline, a portrait of the alleged Ms. Winsome, featuring a fetching blond with a bountiful bosom.

And so it was that Ronnie got his guarantee to come over from Buenos Aires to Punta: the transport, room and board, the company of a beautiful woman, all her contacts, and the clothes she bought him, including a whole new beach ensemble, a white linen suit to wear to the casino, and, as well, a tan one, just imported from Rome, that he might more properly wear when interviewing all the right and beautiful people of Punta. It never even occurred to Luisa Isabel, either, that she was financing Ronnie to do what ninety-nine percent of the men she knew in B.A. would leave their offices unattended all afternoon or their wives and children alone all night to do with her. "Don't

worry, Ronnie, I will not get in the way of your talent,''
she promised him.

Was Ronnie Ratajczak that attractive, that handsome,
that desirable?

Well, not that you could see. Certainly fair enough of
face, but nothing out of the ordinary. He was (possibly)
six feet tall, with all of his hair; for muscles he had posture.
He could put on a bathing suit in public or undress in
private without a worry . . . or, also, without a second
look. More than one woman had told Ronnie what a lovely
neck he had—an odd thing, to be sure, but a nice thing
unless it occurs to you that if you are complimented for a
neck there may not be much encouragement to comment
on other, more traditional parts. No, it was his wit and his
wits that got him by. Of course, a lot of men have all these
things, the whole basic package, save perhaps the neck,
and then they probably own some alternative equal to that:
outstanding hands, say, eyes, or calves; or an ability to
cook omelets or play the piano.

But what set Ronnie apart was his elusiveness. He was
a solid enough man, an enduring professional, but a wisp
of a person. And, as they say in England, at the end of the
day, that was what distinguished Ronnie, what made
women want him and men cotton to him. Most elusive
people frighten us a bit with their mystery, but Ronnie was
mysterious and safe alike, and no one had ever to feel
guarded in his presence.

Well, possibly excepting Felicity.

Ronnie Ratajczak was like a freebie walking through life,
and you could draw out of him whatever you wanted a
quick one of: a drink to pass the time; a nice competitive
game of doubles; a civil argument; a bit of interesting information; the right phone numbers; a raucous night on the
town, a light lunch, or a good screw. For example, it would
have flattered Ronnie—but really not surprised him—had
he known that Luisa Isabel had never been unfaithful before. Yet this woman had all but ravaged him when they
met, back in B.A. It was at the Jockey Club, at the official
Davis Cup party for the two teams. He had been standing

out on the fringe of the polo field chatting with Tom Gorman, the American captain, and Young Zack Harvey, the number-two U.S. Player, when she had wandered over. At first it was clear to Ronnie that she only cared for the players—the celebrities, the heroes—but by the time Gorman left to go meet the ambassador and Young Zack to grab a beer, Luisa Isabel had lost interest in them and was already asking Ronnie if he'd ever seen where the polo ponies were stabled.

Now, in Punta, she brought herself closer to him. There was not a great deal of room where they were, on the chaise, out on the balcony off the master bedroom. But so what? With the full Uruguayan moon and coursing waves, who cared that the premises were not so spacious as the beds the size of putting greens that could be found nowadays in condominiums and franchise motels the world over? If a man was to make love to a particularly beautiful woman for the first time on a midsummer's night at Punta del Este, aesthetics were a damn sight more important than accommodations. A trio of the largest waves of the evening now rolled in, thumping upon the beach, so that neither of them could possibly hear the mere creaking of an upstairs floorboard.

COZUMEL

At that moment, thousands of miles but just a handful of time zones away, Felicity Tantamount, who was really the only woman Ronnie had ever loved, except possibly for the teenage wife he had had briefly so long ago and far away, was in her suite high above the Caribbean. The curtains were drawn open, the view sweeping back to the Yucatán, but the man who was with Felicity had the more enviable vista of watching her put on and take off tennis outfits.

She held up another number and scrutinized it. "A bit too frilly, too twee perhaps," she decided.

"I forget: what's twee?" asked the man in a choppy American accent that clashed terribly with Felicity's British carillon tongue. Among her many attainments—and there were, after all, a great number of people who considered Felicity to be positively the most beautiful woman in all the world—she was able always to speak clearly, yet to do so in a dulcet murmur. Indeed, in one of his more poetic moments, Ronnie had described her voice (first to Felicity herself, then to his readers—on this occasion, *Paris Match*) as "a flaxen melody."

"Oh yes," Felicity said to the man, whose name was Dale Fable. "I forget how circumscribed your limited backwater vocabulary is." And she held up the dress again and examined it once more. "Well, I do like the back."

"What back?"

"Aha: that's why I like it, darling." She took off her bra and beckoned him to hand her another one.

"You know," Fable said, "there are worse things in life than being the man who sometimes holds Felicity Tantamount's bras."

"I should think you would rather say: there are worse things in life than being the man who is able sometimes to hold the things that Felicity Tantamount's bras hold." She winked at him and slipped into the little dress and examined herself in the mirror.

"Do you like it at all?"

"Well, it has possibilities. I like the *direction* they're going. Whose is this?" Fable got up, bade her turn around, and checked the label in the back.

"Allmählich," he told her.

"That's surprising. They haven't shown me anything near as nice so far. Still . . ." She fluffed at the fringe around the bosom. "Even the bloody Germans want to trick everything out so. Just because we're overrun with so bloody many dykes doesn't mean they have to foofoo me all up to prove my femininity."

"I really don't think that's an issue with anybody."

"Well, then, *tell* them, darling. Let them know straight-away that no matter how good a deal I'm offered, I'm not going to take it unless I like the design. I know all your bloody top-dollar American mentality, but I'm not going to agree to wear something I don't like—and like a lot."

"They've all been told that explicitly," Fable said.

"Well, perhaps you should tell them again. What do we have next?"

Fable held up a racy two-piece outfit, which looked more like a bathing suit than tennis wear. Felicity immediately wrinkled her nose at this design. It told volumes about their relationship that even though Felicity Tantamount was standing there before him in nothing but her underwear,

Fable still noticed that she had wrinkled her nose. "You don't like it? You haven't even tried it on."

"Listen, my love, I know a major part of this is to find something new and different, something in tennis clothes that's never been approached before. But, for God's sake, I'm playing tennis, not swimming in some aquacade."

"Won't you at least try it on, sweetie?"

"No, dammit." Felicity examined the top of the outfit more closely. There wasn't much to it. "I'll bet the Japanese did it, didn't they?" Fable nodded. The Japanese company in the competition was Geisha, which dressed Felicity now, and would for another few months, through the final Saturday of Wimbledon, when their three-year contract ran out. "Yeah, I figured it was them," Felicity went on. "Anything that features tits figures to be the Japanese. Nothing they like better than tall, fair Occidental women with big tits."

"And that certainly describes you."

"To a T. But I've done tits, Dale. I did *Playboy* and all that. Let the world know: I am through my tit phase."

"All right, all right. I'll tell Keiko what you're saying. Let's try another one," Fable said. There were still five sporting-goods companies left in the running to dress Felicity—all the great rivals in the world, save those from the United States. Even though Felicity was determined to take design over price, the American companies couldn't even get into the game—not without government subsidies. So that left Geisha, which hoped to get Felicity to renew their contract, and four new bidders: Allmählich from Germany, Triomphe from France, Grazia from Italy, and Banner Day from Korea. Each took turns submitting new designs and upping the bidding, making for a competition that had come to attract a great deal more interest than merely who won the tennis championships—which was inevitably Felicity, anyway.

With Dale Fable as her guide, Felicity was preparing to take the whole concept of celebrity endorsement to a new, high plain. She had leaked the details of their planning to Ronnie, and he had written them in *The Economist*, a revelation that may have peeved Fable—but not so much as the attention pleased him. He had been Felicity's manager before he became her lover as well, and now he sought, with her, to be as much a champion in his field as she was in hers. For Fable it was no longer enough that she drew down millions of dollars a year with Felicity Tantamount shoes and sweaters and socks and underwear, that she endorsed (as a sampling): an airline and an automobile, the resort at Cozumel where they were staying now, rackets, tampons, hair spray, a hotel chain, a ladies' razor, perfume, sweets, and the whole country of Grenada. No, with her new clothing contract he would have her move into a whole new realm. In a way, Felicity was so big that, effectively, she wouldn't be endorsing the product; the product would be endorsing her.

Already, throughout the world, she was known by her first name only: *Felicity*. There was but one. (How many baby girls had been named for her? Felicitys in the kindergarten classes of the late 1980's would elbow aside all the Jennifers and Sarahs, and maybe even the Marias in the Latin countries.) Her identity was universal, and at this one moment in history she was at the confluence of such beauty and athleticism that any appropriate sector of the market which did not ride the crest of her wave would be swept under it.

And now, as Fable watched, Felicity tried on the new Grazia creation. The possibility of landing her contract meant so much to the Italians that when the company had changed hands recently and a new top echelon of management was brought in, it was everywhere assumed that this had foremost to do with trying to win Felicity's favor. But she was left pretty much unmoved by this latest Grazia offering that he handed her. "Try it on anyway," Fable said. "I want to tell the new people exactly what you think."

"All right," she said, stepping into the skirt.

He examined it on Felicity, and he didn't like it either. "You know, darling," he said after a bit, "war is too important to be left to the generals."

"Yes, I know: Clemenceau. But what of it?"

"I've just been thinking. Just maybe, dressing you may be more than the sporting-goods companies can bite off and chew. Where is it written that just because you play in a tennis dress, a tennis-dress manufacturer has to be the one to dress you?"

"What do you mean, Dale?" Felicity said, and she reached around and took the zipper halfway up the back with her right hand, then caught it from the top with her left, zipped it all the way, and posed there in the Grazia.

"I mean: I think we can change all the rules with you," he said.

"Oh, that. I thought I'd already done that." She shrugged her shoulders, and Fable couldn't take it anymore, so he stepped forward to kiss her.

PUNTA DEL ESTE II

Poor Gianni. Had he come directly to the bedroom now, as had been his intention, he would have caught his wife and her visitor in a most vulnerable way, most indiscreetly, but, as familiar, shall we say, as Luisa Isabel had been with Ronnie, they had not yet been intimate—not in the technical, clinical, consummated, adulterous sense. If Gianni had only barged in now, Luisa Isabel could have cried and apologized—and thanked her husband for saving her from the ultimate weakness of the flesh just in the nick of time—and Ronnie could have scrambled for his trousers, snatched up his gorgeous matching luggage that IWOOTP had given him for Christmas two years ago, scurried down the stairs, and made for the airport or the Brazilian line, whichever seemed fastest.

Unfortunately for all concerned, however, Gianni Grande did not do as he originally planned. Instead, as he paused at the top of the stairs, he considered this man Ratajczak, who was seducing his dear, chaste wife. Ratajczak, Gianni thought, must be an uncommon human of many strengths to convince poor Luisa Isabel to give up years of fidelity to award him one night of pleasure. The *norteamericano* must be as physically prepossessing as he was obviously sinister. So, taking all this into account, at the top of the stairs Gianni headed the other way from the master bedroom, into his study, and there he took out his pistol from his desk and began to load it.

At the same moment, Ronnie discovered that Luisa Isabel was a screamer. She cried, she sighed, she oohed and aahed and let loose a stream of Spanish ecstasies that seemed to rend the heavens. Certainly they reached her husband's study, and since Gianni Grande was only too familiar with what brought forth these sounds, he lost all reason, and, clutching his loaded weapon, tore out of the room and down the hall, prepared to smash his bulk against the bedroom door should it be locked. In fact, it wasn't even latched, and when he slammed into the door, he knocked it back against the wall, all but tearing it from its hinges, as well as rocking ashtrays and bric-a-brac and picture frames, sending some crashing to the floor.

Adding to the mayhem, Gianni Grande stumbled over Ronnie's matching IWOOTP luggage, while Luisa Isabel screamed twice in quick succession: first in orgasmic delight, and then in abject fear when she realized who had joined her and Ronnie. As for Ronnie, he rolled off Luisa Isabel at the very height of his passion, and then could only stare at Gianni Grande as he came onto the balcony shaking his gun with anger.

Worse, neither Ronnie nor Luisa Isabel could cover themselves. There was no sheet, nothing on the chaise. Momentarily Ronnie thought about shielding the lady with his own self, but upon reflection, he decided that that was not likely to convey a proper image to the man with the gun. So he just lay there next to a sobbing Luisa Isabel, his own weapon standing straight, shining under the Uruguayan moon.

"*Puta*," Gianni said, and he spit on the floor. *Whore.* And then, to Ronnie, somewhat solicitously: "*Y usted: habla español?*"

"No, not really," Ronnie replied. "Not under these circumstances."

"Then I tell you in English, you son of a bitch: first, I shoot your little thing off"—and he waved the pistol disdainfully at Ronnie's slumping private parts—"and then I shoot you in the face, and then I shoot this trash you try to fuck. Okay?''

And slowly then, purposefully, Gianni Grande began to raise the pistol, aiming it square at Ronnie's crotch.

Damn, Ronnie thought: if this were only journalism instead of the real world, I could offer a retraction. But that was out. So: Jump up and (naked as a jaybird) try to attack a far larger, enraged bull of a man with a gun? No, no, no. That was no more possible than escape, which would merely entail rolling off the chaise, dodging bullets, dashing a few steps to the balcony wall, catapulting over it . . . and then crashing to a patio thirty feet below. Hmmmm.

Luckily, Luisa Isabel introduced a diversionary subject. "Please, Gianni," she cried in Spanish. "Please, this is the only time in my life."

"You promise me?"

"On our children." He paused. God knows he wanted to believe her, and she picked up on that. "On our children. On my mother. On your mother." Luisa Isabel was on a roll. "On the sweet Virgin."

"Okay, then maybe I only shoot him," Gianni declared. "I punish you forever, but I only shoot him. First his cock, then his brains." He turned to Ronnie and back to English. "You understand me?"

"I told you: *comprendo solamente pequeño*."

Right away, Gianni Grande roared. Ronnie should have said *poco*, not *pequeño*. He had said "I understand only small" instead of "I understand only a little." Gianni Grande loved it. Gee, he seemed to have a sense of humor after all. "*Pequeño*, huh? Heh, heh. *Pequeño?* That's the little." And he pointed again at Ronnie's dick, which had, at last, mercifully, stopped calling attention to itself and shrunk to near-invisibility.

"That's gratuitous," Ronnie said.

"What?"

"Hey, come on. You got the gun on me. You don't have to insult me in the bargain." Besides, in his own small journalist's mind, he didn't like the guy playing loose with the truth. From the various comparison shoppers who had shared his bed over the years, Ronnie understood that that part of him measured comfortably in the median range, rather like the rest of him.

But: enough chitchat. "Good-bye, you son of a bitch American."

"Wait, wait," Ronnie cried, even raising his hand in the stop-sign motion. "Don't shoot me because I'm an American. That would be a tragic error. This is no time for irony. I'm not American."

"You're not?"

"Canadian."

Unfortunately, Gianni Grande considered that for only a moment. "So, it was no passport fucked my wife. I still shoot you." And with even more precision, he pointed the pistol, carefully aiming it—whether his head or his balls, Ronnie really didn't care anymore.

"Good-bye," Luisa Isabel said, sobbing all the more now.

"Good-bye?" Ronnie asked.

She nodded. "Yes, when he makes up his mind to something . . ."

So, Ronnie thought, that's it. I better at least try to get away, and if he doesn't kill me in the process and I don't break my legs in the fall, I'll hobble off over the dune and hide in the waves. Or something like that. He closed his eyes, clutched his fists, and prepared to move in the next instant. But by that instant he was too late. The shot exploded in his ears, and he could only imagine that the process of death had begun.

℘

Instead, the bullet sped by Ronnie, and, far out, fell harmlessly to the bottom of the Atlantic.

Stunned at finding himself yet alive, Ronnie opened his eyes, just as Luisa Isabel screamed and Gianni Grande went "oooof!" The big man had not even seen what hit him from the side, so intent was he on aiming at Ronnie's private parts. The man who had slammed into Gianni Grande full-bore had knocked the pistol clear from his hand just as it went off, and then driven him against the side of the

French door with such force that it shattered much of the glass and left it hanging by the bottom hinge.

Gianni Grande was caught completely unaware and now was left totally defenseless. The stranger, who was rather nattily dressed, save for tennis shoes, walked over—strolled, you might even say—and dropped the big man, first with a roundhouse blow to the stomach, and then, when Gianni buckled under that, with an uppercut to the chin. He fell to his knees then, gasping, retching, his eyes bulging as if even they too were searching for air.

At near-leisure, then, the dapper little fellow leaned down, picked up the pistol, and held it on Gianni Grande. Luisa Isabel screamed, and so he turned back to reassure her. "No reason to fear, madam," he said gently in a straight British accent. "So long as he doesn't move a bloody muscle."

Gianni Grande gulped and gasped his acquiescence.

The Brit backed over to the balcony rail and called down, "All square up here, Rudy. Won't need you, thanks. Meet you at the car in a jiff."

"Righto," came the reply from the dark.

"Would have been there to help break your fall if you'd jumped," he said to Ronnie.

"Well, that's comforting to know."

Ronnie hadn't noticed before, but yet another intruder now stood in the doorway. He was as slim as a man could be without being skinny, and from the fine cut of his shirt and slacks, Ronnie thought at first glance that he might be Continental—or Argentine Continental anyhow. But as soon as he opened his mouth, the slim man was revealed as no less English than the others. "I'm sorry, Ronnie," he said. "We had no idea he had murder on his mind or we would never have cut it so close." Then he picked up the nightgown that Luisa Isabel had left on the chair in the bedroom. "Forgive me, señora, but this has happened so fast." Making sure to avert his eyes from her, he handed Luisa Isabel the gown. It was short and flimsy, the sort of thing a lady would choose for exciting a man, but it was better than nothing, and hastily she pulled it on, sat up, and drew up her knees.

The slim man then threw Ronnie his underpants and trousers, and turned back to Luisa Isabel. "Would you feel more comfortable coming with us?" he asked her. "I can have my man downstairs drive you, or we'll escort you. We'll offer you accommodations for the evening—quite safe and private—or choose your own hotel. Whatever."

Luisa Isabel only stared back, trying to keep her eyes from her husband. *"No, gracias,"* she sighed at last in a pale little voice.

"All right," the slim one said. "I'm sure your husband understands that if any harm were to come to you now . . ." He shrugged, allowing the rest to be imagined. From the floor, Gianni Grande nodded.

Then, almost like a soldier making a left-face on parade, the slim one squared up crisply to Ronnie. "And now, Mr. Ratajczak, if you will come with us." Ronnie grabbed up his shoes and shirt, even as the first intruder, the one who had saved his life, picked up his beautiful matching IWOOTP luggage and moved ahead as efficiently as any porter.

For just an instant, then, Ronnie paused. He wasn't quite sure what etiquette was required, but he did manage to shrug while giving Luisa Isabel one of those open-eyed, closed-mouth expressions: That's the way it goes. She studiously looked away, pondering her future as a wife and mother.

℗

In the car, the slim one climbed into the back seat with Ronnie. He apologized for the automobile, which was an old rattletrap. "I'm afraid that the estimable Punta Rent-A-Car offers little in the way of choice," he said. "The rich Argentines who come over usually keep one of their own cars here during the season, you see. So, for such a fancy place, there's very little demand for a hire car."

Ronnie agreed this must be so. Rudy was driving. The other man in the front seat, the one who had saved his life, turned around now. "We didn't forget these," he said, and he handed Ronnie his wallet and passport, cash—even the next-to-worthless Argentine coins he had brought over from B.A. "The rest of your belongings are in the boot."

"Thank you."

"I quite liked that new white suit," the man in the passenger seat up front said, and then he extended his hand. "I'm sorry. I'm John."

"Rudy here," said the driver, signaling in the rearview mirror.

"And I'm Colin," the thin one said, shaking Ronnie's hand.

"Yes, hello, Colin, and I'm . . . Oh, you know who I am."

"Yes, indeed we do, Mr. Ratajczak," Colin said, even to pronouncing it the correct North American way: Sometimes the more nasal A is simply right. Ratajczak, Polish in origin, is such a word. Ratta-jack. To soften it up in the British manner—Rotta-jock—doesn't have near the punch. Or the charm. As British as Felicity was, she always made sure to pronounce it the North American way whenever she introduced Ronnie.

"Never mind the 'Mister,' " Ronnie said to Colin. " 'Ronnie' will do fine."

"You prefer that to 'Ron,' do you?"

"Amongst friends, yes. I do use 'Ron' on some bylines, even 'Ronald K.' on some others who prefer more formality—"

"Yes, I see you're always that way in the *Sunday Times* magazine. I quite liked your piece there on the Dale Fable organization."

They seemed to know everything, but Ronnie let it pass, and just said thank you.

"You see, I really wouldn't know, myself. About names, I mean," Colin said. " 'Colin' isn't the sort of name that lends itself to the diminutive: I was 'Buster' as a small lad, but I never cared for that."

"No," Ronnie agreed.

"Well, enough of that for now," Colin decided. "As you might imagine, Ronnie, we have some business to discuss, but I suspect that after such an unsettling evening it would be better for all of us if we let you get a good night's rest."

Ronnie agreed.

"Of course, now, if you'd like a drink or two to wind down with, we'd be delighted to join you. We're all tennis fans here, you know. Like very much to know a bit of the inside about McEnroe, Felicity, of course, and the little Russian girl."

John turned around: "Always been a big admirer myself of young Wilander. Like Borg before him, so well-mannered."

Ronnie nodded and shifted uneasily: He didn't want to disagree with these fellows, whoever they might be, but, by the same token, after the events of the last incredible half-hour or so, he really wasn't in the mood for small talk and tennis gossip. "Look, if I could take a rain check on that," he said.

"Of course," said Colin. "I don't think I'd be up for a chat if I were you either."

"Thanks for understanding. It's been a very uneasy evening for me. I don't know about you fellows, but I've never been almost killed before."

They laughed, sort of chortled actually, in a way that suggested only one thing: they'd been almost killed all the time. And with that, as the old car banged along, Ronnie's guard came up for the first time. He had only just arrived in Punta this morning, and he didn't know much about the place, but he knew he was being driven away from it. The lights from the high-rises downtown, the casinos and hotels, were fading away.

Now, Punta del Este is simply enough named, the coastal point to the east of Montevideo, seventy-some miles away from the capital. North from Punta, it's another hundred miles or so up the coast to Brazil. Uruguay is a tiny little country, and it exists, the Argentines joke, only at their tolerance—providing, as it does, a convenient safe haven for fleeing Argentine politicians. Punta itself became fashionable only in the last couple decades, as the wealthy of Buenos Aires came to decide that their own traditional Argentine resort, Mar del Playa, had become too overrun with hoi polloi. So in high season, like now, January and February, the wealthy women of B.A. would spend whole weeks sunning on the Punta beaches, with their husbands popping over for weekends.

Ronnie couldn't help but be impressed with the architecture as they sped out of Punta. It was the most eclectic area he'd ever seen: a traditional European house next to a glassy modern, next to an adobe style, followed by some sort of Italian palazzo. But soon that was past, and they were driving through the northernmost part of Punta, from whence there was next to nothing, and then, Ronnie knew, nothing much at all—until finally there was Santa Vitoria do Palmar, in Brazil. He took a breath. It didn't seem like a good place to be alone with some violent strangers, however polite they might be. At last Ronnie couldn't wait any longer:

"If I can ask, where are you taking me?"

"Oh, not far," Colin replied. "We were looking for something away from the hurly-burly, something a bit more secluded. Quaint." Ronnie nodded, as if he had been consulted in these decisions.

"Here's the turn-down now," Rudy said, and he swung the car right, off the main road, down a rutted, rocky drive path. There seemed to be little inns scattered among the private cottages, but near the bottom of the hill, just before the beach, there was a somewhat larger place on the left, and Rudy piloted the old heap into one of the parking places there. The sign said "La Posta del Cangrejo."

"The inn of the crab," Colin translated. "But, I'm happy to say, a misnomer. Really quite nice, indigenous, modified American plan, reasonable, good access to the beach." He handed Ronnie a key as they got out. "We've checked you in already. Just grab what you need, and we'll get the balance of your luggage up to you tomorrow. You're on the second floor in the back, overlooking the ocean. Perhaps not as luxurious as your accommodations with La Señora, but then, here you'll be unmolested."

Ronnie nodded as Colin chuckled at his little joke. Then they all wished him a good night's sleep.

"Good night, Colin," Ronnie said. "Good night, John. Good night, Rudy." And he went up to his room, found it as agreeable as Colin had assured him, and fell fast asleep.

Ronnie awoke with the first rays of dawn streaming in on him, but fear and curiosity would have woken him early in any case. Danger was just not to Ronnie's appetite. He sought nothing that might force a hitherto unknown courage to surface, and he firmly believed that discretion was the better part of everything. Ironically, there was a widespread rumor abroad in the tennis community that Ronnie must be a CIA agent—after all, didn't he travel all over the world, always appear in comfort and the right company?—but anyone who knew Ronnie at all well appreciated that that was patently impossible. Ronnie Ratajczak a spy? The minimum perils attendant on writing about tennis and travel were quite enough for him.

Back in the early seventies he had worked for a time for Reuters in Africa, and he'd been obliged to write about some nasty skirmishes and massacres, but he was the follow-up fellow; he never assumed the intrepid role of the war correspondent at the front lines, dodging bullets for the sake of his readers and the honor of his profession. For Ronnie, camping out meant a Holiday Inn that didn't leave you a free plastic shower cap, and it had not been any jeopardy—simple boredom mostly—that had driven him out of Africa and into more genteel journalistic pursuits.

Ronnie's career had started on a small paper in a small town in Ontario, near where he grew up. One of the things he was assigned to cover was the town's Junior A hockey team. It got beaten in the playoffs—a huge upset, by Oshawa—and that crushed the town. It crushed Ronnie, and it crushed his wife, who taught home economics in the high school. Only, after a while Ronnie said: "This is ridiculous. This is just a boys' hockey team. We can't be this way about a boys' hockey team. We gotta go somewhere else, eh?'' Like most Canadians, Ronnie finished many sentences with an *eh* in those days.

His wife didn't have the foggiest idea why he would say such a thing, and so, finally, they agreed maybe he just better leave by himself. Eventually she married a carpenter and they had three wonderful children, which always proved, Ronnie said, that much good really could come out of a town's team losing in Junior A.

Soon he had stopped saying *eh* and found himself in Lusaka, where he got lucky and landed a job with Reuters. Mostly there he wrote stories about the railroad the Chinese were building for the Zambians. Zambia was landlocked, and the railroad would help them get their copper out. Ronnie wrote all the time about the railroad, until one day he realized the railroad in Zambia was very much like the Junior A hockey team in Ontario. Luckily for him, Arthur Ashe came through at just about that point on a tennis tour that was sponsored by the United States government. He was going all over Africa playing Stan Smith. Ronnie asked if he couldn't just hook onto the tour and write free-lance pieces, and everybody said fine, it wasn't classified or anything.

In his resignation wire to Reuters in Nairobi, he wrote: ''After a while, railroads are just like boys' hockey teams and elections and highway scandals and, I imagine, tennis.'' But, he thought, it would be interesting to find that out, and it rather had been, too, at least until he had almost got his balls and his brains shot away last night.

After lying there awhile sifting these reflections, Ronnie realized he was never going to drift back to sleep, and so he got up and strolled out on the balcony. The sun was already hot, but there was no one to be seen anywhere around La Posta del Cangrejo. There was a little dirt road that ran under his window, between the inn and the beach, but there was not a soul on it. Hmmm, must not be any Americans around, Ronnie thought to himself. Only in America or where The Dollar Was Strong and Americans abounded did he ever see any joggers, and this was clearly the ideal joggers' path. *Ergo:* no Americans.

But at that point Ronnie did see one man come around

the bend, walking. It was Colin, out on what used to be called a "constitutional," and he had gone more native this morning—a sport shirt and shorts, sandals—but Ronnie recognized his thin British form right away and waved. Colin saluted him back, and, so as not to wake anyone, he pantomimed drinking coffee and beckoned Ronnie to meet him on the Posta patio.

ℛ

After breakfast, John and Rudy joined them. They were in bathing suits and carried beach towels and little travel purses, and they all piled into the old rattletrap and headed back onto the road north again, going farther out of Punta. "Where exactly are we going?" Ronnie finally asked, trying unsuccessfully to be casual.

"Oh, now, don't be afraid of us," Colin said. "Surely we wouldn't have gone to all that bother to save you last night if we wished to harm you in the morning."

"Yes, but still, I can't imagine *why* you bothered with me."

"Don't worry."

"Yeah, I know, *más o menos*," Ronnie said.

"What's that mean?"

"The Argentines like to use it, which you might, too, if you'd been through the Perons, the *generales*, eight-hundred-percent inflation, and some disappearing loved ones. It means sort of . . ." He shrugged and waggled his right hand. "It means *más o menos*."

"Oh," said John.

"Yes, Ronnie's quite good with language," Colin told the others. "He ordered breakfast for me this morning."

"No, you only saw me at my best," Ronnie said. "I can order breakfast and drinks and ask what time the airplane leaves in just about every language known to man. But otherwise: nothing. *Más o menos*."

"Well, you certainly sounded awfully good," Colin said.

"I can always *sound* good," Ronnie explained. "I can read a newspaper and *sound* good, even if I don't have the

foggiest idea what I'm reading. But you see, I'm a journalist, and I have a good ear.''

''And they speak English everywhere.''

''Well, that's a *más o menos* too,'' Ronnie said. ''True,
someone speaks it. The airline clerks or the concierges. But
I miss it when I don't hear English around. Words are what
I work with, and if I can't deal with the ones around
me, I'm never really content. It's like beautiful women—''

''What is?'' John asked, suddenly interested.

''Me and words. Beautiful women are dealing foremost
in beauty. So they worry more about how they look, what
they wear. Only rationally, it should be the plainer ones
who would fuss about appearance. They're the ones who
need to. But it doesn't work that way. We concentrate on
what we have the most of or what we do the best with.
Well, my words are my clothes, and I don't ever dress
sloppily.''

''Well said,'' Colin piped in, as, just about then, Rudy
pulled the old heap off the road. They were some miles out
of Punta now, alongside a beach that appeared, from the
road, to be utterly deserted. And, as they saw for sure
when they came over the dunes, it was. ''Unspoiled,''
Ronnie remembered, was the standard word he always
avoided using in such cases for his travel pieces—only to
have the numbskulls who edited put ''unspoiled'' back,
more prominently, into a headline or caption.

They all four tripped along the warm sand, but Rudy
lugged a briefcase, and he separated from the rest of them.
Then he set up some distance from where Colin and John
bade Ronnie to sit down. After a time Ronnie noticed that
Rudy had produced binoculars, and from the dune where
he perched, he spied about—even if no form of life could
be seen anywhere on a beach so . . . unspoiled that even
the waves seemed to take on a static aspect, as if they were
part of a tableau.

''So what's up?'' Ronnie said when they settled down
on the towels.

''You don't have any idea what we want with you?''
Colin asked.

"Well, an idea, yes."

"Oh?"

"Yeah, I'll bet you want me to run cocaine. I travel a lot, I'm not suspected. I'm logical. I'm safe. But, sorry, I'm not inter—"

"A good guess," Colin interrupted, and John nodded assent. "Has anyone on the tennis circuit ever performed that function before?"

"You're asking me?"

"Strictly a professional question."

"It's just that most people only want to know who the lesbians in tennis are," Ronnie said. "It's nice to have a tennis question about drugs instead of homosexuality."

"Well, is there a lot of drug use?"

"Probably not as much as you'd imagine, given a young, affluent international crowd. But you see, it's an individual game, and the player who messes with drugs, loses—and quickly. In any team sport—football, basketball, whatever—you have a whole team to carry you for a while. Still, there was one player a couple years ago . . ."

"Top ten?" John asked.

"Uh-huh. Yeah. He got into cocaine heavy. His game went all to hell. All of a sudden, he couldn't beat anybody. Girlfriend dropped him. Worse: his doubles partner dropped him. So then he started couriering the stuff. I don't know if it was his original idea, but what he did was, he hollowed out one or two of his racket frames and carried the coke in there."

"Anybody ever catch him?" Colin asked.

"Oh no. I don't think he was ever suspected, much less searched. Nobody ever dares touch a player's rackets, anyhow. So he went on carrying the stuff for a year or so, but pretty soon he simply couldn't qualify to play, so eventually he had to drop off the tour. I think he has a teaching job somewhere down near Miami now."

"And that's the only case you know of?"

"Yeah, but I can't vouch for the whole tennis community. There's a lot of people traveling in this sport." Ronnie stopped, and looked square at Colin. "But you won't get me. I won't do it."

"No?"

"No way. I'm not foolish enough and money doesn't drive me that much. Besides, while this may surprise you, despite all my faults, I'm pretty honest. In the things that matter."

"Oh, how well we know that," Colin said, picking up some sand now and sifting it through his thumb and fingers, down the palm.

"You do?"

"Oh yes. Nobody can buy your byline, can they?"

"No, they can't." It was a coup for some small tournament in some corner of the world to get Ronnie Ratajczak to cover it. Promoters vied to bring him to their site, because his presence—even if he wrote critically of the endeavor—signaled a certain credibility—and hence prestige—which could be translated into better players showing up the next year. In a world where hotel rooms and airplane tickets were traded promiscuously, Ronnie flew almost everywhere on the cuff—and often first curtain—and his accommodations were usually taken care of quite generously. He preferred suites. He was invited to all the best parties, and most promoters had their wits about them sufficient to arrange introductions to the loveliest of available local beauties. Even Ronnie joked loudest himself that he was called "The Globe's Guest."

But all that only bought his appearance; it never influenced what he might write. No, no, no. "I'm a scoundrel," he said, rising up off his towel. "But I'm an honest scoundrel. And now, if you gentlemen will be so kind as to take me back to the Cangrejo, I'd like to pack and get out of Punta and set some distance between myself and a certain cuckolded husband."

"Wait, we're not through with you," Colin said.

"No. There is no discussion. I won't carry—"

"We haven't asked you to."

Ronnie said: "This isn't about drugs? You're not drugs?"

Colin shook his head. "All right, show him, John." And the little man reached into his purse and brought out two wallets. He handed one to Colin, and then withdrew from his own a badge. Colin did likewise. Ronnie looked. They were identical, save the identification numbers, both reading "CENTRAL INTELLIGENCE AGENCY," the letters standing out above the eagle and the Great Seal and the other embellishments which signified the government of the United States of America.

Ronnie had to laugh out loud. "Why are you laughing?" Colin snapped, rather irritated.

"Oh, just laughing at myself. It never occurred to me. I guess especially since you're all British."

"Well, after all, you don't need a social-security number to be a spy," Colin said. "And what do you say?"

"Spy? Me? No way. I'd run drugs first."

"Oh, come on now, we're not that bad."

"Nothing personal, Colin. But let me tell you, friend. If I were caught as a drug runner, people would say: that greedy bastard, Ratajczak. And that would be the end of it. It would only be my goose cooked. But as a spook . . . that's what you call it, isn't it?"

"You may if you like. 'Agent' will quite do, though."

"Okay: as a spy, a snoop, an agent, whatever. If I were caught then, then every international journalist in the world would be held in that much more suspicion. I told you I had scruples, and I won't do that to me or my colleagues."

"Very noble of you, Ronnie. But you don't have to be a spy."

"Yeah, well," Ronnie went on, "all the noble bullshit aside; I'm just not brave. I don't like . . . risk. And if ever I had suffered a momentary delusion about that, it was removed forever from me last evening. The real Ronnie Ratajczak was revealed to be a consummate coward. Now, come on, get me to the airport."

Colin literally tugged at Ronnie's trunks. "If words mean so bloody much to you, then listen to me. I just said: you don't have to be a spy."

"Well, fine. I'm not a spy now."

"Yes, but now you don't get paid for not being a spy."

"What *are* you talking about?" Ronnie asked.

"What I'm talking about is that we will pay you not to be a spy."

"Oh. Does that mean I can get more money from the Russians for *not* being a counterspy?"

Colin laughed. "Go on. Sit down. At least hear me out."

Curious now, Ronnie squatted back on his towel.

Colin took off his sunglasses and began: "Now, here's the situation, lad. Very simple. We have a spy who is presently occupied with a very important mission. Now, it just so happens that, in the next few months, as this mission develops—and, we hope, happily concludes—this agent must be in several of the places where the tennis tour will take you. You'll cross paths, even meet now and again . . . possibly. Certainly you'll deal with some of the same people."

"So I'm to understand that the spy—the real spy—is also someone on the tennis tour?"

"You're to understand nothing about our agent. Let's call this person Dana. A nice androgynous name. You are not even to know the gender."

"Why?"

"Because it does you no good to know. Rudy doesn't even know."

"Yeah, and if I'm caught, then they can't torture it out of me."

"Oh, come now, Ronnie. This isn't the bloody Spanish Inquisition anymore. We're in 1986, and there's very little of that sort of dramatics that go on in modern world-class espionage."

"Oh?"

"Listen, you're the one that didn't want to be a spy. Now, a moment later and you want to know who Dana is and what Dana's up to."

"I'm just naturally curious."

"Well, don't be. Just take the money and run."

"What money?"

"The money we're going to pay you not to be a spy."

"So, all right: why?"

"Because, as I started to say: Dana will be operating in your orbit. Coincidence. But John here, who's even more of a tennis buff than I am, put these coincidences together. And he's a great admirer of your work. As I am. And he'd once heard the gossip that you must be a spy. People like to believe that sort of thing. And so he thought: Well, let's take advantage of that and turn him into a spy."

"Life follows rumor," Ronnie said.

"It wouldn't be the first time. Besides, where better to place a spy than on the international tennis circuit? It's perfect. You can move over all the world without attracting notice. No one is inclined to suspect. You have access and a presumed innocence. And secrets are a damn sight easier to carry in a racket handle than cocaine."

"That's all true enough," Ronnie said.

"Absolutely," said Colin. "So if you agree, we'll then put out the word, surreptitiously, erroneously, in all the right places, that Ronnie Ratajczak is indeed a spy, and a very important one. And then, if that bait is taken, the bad guys—"

"The Russians?"

"I leave that to your imagination. Let's just say that it's neither the Portuguese nor the Peruvians. But whoever, those bad guys will follow you. They will watch you and tail you and—"

"And kill me dead."

"Oh heavens no. Why would they kill you, Ronnie? An agent is no good dead. The whole point is that they'll *think* they're onto us because they know you're a spy, and they'll keep watching you instead of Dana and waiting for you to do something, but of course, you won't. You'll just be writing stories and getting laid and whatnot—all the same things you do now."

"And Dana is home-free," John interjected.

"Absolutely," Colin said.

"In other words, I'm a decoy, a wood duck in the water."

"Oh, come on now, Ronnie, that's a wee bit strong."

He nodded. It was. It was just that he kept trying to talk

himself out of this fool thing, and he couldn't. "All right, then, I see. You just want me to be the guy playing the deuce court with a very strong partner."

"How's that now?" Colin asked, his eyebrows arching.

"It's in doubles. I mean, invariably the stronger player, or in any event the more assertive one, plays the left court. That's the advantage court, with almost all the decisive points—thirty-forty, forty-thirty, ad in, ad out. If you ever walk onto the court with someone you've just met for a game of doubles, if that person stations himself in the ad court, he'll say: 'You don't mind if I play this side, do you?' And of course he himself cares very much. He's determined to play that side. He's an ad-court player. Now, the typical deuce-court player is much more agreeable. He'll sort of wander to the middle of the court and say, 'Where do you want to play? I really don't care what side I'm on.' Although, in fact, he does. He wants the deuce court so the other fellow has to play the big points. Basically, you see, the deuce-court player sets up and the ad-court player finishes, for better or worse. It doesn't make any difference, the level of competition, pro or rinky-dink. The principle's the same, and you can tell a lot about anyone from what side he chooses to play in doubles."

"And what about you, Ronnie?" Colin asked. "Which side are you?"

"Oh, it's my nature that I'm one of those rare people who's perfectly happy playing either. I can play the ad court if my partner isn't comfortable there. Or the deuce. Maybe I could even be the spy in the deuce court for you."

"I would hope so. It would be a most lucrative game for you, and one of short duration. And by the time the bad guys figure out that you're not a spy, that they've just fallen for that same old tired rumor, Dana's assignment will be completed, and, I can assure you, the people of the United States of America and its allies in the free world—most particularly including your own Canada—will be most grateful to you for services rendered."

"How long?"

"These things are never precise. Missions don't expire

like American Express cards. But probably six months, give or take a bit. It's almost February now. Possibly as early as June, but more likely July.''

''How much?''

''Five thousand U.S. dollars a month.''

''Not enough,'' Ronnie said.

''Ten thousand,'' said Colin.

''Not enough,'' said Ronnie.

''Yes it is,'' said Colin.

''Yes it is,'' said Ronnie.

''So you'll do it?''

''No. I just said a fair exchange is no robbery. But now that I know the price, I want to know what exactly I have to do.''

''Nothing at all, except—''

''Aha! I knew it: a catch.''

''A very nice catch, thank you. Once a month you must meet us at a convenient location to pick up your stipend.''

''Why?''

''What better corroborates the fact that you are indeed in our employ? For example, right now Rudy has a camera, and at a signal, he'll snap our picture, which will eventually find its way into the right hands.''

''Which is to say, the wrong hands?''

''You're catching on, Ronnie.''

''But he hasn't shot yet? This could be incriminating.''

''Really, Mr. Ratajczak: if I wanted Rudy to take incriminating photographs, would I have revealed to you that he had a camera?''

''No, I guess not.''

''Sometimes,'' John said, ''I think you forget that we saved your bloody life last night.''

''I know. Excuse me. But things are moving quickly. Just as I've never been almost killed before, I've never been almost a spy before.''

''We understand,'' Colin said. ''It would have been easier if we could have caught up with you in Melbourne last month, or Tokyo, when things were less strained for you. But all this business had to be approved in Washington. I'm afraid there's red tape in everything, even in espionage.''

"Okay. And when the assignment is over, what then?'' Ronnie wanted to consider every possible reason not to say yes.

But Colin had every easy answer. "Whatever you choose,'' he said, more agreeably than ever. "You've two choices. First, you can ask us to put out the news, through the same old channels, that you're not a spy at all. They'll quickly forget all about you.''

"Really?'' Ronnie said. Could it be that easy? "You mean it's like Andy Warhol might say, that everybody will be a spy for fifteen minutes?''

"Something like that, yes. Or if you don't like that, the other alternative is that we can just let you lie fallow for a while, and then perhaps in time, if we need you again, we could do this all over.''

"It's too easy,'' Ronnie said.

"Yes. Yes, it is. For openers, there's ten thousand dollars, cash, in Rudy's briefcase.'' Ronnie shook his head. "But you're not any kind of pimp, Ronnie. You're a bloody patriot.''

"You've got all the answers,'' Ronnie said.

"Well, we knew about you. We knew you'd have all the questions,'' Colin said. "But come in with us, help the free world, make a very nice piece of change—and all just for being yourself and keeping a secret.''

"And picking up your payment every month,'' John added.

"Yes,'' Colin said. "Sometimes, Ronnie, it's just a sellers' market in these things.''

Ronnie mused this over for another few seconds. "All right, gentlemen,'' he said. "Bring Rudy over. I accept your generous offer not to be a spy.''

NEW
YORK

The Stuyvesant Knickerbocker Hotel, the refurbished old Stuy-Knick on Central Park South, was headquarters for the Virginia Slims championships, which meant the top eight players in the world—or "Felicity and the Seven Dwarfs," as Ronnie had characterized the cast a couple years ago. Since the Stuy-Knick got to be "headquarters" by giving rates, everyone in tennis was there. Indeed, when Ronnie turned around from the reception desk, he couldn't even point out his own Gucci IWOOTP luggage to the bellman because two identical matching sets sat side by side.

"Prosper," Ronnie called, making a very educated guess, and, sure enough, around the corner, tapping a pack of cigarettes he had just bought at the newsstand, came Prosper Hegginbosch.

"Ah, dear Ronnie," he cried, "our luggage must stop meeting like this." He lit another cigarette. Prosper was always smoking—even sometimes on odd-game breaks when he played—but he was happily tolerated by everyone, which was just as well, inasmuch as he was ubiquitous. A Swiss, Prosper was presently the second vice-president of the World Tennis Organization, and, the way these things were ordered, he would become first vice-president at the next meeting of the WTO, and president the year after that. The WTO ostensibly ran the sport, although whenever the demands of the major tournaments or the major promoters or the major stars conflicted with what the WTO had in mind, it was the WTO which artfully practiced capitulation.

Hegginbosch was the ideal tennis volunteer. Most recently, as an "observer" on the WTO Davis Cup Committee, he had successfully observed the matches in Buenos Aires. Among the handful of people that Doreen Whitridge, the executive director of IWOOTP—"Eye-Woofy," it was always called—had seen fit to give the expensive luggage to were Prosper and Ronnie, which was certainly appropriate inasmuch as no one not officially in the women's game saw so much of the ladies in action as these two travelers.

"Don't tell me you were on that flight from B.A.," Ronnie said. "Oh no," Prosper said. "I left the Argentine several days ago because I had to go up to Guayaquil. The Ecuadorean federation wanted an officer of the WTO to come and talk about the possibility of their hosting a South American clay-court championship. Very exciting stuff."

"Sounds like it," Ronnie said.

"Now, now, dear Ronnie: off the record for the present."

"My lips are sealed," Ronnie replied, well aware of the fact that the reason it was off-the-record was that anything Prosper said was sure to be patent nonsense. Prosper just drifted about the world building up frequent-flier mileage and proffering excuses about how he had to "serve international tennis."

Of course, it would have rocked Ronnie's ego a bit had he learned that the real reason for Prosper's going to Guayaquil was to rendezvous with Doreen Whitridge. Ronnie labored under the delusion that other than the aging Mr. Herbert Whitridge, only he shared Doreen's favors, just as Prosper believed that he alone was Doreen's lover outside of wedlock. But no, it was not only their devotion to women's tennis that had earned Prosper and Ronnie their magnificent matching IWOOTP luggage; it was, as well, their sustained personal service to Madam Executive Director.

But then, on this occasion at the hotel, poor Prosper was being bamboozled once again. No sooner had he and Ronnie made sure that they had the correct suitcases (they were actually switched in Tokyo once) than did the clerk at the front desk very quietly slip a note to a gentleman with a pencil-thin mustache who just happened to be moseying through the lobby. It was a short note, written on it only the four digits of the room number just assigned to Hegginbosch.

As for Ronnie, as soon as the bellman had shown him how the television set worked and then departed, he went directly to the phone and called Felicity. She owned a co-op on Park Avenue for her New York sojourns.

Dale Fable answered and went through the motions of inquiring about Ronnie's well-being. "I'll put Felice on," he said, "but we're literally going out the door right now to head down to the Garden and practice."

This was not precisely true. Felicity's limo was waiting downstairs to run her over to the Garden, but the newest design in her tennis-dress competition—Banner Day, the Korean company—had just arrived, and she and Fable wanted to see it on her. In fact, Fable had picked up the phone himself because Felicity happened to be slipping into it at that moment.

The new contract was becoming even more crucial with time. After all, Felicity had won nineteen consecutive Grand Slam singles tournaments. If she won the French championship at Paris early in June, it would be five in a row there, breaking Suzanne Lenglen's record, and then, if she won at Wimbledon a month later, it would be six in a row there, one more than the five straight Lenglen had won—and, effectively, be the last of the fields for Felicity to conquer. Oh yes, she was still only twenty-eight years old, and she might pile up a few more numbers here and there, but the fact was that Felicity had once played for herself, and now—through this Wimbledon—she was playing for history, and then, after that, Felicity would be playing for fun, until she left the game and went on about the rest of her life.

For what seemed ages now, she had overwhelmed the whole of women's tennis, and the fact that she stood five-feet-eleven and five-eighths in her panty-hose feet inevitably encouraged the men with microphones to intone that she was "larger than life."

Fable heard her tell Ronnie over the phone that she would meet him after practice, and he scrunched up his face in disgust. "There's really no need for that puerility," Felicity told him as soon as she hung up. "I was going to call him if he hadn't rung me. We loved each other once, and we've always been friends, and I want to tell Ronnie myself."

"There goes the secret," Fable groused. They were going to announce their wedding-to-be in just a few more days.

The first Mrs. Fable had agreed to a divorce, with a settlement that would rival the gross national product of several island nations, and so he and Felicity could be wed. The day was set, the first Monday in July, on Centre Court at Wimbledon, two days following the culmination of Felicity's career, when she would win her twenty-first consecutive Grand Slam title and celebrate her final vanquishing of Mlle. Lenglen with a sixth straight Wimbledon.

"Don't be snotty," Felicity snapped at Fable. "If there's one thing Ronnie can do when he's asked to, it's keep a secret." She turned her back to him so that he might zip her up. "Why does Ronnie bother you so?" she asked over her shoulder.

"I don't know. You loved him. That's enough."

Zipped, Felicity turned back to face him. And hugged him. "Well, stop thinking that, because I love you and we're going to be married for the rest of our lives. There's simply no one else, darling."

He squeezed her harder, burying his head in her hair. Felicity's hair. The color had been described so many times that there was no original way that a man encountering it for the first time could explain it. How many different ways can you say red? Fable (perhaps because he came from the Sun Belt) thought now of shining charcoal briquets. But whatever, it was utterly red, perfectly red, nothing but red. It was red like in the comic strips. That red. And because no one had ever seen a redhead quite like Felicity before, it led grown men (and women too, for that matter) to actually speculate about her pubic hair. It was reputed to be as fiery as that on her head, but fine and silky, a damask.

Even before all the talk got around, too, Felicity knew.

When she turned the tennis world (and several other worlds) on their ear by posing in *Playboy* when she was only twenty and had just won the first of her Grand Slam titles, she had no compunctions about going topless, but not for a moment would she reveal her nether regions to the photographer. Even now, too, she could drive Dale Fable crazy by threatening to pose in the altogether.

That time she did pose topless, Ronnie was traveling with the men's tour when *Playboy* came out, and of course it was all the talk there, in the locker rooms. When he finally did catch up with Felicity, a couple weeks later, in Hong Kong, he made the mistake of telling her that he couldn't stand looking at the photographs . . . and hadn't. She had come in a couple days early—it was just a four-woman weekend exhibition—and set aside a day to see the sights with Ronnie. She'd never been to Hong Kong before, never been anywhere in the Far East—this was shortly before she played in Australia for the first time and won her first Grand Slam title there at the Open in Melbourne—and she was still gaga-eyed at it all. After a rickshaw ride and Ladder Street, the trip on the Star ferry, all that, he had her hop on a public bus, and together they rode the rickety old doubledecker, winding down along the mountain road toward Repulse Bay.

Felicity was just acceding to number-one in the world, and of course she was a *cause célèbre* because of *Playboy*, but she wasn't universally known yet and could still do things and go places without being swamped. Because she was so beautiful and so striking, people assumed she had to be *somebody*, but that was a fun time: stares and whispers without the questions and autograph requests and general harassment. So she went everywhere; and because Ronnie had already been everywhere once before and because he loved her, it was as often as not he that she went everywhere with. Even now when Felicity returned to someplace, she would usually think first of Ronnie, because her memories of the place were invariably tied up with him—of eating and drinking with Ronnie, dancing maybe, shopping and sightseeing, doing all the things that lovers do. Except making love. That never

worked out. It was funny, though. It somehow made them
all the more complete that they weren't, but that everyone
else thought they were. It was their secret that they really
didn't have a secret.

This time, on the bus in Hong Kong, when they got to
Repulse Bay, he suddenly yanked her out of her seat and
down the steps. "Come on, we're going swimming, Felice." There was a wide public beach there, and, across
from it, a magnificent old hotel.

"Silly, I don't have a bathing suit."

"Oh, you're a fine one. You go around showing your
boobs to the world, but you hesitate to give a little peek to
a few sunbathers."

She couldn't tell whether he was kidding. He was. Only
they didn't know each other quite well enough just yet.
Ronnie took her into the Repulse Bay Hotel, which had
vintage Sydney Greenstreet ceiling fans, and they bought
bathing suits at the shop there, then skipped back over to
the beach and changed in the public bathhouses. Then they
swam and sunned. "Why did you pose?" Ronnie asked
after a long time, raising up on an elbow and looking down
upon her where she lay on her back, eyes closed tight to
the sun. Notwithstanding the red hair, Felicity never had
any freckles, and she tanned as smartly as any brunette.

"What?"

"I said: why don't you burn?"

"No you didn't. You said: why did I pose?"

"Well then, why did you say *what*?"

"I don't know, really. Buying time. Why did you change
the question?"

"I looked at you. You have red hair. You should burn."

"I also have green eyes."

"Oh?"

"If you have green eyes, you won't burn, no matter
what color your hair."

"Is that so?"

"That's what someone told me. And I don't burn."

"So, why did you pose?"

"To make a statement." "Statement" was a big word then.

"Come on," Ronnie said. "Bare boobs are a statement?"

"Well, maybe they are when your father's a man of the cloth," Felicity said. And then: "All right, why do *you* think I did it?"

"To upset me."

"Conceited. Don't you wish?"

"Uh-huh."

"Well, actually, love, I want very much to be the greatest tennis player who ever lived."

"What's that got to do with showing off your boobs?"

"Listen to me."

"Okay. I'm sorry."

"I mean, I don't see any reason why I can't be the very best that ever was."

"Oh, come on: better than a man?"

"Of course not. Not in the sense that I could beat Connors or Borg or Vilas or anybody. But I mean that I could be so much better than all the other women that, years from now, if there were some great, great men's player, people would say he's so much better than the other men that he's like Felicity Tantamount was amongst the women. That's what I mean. That's being the best of all, no matter what my plumbing may be.

"And so, years from now, someone will say: Well, how bloody good was she? Really? And they'll say: Well, she had the best forehand ever, and the—"

"Yes, yes." Ronnie picked it up. "And she had the best serve and the best overhead and the best volley. And she was strong and fast and smart as anyone who ever played the game, and she had courage and stamina and a terrific backhand—"

"That's right!" Felicity said. "*Only* a terrific backhand. Not the best. My bloody boobs get in the way. I can't hit a high backhand nearly as well as I can everything else. Especially down the line." She pantomimed trying to hit that shot for him, as she raised up on the towel.

The other players always tried to serve Felicity wide in the back court, kicking it up high if they could, and if they came in to the net, they would cover against her chipping crosscourt and force her to try to reach back and go down the line. "I would just want everybody to know what it was I was working against when I had to hit a backhand down the line."

Ronnie scrutinized her carefully. Was she putting him on? "Are you putting me on? You're telling me you posed topless so that tennis generations yet unborn would see, graphically, how difficult it was for you to make that one shot?"

"I told you I was making a statement." And she lay back down and smiled and closed her eyes again, and pretty soon it seemed that she was asleep, or at least in that sort of twilight fade that comes from lying in a bright sun in the middle of the day. On an impulse, Ronnie got up and walked back across the road to the Repulse Bay Hotel. There was a little gift shop there, nothing fancy, but he found a pretty little bracelet he liked, gold-plated, with a few shiny bijous, all very thin and plain, only thirty U.S. dollars. He brought it back to the beach.

She didn't even flinch when Ronnie's shadow crossed in front of her eyes, so he knelt down and very gently kissed her closed mouth. She stirred at that. "Why did you do that?" she asked him.

"You always hear about men stealing kisses. I never *stole* a kiss before." She sighed. "Come on, Felicity, run off with me."

"Oh, there's no point in that," she said, her eyes still closed. "You've already run off with yourself, and I'd just get in the way." She raised up on an elbow then and looked him square in the face. "Look, if I wanted to marry someone who was always moving about but not going anywhere, I'd marry another bloody tennis player, and then I'd have a man to hit with all the time."

He had to smile a bit at that, despite himself. For all the work he did in tennis, for all the tennis people he knew, he never let any of them see him play—much less actually go on the court with him. Felicity had tried, on all sorts of occasions, to get Ronnie to play some hit-and-giggle doubles with her, but he'd never even pick up a racket that was lying about when he was around tennis players. "Never play another man's game," he would say. "Especially if you're going to write about that man. Never eat with a gourmet, joke with a comedian, sleep with a whore, or swim with a swimmer." He liked to play tennis, too. He really did. But he never played around Felicity or anybody else in the game. He wouldn't even play with Prosper Hegginbosch—and he was sure he could bagel Prosper.

Quickly, though, he dropped the smile and looked directly at Felicity. "Is there really something wrong with having a job that keeps me on the move? That's a damn sight better than some nine-to-five routine in the same little dusty corner of the world."

"Rubbish. You don't move about because of your job, Ronnie. You move about because you don't want to stay still." Felicity reached out and with an index finger drew a line down his chest. "Understand, now, I do think you're really quite wonderful."

"You love me?" he asked.

"Oh, I should. And perhaps I do. But then, so what? Everybody loves Ronnie Ratajczak. You're so bloody charming. It's such a doddle for you, so easy. And it's quite wrong, really."

"What is?"

"To live off one's charm. You're a promiscuous person, Ronnie. I mean, even if you never went to bed with a soul, you'd still be promiscuous."

"Which is why you won't go to bed with me?"

"That's some of it, yes."

"And it's final?"

"Yes, we must only be friends. Good friends. Dear friends. The best of friends." She kissed him on the cheek. "Friends."

"All right, here, friend," Ronnie said, and he took the little bracelet out of the tissue paper and slipped it onto her wrist. "It's appropriate: something cheap to remember me by."

Felicity was up to the challenge. "Oh no, not cheap, my love. But yes, quite like you: lovely and flashy and unsubstantial." And she turned the bracelet around to catch the sun, then dropped her wrist, with it, across his knee. "I won't tell you anything foolish like I'll wear it always, forever and a day. But I'll wear it a lot. I'll even wear it when I play. And I'll never let on where it came from."

They looked at each other for a moment more, and then Felicity took his hand, and they hopped up and ran, broken-field, through the other sunbathers, into the warm waters of the South China Sea.

℧

At her co-op now, Felicity stepped away from Fable's lingering embrace. "Well, darling," she said, "whatcha think of the dress?"

"You know, I kinda like this mother," he said, fingering the fabric.

"Me too." The dress was essentially white, but there was red woven into it, cleverly, just enough to pick up Felicity's own highlights. "Would they allow this at Wimbledon, or is it too red?" she asked.

"Probably too red. But then, how much does that matter?" Fable said. His plan was to introduce Felicity's new dress in September, at the U.S. Open, and there—as in every other tournament in the world except Wimbledon— it was of no consequence whether or not the clothes had color in them. Only at Wimbledon, at the Championships, at the Fortnight, at the All-England Club, was it still required that the players dress "predominantly in white." Moreover, the way Fable had it figured out, by the time Wimbledon came around again next June, Felicity would be so much one with her new tennis dress that if the All-England required her to play in something else, that fiat would create even more interest in what she *hadn't* been allowed to wear.

Fable perceived his fiancée's new clothing contract as something revolutionary. It was not merely the money—literally millions more than anyone had ever dared ask for an endorsement. Felicity was going to turn the whole business upside down, for not only was she going to be wearing an outfit that had never been seen on the tennis courts before, but also she alone, in all the world, would be wearing it.

The way it had always worked before was exactly the opposite. The traditional conventional wisdom was that the star would be signed, in effect, to be a mannequin. The best players were commissioned to wear everyday tennis clothes, the idea being that someone who saw Ivan Lendl wearing harlequin shirts would pop over to the mall and rush into Sears and buy an Ivan Lendl harlequin shirt. Felicity's ploy meant the opposite, that no one would be able to buy a copy of her outfit for months. Oh, to be sure, cheap Taiwan knockoffs would probably start to appear, but Felicity's original would be so rare, so rich, so extraordinary, that no one would be fooled by imitations. And when the real design finally went on the market, the most fashionable players would be knocking each other aside in order to be the first at their club to own a Felicity.

Dale Fable was even demanding that whatever company signed Felicity could dress no other player, male or female. Grazia, the Italian bidder, had already advised Polly Hutton, who was the number-two player in the world, that if they won the competition to sign Felicity, they would have to buy up Polly's contract. This left Polly absolutely livid; she had been with Grazia for years. It was bad enough to be number-two to Felicity year in and year out, but now, to be tossed aside like an old shoe, to have her famous Polly Polka-Dot separates trashed, have her signature clothes all but ripped off her back, was the ultimate indignity. But the new management at Grazia was unmoved. Whatever company won the right to dress Felicity could have only her alone; she would be the epitome of institutional advertising, of class and beauty.

LONDON

In Chelsea, toward Earl's Court, off Brompton Road, up a dim flight of stairs, over a pub, Colin and John and Rudy entered the sparsely furnished office in the back. It was hardly the sort of place you would imagine for a CIA office, but then again, the CIA is not likely to hang out signs that say "CIA Headquarters" next to the Burger King at the Interchange Shopping Mall.

The only other man in the office was Gerry, British, like the others, a large hirsute fellow with Pickwickian puffs of hair sprouting out of his ears and massive eyebrows that dominated a fleshy, marsupial face. His voice, though, was uncommonly high, belying his size and his position. He was the man in charge. "Well," he piped up as soon as his colleagues entered the room. "Got a touch of color, did we?"

"Has some nice beaches, Punta," Colin replied. "We should have demanded it when we beat the bloody Argies out of the Falklands."

"A bit warmer than Bournemouth now, eh?"

"Rather," said Rudy, shaking Gerry's hand.

"And a lot of good-looking Argentine birds?"

"Well, as a matter of fact, we did get a bit lucky the last night," John said. "So nice, we stayed over an extra day."

"Have to get Washington to dock you boys a day's pay." Gerry laughed, and the three sat down in front of his desk, chuckling deferentially. That desk was about the only substantial item in the room, and on a gray February day the place was grim and colorless.

"Well, it's a bloody good thing all three of us made the trip," John said.

"That so?" said Gerry.

"Yes, our friend Mr. Ratajczak is quite a swordsman, and he got himself in bed with a lady whose old man appeared—with a gun, no less. Took a bit of a dust-up to extricate our lad."

"But you did?"

"Oh yes. And of course that left him quite in our debt. I think he would have gone along with our proposition anyway, but under the circumstances, he was more inclined to favor a CIA that saved his bloomin' skin."

"What did you make of him?"

"Quite what we expected, Gerry. He's direct, instinctively charming though—and notwithstanding that inclination to dip his wick, a man of some discretion, it seems. I think he'll be ideal for our purposes."

"Did he have any particular suspicions?"

"Not that you wouldn't imagine. Obviously, he wanted to know who the real spy might be," Colin said.

"And what did you tell him?"

"I told him that for his own sake, he'd best not know."

"Good."

"But certainly Ratajczak suspects that the real spy is involved in tennis, on the tour."

"A logical conclusion," Gerry said.

"Righto. So I told him that we would only refer to the spy as Dana and that he would never know even the correct sex."

"And he accepted that?"

"To a degree. He is a journalist, after all, and he'll keep trying to figure out who Dana is."

"So let him," Gerry chirped, and they all four laughed.

"And what's new at this end?" John asked.

"Well, unless you chaps can convince me otherwise, I've absolutely decided that we must act here—"

"Not Paris?" asked Rudy.

"No, we're home here, more familiar. I only think we'd add another layer of difficulty by trying to pull it off over there. Another month won't make that much difference."

"Well, it's another month to pay Ratajczak ten thousand dollars," Colin said.

"Money well spent," Gerry said. "Let's not be penny wise. By the time, uh, Operation Dana is over, Ratajczak's cost will seem small. We've got to hire a plane, we know that. The rent for the farmhouse. Some bribes, I might imagine. We still need to work it out properly at the right airfield. Besides, here's one more item I chanced upon yesterday."

He passed a folded copy of the *Telegraph* across the desk, and all three of the other men could see that Gerry had circled an advertisement for a house in Merton, the suburb that abuts Wimbledon. The owner was offering to rent during the Fortnight. "I think it would be an excellent idea to try to get this," Gerry said. "Have Cynthia answer the advert, tell the real-estate agents that she represents a top player who wants it during the Championships, and then have her put a binder down out of the special account."

"Anything else?" John asked.

"Yes indeed. We need to get some sort of a rundown on Dale Fable."

"Who?" Rudy asked.

"You know," said Colin. "Felicity Tantamount's manager."

"Quite a bit more than that, too, it seems," Gerry said. "It was in the *Star* the other day that Fable's divorce is going through in the States, and the betting is that he might well be Mr. Tantamount before too long. In any event, he's obviously very much at the center of things, and I'd like to know more about his finances. Also: his routines, habits, and weaknesses.

"Well, you can be damn sure he's not chasing other women," Colin said.

"No," said John. "Not the man who's in Felicity Tantamount's knickers."

NEW
YORK II

In her limousine, Felicity came over to meet Ronnie after practicing at the Garden. She rode with Amanda Cross, the publicity director for IWOOTP (who was also probably Ronnie's best friend), and a writer from *People* magazine, who had been harassing Amanda about the rumors that Felicity was going to get married. Felicity had to parry a couple extra minutes in the car with the reporter, but even then, she was right on time for Ronnie. But then, she never went long in practice anymore. What was the incentive? Felicity could never overcome the excess of her anatomy and get the backhand down the line perfect, so what otherwise was the point of spending an extra half-hour hitting endless practice shots so that she might beat the second-best player in the world 6–2, 6–2 instead of the current 6–3, 6–3?

Ronnie was alone at the bar when she came through the door. This was one of his favorite hangouts in New York, an Italian restaurant on the West Side that was warm and comfortable inside, but located amid a lot of litter and streetwalkers and general honky-tonk, so almost no one passing by would ever be the wiser. At this hour, too, the regular clientele was absent, for the business-lunch crowd had cleared out, and the early theater people wouldn't arrive for another couple hours. There wasn't even a bartender around to serve them—just Lino, the manager.

The last of the winter afternoon's light glinted in Felicity's glorious hair as she swung through the door, and, rapt at the sight, Ronnie only turned on his stool and watched her approach him without rising. "Oh, don't get up for a lady?" Felicity cracked. "Were you raised in a rabbit hutch?"

"I was only like a camera upon a tripod, rooted still, drinking in your surpassing beauty," he replied, rising at last, kissing the hand she proffered. Felicity wore a long fur coat over a canary-yellow tennis warm-up, snug winter boots, with her hair caught up in pins. Lino stepped in to take her coat. "Lino, this is Felicity Tantamount."

"Oh, I know Miss Tantamount," Lino cooed, kissing her hand. "It is my honor."

"It is everybody's," Ronnie said.

As Lino slipped the coat from her shoulders, Felicity arched her back. It was for no good reason, but the gesture was magnificent. "What can I bring you?" Lino asked her.

"She'll have a beer, just like yours truly," Ronnie said. "Felicity can be remarkably plebeian, and, notwithstanding the topography, one of the boys."

"You seem more acerbic than I remember you, love."

"Oh, it's nothing really," Ronnie replied, heaving resignation. "It's only that I just figured out why you're here. You're going to tell me that you're actually going to marry the son of a bitch." Felicity turned sharply and glared at Ronnie. He had the sense to dredge up enough grace to apologize. "I'm sorry—he said grudgingly," he said grudgingly.

"Don't worry," Felicity replied. "Dale understands you no better. He lives by power, you by wit. He lives by the year, you by the day. He—"

"—has you, I don't."

"Oh, Ronnie, don't rake the ashes again." He nodded. Lino poured her a beer, and another for Ronnie, who toasted her with a pilsner glass.

Her eyes said: Of course I remember.

The first time they were together, they drank beer, in Paris. Whoever thinks of Paris and beer? Would you buy a German perfume? Well, Ronnie and Felicity thought of Paris and beer. She was just short of her eighteenth birthday then, the day Ronnie discovered her. Almost nobody else knew she existed, as player or woman—and not only because she became them both almost at once. Every other female tennis player of any consequence in the world was ranked in the top ten before she menstruated, but Felicity had never even played the game as a child, and when she did take it up, she was all arms and legs, and it wasn't until her seventeenth year that she began to bring herself together.

Ronnie passed through London that March, writing about a men's doubles championship at the Albert Hall. It was the usual stuff, and when Panatta and some other Italian came on in the quarters against the Lloyd brothers, Ronnie snuck down the street to a pub. Another refugee from the doubles was there, an old Aussie second-stringer named Robin Truesdale, who had never won a place on the traveling squad with Harry Hopman but who always managed to get in enough draws to make people assume that he must have been one of the greater Aussies.

By now, Robin could always get one job or another, coaching—pro at a resort in Majorca for much of the year, summers in Gstaad, and a few extra bob from the British Lawn Association, helping the girl juniors. It was a paradox, but like many second-rate Aussies, Truesdale played a superb game of mixed doubles, even though the Australians were renowned as the worst chauvinists in the English-speaking world. They'd slough their poor women, whom they invariably referred to as Sheilas, over in a corner of the bar all night, down round after round—"shout" after "shout"—of beer by themselves, then scream out, "Come on, Sheila," and yank the lucky lass off to bed. But they could play mixed, the mates, and the second-stringers like Truesdale were in particular demand, because the top Aussies had singles and men's doubles to play and couldn't be bothered. Truesdale had an especially fine way of teaching young girls, and the British called on him.

Ronnie had known him for a while, matched a few shouts with him, chased a few Sheilas, and he was glad to find such good company, away from the desultory action in Albert Hall. "What's new?" he asked.

Truesdale thought for a moment, cocking his head, and then, with a studied air of portentousness he declared: "Take your bloody pad out, mate." Ronnie hesitated, but almost before he had the pad out of his pocket, Truesdale had snatched it from his hands, grabbed his ball-point, and in large letters that filled up a whole page, written down Felicity Tantamount's name. Ronnie studied it baffled. "That's the greatest women's tennis player in history," Truesdale declared.

"I never heard of her, Truedy," Ronnie said. The Aussies, in their prolonged adolescence of trooping the world, playing tennis for "expenses," always called themselves by schoolboy diminutives: Hoadie and Emmo, Dibbles, Dave-O, Newc, Rochie, Truedy, and so on.

"That's because nobody's heard of her, mate. She's only ranked eighth amongst the British girls. But she's almost ready. You write about her now, and they'll think you're a bloody genius."

Ronnie nodded, they had another beer, and after a while he forgot all about Truedy's tip and went back to suffer through the doubles. Truedy left for America a few days later, to take a job coaching the Omaha-Des Moines franchise in something called World Team Tennis, while Ronnie headed off to Greece to dash off some travel pieces about some unspoiled new Aegean beaches.

But then, later that year, one fine spring day, the second week of the French Open, Ronnie happened to glance at the schedule. It wasn't very scintillating—Kodes against Okker and Billie Jean vs. Morozova in the feature matches—so he glanced down the sheet, and sure enough, one name jumped out at him. Mlle. F. Tantamount, from Staunton-on-Swale, England, would be playing on some court in the farthest reaches of Roland Garros in a third-round junior match against the fourth seed, a chubby pre-pubescent blond from a place in Florida that had a "beach" at the end of its name. He remembered her: she hit two-handed backhands, just like Chris Evert, and won by attrition. And, more, he remembered Truedy's tip.

He ambled out there. Apart from the umpire, there were nine other people present.

Ronnie was immediately overwhelmed:

Felicity was gorgeous even then. He simply stared at her for the first few games, stunned that any of God's female creatures could embody such definition of prime musculature without taking anything away from the soft, graceful lines of traditional beauty. "My God," Ronnie said to himself, "you couldn't even order this with a credit card."

When he finally gained control of his senses sufficient to notice the tennis, he gathered that Felicity had lost the first set 6–2 and was down 3–0 in the second. She had no idea what she was doing on the slow and unfamiliar red-clay surface. The plump little blond from Florida just stood back and literally seemed dug in, the grubby dust from the courts covering her shoes, her socks, and nearly up to her calves, pounding passing shots by Felicity as she roared to the net, headstrong, point after point. Except on those occasions when her big serve won the point outright, Felicity was fodder against the little American. But Ronnie knew enough about tennis by this time to understand what Truedy had told him: Felicity had all the equipment. To be sure, she was at sea on this slow Continental surface, but play the same match indoors or on grass, on anything fast, and he knew the scores would be reversed. Besides, even in abject defeat there was a majesty to Mlle. Tantamount. Whereas her opponent was covered by the red dust, Felicity was barely nicked by it. It was as if she had played the two sets a foot above the ground, and even at the end, when she ran up to congratulate the victor, her shoes and socks remained pristine white and her tennis dress bore not a mark of perspiration.

Ronnie went up and introduced himself to her, saying he wanted to do a story about her for the London *Sunday Times*, which, so far had never printed a word of Ratajczak's.

"But I'm the one who lost," Felicity said.

"Yeah, but it won't happen again."

She considered him for a moment, and then she said: "I didn't know that anyone knew that but me."

Afterward he met her back at the little hotel where all

the British juniors were staying, and he took her over to
the Left Bank and interviewed her there. She wouldn't have
any wine because she had a doubles match the next day,
but she did chance a beer, because she had heard Truedy
talk often about how the Aussies swilled Fosters all night,
even before big matches, and then "pissed it all out of
their system." Felicity talked and talked—nobody had ever
asked before—spilling out all that was soon to become leg-
end, as first Ronnie and then everybody else wrote it:

Her growing up, a surprise only child, her father the
rector of St. Andrews of the Stream, Staunton-on-Swale—
The Vicar's Daughter, Ronnie dubbed her—a little river-
side town in Yorkshire. She never even held a racket till
she was twelve, when a parishioner died and left some odds
and ends to the church, and then Felicity taught herself the
game, picking up the rudiments from matches she saw on
the telly, practicing serves against the front door of the
church when her father was out on his pastoral calls. Then,
as she got better, Felicity cut the grass herself out in the
graveyard, tended to it and smoothed in the dips, then hit
against the tombstones, developing extraordinary accuracy
that way—hitting crosscourt, as it were, over to the Fow-
lers' large monument, down the line to the Barretts' smaller
stone, swinging topspin deep to the Thompson-family
markers, volleying off Lord and Lady Tucker's double-
width monument. Miss, and the old balls would scatter
away, demanding a long chase; with accuracy, they would
bounce back. Felicity learned to be very accurate indeed;
when she finally got a chance to play on a real tennis court,
it was amazing how easy the game seemed.

All this she spilled out to Ronnie in Paris, and all this
he scribbled down as fast as he could, sitting there with
their beers in the little café, until even early in June, only
a few weeks from the summer solstice, the night finally
crept in, and he had to walk her back to her hotel to honor
the team's curfew. After she was eliminated in the doubles,
he told her, he would take her out for a proper dinner.

That was a mistake: Felicity promptly lost the next day
in the doubles, dragging her poor partner down with her.

She had a terrible crush on Ronnie. He was just short of thirty then, the most stylish older man she had ever met in her life. She was almost eighteen, in Paris for the first time in her life, and as soon as she met him, all she wanted to do was cap the trip properly by going to bed with him.

℘

But now, in New York, at the bar, Felicity asked Lino to get her another beer, although she studiously announced to Ronnie that it would be her last. The news about her marrying Dale Fable had sat even worse with Ronnie than she had imagined, and for one of the very few times in their life, they were uncomfortable together. Desperately Ronnie changed the subject to shop talk, and she was glad to take the bait.

"Really, Felice: can anyone beat you? I mean, in the near future?"

"Oh, indeed, there's one," she replied devilishly.

"Who?"

"Come on, you're the bloody expert."

"Hmmm, not Polly?" he asked, fishing really.

"Hutton? She's chased me for so long that she has the least chance of the lot. If some night I was really off my game—a pulled muscle perhaps, the flu, jet lag, had my period terribly, whatever—Polly would be the one least able to take advantage."

"But she's the only one who even comes close to beating you."

"Ah, yes. I didn't say Polly couldn't come close. I just said she couldn't beat me. She's programmed to come close."

"I know. And close doesn't count except in horseshoes, hand grenades, and drive-in theaters." Felicity shook her head in mock agony. "How about Tiffany?" Ronnie asked.

Tiffany Rogers was the newest blond two-handed backhand specialist from the Sun Belt, just now moved up to fifth in the world, age seventeen. "No, not yet," Felicity said. "In fact, she'll probably slack off before long. The glamour's beginning to wear thin, and her mother's starting to drive her crazy, traveling with her. Only after the tedium of the tour sets in will we see what Tiffany's made of.

Already she talks in the locker room a lot about how she's ready to get laid. That's usually a tip-off that the routine is getting to her.''

"Well, at least she's straight."

"Oh yes, very much so," Felicity said. But then, with a sigh: "For now."

"And what does that mean?"

"Oh, come on, Ronnie, you know how it is. To be a woman athlete is still to be a contradiction in terms."

"You are some kind of feminine contradiction?"

"Obviously there are exceptions. But for most of the girls, they come out on the tour, and if they pop into a bar like the guys do, they're trash, and if they get laid like the guys do, they're nymphos. And if they don't: they're dykes. And after a while, it can almost be self-fulfilling. They find out that any guy they meet is just out to take advantage of them.'' She switched deftly to an American accent. '' 'Let's get it on, hon. Why not? Tomorrow you'll be in Kaycee.' Besides, the girls know that almost everybody is calling them leses behind their backs. And so, one night, somewhere, after a tough loss or a canceled flight, they'll be with some other player, and they'll realize for the first time how safe they feel with her, and loved. And so, what the hell, they choose that.'' Ronnie signaled for another beer. "There's an old French expression that says that an actress is more of a woman, but an actor is less of a man. The inverse is true with us: an athlete is more of a man, but a woman athlete is less of a . . ." Felicity stopped. "I thought we were talking tennis for a change."

"Oh yes: who can beat you? Well, since we're speaking of ladies of that persuasion, how about Consuelo?"

"Never."

"Diane?"

Felicity almost gagged. "Oh, come on, love, you're bonkers. You haven't the foggiest, have you?" Diane Bishop was the *other* topranked British player, all the more intimidated by Felicity for being linked by citizenship.

So Ronnie tried again. "Marissa took a set off you last time, in Houston."

"Uh-huh. And I had to fly up to Dallas that day for a photography session, and when I came back to Houston, Dale had just popped in from Tokyo, full of the most impatient ardor, and—"

"For God's sake, Felice, don't rub it in."

"It really wouldn't have mattered. Marissa is like so many other girls—or boys—who come onto the tour from some out-of-the-way place. She's just so glad to be playing tennis, on tour, away from Bolivia, that she's perfectly content just to get by. You see, that's the main difference between the Americans and the rest of us. If you're not from America, the goal is to stay on tour and spend all that time in the States. But what do the bloody Americans care about that? If they're not playing tennis in America, they're doing something else in America, like going to graduate school or selling real estate. So being on tour doesn't mean to Americans anywhere near what it does to the rest of us. What matters to them is *winning* on tour. It's a totally different perspective."

"God, I gotta write that down," Ronnie said, pulling out his pad. "I can use that somewhere." He looked up from his notes. "I'm reduced to picking up the pearls of wisdom that Miss Tantamount drops at the bar."

Felicity froze him before she spoke. "You know, Ronnie," she said at last, "you don't wear self-pity at all well."

He stiffened at that, mostly because he knew she was right, so then he took her hand and slapped his own face with it. "I'm sorry. Whatever, I've never been a whine."

"No."

"But I still can't figure out who it is you think can beat you."

"*Might* beat me."

"Ludmilla?" That meant Ludmilla Koryamov, the young Russian, just inside the top ten.

"No, the poor little thing."

"Little? She's damn near as tall as you."

"Yes, and I suppose that says something that I think of her as so fragile out there, so at a loss."

"At a loss for what?"

"For anything in tennis." Ludmilla had, in fact, started out as a basketball player, but then, at some Soviet sports academy, the psychologists and the tests had decided she would serve the USSR better as a tennis player, and so, overnight, they had stripped off her high tops and her satin shorts and put her in sneakers and separates. Ludmilla was such a natural athlete that she could beat most players, but she lacked an instinct for tennis, and that sort of spontaneous sense and feel for the game could never be installed by the Soviet sports mechanics, no matter how long they worked with her. Ludmilla traveled with a chaperone-coach named Nushka, who shared a room with her young charge and rarely let her out of her sight.

"You know, in fact, that she quite adores you," Felicity said.

"Who adores me? Present company excepted."

"Ludmilla. Almost any Western gentleman could deflower her with a pair of designer jeans or a trip to a disco. But you, Mr. Ratajczak, are part of a select group of sex symbols that includes Sting, Stefan Edburg and the guys on *Miami Vice*, who could have a go at Ludmilla without even troubling with the jeans or a visit to Studio Fifty-four."

$$\Omega$$

In fact, at that very moment, a few blocks away, on the twenty-seventh floor of the Stuyvesant-Knickerbocker, in the room Ludmilla shared with Nushka, the younger woman momentarily left the surveillance of the older and went into the bathroom. Wrapped in a T-shirt she carried, Ludmilla had with her what meager jewelry she owned, her papers, and perhaps two hundred dollars in cash. She took it all and stuffed it here and there about her person, into the pockets of her Triomphe sweatsuit, into her bra, her panties, wherever it wouldn't stick out. She came out of the bathroom then. Her purse was on a table across the way, and Ludmilla let it remain conspicuously there. Nushka was in a chair, glued to *The Price Is Right*, her favorite show next only to *Lifestyles of the Rich and Famous*. Nushka's colloquial English had picked up considerably, watching such shows, and she was obviously enthralled as Bob Barker welcomed another madcap American capitalist who had *come on down* to go for the Showcase. The question was: how much did a new portable microwave popcorn popper cost?

"Auntie," said Ludmilla as casually as she could, "I must get some Tampax."

Annoyed at this intrusion, barely glancing up, Nushka snapped: "That is three more days away for you."

"No, Auntie. This month it has begun already."

"Then use mine."

"You know yours are not best for me. Let me go down to the shop and buy some. I'll sign for it and come right back."

"Well, all right, but do not be long." Nushka had been accompanying Ludmilla for almost three years, and occasionally, in harried moments such as this one, with a Showcase on the line, she had come to permit her ward to move about by herself.

"Would you like some chocolate or something?"

"Yes, a Butterfingers or Snickers would be nice," Nushka said, and Ludmilla promised to get her one. Then she went out the door, and as soon as she had closed it behind her, she literally jumped up in the air and dashed down the hall to the elevator. When she pushed the down button, she immediately began to mutter. "Hurry, please, please," she said in Russian. And then: "Please, please," in English too, and "Thank you" when it came. Ludmilla was, of course, in the process of defecting.

॰

Ronnie was going bananas trying to discover the one player Felicity truly feared. He tried a few more names. "Come on," she said. "You're better than that. You knew I was good before anybody else did."

"Oh, that was just because Robin Truesdale tipped me."

Felicity put her hands on her hips and spoke like a schoolmistress. "You never told me that."

"Of course not. I never reveal my sources. Besides, Truedy had stopped coaching you by then."

"That was because he'd tried to get in my knickers."

"You never told me that."

"Of course not. I never reveal the names of the gentlemen who try to get into my knickers."

"Thank God. I couldn't live under the sheer weight of those numbers. You also haven't told me the name of that one player you think can beat you." Felicity crossed her arms and looked inscrutable. "God, who haven't I named?" Ronnie considered the list again. "Wait," he said. "Rina. Did I name Rina?"

"No."

"Is it she?"

"It is."

"Rina? But she's going backwards. What is she down to now—ninth or tenth?"

Felicity only shrugged. Rina Rodanya was from Bulgaria, and while she wasn't quite yet twenty, she'd been a regular on the tour for three years, having exploded out of nowhere. In fact, the first time she played Felicity, on clay in Florida, Rina caught the champion off guard and actually beat her. That turned out to be the only time Rina ever defeated Felicity, but it was enough to give her confidence, and soon she was in the top five, a semifinalist at both Paris and Flushing Meadows. Rina was a wonderful athlete, and unlike, say, Ludmilla, she had a sensitive feel for the game, and before long she began to exhibit even more of an aptitude for fast courts than for the slow clay on which she'd learned to play.

"Don't be put off by her slump," Felicity said. "Rina's just going through that phase when the excitement of seeing the world has faded and hasn't been replaced yet by the joy of greater success. I told you it would happen to Tiffany. It happens to just about everybody who travels . . . well, except you perhaps. You're the one strange duck who never seems to tire of the road, the pace, the—"

"We've gone through all that before, thank you," Ronnie said.

"All right, fair enough. Anyway, with Rina, the only real problem is Libor."

Libor Rodanya, Rina's coach and father, was a brute of a man, swarthy and mean, even occasionally smelly. Against odds of station and geography, he had somehow learned tennis and then had taught the game to his pretty little daughter—and all this up in the mountains, near the borders of Greece and Turkey, the most antediluvian reaches of Bulgaria. So Rina wasn't just a prodigy, she was *his* prodigy, and the government and the Bulgarian sports federation allowed Rina to go out on tour only because her father traveled with her.

"Even if he's her father, even if he taught her the game, I know she despises the bastard," Felicity said. "I can see it whenever he's near her. Some of the other girls are even quite sure he beats her when she plays poorly. One night . . . it was in Chicago after Marissa beat her in the quarters. Rina had been up a set and two breaks, and she still lost, and Ludmilla came up to me in the locker room and told me how scared Rina was, and she asked me if I could do anything."

"Could you?"

"I tried. Back at the hotel, I contrived to run into Libor in the lobby and ask him if he wouldn't join me in a nightcap. The bloody swine: you could see the smoke coming out of his ears, he was so mad. But he was flattered that I spoke to him, and I rather expect he thought I was propositioning him, so he let Rina go up to the room while he met me for a drink. I got him to talk about Bulgaria, and I told him what potential Rina had and how she must be treated gently—I emphasized that part—and, I don't know, it might have done some good. Maybe that one night he didn't beat her. Who knows? Anyway, the next day Ludmilla thanked me for Rina, for the effort."

℘

By now Ludmilla had reached the lobby of the Stuyvesant-Knickerbocker. She came off the elevator and headed left to the main lobby, which opened onto Central Park South, where she knew there was a cab rank. She knew she had to get a taxi right away, for she hadn't been able to bring an overcoat with her and couldn't go out in the freezing cold and search for one. It was February, the ice and dirty snow lingering from a storm three days previous.

And, indeed, as she neared the revolving doors, Ludmilla could see a couple of taxis waiting. But then, when she was only a few steps from the door, and freedom beyond, they came through the doors, disgorged smack in front of her. Rina and Libor.

Rina came first, carrying her rackets and gear. Libor was behind her, wrapped in a great furry coat, stomping against the cold. But as soon as he got into the lobby, he spied Ludmilla and stopped, glaring at her. She withered before him. The jig was up.

"Where is Nushka?" he growled.

"Upstairs. I only came down to get some things at the drugstore."

"Nushka should be with you."

"I'm a big girl, Libor."

"Perhaps too big, eh? You stay right here. I will call Nushka." And he marched over to the house phones across the lobby. Ludmilla looked at Rina, and their eyes caught in sympathy, and for an instant Ludmilla even thought to grab her hand and run out the door with her. She was sure Rina would come. But the taxis might be gone, and the thought of Libor running her down was somehow more frightening than being caught by the whole KGB. Suddenly another thought sprang into Ludmilla's mind. She dashed the few steps over to the reception desk.

"May I help you?" said the clerk.

"Meester Ratajczak's room, if you please," Ludmilla said. She looked back. Libor had slammed down the phone and was approaching.

"I'm afraid we can't give that information out."

"Oh, please, please. I haff very important interview. I am tennis player and Meester Ratajczak is journaleest. Please. He will be expecting me recently."

The clerk looked over at the guy he was working the desk with. It was certainly apparent that she was a foreign-kid tennis player, and not at all likely to be a jewel thief.

And she seemed so beside herself. "Ahh, give it to her, Dougie," the other clerk said, and Dougie punched up the question on his computer screen.

"Twenty-eight-fourteen," he said, and Ludmilla thanked him, turned around, and almost bumped into Libor.

"I just talked to Nushka. I will take you to shop," he barked, grabbing for her arm.

Ludmilla made the tears come and slapped at his hand. "No. You upset me so, I go back to Nushka," she sniffed, and before he could react to this affront, she tore past him to the elevators. But still, Libor was proud of his vigilance, and he was content to stand there and watch smugly until Ludmilla was safely boarded on an up car. Only then did he turn to fetch Rina.

Momentarily Ludmilla's finger paused before the light that signaled twenty-seven, her floor. But quickly she passed over it and pushed twenty-eight, and when she got off, she rushed to 2814 and knocked on the door. Then she banged. But of course Ronnie wasn't there. Ludmilla looked about desperately. She had called Rina the day before—in another room on this very floor. Before long, Libor would be alighting down the hall. She was trapped.

Luckily, however, at just that instant, down the corridor from the other end came a maid pushing one of those aluminum carts that hold such sundries as towels and Kleenex and sheets and shampoo samples and soaps and shower caps and strips of paper that prove the toilet seats are clean. Ludmilla sprinted down to her.

"Please, missus," she cried. "Forget key. Please, please!" And she signaled back toward 2814 while cocking an ear, waiting for the awful sound of an elevator arriving. The maid looked at her dubiously; she couldn't understand, inasmuch as this was New York and therefore such employees never speak the nation's official language. If this had been Brussels or Santiago, Djakarta or Rome, the maid would have known a few words of English. But it was only New York, and so there was a language problem. *"Qué, qué?"* she said. *What, what?*

"Yes," cried Ludmilla. "Key, key!"

"*Sí*, key," said the maid, pleased with herself.

"Yes, please."

"No, no," said the maid. "Key—lobby."

"Oh no, please, lady," Ludmilla said, and then, inspired, she grabbed her crotch and twisted her legs (and her face, too) and cried, "Period, period! Must go my room." And then, to cap off the performance, she made some sort of inserting motions.

That did it. Their shared biology bridged the language gap. "*Sí, sí, menstruo, menstruo!*" the maid cried, and suddenly she was an angel of mercy, abandoning her cart, brandishing her key ring, racing down the hall. They passed the elevator bay only seconds before an elevator arrived and Rina and Libor got out.

At 2814, Ronnie's room, the maid put the key in, turned the lock, and Ludmilla rushed inside, heading for the bathroom. As soon as she heard the door close, she came back out to the bed and fell across it, gasping. Libor had almost caught her.

Hardly had the maid let Ludmilla into Ronnie's room than Libor and Rina came off the elevator, turned the corner into the corridor, and entered their room down the hall. The phone was ringing, and Libor rushed to grab it. It was Nushka. *The Price Is Right* had just ended, and she wanted to know what was keeping Ludmilla.

♀

"Hey, Lino," Ronnie said, and the barman took his glass. "No, no, no. Not another one. Gimme a white wine."

"A white wine? You, Ronnie?"

"Yeah, I'm remembering something." Felicity had just left and he was remembering that night in Paris when they had their first proper evening together. She had tanked her doubles match and was out of the tournament, so she was sure it would be all right to have wine that night—and that's what they drank, and that's what Ronnie remembered.

They both had had just enough wine to reach that perfect estate between happy and tipsy—what used to be called, so neatly, "gay," before that came to mean something else—

and Felicity was going on and on about her life and her dreams, and in his own mind, Ronnie was trying to sort it all out, what he would put in the story for public consumption, what he would never share with anyone, all the time trying to keep in mind that she was still only seventeen, even if she was already the most beautiful woman he had ever met.

They walked back from the little café, and she was the one who made the advances, such as they were, now laying her head upon his shoulder, taking his hand for a moment, telling him how wonderful the evening was, giving him the credit for how magnificent Paris was, generally talking in that code that women have learned to use to signal men that they can start things. But Felicity could tell Ronnie was reluctant. She didn't know why, but she could sense that he was. So she would help him. She told him that she thought she had some photographs that someone had taken of her playing amid the tombstones back at Staunton-on-Swale, and she could lend them to him for the story.

It was a ruse. But Ronnie bit, of course, and he came up the stairs to her room. Now, as hotel rooms go, this was a quaint one. It was too warm, and the rug was a bit threadbare, but the shutters were perfect and held out all the light. European hotel rooms are always darker than American. Americans have invented just about everything to improve the light, but nothing to improve the dark.

Lino brought Ronnie the wine, but he barely noticed it before him. Instead, he was hearing Felicity close the shutters when she went into the hotel room in Paris at the top of the stairs. He had told her he would wait outside the door while she got the pictures, and that surprised her, inasmuch as she had gotten him this far, but then he surprised him by closing the door—only, of course, that didn't surprise him nearly as much as when she opened the door a few minutes later and stood there, not in the clothes she had worn to dinner, but clad only in a white peignoir that revealed everything, including how much she wanted him.

"You don't have to worry, Ronnie. I've had a boyfriend. I slept with him. I have the pill. It's all right." She drew him to her as she whispered the last sentence in the way people say those things in movies, although they never do in real life. But at this point Felicity had seen more of movies than she had real life.

"Listen," Ronnie said, making himself talk, because he knew that as long as he talked he could control himself, but once he stopped, he was a goner. "Listen, that's not all of it. I know you're only seventeen—"

"Actually, I'm almost eighteen. I do wish you'd look upon it in that way."

"Well, I certainly will. I'd *like* to look at it that way. But as I was saying: that's not the only thing. You see, there are scruples, Felicity. I mean, I know there're not many around these days, and you probably think journalists don't have any at all, but the fact is, I do have some, and when you're doing a story on someone, you don't sleep with her. Even as much as you'd like to. I want to write about you, and I'm going to be the first person ever to do that, and I want to get it right—exactly. I mean, for history and everything. And I can't do that if I make love to you."

"When will the story run?"

"Around Wimbledon, probably. When you get to Wimbledon, on the grass, you're going to beat somebody. I know. And you're going to be a big story, real fast."

"Can we make love then?"

"I think so," Ronnie said. "It's just that right now, 'The time is out of joint—' "

" '—O cursed spite, that ever I was born to set it right!' " Felicity said, picking up from him and finishing the quotation.

"You see? It's just the time. It's not you and it's not me and it's certainly not Paris."

"Yeah, I see. Ronnie?"

"Yes?"

"I don't know many men—grown men, as it were—but you're very different, aren't you?"

"Yeah, I guess I am. I don't know whether I'm good or bad, but I am different."

"I thought so."

"But then, you're very different too, Felicity. And I know for certain that you're neither good nor bad. You're great. And you remember that." He held her just a little bit closer then. "Now, kiss me . . . quickly," he said, and he pulled Felicity all the way to him, feeling her breasts crushed upon his chest, feeling her shake in his arms, feeling himself go limp all over except in the one place which acted altogether in opposition to the rest of him, and for just a moment he opened his mouth upon hers, and their lips swarmed upon one another, and tongues the same. Sharply then, without any warning, Ronnie broke free from her and turned away, opening the door, pausing only to look back and say: "Someday soon."

The whole way back to the hotel, Ronnie hit things: mailboxes, lampposts, trees, the palm of his other hand, whatever he could. "Fucking scruples," he said occasionally, out loud.

ॐ

That evening was a learning experience for Felicity, too. It was to be the only time in her life that a man ever resisted her, and she didn't care for it. But then, just as Ronnie had told her, she turned Wimbledon on its ear three weeks later, and by the time Billie Jean finally beat her in the quarter-finals, she was a sensation. It was "TANTAMOUNT TO VICTORY," "TANTAMOUNT TO GLORY" "TANTAMOUNT TO BEAUTIFUL," and every conceivable headline variation on this theme, the world over. Ronnie's piece in the London *Sunday Times* ran at mid-Fortnight, the day after Felicity clobbered Françoise Durr in the round of sixteen, and was devoured by everyone. Moreover, since Ronnie was suddenly identified as the only Tantamountologist extant, he was soon hired by other publications the world over to bring the tale up-to-date, add a new angle or two.

But just as quickly, she was gone from him—signed by Dale Fable and whisked away from Wimbledon by Fable Associates associates, flown to New York to spend the summer signing contracts and turning heads. She called Ronnie a couple of times, but before he even saw her again, a month later, early in August in Toronto at the Canadian Open, Felicity was already having her first real affair, with a young talk-show host she'd met as soon as she got to Hollywood.

Ronnie told her he could accept almost anything from her except bad taste. It wasn't long after that she agreed to pose for *Playboy*.

All of this was in the wine, and only Ronnie could see it. Finally he left it there, every drop of it. "Lino, sometimes wine is just for remembering, not for drinking," he declared. Outside, then, he let the arctic wind catch him and carry him up to the Stuy-Knick. He was freezing by the time he got inside. Worse, Libor Rodanya spotted him right away and ran up to accost him, stabbing a stubby finger into his chest. "All right," he sputtered, "where iss she?"

Dumfounded, Ronnie looked around—if not for support, then at least for some explanation. Instead, there were only three other men in the immediate area, and all of them seemed, to Ronnie, to be with Libor. And they were— rushed over from the Soviet embassy as soon as Libor had called with news of Ludmilla's defection.

"This is the one who knows," Libor told them stoutly. And, to Ronnie: "I know who you are and who you work for."

"Libor, what *are* you going on about?"

"You tell us where she is stay. In your room maybe? I know she no leave hotel."

Ronnie held his hands up to quiet Libor—not so much to accommodate the man in any way, but simply because he was curious. "Now, Libor: just first, you tell me *who*?"

"Ludmilla! You know this."

"Ludmilla? Now, you get this straight. I just got in from Buenos Aires. I haven't seen Ludmilla for three weeks. I don't know where she is or what you're talking about."

"You lie."

This time it was Ronnie who laid the finger on the other man's sternum. "Now, don't say that, Libor. Don't ever say that to me. Because let me tell you: I know all about you, pal."

Libor straightened, bristling at that. "What you know?"

"Oh, I've heard all about your ass. You and Rina. Don't push me, mister. Or I'll write what kind of a father you really are." Libor gulped. Felicity must have had it right on the button. The Bulgar shrank back, silenced, and Ronnie brushed past him to the elevator, on the way to his room, where, of course, he found Ludmilla, still sprawled on his bed.

℘

"Oh my God," Ronnie said. "What are you doing here?"

"I defect."

He slumped down on the bed next to her. "Ludmilla, that's terrific. But why did you defect to my room?"

"Because I hear you are spy," she said cheerfully. "Nushka and Libor say: Ronnie Ratajczak work for CIA."

"Well, Colin and his boys certainly get the word around fast," Ronnie mused. "They could give advertising lessons to Madison Avenue."

"Say what?"

"No, no. Just talking to myself."

"It hokay if you screw me, too," Ludmilla announced then. "That be hokay if you help me." She raised her hand to the zipper of her sweatsuit, but Ronnie reached up and drew it away.

"Ludmilla, let's work on one thing at a time, all right? You know, like at practice. Today we concentrate on the serve, tomorrow the backhand crosscourt. Today we concentrate on defecting."

"Screw maybe later?"

"Rain check," said Ronnie. The phone rang. The voice was clear, modulated English, enunciated precisely, the way it had been learned in school somewhere.

"Is Ludmilla in your room, Mr. Ratajczak?"

"Who is this?"

"This is a friend of Ludmilla's."

"Well, listen, friend of Ludmilla's, as I told Libor, I haven't seen her in three weeks, and I'm tired of being harassed. So if you will please leave me alone." And he banged the phone down.

"Who wass that?"

"Ludmilla, the problem is that if you heard I'm with the CIA—which I'm not, of course—but if you heard it, and Libor heard it, then a lot of people have also heard it, and that was, uh, somebody else who heard it."

It was fairly obvious that everybody from the Soviet consulate and the Soviet mission to the United Nations and every spare KGB operative assigned to the greater New York area had been called to the Stuy-Knick, and any minute they were going to stop being polite, and they were going to come up and bust into Ronnie's room, and so what if they were wrong and Ludmilla wasn't there, because then they'd just pay the hotel the couple hundred bucks' damage to the door. What was the worst that could happen if they busted a door down, irritated a Canadian journalist, and took a confused young tennis player back to her family and friends in Volgograd? Was the President going to cut off wheat sales and invade Afghanistan in retaliation?

Ronnie was thinking fast. If he called the police emergency number and explained that someone was defecting and he was expecting the KGB to invade his room, he might get a patrolman to visit Thursday week. Call Colin in London and tell him to contact the CIA in Manhattan? No, no, no. He was the one. He picked up the phone and dialed the hotel operator. "Connect me with Mrs. Amanda Cross, please. . . . Oh God, Manda, be there." She was. "Manda, it's Ronnie. Now, listen to me, sweetheart. I need you, and right now. Don't ask me any questions, just leave whatever you're doing and get down to my room: 2814. Yes, of course it's important. Right away. Wait, wait, wait. I want you to bring one thing with you—the sexiest, flimsiest nightgown you own . . . No, I'm not going to try to reconvert you to heterosexuality. Just, for once, do what I say and get your ass down here."

And, out of curiosity, she said yes and he hung up.

If Ronnie had a close friend on the tour, in tennis, in all the world, it was Amanda Cross. She was the public-relations director for IWOOTP, traveling to most of the tournaments, a lady who could be as bitchy as she was independent. It was no wonder they got along so well. Until five years before, when she had been thirty-five, Mrs. Cross was a respectable member of the Indianapolis Junior League, the mother of two well-scrubbed children who played tennis and soccer, went to ballet class and Sunday school, and listened to their mother read them stories before a roaring fire at night. Manda's husband was the affable Charles, known to all his friends at the Phi Delt house in Bloomington, where he had met Manda, as (of course) Chris. Chris Cross. It was a terrific way to start off on the telephone when he sold insurance: "Hi, this is Chris Cross." He always made the president's Round Table for selling seven figures a year. But . . .

. . . something was missing in Manda's life.

She tried volunteer work and one summer joined the Hostess Committee for the National Clay Courts, which were held in Indianapolis in the caldron of July every summer, the idea being to find out what South American dirt specialist could come to mid-America and win the clay-court championship of the United States when it was a hundred and twelve in the shade and all the good American players were playing in a hard-court tournament along the cool shores of Lake Winnipesaukee in New Hampshire. As a consequence, in succession, the U.S. Clay Courts was won by Gómez, López, Valásquez, Márquez, Narváez, and Ramirez, making this American national title look like the jockey standings at Aqueduct or Agua Caliente.

Also, in the name of true Midwestern hospitality, the Crosses agreed to "put up" a player at their house. Tennis players earn several hundred thousand dollars a year, but whenever they can, many of them will spring for a free bed and breakfast. Most particularly this included Felipe Miguel Jesús Luis Miranda, who brought new meaning to the word "freeload."

And, as the zephyrs of fate blow, Chris Cross was called away to a term-life seminar in Terre Haute for two days, and before Manda knew what had happened, she had gone to say good night to Felipe and tell him where the extra towels were, and she ended up in his bed, the first time in her fourteen and a half years of marriage that she had been unfaithful.

Teddy Tinling, the famous tennis-dress designer and the chief of protocol for the sport, has written that a person's sexual instincts are best revealed by his or her serve. Essentially, Tinling suggested, and certainly with regard to males, a serve is analogous to the act of insertion, and if ever this was proven true it was by Felipe Miranda, who could smash the boomingest serve ever seen, but who, in the vernacular, then did nothing with it. He wouldn't follow his serve in and try to work off it, but instead, after he unleashed this monster thrust, he would take a step back and begin to rally languidly from the baseline. And such was the manner in which he seduced Mrs. Cross, a development which left her with the worst of two worlds, disappointed and guilty alike. And so, by the next evening, when she found herself at a party given by the committee for the competitors, Manda was in a most vulnerable state.

There were almost no male players there, as is invariably the case at these affairs, but the female players had come out in abundance. The male players, wherever they be in the world, take off in all directions, abandoning the tennis environs, while the women huddle together, finding solace and company from each other—in the manner Felicity had described to Ronnie. A lot of promoters prefer to put on a men's tournament rather than a women's simply because they don't have to trouble doing a lot of extra things to entertain the men. It's like that old joke: what's the difference between drunks and alcoholics? Drunks don't have to go to meetings. The women players go to meetings.

And, wouldn't you know it. At the cocktail party, Manda struck up a delightful conversation with Patti Cabell—old Patticakes, who was still then number-six in the world. Patticakes was herself in a bit of a stew, inasmuch as she had just now broken up with Connie Guardina. Connie was a transsexual, originally Carl Guardina before the operation, but to her dismay, Connie had found that she had retained an interest in women even as she had become one herself. You could take the boy out of . . . As Ronnie had said one night in Perugia:

"Connie is the first case of penis nostalgia on record." In any event, Connie and Patticakes had traveled together for a year or more, that relationship crumbling only recently, and now here comes Patticakes to the party in Indianapolis, and there is Manda Cross, juicy and blond, tanned, a little plump perhaps, but only in a perfectly wholesome way—but so upset about something, so distracted, so open, so helpful, so naive she didn't even understand that she *might* be a latent homosexual, even as Patticakes talked her back to her hotel room and told her so and showed her so.

Manda was simply flabbergasted at what transpired. Felipe Miranda the night before, not to mention Chris Cross for almost fifteen years of nights, had never once managed to come close to achieving what Patticakes did in an hour. Patticakes turned Manda's pink parts into software, and not only that, Manda knew that Patticakes could put it back into the computer and punch up the best stuff whenever it was required again. "How?" Manda asked, as she lay there gurgling.

"Takes one to know one," Patticakes replied smugly.

So Manda owned up to what she must be and ran off from her husband and children two weeks later. The first time around the world as a woman's kept woman, it was terrific, but then it began to pale, and one night in Hilton Head (or was it Stuttgart?), Patticakes caught Manda on the training table with Mary Catherine Costello, the tour trainer, and that ended that.

Most housewives, when they become liberated, change their everyday life and go to work selling real estate, but Manda had evolved a great deal more, and now that she wasn't with Patticakes, she didn't just want to switch over and start bunking with Mary Catherine; she didn't want to be a tramp, for goodness' sake. But she couldn't just go back to old India-no-place, Indiana, either. Luckily, about that time the assistant publicity director for IWOOTP quit to take a job promoting an ice show—"It's a good change of pace," she said, "because in the ice show all the men are gay and the women are straight"—and, encouraged by Ronnie himself, Manda applied for the job, and was given it, on a temporary basis anyhow.

As Ronnie had expected, though, Manda was terrific at the job, and within a few weeks she was hired permanently. Not only was Manda clever and efficient, but all the new male writers would take a shot at her, and all the ones who knew she was a lesbian figured she only needed one night with yours truly to get her head back on straight, so with all this attention paid her, Manda got a lot of great publicity for the IWOOTP and for women's tennis, so eventually she was promoted and became the chief publicity director.

Ronnie and she got along wonderfully, right from the start. He never even talked about getting into her pants; he never even had a few drinks and got *theoretical.* "I've just never been much of a missionary," he told her one night in Rio, at the Federation Cup, and that was that. And he was vital to her. She had gone through so much in such a short period of time, and she needed someone she could talk to—without all the leering and speculating and patronizing that all too often happened when she dared unburden herself.

Every now and then, in fact, when accommodations were tight or Ronnie couldn't get the promoter to set him up with a freebie, Manda would let him share her room. Once even, in Johannesburg, when there was a drought, Manda and Ronnie shared showers, soaping each other's backs. They had become very good pals, and they used each other in all the right ways. So when he asked her to come to his room at the Stuy-Knick, Ronnie knew she would.

She not only showed up immediately but also brought a wonderful negligee. It was peach-colored, flimsy, with lace, and a string that tied easily at the bodice, for quick access. "Perfect," he said. "Come right in and slip into that."

"Now?"

"Right this very moment." And Ronnie pulled Manda into the room, where, of course, she immediately spotted Ludmilla lying on the bed in her sweatsuit. The two women went bug-eyed at each other.

"My God, Ronnie," Manda said. "I never thought you'd go kinky. But I'll say this for you, kiddo: for a rookie in *ménage à trois*, you're an all-star: a Communist virgin and an Indiana dyke."

He answered in his best mock-melodramatic voice: "You must believe me, darling, that this is not what it appears to be."

"I'll still respect you in the morning," she said, kicking off her shoes and unzipping her slacks.

"It's all right, Ludmilla," Ronnie explained. "Manda and I used to share the same foxhole when we were in the Israeli army together."

Ludmilla was not fazed. "You want me take off my clothes too?"

"No, dear. I'm just going to want you to get *under* the bed."

Manda considered that. "Ronnie, before I expose my person any further, what the fuck is going on?"

"Tell her, Ludmilla."

"I defect."

"Not today you don't," Manda shot back. "You play Hutton in the second match at the Garden tonight."

"Sorry," Ronnie said. "You'll have to scare up a replacement doubles or an old-timers' match. Ludmilla either defects or Ludmilla gets caught. Either way, Ludmilla doesn't play any tennis tonight."

"Well, okay, but why is she here? Why didn't she go to the American embassy?"

"Because we're in America, and there are no American embassies in America."

"All right, all right. How 'bout the Swiss embassy?"

"Come on, be serious, Manda. Just keep taking your clothes off and listen. Because we've got to get Ludmilla out of here—"

"What's this *we*, Kemo Sabe?"

"You and me. And it's not going to be easy because every Russian cowboy in New York has been sent over here and they're searching this hotel right now, and worse than that: our dear Bulgarian friend is convinced Ludmilla's in this room."

"A good convince," Manda said, throwing her slacks on a chair and pulling off her turtleneck.

"Right, so the first thing we've got to do is con Libor

and the others into thinking she's not here so that after that we can get her the hell out of here.''

''And how are you going to do that, pray?''

''Well, I've got an idea. I may not know anything about espionage, but I do know hotels, God knows. Only I need you.''

''Okay, I can get a good press release out on it,'' Manda said, and she undid her bra and slipped out of her panties. Ludmilla watched with fascination. ''Anything for PR, kid.'' Ronnie chucked her the negligee then, and she started to tie the bow at the bodice.

''No. Leave it untied,'' he said. ''We're supposed to be making love.''

''We are?''

''Yeah. Lace untied. And tousle your hair.''

''Tousle it?''

''Tousle it.'' Ronnie ruffled his own hair then, and took off his shirt. Then he sat down on the bed and started on his shoes and socks.

''Be still, my heart,'' Manda cooed. Ludmilla watched, much more involved now in Ronnie's undressing than in this business about defection.

''All right, Ludmilla, as soon as we hear someone at the door, you go under the bed, and all my clothes come off. You understand?''

''I sink so, yes.''

Manda frowned. ''Under the bed? That went out with high button shoes.''

''We gotta put her somewhere and hope we can bluff 'em,'' Ronnie explained, pulling off his pants, getting down to a pair of skimpy powder-blue briefs.

''Hmmm, not a bad neighborhood,'' Manda said, gesturing to his loins.

''Too bad you can't ever get a place to stay there,'' he replied.

That was when the knock on the door came.

Ronnie pointed under the bed for Ludmilla. ''Go away!'' he cried out, sounding as irritated as he possibly could.

''It's very important,'' said the voice. It was a man's.

Ludmilla climbed under the bed and then Ronnie pulled off his underpants and beckoned for Amanda to get into the bed.

"We don't need the room to be made up now," Ronnie called out, and as he did, he took the sheets and threw them about, knocked a pillow on the floor, and mussed up his hair some more.

"This is not a maid. This is urgent, Mr. Ratajczak," the voice said, sounding all the more demanding. "The manager requires you to open."

"All right, all right," Ronnie said out loud, and then, pecking Manda on her cheek, he whispered: "The rats are taking the cheese."

At the door, he cracked it as much as the chain would allow. He could see one well-dressed fellow, only guessing how many more there might be out of his view. "It is imperative that I talk to you," the man said.

"But this is not the time. You've interrupted me."

"You must open the door."

"But I haven't any clothes on."

That was when the barrel of the pistol came through the crack, pointed directly at his head. "Open." Ronnie closed it just enough to get the chain off, and as soon as he did, the man with the gun and his two colleagues barged through the door. Ronnie crossed his hands over his privates in an excellent display of modesty.

Manda was even better. First she shrieked. Then she cried out: "Help me, darling!" And then she tossed the sheet back, grabbed for her negligee, and holding it before her as best she could, her large bosom bouncing spiritedly, she scrambled out of the bed, losing her balance as she hit the ground running—so neatly that Ronnie, in admiration, couldn't tell whether it was a planned part of the act or not—then regaining it, hopping for a stride or two on the right foot, obliquing to find a hiding place behind Ronnie. Fearfully she peeked out at the Russians behind Ronnie's bare ass.

By now the intruders were already retreating from the room, bowing, gulping, apologizing. They were going to raise hell with Libor for this. "I'm sorry. Please excuse us, madam," the leader said. "We have made a terrible mistake."

"Get out of here, you pigs," Ronnie cried then, all bravado now, slamming the door and locking it after the Russkies. By the time Ludmilla scurried out from under the bed, she faced the rather unlikely vision of a man and a woman standing starkers in the middle of the room embracing each other in warm partnership, laughing and hugging in fraternal delight.

⁓

After Ronnie and Manda got their clothes back on, he bade the ladies to wait, and then he went down the hall till he found the maid, a tiny little thing, tidying up 2822 while she concentrated most of her attention on a rerun of *Little House on the Prairie* on Channel 11. *"Un momento, por favor?"* Ronnie said, and, by displaying his key and suggesting a sense of urgency, he got her to follow him back to his room.

There Ronnie introduced the maid to Ludmilla and Manda, happily eliciting the information that her name was Pilar. From years of interviewing, Ronnie had discovered that people tended to be more forthcoming if personal address were applied. It certainly wasn't rational, but it was human nature. "Pilar," he said, laying a hundred-dollar bill in front of her, "Pilar, *por usted*, Pilar. For you." But, even comforted by the sound of her name, the maid eyed Ronnie suspiciously.

"Qué? What I do?"

Ronnie beamed. "Do, Pilar? Do? *Nada*, Pilar. Nothing at all." And for emphasis he turned to Manda. "Right? Pilar doesn't have to *do* anything, does she?" Manda nodded, and so, for that matter, did Ludmilla, although, in fact, since Ronnie had neglected to advise them what he was up to, they didn't know. And it was getting harder, because he couldn't remember the word for "dress," let alone for "borrow"— which made it very difficult for him to tell Pilar that he wanted to pay her the hundred dollars to borrow her dress.

So instead he went and got his own bathrobe and showed it to Pilar. "Pilar, you take this for *treinta minutos*. And the hundred dollars, Pilar. You keep the hundred dollars,

Pilar. Understand, Pilar? And all we want is . . . your clothes, your *ropas*—I mean, just your dress, Pilar.''

Well, it was a good try, anyway.

"*Ropa?*" Pilar screamed, crossing her arms across her breasts. Her worst fears had been realized: she was in the clutches of a kinky SM gang. They wanted to take off her clothes.

"No, no, Pilar," Ronnie said. "Switch, borrow. *Solamente treinta minutos,* Pilar. No touch you." Only, unfortunately, just as he said this, Pilar decided to bolt for the door, and as she did, Ronnie instinctively reached out to stop her, touching her—holding her—by the shoulder. Promptly she began to scream. Bloody murder.

Ronnie didn't wait. With one hand he reached behind and threw the door closed. With the other he grabbed Pilar around the waist, and then, pulling his free hand back from the door, he clapped it over her mouth. Pilar tried to scream, she tried to bite him, but he was able to hold the tiny woman at bay.

When Manda finally gained her senses, she said, "Ronnie, what the fuck?"

Ludmilla, not being so articulate in English, could only stand stock-still, gaga.

"For Chrissake, will you two stupid broads help me?" Ronnie said. "Get me a towel."

"Oh sure," Manda said. "Then I'll be an accomplice."

"Don't be technical. It's gonna be okay." And then he twisted his head around to where he could show Pilar how sincere he really was. "I promise you, Pilar, it's going to be okay, Pilar. And you drive such a hard bargain, you're going to make a thousand dollars. A thousand *dolares*, Pilar." He couldn't remember the word for "thousand," either.

Unfortunately, Pilar's terrified eyes did not suggest that she believed this promise, and neither was her faith strengthened when Manda came back with a face towel and Ronnie jammed it, as a gag, into Pilar's mouth. "Now what, leader?" Manda asked.

"You and Ludmilla have gotta get her out of her clothes."

"*We* gotta?"

"That's right. We don't want this to look wrong. I can't be here for a thing like that. I'll come back when you've got her in my robe."

"Oh, great. We kidnap a maid, grab her, manhandle her, stick a towel in her mouth, and then you're worried about propriety."

"Look, Pilar's going to make a thousand out of this." And he reached deep into the recesses of his wallet and pulled out a wad of bills, which had been part of his initial CIA payment.

Manda drew back. "What the hell are you doing carrying that kind of cash around, hucklebuck?" she said.

"Never mind. I hit the number. I won the daily double. My ship came in. My rich uncle died. The main thing is: Pilar's going to walk away with a lot of this in a half-hour. So just get her clothes off and get her in my robe—and then you put her stuff on."

"Me?"

"That's right." Pilar's uniform was a rather plain gray outfit, but the blouse hung out over the slacks and Manda should be able to squeeze into it.

"What are you going to do now?" Manda asked him.

"I'm gonna do what we used to call casing the joint. We're gonna bust Ludmilla outta this big house, so you just change clothes, keep her quiet, and sit tight till I get back."

Ronnie opened the door then and yanked the maid's cart inside so that no one would guess Pilar was in 2814. Then he smoothed down his hair and went back out and down the hallway. He was looking for the service elevator, but when he passed the guest elevators, he saw a man in a lumpy suit just standing there. Neither of the call buttons was lighted, so almost surely he was yet one more of the KGB boys rushed over from the Soviet embassy, to be posted on guard duty, looking for Ludmilla or clues to her whereabouts. Since Ronnie appreciated that he very much fell into the latter category, he suddenly changed his plan and casually walked over to the passenger elevator and pushed Down. Then he whistled and looked about, trying to appear as innocent and conspicuous, alike, as he could. When the elevator came, Ronnie even made a point of holding it for the man until he finally said, "No, I'm just waiting for someone, sank you." As Ronnie had guessed, there was indeed a touch of an accent.

He was alone on the elevator. First he pushed L, for lobby, but as soon as the elevator started down, he quickly pushed another floor at random: twenty-one. He got off there, pleased to discover that no KGB scout was lurking on that floor, and so he went down the corridor and through the swinging doors to the service elevators. He pushed the Down button and waited impatiently, praying nobody else would be on his elevator when it came.

It arrived and the doors slid open, and silently Ronnie cursed his luck—there was a man on it. His head was ducked down and he didn't see Ronnie right away, but the die was cast, and for Ronnie not to get on now would appear even more suspicious. If this guy were also KGB, he could easily enough imagine that Ronnie was scouting Ludmilla's escape route. So Ronnie stepped forward. And the doors closed behind him. Then the man raised his head.

"Jesus," Ronnie said. "What? You?"

It was Young Zack Harvey, the seventh-ranked men's player in the world, whom Ronnie had just seen at the Davis Cup matches in Buenos Aires. "How ya doin', Ronnie?" Young said, as if they always met in service elevators.

"Well, I'm fine. But what are you doing . . . in New York?"

"Oh, I just had some business with Dale here."

Now, it was true that Dale Fable was Harvey's agent, and his office was in New York and Fable was there himself now, but it was also a fact that only two days before, Young Zack had flown all the way from B.A. to Palm Springs, where he was beaten in the first round, and his next tournament was starting Monday in La Costa, near San Diego, and so for a kid to fly all the way across the continent to conduct a spot of business with his agent between California tournaments was, to say the least, an odd procedure.

Besides, Harvey had been on a hot streak—well, at least

until the last couple of weeks. He was an exceptionally bright player, very sensitive, and nobody really understood how good he might be, because he had blossomed so late, never really concentrating on tennis until his senior year at Yale, when he had come out of nowhere to win the NCAA's—and then, boom, like that, qualified for Wimbledon a couple weeks later and got all the way to the sixteens before Wilander beat him. Everybody had taken to calling him Young Zack—and soon just Young—because he was so old a newcomer and so intellectual an athlete. And now, here he was, barely a half-year later, already up to seventh in the world, riding a service elevator in New York with his head down when he should have been practicing his backhand approach in Southern California.

So, right away, Ronnie pushed the button for another floor, which happened to be eleven, and when the elevator stopped there, Ronnie pulled Young Zack off. They were alone. "All right, Young, I want you to do me a favor," he said. "You do something for me, and I've already forgotten that you're here in New York. All right? I never saw you, it won't ever be in anybody's newspaper, and it won't ever make anybody's cocktail conversation. Okay?" Harvey nodded gratefully. "Now, all I want you to do for me is pretty much what you were already doing anyhow, which is to get back on this elevator—"

"This one? The service—"

"That's right. And you take that down to the basement. And when you get off, you find out for me exactly what a person does, where a person goes, if he gets off the service elevator and goes out the service entrance. Then you come back and tell me that."

"Here?"

"Right here. Got it?"

Young gave Ronnie a mock salute and took the next service elevator down. Ronnie had always liked the kid. As a player, Harvey was something of a throwback physically, for he was tall and rangy, with a big booming serve and slashing volleys—quite a contrast to most of the other top players, who were relatively little guys who scampered about. Agility had become the hostage to size; Felicity was taller than many of the men stars. But Young Zack was quicker than he appeared, and instinctively he was able to adjust enough to keep his smaller rivals off balance until he could gain the upper hand with his big shots—and blow them away. What especially appealed to Ronnie was that Harvey took a much greater interest than his compatriots in the places he played and in the players from other countries. Ronnie was always pleasantly surprised that, in those weeks when there were two big tournaments scheduled at the same time, one in America and one somewhere else, Harvey would invariably be one of the few Americans who opted to play overseas. Whenever he and Ronnie talked, they discussed politics instead of tennis, and Young Zack still planned to stay on tour for only five or six years, at which time he would enroll at Harvard Law, where he had been accepted before he found out how good a player he happened to be. His specialty would be international law.

In only a few minutes the elevator opened and Harvey reappeared, brushing past a waiter with a large room-service order. "What's the deal?" Ronnie asked.

"Very simple. When you get off, turn to the right. You come to the kitchen. Take a left there. It's easy. After a bit, you see a ramp there, alongside some stairs. That leads up and out to the street."

"Which one is that?"

"The back. Fifty-eighth."

"Good. Was there anyone around, you know, like *lurking*, shall we say."

"Yeah, I was gonna tell you that. There was this guy in a gray suit, big fur coat over top of it. He checked me out when I came off the elevator, and then he turned away and pretended like he was doing something. He's waiting right there as you get off."

"Okay, that's great, Young. Thanks."

Ronnie shook his hand and headed for the regular passenger elevator. "Ronnie," he heard Young call as he got to the swinging doors, and he turned back.

"Yeah?"

"I hope you get her outta here."

"How'd you know that?"

"Oh, everybody's heard about Ludmilla by now," Young said.

Only, of course, Ronnie was sure that next to nobody had heard.

Back in the room, poor Pilar was still bound and gagged, although Ludmilla was soothing her, patting her forehead with a damp cloth. Ronnie took Manda aside and let her in on his escape plans. "You know," she said, gesturing toward Pilar, "this sort of thing is totally against the law. I mean, if we were Puerto Ricans or something, we'd get ten to twenty in the slammer for this."

"Naw, we'd plea-bargain it down to a traffic fine," Ronnie said.

"Still, it's never going to look good on my résumé," Manda said, tugging at Pilar's blouse, which she had put on herself. It was very snug up top. But she managed; she even got into Pilar's shoes, too.

"Hey, I know all that," he said, taking out an envelope and letter and printing on them. "That's why we've got to make this work. If we get Ludmilla outta here, then we're heroes, and the end justifies the means. Ludmilla's got asylum and Pilar's got a thousand bucks." This time he handed Manda the bills. "Now, as soon as you come back here, you give this to Pilar."

"Right, boss," Manda said, and she tucked it into her bra.

"Okay then, girls," Ronnie said. "Zero hour. You stay here till you hear an alarm go off, give it a couple more minutes to make sure I can get a cab, and then take off. Okay?"

"Even better, hucklebuck," Manda said. "We don't need a cab. I'll call you a courtesy car." The Virginia Slims tournament, like most in tennis, had cars with drivers available for the players to go to practice and the like. Manda phoned down to the tournament office and was assured that a courtesy car would be awaiting Mr. Ratajczak at the front of the hotel.

"I think this is a first," Ronnie said. "I don't think anybody's ever defected in a courtesy car before." And then he looked around at his three lady friends. First, he patted Pilar—as asexually, avuncularly as possible, on the knee. "Pilar, old pal, just sit tight. Another *treinta minutos* you're going to be a thousand bucks richer—tax-free. Defection work is strictly off the books."

Then he stood back up, shook Ludmilla's hand, and kissed her on the cheek. "I hope this caper works," he said. "You're a good kid, Ludmilla, and you'll make a fine American. You're warm and greedy."

He just hugged Manda.

She said: "Oh, Ronnie, if only you were the man I met before I met other men."

"Yeah, we could have worked something out."

"Someday I'm going to get drunk and tell Felicity what an asshole she is."

"Yeah," he said, pinching her chin. He put on his overcoat then and picked up a package—something he'd wrapped in hotel envelopes and a plastic laundry bag. "Okay, team, remember: there's no tomorrow. And: when the going gets tough, the tough get going. And, as you know: a winner never quits; and a quitter never wins. And above all, never forget: the biggest room of them all is the room for improvement!" And he swept off. It was a go.

ℛ

The lobby was abustle with Russians shuffling about, watching every elevator, monitoring every door. If Ludmilla were still in the Stuy-Knick—and nobody had seen her come down and go out since she went up on the elevator—then she was not going to leave.

Libor was in the middle of it all, and Ronnie politely tipped his fur bonnet—a Russian model, as a matter of fact—and smiled sweetly at him as he walked toward the front door. Then, almost as if it were an afterthought, Ronnie turned and handed Libor the package he was carrying. "Oh, Libor, this is for you."

"What iss this?"

"I can't tell you. But, whatever you do, don't open it now, my friend. Not till I leave."

"Why iss that?"

"Just do what I say," Ronnie shot back, quite sharply in fact, pushing the package more firmly into Libor's grasp. He was sure that the Bulgar would accept the package if he spoke with command—no matter that he had no right to give orders—because Ronnie had discovered with his travel that the less freedom a man has, the less he will question authority. Even presumed authority. And, indeed, Libor held the package dutifully. Had he brought it to his ear, he would have heard it ticking. It included an engraved travel clock, Ronnie's second-place award in the 1981 IWOOTP Feature Article of the Year Contest, one he had written for *Redbook* about Felicity's clothes.

Ronnie then walked directly to the desk and spoke to the clerk there. "I'm afraid I have a room theft to report," he said.

"Oh, I'm terribly sorry, sir. Let me call Security."

"Thanks, but I'm going out right now. I'll speak to them when I get back. Luckily, it seems that only one item is missing, but it just happens to be an object of considerable sentimental value. A clock—engraved—that was awarded to me once. Here's a description."

"Oh, I'm so sorry, sir. I'll take care of it."

"Thank you so much," Ronnie said, and then he walked over to the bell captain's post and handed him an envelope. "You see that guy over there, the burly fellow with the package?"

"Yeah, I see him," the bell captain said, looking at Libor.

"A foreigner of some sort," Ronnie went on. "Very strange man. Keeps looking at his watch. Seems very nervous. He accosted me just now as I came off the elevator and asked me to deliver this envelope to the manager. Could you get it to the right person?"

"Oh yes, sir, thank you," said the bell captain, and as soon as Ronnie turned away to go through the revolving doors, he looked down at the envelope. It said "Mannajer" on the outside, and when the captain opened it up he was shocked to read:

> WARNING TO ALL PEOPLES. At
>   6 oc'lock BOMB
>   will GO sommwher in yur hotel.
> FREE UKRANIA!
>
> 23 August MOVEMENT

(Ronnie was particularly pleased with the 23 August Movement signature. He thought that was an especially nice, authentic touch. There wasn't a country he'd been to lately that didn't have a revolutionary group named after a day—and invariably, they were the folks with the bombs.)

The bell captain said, "Cover for me, José," and sprinted toward the manager's office, checking his watch on the run. It was now 5:35.

Outside the hotel, Ronnie saw the courtesy car parked on Central Park South. He went over and spoke to the driver, who wore a sash, like a beauty queen. "Hi, I'm Ronnie Ratajczak, and Amanda Cross just called about me. I have to duck in to make a phone call, but stay here, I'll be right back." He found a booth in the drugstore, and dialed the hotel. "The manager, please." He was connected to the man's secretary. Then, in a gruff, heavily accented voice, Ronnie said: "I must talk manager."

"I'm sorry, sir, he's in a meeting now."

"Very important. Must talk *now*!"

"Could you tell me your name and what this is in reference to?"

"This is Twenty-third August Movement and is in reference to bomb is what."

"Excuse me?"

"Bomb. Big bomb. Go boom."

"Did you say bomb?"

"Yes."

"What bomb, sir?"

"The one go off in your nice hotel at six o'clock."

"Just a second, sir." The secretary dashed into the manager's office and brushed in front of the bell captain. "Mr. Pollard, there's a very important call for you on twenty-seven."

The manager didn't even look up from the note. "I don't care how important it is. Tell 'em I'll call back."

"I'm sorry, sir—"

"Didn't you hear me, Linda?"

"Yes, sir, but he said something about a bomb. At six o'clock."

"Jesus," said the manager, and he pushed the button on his phone and picked up the receiver. Nothing. Even now, Ronnie had hung up and was walking toward the courtesy car.

The manager rang the secret buzzer for Security. Then: "Linda, get the cops here pronto. The whole Man-fucking-hattan bomb squad." The head security man ran in. "Carlos, we got a bomb scare, and this baby looks for real. A phone call. This . . ." He tossed him the note. "Go for the alarm. I want the whole building ee-fucking-vacuated. We only got twenty-three more minutes before this mother is set to go off."

"Yes, sir."

"And get a couple of New York's finest and go with Hector here. The guy who gave him this note is still walking around in the lobby. With a package. With a bomb-fucking-sized package."

"Yes, sir."

They ran out, the security man found the first cops coming through the door, and they all drew their guns on Libor. They would have banged him up against the wall, except he was still carrying the package. "Be careful, boys," said the security man. "Don't jar that mother."

"Get it over to the park," hollered a cop.

"Get his ass over there, too," yelled the security man. "If it blows, I want him going up in smoke too."

About a dozen Russian agents converged on the scene.

But even as Libor beseeched them for help, they all seemed to hold back. Nobody had told them about any bomb, either. Besides, it was at just that moment that the hotel alarms all started going off, and guests and bellmen and clerks were all running around and getting stuck in the revolving door, and a few of the KGB guys even took the opportunity to fade into the crowd and put a little more distance between them and Libor, with his bomb.

"There it goes," Manda said. The alarm screamed into 2814, as it did everywhere in the hotel. "Get ready, Ludmilla. Ronnie said to give it a couple more minutes to let it get completely chaotic, then we move out." Then Manda leaned down to Pilar and spoke slowly. Pilar still didn't understand, but it helped soothe Manda's conscience. "Now, don't worry, Pilar. That's not a real alarm. I mean, it's a real alarm, but it doesn't mean anything. Now, I'm going to be back in a few minutes, and then you can have your uniform and your cart—and you get a thousand dollars." She waved the bills, extracting them from her bra. "See, this is just like television? Okay? It's just like a game show."

Pilar did at least nod when she saw the bills again, and, on either side of her gag, there may even have been the hint of a smile.

Ludmilla was all set. She climbed into the bottom part of the maid's cart—where the towels are stored. She had to squoosh up some, but she managed to fit all in. Manda took some of the towels then and draped them over the side. She stood back and inspected the cart. It was perfect. There was no sign of life there at all. "Okay, here we go to freedom," she said, and pushed out into the hall.

The alarm bells were going off all over the place, and guests were starting to pour out into the hall. A few of the more prudent ones were, in fact, actually taking their coats and heading for the elevators. "What is it, miss?" a man asked at his door as Manda wheeled by.

"Ees a bomb scare, sir," Manda said.

"Is it real or just a scare? I got L.A. on the line here."

"I am scared plenty good," Manda said. She was working on a nice Spanish accent.

"Goddamn New York," the guy said. "Nothing works anymore."

There were a few people piling onto an elevator just as Manda got there. The Russian agent watched them go. He didn't know what to do. "You must go, sir," Manda said.

"I'm supposed to stay here," he said.

"Ees a bomb," Manda said, and, for more emphasis, threw up her hands and made a bomb noise. The agent turned then and ducked for the elevator, just as four more guests showed up. The Russian didn't even glance at the maid's cart.

Ronnie's courtesy car had been just about ready to pull away from the curb when more New York police arrived and stopped all traffic. He hadn't counted on this. Suddenly, then, from inside the hotel a whole escort of cops appeared, convoying Libor across Central Park South. He didn't even have a jacket on, and was freezing in the cold, but at least he had all sorts of cops pressing to him, guarding him—and staying as far away as they could from the one young patrolman who had been detailed to carry Libor's package. When they were all safely across to Central Park, the officer directing traffic waved the automobiles on, the courtesy car included.

The driver with the sash pulled away from the curb. "Okay," Ronnie said, "for right now we're just going to pick up somebody else, around at the service entrance on Fifty-eighth Street. All you have to do is turn down here, then go over to Sixth and park there at Fifty-eighth."

On the twenty-eighth floor, the service elevator came. It was fairly crowded with hotel employees escaping the bomb. But Manda had no choice. She got on and started to pull the cart on after. "Hey, leave the cart," a guy in the back said.

"I can get eet on hokay," Manda said, yanking it.

"So all right, come back for the cart," the guy said, and

there were a lot of other murmurs of support for his position. Uh-oh.

Manda figured she better drop the quaint Spanish bit. She'd go strictly New York native instead. So she turned and faced the man in the back who was complaining. "Lissen, asshole," Manda said. "It's my fuckin' cart, and if I lose it, I ain't got no fuckin' insurance."

"Awright, awright," the guy said. "How did I know you didn't have no insurance?" People in the United States will let you get away with anything if you bring up insurance.

"Let her on with the cart," an old lady up front said. "She don't have no insurance."

So the people made some space and Manda pulled the cart the rest of the way on, rattling all the little free shampoo bottles and soaps, spilling a few plastic shower caps, and, incidentally, banging Ludmilla's head against the aluminum. The elevator doors finally closed, and the car sped to the bottom, where everybody began to crowd off. Manda stayed in the flow.

Of course, she saw him right away, as soon as she glanced up. Even if she hadn't known he was a Russian agent, she would have suspected it. Just as Young Zack had told Ronnie, as Ronnie had told her: big guy, in a gray suit, with a fur coat. The alarm was still clanging away, and everybody from the kitchen had deserted the building, but he hadn't moved from his post. He looked at all the faces as they came off the elevator, letting Manda pass.

She wheeled to her right. It was exactly as Young Zack had reported it would be: the kitchen ahead, only a few steps, and she got there and swung left, and sure enough, straight ahead lay the steps and the ramp, and beyond them, the doors to Fifty-eighth Street and Ronnie waiting in the courtesy car.

Everybody else from the elevator had melted away by now, and Manda had only to steel herself from being undone by curiosity and looking back to see if the KGB man was still looking after her. Had she, she would have seen him still standing there, but puzzling after her. At first he had thought: something is wrong, but I don't know what.

And then slowly, it came to him: not that Ludmilla *was* in that maid's cart, but that yeah, maybe you *could* put someone in a cart, and he hadn't seen any other carts down here around the kitchen, but he certainly would have to check out the *next* cart that came along; and then he thought, well, why not, maybe I can still check out *this* one. And so he started to jog after Manda. She was halfway up the exit ramp when she heard him call: "Miss, please wait. Miss, maid, wait."

Manda tried to figure out what best to do. If she suddenly broke for the door, it would be obvious what the situation was, and Ludmilla was a dead duck. But Manda assumed the Russian was still some distance behind her, and his call had been tentative, and so she just pretended not to hear him, and plodded ahead. But now the KGB man grew more suspicious, called out again, and picked up his pace. By the time Manda was able to push her heavy load almost to the top of the ramp, the Russian had reached the bottom.

She could hear his breathing clearly now. She could sense him looming. She knew that the only hope was to get over that final little bump where the ramp topped out and then crash the cart through the door like a battering ram. "Stop!" he cried. "I know you! Stop or I shoot you!" Manda pulled the air into her lungs and prepared for the final assault, Underneath, Ludmilla began to sniffle.

And then Manda saw a face in the window of the door ahead—and whoever it was, it clearly wasn't Ronnie, so it wasn't help. Then the door flew open, and the face was attached to a tall man, a giant, it seemed, in his parka, and Manda sighed in relief as much as fear, because now she was trapped and it didn't matter anymore.

The man in the parka burst toward her.

"I'm sorry, Ludmilla," Manda said out loud. "I tried."

It happened so fast then. The man in the parka didn't grab her after all. No, no, no. He didn't. He brushed right by her, and only in that moment could she see that it was Young Zack. Quickly Manda glanced back, and she saw the Russian's eyes grow wide. He was looking right at her. He was sure now. But he was too late. As she pushed the cart over the hump she heard Young saying: "Hey, buddy, where's the Jimmy Walker Ballroom?"

"Excuse me, please," said the KGB man.

But Young made sure he stood square in his path. "I said, where's the Jimmy Walker Ballroom?"

Manda pushed the cart against the door, Ludmilla's head rattling against the aluminum, more shampoos and a whole box of matches falling to the floor.

"I'm sorry, but I don't work here." He tried to hop around Young, but the kid shifted with him and blocked his path again.

"I don't care where you work. You goddamn New Yorkers don't have any manners. This is the Stuyvesant-Knicker—"

"Take your hands off me!" the Russian roared this time, and in one motion he threw Young Zack aside and pulled out a gun, holding it high to make sure that the pest bothered him no more.

Manda was outside and looked around. The cold February wind blew a colder fact in her face: There was nobody there—no help, no Ronnie, no courtesy car, nothing.

The Russian was just starting to open the door behind her.

Suddenly she heard the cry: "Mandaaaa!!" She looked. Down at the bottom of the incline, where Fifty-eighth Street crossed Sixth Avenue, she could make out Ronnie. He was jumping up and down and waving. And she could see the police cars lined up. The cops had the whole block cordoned off because of the bomb scare. They wouldn't let any cars near the hotel. "Mandaaa! Run! Hurry!"

So she took off, pushing the cart smack down the middle of the empty street. "Hurry! Manda!" Ronnie screamed, and this time she could sense a new urgency in his voice, and sure enough, when Manda glanced back, she saw the Russian beginning to start after her.

"For Chrissake, help her!" Ronnie screamed at the nearest cop.

"Nobody goes up this street, buddy. That's department orders."

"But you gotta help her."

"You don't understand, mister. You don't tell me what to do. I'm the one tells you."

"But she's defecting, dammit," Ronnie cried. "From the Commie Red Rats!" And with that he broke past the cop, scurried around a patrol car, and ran up the slope toward Manda.

"I hope you got bomb insurance," the cop called after him.

Manda was practically out of control by now, the cart careening down the hill, Ludmilla banging around inside like one of the three little pigs who got away from the wolf, rolling down the hill inside a butter urn. But even so, the Russian was fast, and he was gaining step by step.

Manda saw Ronnie breaking toward her, and with a gentle push she let the maid's cart go. It careened the last few dozen yards down the incline. Ronnie braced for it and managed to deflect it into a police car parked there.

Ludmilla fell halfway out, dazed and banged about, but apparently whole.

The Russian could only watch, still holding Manda by her jacket. "Help me! Help me!" Manda cried, "Help me, officer! This man is a card-carrying Communist, and he's got a bomb."

"He does?" said the cop. He reached for his revolver, and the Russian dropped his, and in that instant Ronnie yanked Ludmilla the rest of the way out of her cart, dragged her over to the courtesy car, and threw her in. "Come on," he said to the driver with the sash, "let's get out of here."

"Where to?" she asked.

"Studio Fifty-four," Ludmilla said, coming to life.

"The Statue of Liberty," Ronnie said.

The last he saw of the scene as the courtesy car pulled away, was Manda pushing Pilar's cart back up the hill, giving the Russian the finger as she passed him by. The cop was demanding to see his gun permit.

GRENADA

Grenada had a problem. Yes, Grenada, the country, that Grenada. An image problem. A couple of years ago, nobody had heard of it except for a few medical students who couldn't get into school in the U.S. But now, after the invasion, everybody had heard of Grenada, only the wrong way. Something had to be done to put a new shine on Grenada's grimy face.

And so it was that the commuter from Connecticut who handled the Grenada public-relations account in New York, who was an enthusiastic weekend tennis player, thought: If we can hold a big tennis tournament in Grenada and nobody gets shot or anything, this will be a step in the right direction.

Naturally, the first man the public-relations expert called was Dale Fable, who advised him that while a real tournament was out of the question, for the right price he could have Felicity Tantamount herself to play in an informal exhibition tournament. Grenada went for it. Even better that they would have the women playing instead of the men. If females were shown hitting tennis balls and having a good time in Grenada, that spoke for the safety of the island far more than would McEnroe and Connors and Lendl and that bunch of sullen brutes. Felicity was guaranteed a two-comma payoff, and because it was Felicity,

NBC agreed to televise the finals, putting tennis on instead of refrigerator races and the weekly junior flyweight championship bout from Atlantic City; and because it was Felicity, all sorts of publications felt obliged to cover the event. That it just happened to be February in the Caribbean also did not deter the men and women of the fourth estate from their obvious journalistic responsibilities.

It was an eight-women tournament. Besides Felicity, Fable brought in Polly Hutton, Tiffany Rogers, Rina Rodanya, and four other bozettes he had under contract who would be sacrificial lambs in the first round.

The tournament was named the Granada War Memorial. Naturally, Ronnie was invited to cover the show. He was assured a chair up in first curtain and a lanai room opening on the pool. He also set up some travel pieces he could do, including: "Grenada Reborn"; "Grenada: The Beaches and the Battle"; and (for a Japanese airline magazine) "Grenada—The Okinawa of the Caribbean." It was going to be a good week for him.

The one new hotel in Grenada, the Ritz Plaza in St. George's, had been rushed to completion in order to accommodate the tennis caravan. Courts, even a small stadium, had been constructed adjacent to the hotel gardens, although the workmen were still tapping out the finishing touches when Ronnie arrived on Thursday, the day before the first-round matches.

He was hardly settled in his room when the phone rang. Since the defection, he had become something of a hero, and he was finding out how the other half lived—the press was always running him down and harassing him, especially since Ludmilla had been tucked away for safekeeping for a while. But this time it was a familiar voice calling from London. "Colin here," it said.

"Well, I've certainly got to hand it to you fellows," Ronnie replied. "You sure do get the word out."

"How's that now?"

"How's that? I was hardly off the plane in New York before the Commies knew I was working for you boys."

"Now, now, wouldn't want to be associated with slow spies, would you?"

"Will I get my next month's pay that fast?"

"Don't be impatient now. It's only yet the middle of the month. I just have a bit of a favor."

Ronnie broke in. "I knew it. You promised me there'd be no strings attached."

"Indeed. This is only a personal request, Ronnie. I've a chance to cash something of a nice bet, and for your help you'd be on for a third of the winnings."

"But of course, dear Colin, my friend. What's on your mind?"

"Just the answer to a simple question."

"Shoot."

"Is Felicity Tantamount going to marry Dale Fable?"

Ronnie was taken aback by that. At last he said, "What's that got to do with the price of eggs?"

"Well, there's a rumor to that effect, it's been in the press here, and now Ladbroke's and Hill's both have lines on it."

"You're kidding."

"Oh no indeed. It opened at four-to-seven *for* the nuptials, and now it's down to two-to-five. You know how it is here. Anything to do with Felicity interests the bloody public."

"All right, Colin. A certain lady has asked me not to say anything about this particular matter, but, as strictly a point of financial counsel, I would advise you to bet all you can on such a marriage."

"Well, thanks lots."

"Wait a minute," Ronnie said. "How 'bout putting my whole March payment on it?"

"Ten thousand, U.S.? Sorry, the bookies would never take that sort of swag. Just a few bob or it goes off the board. I'll get down for you what I can."

Ronnie paused now. "Colin?"

"Yes?"

"No, never mind. I started to ask you something, but you wouldn't answer, would you?"

"I told you in Punta, the less you know, the better."

"All right, then. I'll see you in a couple of weeks, some-where."

"We'll be in touch."

"The money will touch me fine, thanks," Ronnie said. Still, when he hung up, he was sorry that he hadn't asked *the* question. So what if Colin wouldn't answer him? His reaction alone would have told something. It was all so preposterous, but then, this was the second time Colin had asked about Felicity. Was it really possible that she could be the spy? Felicity be Dana? Felicity Tantamount? Why would she do a thing like that? Still, you never knew.

Felicity did everything else, didn't she?

Ω

For the pool, then, Ronnie selected his blue Stubbies from Australia, his buffalo sandals from Tanzania, and a T-shirt from South Korea. He found the pool in the shape of Gre-nada itself; his chaise was over near Point Saline, and as he was taking off his T-shirt and exhibiting the nice tan he almost always had, he saw, across the way, a beautiful, shimmering woman, and what she appeared to be doing was looking at him. Now, every man's fantasy is to go to a pool at a fancy resort, and no sooner does he start taking off his T-shirt than the most beautiful woman there starts looking at him. Also, the most beautiful woman is by her-self, and momentarily she will come over and introduce herself.

Being well-acquainted with this fantasy, Ronnie promptly put it out of his mind and lay down to catch some sun. The best he had ever done in real life was that maybe the third-or fourth-best-looking woman chanced to look at him, and even then, she was not alone and she certainly didn't come over to introduce herself.

You can imagine, then, Ronnie's surprise when he felt somebody blocking his sun, and when he opened his eyes, there she was, the gorgeous creature, standing there look-ing down upon him, exactly as if he were a goddamn sex object or something shameful like that.

The first thing Ronnie wanted to assure her, in fact, was that there was a lot more to him than just his looks. Just because he had a nice tan didn't mean there wasn't a lot of fine stuff inside him, as well. But she spoke first: "Excuse me, but wouldn't you be Ronnie Ratajczak?"

The remark really set him back, but notwithstanding his chagrin, he managed to rise to his feet and acknowledge his identity. Ronnie certainly didn't want to tell her that he thought she had come over to meet him because she liked the way he looked, and now he was upset because she merely knew who he was, so he put on his best face and drew up a chaise for her, next to his.

They both sat down. "I'm Lia D'Antonini, and pleased to meet you," she said in that perfect rounded Continental tone that somehow balances English exactly midway between the British and American accents, without any inflection whatsoever. "From Rome."

"I would have said Milano." It was reflexive, a small flattery based on that most banal of stereotypes, that northern Italians tend to be more intelligent than those from down the boot.

Lia was, in fact, also rather dark—which, the other stereotype has it, northerners are not supposed to be—but Ronnie had been lucky and had winged her with the right arrow. She was caught short, too. "Yes, I was born nearby. In Como. How ever did you know?"

Ronnie shrugged smugly. "Your accent. More Lombard." It was the perfect thing to say—making him so blithe and commanding and herself so defensive . . . especially after years of practicing to speak totally without accent.

"You have a good ear," she said, making the best of her disappointment.

"Well, I've been everywhere in the world once, and I know a little something about every place."

"Oh, and what do you know of Lombardy?"

"I know that Stendhal was French, he was very popular in England, and his heroines were Lombards, and"—Ronnie added a bit of a benign leer—"now I know why."

Lia let the last part go. ''What else do you know of Lombardy?''

''Not much. I don't know anything else about Stendhal, either. I told you: I just know a bit about everything. I'm a journalist. If I really knew a whole lot about something, then I'd be a professor or a concierge. Journalists are the travel agents of truth.''

''Oh.''

''But, enough of me,'' Ronnie said. (He was on a roll.) ''What about you?''

''For our purposes, it's really quite simple,'' Lia replied. ''I'm the new executive vice-president of Grazia.''

''The tennis clothes?''

''Yes, that.'' It made him pay attention to her own attire now: a one-piece white bathing suit with a pattern of purple flowers played across it diagonally, down from one breast to the hip. Lia's toenails were painted the same shade as the pattern; very few women could pull that off. She went on: ''I shall be very direct, because it's no secret anyhow. I have been given this position to sign Felicity Tantamount to a Grazia contract. That is my assignment, and it's fair to say that if I succeed at that one thing, I am a success, while if I do not, I'm a failure.''

''Nothing else matters?''

''Effectively, no. We want that contract, and I'll do all within my powers to obtain it. Understand, Mr. Ratajczak—''

''Ronnie.''

''Yes, Ronnie. Understand: there has never been anything in this field so important as who will dress Felicity. A Wimbledon championship, six Wimbledons—nothing compared to what she wears. This is the only real championship. Do you see?''

''Oh, I know enough to believe that,'' Ronnie said. ''So, what do you want of me?''

''Only what Americans call an edge.''

''And how can I be your edge?''

''I know you're very close to Felicity, and—''

Ronnie held up his hand like a traffic cop. "Stop right there. I don't trade in friendships."

"Nor would I expect you to. And neither would I expect that it would do me any good. I understand that Mr. Fable is the only one she any longer listens to in matters of business."

Or, Ronnie thought, in matters of the heart.

"No, I value you," Lia went on, "because so many people tell me that you know more about this, ah, community than anyone else, and that you can deal with it utterly professionally, without any hatchets to grind." Ronnie let that pass. "I only want your expertise. This tennis is a new world for me, and I suspect you could tell me more in an hour or two than I could find out in weeks. You can make a fair price for yourself."

"I'm not an informer."

"Please"—and she reached out and touched his knee in a show of their intimacy—"it's not gossip I want. I need background, a small-cut."

"Shortcut."

"Yes. And I will pay you, of course."

"Of course."

"Then you will have dinner with me this evening?"

"Perhaps," Ronnie said. "I may be free. Wait here, please." He crossed to a house phone at the bar and dialed the desk, asking if Mrs. Whitridge had checked in. She hadn't, and there was no word on her arrival, although the desk concurred that she had indeed been expected that morning. So Ronnie came back to Lia. "This evening would be fine," he said. "Shall I make a reservation?"

"No, thank you. I'm more interested in the quality of the conversation than in the quality of the dinner. We'll be served in my suite. Be there at seven. Number thirty, on the garden side."

"All right," Ronnie said.

"Will two thousand dollars be all right?"

"Yes, that's a fair enough price to pick my brains." What the hell, Ronnie thought, if he could be paid not to spy, he could also be paid not to give away secrets.

Besides, more important, Signorina D'Antonini was what used to be called ravishing.

🙞

Not until Ronnie was almost finished dressing for dinner did Doreen arrive at her room and call him. "I'm sorry," he said, "I'd given up on you for tonight."

"Don't blame me, mate," she replied, "but an honest banana bender must sometimes place her vocational obligations above the social. I had to make a side trip to Venezuela. We might put the Fed Cup there."

Doreen, she of the luggage largess, the executive director of IWOOTP, was from Brisbane, in Queensland, where the natives are referred to as "banana benders" by other, more sophisticated Aussies, such as the "crow eaters" of South Australia. As Doreen Masterful, she had been a run-of-the-mill player, but smart, with a volley, so Margaret Court used her occasionally as a doubles partner, even if they had nothing whatsoever in common as people. But playing with Margaret and pulling off the occasional upset on grass kept Doreen on tour long enough for her wonderful exuberance and bitchy wit to win the tennis world at large, and, in particular, Herbert (Hobby) Whitridge—he being a widowed old tennis volunteer from Tampa who exhibited the same sort of classic traits of freeloading that Prosper Hegginbosch would display so blatantly twenty years later.

Doreen married Hobby, but she had always been the sort who needed problems—as a player, she had lost a lot of matches only because her interest would flag if she got ahead; she played her best on the brink of defeat—and she quickly grew bored with the comfortable existence of stockbroker's wife. So Doreen helped promote a tournament that came to Tampa, and then ran an exhibition round-robin all by herself, and one thing led to another, and before she knew it—and certainly before Hobby knew it—she had been appointed executive director of IWOOTP, Eye-Woofy.

Doreen relocated Eye-Woofy in Tampa (it really doesn't

matter where anything in international tennis is, so long as it's near an airport) and began to travel the world again—although less and less with Hobby, as he crossed the bar into his seventies. And so it was that, most discreetly, she began to take up first with Ronnie, then with Prosper—although, as we know, neither was aware of the other's common role, and neither did anyone else have an inkling that Doreen could be unfaithful to dear old Hobby.

"I can drop by after my dinner," Ronnie suggested.

"What's the matter with the Sheila you're having dinner with?" Doreen talked like one of the mates, one of the blokes. She called almost everybody she liked and everything she enjoyed—be it a meal, a screw, or even an old-fashioned barroom brawl—a Blue. And since Australians often refer to anything especially red as blue, she also called Felicity Blue. Or the Great Blue.

It could get confusing. Anyway, Ronnie said: "No, it's a business Sheila."

"Travel or tennis?" Doreen fired back.

"Do I have to tell you?"

"Would you want me to find out from the wrong people, son?"

"No, mother. You may have heard of her. She's the new Grazia—"

"Oh, bugger you, Blue. Business, my arse. Everybody's heard about the beautiful and mysterious Lia D'Antonini. The Italian Ice, they already call her."

"Bad news travels fast, huh."

"No, it's just that I worry about you, Blue. The lady has only one purpose in life—to sign up the Great Blue. Don't think for a moment that it's either your charm or your cock she's after."

"I'm aware of all that, thanks."

"Only offering you wise counsel, lover boy. You know, mate, you're really not as attractive as you think you are."

"No?"

"No. You only do so well with the bloody Sheilas because not only do you have a pecker, but you can think like a woman."

"I'm effeminate?" Ronnie shrieked in falsetto, playing along.

"You? Don't put me on. But mostly you're just a shrewd bloke. And in this modern adrogynous world, to have a pecker and think like a woman is a devastating combination."

Ronnie told Doreen he'd see her after dinner. She told him that she had the cigarettes.

♀

Lia was in lavender, with a flower in her hair. There's nothing more difficult for any woman to try, because it's almost impossible for her not to look like some silly native girl from the South Pacific. But the lady pulled it off so well that Ronnie couldn't help but say, "I like your flower," before he said anything else to her.

She was even prettier than what he remembered from the pool, sexier somehow in her clothes, now that he was able to notice all of her and not just the erogenous parts. Lia was slim and full, alike, with long black hair that he wished (for some subconscious reason) that she would wear down over one eye; she had wine-red lips and a lustrous olive skin that was so perfectly burnished that it seemed she had no pores, let alone blemishes. Strange, perhaps, but Ronnie couldn't help but think that Lia was the most extraordinarily *tasteful* thing he had ever seen. If you could, say, buy Felicity off the shelf, friends would be knocked back by the sheer beauty of your purchase, and the luxury of it. But could you buy Lia, everyone would compliment you on your taste.

She pointed to a bar and asked what he wanted. "I have all sorts of possibilities," she said.

"Oh, I'm not much for experimenting with tropical concoctions. Never take anything with fruit, straws, or little paper parasols in it."

Lia picked up a folder that lay conspicuously on the table there and held it up. "It says you don't like wine," she announced, and then she laid it back down.

"Oh, it does, does it? Well, I like wine enough. I told

you I know a little bit about everything. It's red with fish, white with pigs-in-the-blanket, and rosé with buttered popcorn. I'm planning on writing a series of how-*not*-to books. My first will be: *Not To Be a Wine Drinker*." He pointed at the vodka bottle and said: "Tonic," and she picked up a highball glass for him. "Did you ever play poker?"

"No, not really," Lia said.

"Me neither. I'm also going to write *Not To Be a Gambler*. And then the sequel: *Not To Be a Backgammon Player*, although that's known in some languages as *Not To Be a Bore*. Same thing."

"Yes," Lia said, laughing.

"Anyway. Cards. There's a game called high-low. There's two winners with every pot. The best hand and the worst hand. Only card game I ever liked. And most people go high, so if everybody's going high, it's easier to win low. My experience is that that works even better in general than in poker. And nowadays every bozo with a pocket computer and a frequent-flier number is an expert on wine: bouquets, aroma, character, and Chablises. Why should I bother? There's always somebody else there at the table who has devoted his life to the subject and can handle the task."

"Suppose you're alone?" Lia asked. She held up a lime, and Ronnie shook his head.

"Oh, I wouldn't drink wine if I were alone," Ronnie said. "I think it gives you the gout."

"Suppose you're alone with a lady?"

"Well, then I tell the lady I really don't know much about wine and let her decide."

"About the wine?"

"No, about me."

Lia handed him the vodka. She also gave him the check, too: $2,000 U.S. And then she led him out onto the lanai, and they sat across from each other, and although he tried to talk some about her, she diverted his every parry, and kept him on the subject she had paid him for. In a while, a waiter brought dinner, which Lia had him set up in the living room, but the conversation went on as before, and

Ronnie only talked of tennis: who had the power; who appeared to, but didn't really; the same thing with brains; who was connected; who liked each other; who didn't; who could be trusted; who could influence Felicity—and, for that matter, who could influence Fable. Lia knew what she wanted to know, and she asked it directly.

But then, Ronnie knew a great deal, and when they moved back outside for amarettos, he said: "I think I've given you a very good survey course: Women's Tennis 101."

"Oh yes." And she tapped her watch. "I won't keep you anymore."

"Oh, you're not keeping me. You paid for my knowledge, and I'll give it. And my company goes with that. Only, I'd rather, if I stayed, talk about things other than business."

"No, not now. Forgive me. I still have a bit of jet lag." Ronnie nodded and rose. No one ever argues with anyone who says she has jet lag; it's the accepted and universal excuse.

"Maybe Sunday?" he asked. "Dinner, after the matches."

"Yes, maybe," Lia said, escorting him to the door. "There is still the one thing you didn't tell me tonight."

"What's that?"

"Did she break your heart?"

He gulped a bit, with surprise. "Oh, you knew that?"

"Shall we say that it plays a somewhat larger part in your dossier than how you feel about wine."

"Well, I won't elaborate on what the dossier says"— and he waved disdainfully at the folder on the table.

"No?"

"No, I won't tell you, because no beautiful woman bothers to try to break the heart of a man if she knows he's already had it broken by another beautiful woman. And I'd rather you have a go at it." And with that he reached into his pocket, drew out the check she'd given him, and tore it up before her.

"You earned that," Lia said.

"I'd rather earn you, thanks," and Ronnie reached down, and before Lia knew it, he'd taken her hand and brought it up and kissed it, not in any sort of parody, but precisely in the way men used to kiss women's hands in another time.

"That's quite good, very nice," Lia said.

"Yes, it's a Ratajczak 1986. I learned that when all the other boys were out swilling grapes." And then he was smart enough to turn on his heel and stride away.

When he was gone, Lia wished that he hadn't. She wished that she hadn't told him she had jet lag, but had said it was a headache or her period or something like that—an excuse that he might not have accepted without some dispute. She leaned down and picked up the pieces of the check. Then she reached up under her skirt and unbuttoned the holster that strapped about her thigh. It carried a dandy little pistol. She hid it under some purple-tinted underclothes in a drawer, and then she called down to be awakened at seven. She had to speak to London then and give them her first report on Ronnie Ratajczak.

φ

Ronnie called Doreen as soon as he got back to his room, and she invited him over. With circumspection, then, he cut this way and that to reach her. Her room was in the new wing, catercorner behind the main part of the hotel, and Ronnie had to pass through some gardens with garish lighted fountains, and in the middle, where several paths converged, a gazebo.

He was walking by briskly when he chanced to glance into the gazebo, and he was stunned to see a form there inside, on a bench. His first thought was that it must be two lovers, closely entwined, but on closer inspection it proved to be only one large person. Ronnie stopped and drew closer then, peeking through the latticework. Even though he couldn't make out the face at that distance, the form, heavy and rumpled and sodden, looked familiar enough, and then, in the lights reflected from the fountain, he could see that it was indeed Libor Rodanya.

It was apparent that he was drunk, passed out, and so, with a shrug of good riddance, Ronnie resumed his journey to Doreen's room.

By arrangement, she had left the door open, and with a glance around to make sure no one was watching, Ronnie pushed quickly in. Doreen, in a sea-green see-through gown, immediately handed him a vodka and a wet kiss on his mouth, and when Ronnie didn't respond to that with his usual enthusiasm, she stepped back—not so much rejected as surprised. There was no longer much coyness to their relationship. No, no, no. What Ronnie and Doreen practiced was recreational sex—just as 280-pound defensive tackles at the University of Nebraska are playing recreational football.

Ronnie apologized. "Sorry, Sheila, but I'm a little distracted."

"A passing diversion, I trust."

"Literally. On the way over, I walked by that gazebo out there, and inside—"

"Libor," she said.

"How the hell did you know that?"

"He must have been passed out there for an hour. Before that, I was in the bar having some grog with Manda, and we saw Libor over in the corner with some people. They were white, but they seemed to be islanders—two guys and a . . . lady. I may not be an authority on whores, but there was no doubt about this one. I glanced over once, and I'm quite sure she was giving him a hand-job under the table. Libor, of course, was his usual gross self—"

"Of course."

"And I reckon he was putting away buckets of rum, too, because all of a sudden he toppled forward on the table. This being a class joint, the barkeep wanted him carted away, and his new friends were so kind as to volunteer for the task. We assumed they'd take him back to his room, but, as you saw, they just dumped him out there in the garden."

"Did you call Rina?" Ronnie asked, sprawling in a chair.

"Hmmm, that's a thought. God, he so seldom lets her out of his sight. But then, she's probably thrilled just to have a few hours without the bloody swine."

"I've heard he beats her, too."

Doreen stopped in the midst of pouring herself another rum. "I was afraid that might get out. I would hope you wouldn't print it."

"Maybe it would be good if I did."

"Rubbish. The Bulgars wouldn't stand for it. They'd yank them both back home, never again to leave. Never forget, mate, Libor is not only her father, but he taught Rina this game, he ushered her out of nowhere into the wide world. As dreadful a creature as he is, she owes everything to him. Poor devil."

Ronnie started to respond, but instead, Doreen leaned down and jabbed him in the stomach. "Enough," she said. "If you want to speak to me about the state of the game, call my office for an appointment. On the other hand, if you want to root, then for God's sake, get at it."

"Root" is the Australian word for "screw," as "barrack" is the Australian word for "root." You go to the stadium to barrack for the home team, and then you go to the bedroom to root your Sheila. Occasionally, on account of this idiosyncrasy in the language, international problems may arise. Doreen had been there on the occasion in Melbourne when, at a huge black-tie dinner before the Davis Cup, a new American player arose, declared how delighted he was to be in Australia, how much he liked the country and the people, even how pleased he was to have met some lovely Aussie girls, and, he said, "Even though we'll be playing against your countrymen, we sure hope that at least some of you girls will come out and root for us."

A hush fell on the ballroom.

There was no such problem in Doreen's room. She was already unbuttoning Ronnie's shirt. Doreen was enthusiastic. Also, Ronnie thought, she was generally amoral. That was what made their relationship so special.

Since Doreen had retired as a player, she had grown almost Rubenesque—at least by the standards of the world

Ronnie inhabited, wherein resided women who jog, diet, stretch, and get tummy tucks. Doreen, though, owned animated globular breasts, and overall, warm, fleshy folds, and sometimes when she held him he feared she would never permit his escape. But then, he knew that she would want a cigarette soon enough. It had been five years or more since Doreen had stopped smoking, and almost a decade since last Ronnie had lit up, but in the moments following their first consummation they had talked about how the best cigarette was the one you shared after making love, and so the next time, at Wimbledon, Doreen and he split a Virginia Slims. Ever since, they had certified the act by having one cigarette, and it was all the better, inasmuch as they never otherwise partook, and the smoke they drew in left them a bit giddy. "God, this is wonderful," Ronnie said as he inhaled.

"I know," said Doreen. "And if we work at it here together, Blue, we can get up to a pack a day."

In fact, it was two more cigarettes and two in the morning when Doreen pushed him out of bed and sent him on his way. Ronnie was partway across the lawn, approaching the gazebo, when suddenly he heard a door open somewhere behind him, and, not wanting to run into anyone he knew, he vaulted over a little bench and ducked behind a bush.

Just in time. He saw the figure approaching from down the path. There was a spring in its step, a long stride—hardly what might be expected from someone wandering around a hotel after two o'clock in the morning. The figure neared, long and lean, and as it passed in front of Ronnie's hiding place, became Young Zack Harvey.

Fascinated, Ronnie watched as Young approached the gazebo. There he stopped, looked in, and saw—Ronnie assumed—Libor. But Young Zack must have seen the Bulgar there on an earlier peregrination, because he obviously wasn't the least bit surprised. Instead, very deliberately Young took a couple steps toward the sleeping hulk, and then he stopped and, clear as a bell, spoke: "You miserable Communist cocksucker."

Now Ronnie saw Young reach into his pocket and pull out a pistol, which he carefully aimed at Libor. For an instant Ronnie froze, but then he burst out of the bush, waving his arms and screaming Young's name.

Immediately Young whirled around so that now the pistol pointed directly at Ronnie.

Ronnie threw up his hands. "No, no, Young. It's me. Ronnie Ratajczak."

Young Zack let the pistol drop, and when he spoke, it was with a certain irritation: "What the hell are you doing here, Ronnie?"

"What am *I* doing here? I'm working here. What are *you* doing here? That's the question."

Young only sighed as he put the gun back in his pocket. "You didn't have to worry. I wasn't going to kill the bastard. You know I couldn't do that, Ronnie. I was just imagining."

"Oh sure. If you could imagine that well that you could hit a backhand down the line, you'd already be champion of the world."

That got Young Zack's back up some. "It's my business why I'm here."

Ronnie came closer, stepping into the gazebo. The fountains were turned off now, and the only light came from the starry Caribbean heavens. "You know, Young, I truly appreciate what you did in New York. If it hadn't been for you, Manda couldn't have gotten away with Ludmilla. And, like I promised you, I didn't say anything." Young Zack nodded his thanks. "But there's a point where it's simply asking too much of me to keep bumping into you at odd places around the world and expect me to suppress my instinctive curiosity—let alone my professional concerns."

"Look, I understand, Ronnie. But this has nothing to do with tennis."

"No, it's not that easy, Young. Last week you lost in the first round Monday in California and a couple days later you pop up in New York. Then you go back to California and three days later I run into you in Grenada—and I know in three more days you're supposed to be in Osaka for an exhibition with McEnroe, and then Manila for the mixed doubles.

"Now, a man might think, Young, that you merely have an imaginative travel agent, fueling your taste for covering ground, but a more cynical bastard, like myself, for example, might come to the conclusion that the reason you keep losing tennis matches you should win in the first round, and the reason you're about to drop out of the top ten after your quote meteoric rise to dizzy heights unquote is because you're flying all over the fucking world and riding up and down on service elevators and carrying pistols at two-thirty in the morning."

"Yeah, I guess it looks suspicious, Ronnie."

"Young, it looks, to say the least . . . unusual."

"Just don't say anything, please?" Young Zack said, even taking Ronnie by the shoulders. "I swear to you, all this stuff is going to be over in a few months, and then I'll give you the story. I promise."

"Young, I don't want the story. I mean, sure, I always want the story. But I don't want to see you all messed up."

"I'm all right, Ronnie, I swear." And he smiled then—positively beamed—at some secret thought. "In fact, I've never been better in all my life."

Ronnie shook his head. "Okay. Just one question: do you work for Colin?" Young Zack cocked his head quizzically. "Are you Dana? You are, aren't you?"

"What are you talking about?"

Ronnie just clapped Young on the shoulder. He didn't expect him to level with him, but he wanted Young to know what he knew. And he wanted to see his expression. "You're a good actor," he said. "Now help me. The least we can do is get this fat mother back to his room." He gestured derisively at Libor.

"You actually want me to help him?" Young asked incredulously.

"Look, no one in the world could despise him any more than I do, but everybody deserves a certain expression of charity from his fellow man."

Young Zack shook his head. "I don't want anybody to see me."

Ronnie took his arm. "Okay, that's fair. But I can't drag the big prick by myself. You're a big strong professional ath-a-leet. You help me get him to his room, then you duck away, call Rina in the room—anonymously—and then she'll open the door, and the two of us, Rina and me, will get him in. Okay?"

Young reluctantly nodded agreement. Ronnie reached down and began to go through Libor's pockets. Young asked him what he was doing.

"Seeing if I can find his key. You don't know his room number, do you?"

"Who, me?" Young said. "Why would I know that?"

"I don't know. I just asked. Never mind, anyway! First pocket." Ronnie held the key up, and then they began to position themselves to lift the fat man up. He was still deadweight. "You know," Ronnie said, "I don't think our friend here had a few too many. I think his pals back in the bar slipped him a Mickey Finn."

"What the hell's that?" Young asked, trying to wrap Libor's left arm around his shoulder, as Ronnie attempted to do the same thing with the right.

"God," Ronnie said. "You mean the younger generation doesn't know what it is to give a guy a Mickey?" They had the body up between them now, although the arms kept flapping uselessly, with the big ring on Libor's hand slapping back and forth into Ronnie's face. "A Mickey Finn is a drugged drink—slip a few knockout drops into the booze. I'm afraid dear old Libor thought he was getting himself a piece of ass, and instead they took him for a ride. They probably relieved him of every nickel he had, and then dumped him out here."

Luckily the Rodanyas' room wasn't far away, at the back of the garden, on the ground floor. Ronnie and Young Zack got him propped up and Ronnie held him there. Then he winked at Young. "Listen, three strikes and you're out. If I run into you next week at the last base camp on Mount Everest, I'm writing about it."

"Thanks, Ronnie," Young said. They couldn't shake because it took both of Ronnie's hands to hold Libor up, but Young patted him and ran off. In time, Ronnie heard the phone ring inside the room and moments after that Rina opened the door. She had thrown a little shorty bathrobe over her shorty pajamas, and, Ronnie thought, she never looked cuter. But then she came out the door and she saw her father, and her eyes turned wide and sad.

Whispering, Ronnie instructed her how to help, and together they managed to drag the form the few feet through the door and to the bed, where they let him fall out onto it. Libor was still completely out. "He's going to have a terrible head tomorrow, Rina. Whatever somebody gave him was mighty powerful."

"Thank you so very much," she said. "I will tell him who he was that bring him home. After New York, he be much surprise that it is you."

"Yeah, well, get your sleep. Who do you play tomorrow?"

"I play the little thirteen-year-old from Chicago, Illinois. And then, I beat her, I play Felicity in the semis."

Ronnie wished her luck and left for his room.

Had he stayed, he would have been very surprised at what Rina did next. First she pulled off her father's shoes, which was nice of her. Then she reached into his coat pocket, found the gun he so often carried, and put that in the drawer where he usually kept it, under his shirts. But then she reached back into his jacket and took out his bill-fold, extracting what money there was from it. Then Rina unbuttoned her father's shirt and reached down to his money belt, which, of course, she knew he always wore. She took all the bills from it, every last one. Next she unfastened the gold chain from his neck, and after that she began to try to remove the huge signet ring from his right hand. It was a struggle so Rina finally had to use soap.

She then jammed all the bills, as well as the chain and the ring, into an envelope. Then she waited, sitting at the foot of the bed, until she heard a soft knock on the door and heard her name being whispered in a voice she rec-

ognized. Without even looking, she opened the door a
crack, said not a word, but slipped the envelope out, closed
the door, locked it, turned out the light, and went to bed,
smiling broadly, her whole body tingling.

Ronnie watched Rina play the next afternoon with special
curiosity. It wasn't just that Felicity had tipped him off to
her true potential, but naturally, his interest was further
piqued by the events of the previous evening. Libor was
nowhere to be seen, either, and as far as Ronnie knew, this
was the first time the daughter had ever played away from
her father's vigilant gaze. Notwithstanding—and despite her
interrupted sleep—Rina played better than ever, with an
ease and an enthusiasm Ronnie had never seen previously.

Felicity came over and sat down next to him. "What did
I tell you?" she asked smugly.

"Well, true enough, but consider the opposition," he
replied. Rina was playing a little thirteen-year-old, the
daughter of a dermatologist from Lake Forest, Illinois. On
behalf of Eye-Woofy, Doreen had begged the doctor not
to rush his child into a professional career, but he announced that he would sue if IWOOTP attempted to de-
prive his little darling of the right to livelihood. So Dale
Fable rushed in and got her a training-bra endorsement,
and the father solemnly assured everyone that his daughter
would travel with a nanny and a tutor; he had his priorities
in order.

Felicity sneered back at Ronnie. "Don't give me that,
ducky. Rina could beat anybody the way she's playing today." Rina ran out the child at one and love.

"Anybody?"

Felicity answered that only by tossing a provocative
shrug at Ronnie as she walked away from him.

He hurried to catch up with Rina. She had finished tap-
ing a brief interview with Bud Collins for NBC, and was
walking by herself back to her room. When she saw Ronnie
she greeted him with a broad smile—something he was sure
he'd never seen before. Previously, Rina had smiled only

fleetingly and furtively. And now, more than a smile, she also suddenly pecked Ronnie on his cheek. "Thanks for Papa last night," she said.

"Oh, any paragon of virtue would have done as much. Have you got a couple minutes to talk?"

Rina's mouth turned down. "I am sorry, but Papa will not ever let me talk with you once more. Not after New York and Ludmilla."

"I understand, Rina. Of course."

"But"—and she jabbed him—"I quick talk to you now before Papa catches us." And she steered Ronnie over to a little bench behind a low chaparral of Caribbean plantings. Especially since she was doing him such a nice favor, Ronnie restricted his questions to tennis, to the clichés of shots and potential and playing the big points—hoping that Rina might volunteer some revelations about her personal life, but not really expecting that . . . and not getting it either.

But she was such a nice kid, so cute, so sweet to risk her father's punishment by giving Ronnie this interview, that when they stood up to go, he playfully offered her his notepad. "I want you to interview me now," he said.

"Oh, what I ask you for quote?" she said. Rina had adapted exceptionally well to the Western world, to its nuances and inflections as much as its blue jeans and french fries—and quickly now she got into the game, snapped his notepad away, and held his pen, poised, to write.

"Well," Ronnie said, "I would just like the press to know that I've never seen Miss Rina Rodanya prettier than she is right now. You've changed so in just a few months. The way we say it is: she's blossomed."

Rina ducked her head and beamed. She knew Ronnie wasn't trying to make a pass at her, but she also recognized that he wasn't some old fogy who said that sort of thing to all the girls under the age of social security. Besides, she was damn sure he was right. She felt pretty. "Maybe someday soon I be second-prettiest girl on tennis tour," she said.

"Maybe already," Ronnie said, and he took the notepad

back and turned to walk away. That was when he heard Rina gasp, when he felt the pain chop into the base of his neck, and when he found himself bouncing off the bench and skidding across the lawn into the flowers.

When Ronnie reconnected his head to his shoulders and peered up through the ferns, Libor had his dukes up and was begging him to mix it up. "I tell you, I tell Rina," he snarled—for effect, he swept one hand toward her as he said that, rattling her in the shoulder—"never you talk to her. Never. I find you talk next time, you not never get up, you focking CIA, you."

Ronnie decided to stay down, occupying himself with brushing the dirt off. Rina started to sob a little, and yanked at her father's shirt, pleading with him in Bulgarian. At first Libor didn't listen, but then he jerked his head in some astonishment. Ronnie, carefully holding his assigned place in the flowers, figured, correctly, that she was telling her father about last night. Libor turned back to Ronnie. "You bring me home last night?"

Ronnie took this relatively civil remark as an excuse to pick himself up. "I found you passed out over there in the gazebo."

To express his gratitude, Libor took a menacing step closer to Ronnie and shot his hands up again. "You steal from me, huh? You steal my ring?"

Ronnie gulped and prepared to defend himself. Probably by running away, fast. But Rina jumped in between the two men and grabbed at her father. "He helped you, Papa. He helped you!"

"Him, CIA, *help*?" Libor spit on the ground in the general direction of Ronnie. "What I say to you is: fock you and fock the horse that bring you."

Nice grasp of the idiom, Ronnie thought. Libor yanked roughly at Rina and pulled her away, tussling her toward their room.

☙

Ronnie and Manda met for drinks that night after the evening's matches. It was a little late. Felicity had won the featured match love and love, but Tiffany Rogers was having her period and needed three long sets to beat somebody named Sarah Thomsen from Barbados, who was ranked one hundred and eighty-seventh in the world. Sarah had been included in the War Memorial Invitational only because she was the best professional from the Caribbean, and Fable figured they could use some local interest.

"I didn't know Tiffany had problems with her period," Ronnie said. He and Manda had gone to a little bar called the Nutmeg, in the Carenage area of St. George's.

"Oh, she doesn't—not in the usual sense," Manda said. "It's just that she lost her cherry a couple weeks ago to some rock guitar player, and she convinced herself that she must be pregnant, and so when her period did come—and right on time—it caused her such gratitude, she had difficulty maintaining her consistency, keeping momentum, concentrating, and—"

"Playing the big points well."

"Yes, absolutely, thank you."

"Don't worry, I won't write a word of this," Ronnie said.

"Au contraire, mon ami," Manda said. "As public-relations director of Eye-Woofy, I'm buying you all these alcoholic beverages in an effort to influence you into writing, in all your stories, not only that Tiffany got laid—by a man—but that she liked it immensely, plans to do it again, and to remain heterosexual for the rest of her life."

"Absolutely. I'll headline it," Ronnie said.

"I think Doreen's planning to videotape it the next time Tiffany gets screwed so that we can put it in our highlight film that we show sponsors. Cute as she is, hucklebuck, it would have really been a tough one for us if she'd come up dyke."

"Well, I'm glad you're happy, because I'm depressed."

"Oh, great," Manda said. "I came out with you tonight because I was depressed, and now you're going to depress me more."

"Hey, there's no law that says I can't have my time of the month too, you know."

"Okay, so what are you depressed about?"

"Felicity's going to marry Fable."

"So what else is new?"

"Libor knocked me into a flower garden this afternoon."

"That depresses you?"

"Well, that and what I did."

"What did you do?"

"I lay there and cowered, possibly even whimpered."

"That depresses you?"

"I think it means I've lost all my macho. You know, like you lost your heterosexuality or Peter Pan lost his shadow."

"Don't worry, Ratajczak. Unlike what me and Peter Pan lost, you never had much macho to lose."

"Thanks. There goes all my self-esteem." Ronnie ordered another round. "Besides, what really depresses me is that Libor will probably beat Rina up because she talked to me. You know, I'm the Mr. Nice Guy who was kind enough to drag his fat ass back to his room last night."

Manda nodded. By now everybody had heard of Libor getting Mickey Finned. "Oh, you should have heard him tonight," Manda said. "All he could keep talking about was his ring."

"What ring?"

"You know, that monster gold ring of his. His pride and joy. The first prize money Rina ever made in the free world, he made a side trip to Amsterdam and bought that ring for himself."

"He bitched about that ring to me," Ronnie said. "But it can't be. When I was lugging him, that big ham hock of a hand was hanging down like this"—Ronnie parodied a limp wrist, slapping the one hand with the other to emphasize how loose it was—"and it was the ring that kept banging into the side of my face, like this."

"Look, I don't know. But that's all he was pissing and moaning about—not the money he lost, not the gold chain. The ring."

"Damn," Ronnie said, and he banged his glass on the

table. "I mean, that doesn't make any sense. He had that ring on. You think maybe he's trying to work some insurance scam?"

"Hey, I don't know, hucklebuck. He got rolled last night and he hasn't got the ring today."

"Wait a minute," Ronnie said. He closed his eyes and mused.

"What are you doing?"

"I'm musing. Deep musing." He tried to think back, to reconstruct the scene, to visualize Libor—and every time he saw him, not only did he have the ring on, but also the gaudy chain was around his neck. And wait: when Ronnie saw himself reach into Libor's pocket for the key, wasn't there something else in the pocket he had to reach around? It felt like a wallet, didn't it? It wasn't a pack of chewing gum, was it?

"All right, what are you musing about?" Manda asked.

"I'm just musing that if he had the ring . . . and his gold chain, that crap . . . and I think he had a wallet too . . . and if he has all that when I pick him up and take him back to the room, and he doesn't have it the next day, then . . ."

Manda shrugged. "Then Rina stole it from her father. Is that what you're saying?"

Ronnie said, "Yeah, and I guess that doesn't make much sense, does it?"

"No." The new drinks came and Ronnie took a long pull on his. "And anyway, it doesn't matter. All that matters is that if he feels like it, the son of a bitch is going to beat up that great little girl of his."

Manda reached out and touched his hand. "Listen, I'll tell you something if you can keep it under your hat."

"Okay."

"Felicity's going to try something. She's getting Dale to offer Libor an extraordinary management contract for Rina. She figures if we can give the rat bastard a whole potful of money, maybe we can buy him off some, ease him out a little—maybe bring in a new coach for Rina, break the stranglehold. Dale's going to present the whole package to Libor in Manila."

"You mean it's a bad contract for Dale?"

"Right. No way he can make any money off it. But Felicity's making him do it."

"That's very sweet of her," Ronnie said.

"I know. She's an asshole only when it comes to you."

"Thanks. So what's depressing you?"

Manda leaned back in her chair. "I have a few days off before I have to be in the Philippines, and I was going home to see the kids."

"Well?"

"Well, Chris doesn't want me to do it."

"You have visitation rights, don't you?"

"Yes, but he just got married, and she doesn't want anything to do with me, and it'll be very upsetting to the kids, and so it isn't worth it."

"Are you sure?"

"Yeah, I'm sure. Not for just two or three days. Only, of course, that's all I wanted, the couple of days I had."

"Okay, so where are you going instead?"

"I don't know. Hawaii maybe. Or I could just go on ahead to the Philippines early. I hear there's some great beaches down on Cebu."

Ronnie slammed his hand down hard on the table. "No. No, you're not."

"I'm not what?"

"You're not going to Hawaii or Cebu."

"I'm not?"

"No, because you're going with me. Sugah chile, we're a-goin' to the Mardi Gras."

"We are?"

"That's right: Fat Tuesday, you and me. New Orleans. N'awlins. We'll go straight from here. I'm doing a travel story. You see, last year I went to Carnival in Rio, and now I'm doing Mardi Gras this year, and then I'll write a story comparing them. It's a natural. I can sell versions all over. Only some places it'll be entitled 'Carnival! The

Mardi Gras of South America!' And other places it'll be
'Mardi Gras! The Carnival of North America!' "

"Really?"

"Absolutely."

"But I'll never be able to get a room," Manda said.

"Dammit, you'll stay with me. We'll pretend to be living in sin, and we will, in every whicha way. We'll drink
like fish, we'll jam in the red beans and rice, we'll party
all night all over the Quatuh—"

"The where?"

"The Quatuh. The Quarter. The French Quarter. For reasons that have never been clear to me, they speak with a
Boston accent way down yonder in New Orleans. The Quatuh. Redfish at Mr. B's. And hey: you ever had mud bugs?"

"What?"

"Mud bugs. Crawfish. Crawfish pie and jambalaya. And
every night, Manda, every night, instead of screwing, we'll
trade the most magnificent back rubs."

"Hey, I like that."

"You know," Ronnie said, "sometimes I've been with
a beautiful, wonderful woman, and she's good with the
tactile stuff, and she's giving me a glorious back rub, and
all I start thinking is: damn, it's too bad this has got to end
in a while, because we've got to get around to screwing.
But for once I won't have that dilemma."

Manda considered Ronnie. "Are you all right, Ratajczak? Either you don't know how to screw or I don't know
how to enjoy a back rub."

"Well, all right, I was dealing in a little hyperbole."
And then Ronnie jumped up from his seat, took both of
Manda's hands in his, and in a firm clear voice said:
"Manda, dear, will you do me the honor of comin' with
me to the Mardi Gras in N'awlins, Loosiana?"

"I surely will, hucklebuck," Manda replied, and many
of the patrons applauded this touching love scene.

As the ranking WTO officer present, Prosper Hegginbosch
was called upon to make the victory presentation to Felici-

ty. She had been the picture of slashing grace, one of those days when she used every shot and every part of the court, varying her styles and her strategies as if she were displaying her repertoire and wasn't really terribly interested in whether she won or lost. But, of course, she won in straight sets, three and four—and clearly could have dispatched Polly Hutton faster had she wanted to.

Prosper congratulated Felicity on her victory, her one hundred and thirty-eighth in a row, and he also took the opportunity to congratulate Mrs. Doreen Whitridge on the magnificent job she was doing as director of the IWOOTP (although neglecting to inform the assembled that she had spent the previous night in his bed), and, as well, Prosper praised the emerging nation of Grenada for the wisdom and spirit it had exercised in holding this magnificent new event on the tennis calendar.

In the press section, Ronnie whispered to Manda: "Here it comes. Peace and brotherhood through tennis." And, sure enough, Prosper did not disappoint. With the Grenada War Memorial—or actually, suddenly it was now "the first annual" Grenada War Memorial—there was clear-cut evidence that, "If we can solve our differences upon the courts, as we did this week here, then certainly it is but one more step to discovering peace in the chambers of our world governments."

The fans applauded these insights heartily, and Prosper proceeded with the ceremony. He was ideal for his position in the World Tennis Organization, his qualifications being that he was a wealthy middle-aged businessman who enjoyed playing social tennis and traveling first class. This made him a "volunteer." Now, there are a number or organizations, of religion, of culture, of health or social concern, whose volunteers are inclined to eleemosynary or good-spirited instincts; and then there are other individuals who seek to serve their fellow men by wearing blazers and working for sports. Nowhere has this been raised to such a fine art as with the Olympics, golf, and tennis.

"Now, everybody join in," Manda whispered, and, like an orchestra leader, she conducted the press in a chorus with Prosper, as he intoned: "For, yes, the boy—or girl, as the case may be, of course—that young person with a tennis racket in his or her hand cannot also be carrying a machine gun or a firebomb!"

The climax. More applause. Modesty overcoming him, Prosper bowed his head that these original sentiments of his were so well-received. Then he nodded across the court, and Ronnie could see Bud Collins of NBC start to move out, carrying some red roses; behind him were Felicity and Fable, walking hand in hand. "And now," Prosper said, "ladies and gentlemen, please don't leave us, because, while this is the end of one tournament, it is the happy beginning of a much larger enterprise, and I'm proud now to turn the microphone over to Bud Collins, who has a very special announcement."

Maybe Ronnie could have stayed. He was prepared to. Only he could see that Fable was actually carrying a little ring box. He was going to slip the goddamn ring onto her finger right on TV, for the world to see. That was too much. Ronnie brushed past Manda and the lady from the Boston *Globe* and the one from *L' Equipe* and the stringer from *The National Enquirer* and the guy from the *Guardian*, and got to the end of the stand and climbed over the rail and jumped down. It was enough that he could hear the damn thing blaring out over the public address.

And finally, it was done, and he went to the press table, set up behind the courts, to write. Bad enough, too, that he had to write about Felicity's engagement to another man, he had to write it three times, for a Japanese paper, for a German paper, and for *USA Today*. He paused before diving into the second paragraph. It came slowly.

After the match, Tantamount told Bud Collins, the NBC commentator, and a worldwide audience that she and Dale Fable, her manager and the man who is generally accepted as the single most powerful force in the game, would marry at Centre Court of the All-England Club on Monday, July 7, the day following the conclusion of the Wimbledon championships. It will be the first marriage for the champion, and the second for Fable, who put the engagement ring on his intended's finger while the crowd cheered.

The bride-to-be also was presented with a diamond pin to commemorate the happy occasion, and then she told the excited crowd, "I . . ."

Ronnie stopped. The words wouldn't come—except for the fourletter ones that kept forming in his mind. He had set up at the end of the press table, and all along it, the other typewriters and word processors were going at a breakneck pace, especially the British, as they rushed to make their Greenwich Mean Time deadline. Fable had thought of everything. By making the announcement on a Sunday afternoon, he and Felicity had caught live American TV, as well as all the Monday-morning British editions. Already, back in London, the editors of the tabloids had bounced the latest IRA outrage off the front page and were busily writing Felicity marriage headlines.

Manda came over and rested a hand on Ronnie's shoulder. "I never saw you with typewriter block before," she said.

He clapped her hand over with his own. "Thanks, buddy. But then, I never lost the girl of my dreams before, either."

"You knew about this," Manda said.

"Yeah, but somehow . . . now that the whole fucking world knows . . ." He got up and headed over to a cooler to grab a beer.

"I'm not any help, am I?" Manda asked.

"No, not even you, babe," he said, and she punched him softly on the shoulder and left him to go back to work. He began typing again:

. . . and then she told the excited crowd, "I really love Ronnie Ratajczak, the famous writer and sophisticate, and regret any embarrassment that I have caused you, Dale, or my many fans." Ratajczak, more devilishly handsome then ever, then strolled confidently onto the court, swept Tantamount into his muscular arms, and carried her away to an undisclosed love nest as the startled crowd oohed and aahed its appreciation.

He tore that up and began again:

. . . and then she told the excited crowd, "This is so terribly hackneyed, but I can only say that I am the luckiest woman on this earth, that this wonderful man would want me."

The wedding has been rumored for several weeks in the tennis world, and in fact, recently in England, where betting is legal, bookies have offered odds on the probability of nuptials.

Ronnie stopped then and called down to the man from the *Times* of London, "Hey, Rex, excuse me, but what odds were they posting on the marriage?"

"Sorry, Ronnie?"

"You know, Hill's and Ladbroke's, Mecca, whatever—what were the odds they were offering on Felicity marrying Fable?"

"Ronnie, there was a lot of gossip about it, but nobody ever got round to setting any odds. However popular Felicity may be, that sort of thing only happens with the royal family."

"Are you sure?" Ronnie asked. "I mean, didn't one shop do it—just small bets, for the publicity?"

"Ronnie, I'm positive I'd've heard if that had been the case. Wait a second. John . . . John . . ." The man from the *Times* called over to the man from the *Telegraph*. "There weren't ever any odds offered on Felicity marrying Fable, were there—with the betting shops?"

"Nothing of the sort, no. A great deal of talk about it the last fortnight or so, but that's all."

"You heard that, did you, Ronnie?" the correspondent from the *Guardian* asked.

"I thought I did, yeah," Ronnie said, "but I guess I must have imagined it." And he went back to his story, crossed out the line, and struggled to write the next paragraph. But it was weird. It was just one more thing. Ever since he had agreed not to be a spy, things kept happening to him that didn't make any sense.

♄

Had Ronnie been aware that Lia had worn a gun the first time they had dinner, he would have taken a special pride in watching her dress for their second dinner date that Sunday evening. She pulled on her dress—a creamy white, pleated, trimmed in violet with a matching belt—and then she lifted her leg up on a chair so that she might strap on the holster. But suddenly Lia stopped and put the gun away in her drawer.

Ronnie had the driver deliver them up-island to a little restaurant called the Bosun's Hut. It was billed as the most romantic in Grenada, and surely it was—intimate, a piano playing, Mount St. Catherine behind them while they overlooked the Caribbean and Grand Anse beach. They chose the lobster and curried conch, and Ronnie had Lia order the wine.

They laughed at that and at a lot of other things. He already knew she was smart (and ravishing), but now Lia was revealing herself to be warm and fun, as well. It frightened him a little, because Ronnie knew that women like that are complicated . . . especially for the men who dare prize them. Ronnie made Lia talk about herself then, which she did, comfortably, and truthfully, too, except for the parts she left out.

Her father was a professor of art, she began, and she herself had been inclined toward an academic life until she came down to Rome for college and got caught up in the rebellion of the late sixties. "I moved in with another student," she said.

"A boy?" Ronnie asked.

"I don't know."

"You don't?"

"Well, actually, I thought he was a man then. But maybe he was still a boy. Anyway, boy or man, I loved him, and we were going to marry."

"Did you?"

"No, he was killed."

"Oh, I'm sorry."

"I'm not," Lia said straightaway. "Wait . . . I know that sounds terrible. I mean only that I'm not sorry for me. Of course I'm sorry for him. But Paolo was so unyielding. He believed in revolution, and in violence—"

"A Communist?"

"Not the way you think it, no. The Brigate Rosse, the Red Brigades—we might have called ourselves Communists, but we lacked the ideology. We were drifters, political and intellectual hobos. The KGB just used us. We were anxious little terrorists. And Paolo never would have changed—and I'm afraid that I loved him so, that I never would have either. I'd still be a terrorist, and we would have kept living on the run—hiding, plotting, killing maybe. I know that now."

"But then you loved him?"

"Oh yes. When I heard the news . . ." She paused. "There was this kidnap, but someone had told, and the police were ready for us, and he was killed quickly by a fusillade, and I was so hurt, so destroyed, that I . . . I'm sorry, what is that word when you lose a child?"

"You mean miscarry?"

"Yes. It was almost three months old. And, as horrible as that was too, sometimes I think it saved me, for I was prepared to do something—anything—to avenge Paolo, but when I lost the child, his child, our child, it left me so empty and—"

"Lia, you don't have to tell me this."

"No, it's very easy, Ronnie. I don't tell everybody, of course, but it is no trouble when I feel like it, because it's like I'm telling a story about somebody else. That girl, that silly little pregnant bombthrower, that is not the woman who orders your wine."

He took the cue and toasted her. "Well, all right, thank you for . . . telling me so much."

"And you are not what I expected, Ronnie," Lia said.

"Oh, what did you expect?"

"Never mind. For now, I would prefer to enjoy the unexpected.'' And then she told him more, about a life slowly coming back together after Paolo died; about a return to school and art, and a new interest in business. After graduation, she went to work as an interior decorator, so she could combine her interests. Eventually she moved into *haute couture*—not as a designer, but strictly on the business side. When Grazia was taken over, she was brought in as a vice-president, and was now executive vice-president—a high position for anyone so young, but especially for a woman in a Latin country.

She saw Ronnie raise a suspicious eyebrow as she related this. ''Oh, are you wondering?'' Lia asked. ''Don't. I slept with no one to get promoted.''

He chuckled. ''Oh no, I wasn't wondering . . . much.''

''Of course, I might have. You never know. Perhaps in the United States, where there are so many women in competition now, you must sleep with someone to gain ground. But that's not yet the case in Italy. I was afraid: I sleep with one, I would have to sleep with them all, because there are no other ladies to do it.''

Outside, Ronnie told the driver to wait, and he and Lia took off their shoes and walked along the beach. As soon as he picked up a stone and skipped it on the water, she laughed.

''Why did you laugh at me?'' he asked. He thought he'd thrown it quite well, thanks.

''Not at you. I was only laughing that you threw the stone. Now, I don't want you to think that all Lia does is walk along beaches with men, but I'll tell you, if you walk with an American, he'll throw stones—''

''Dammit, I'm Canadian.''

''Forgive me, of course. But for these purposes, the same. North Americans. You throw.''

''Is that unusual?''

''Oh yes. The European boys. They do not grow up throwing. They kick. If you were a European, now you would be pawing at the sand, kicking the foam off the waves. You all make love the same, you know. No bloody difference. I mean, yes, some good, some not so good, some bad. But all the same. The difference is only: you throw, they kick.''

Instantly then, as soon as she stopped talking, he threw a shell and then he grabbed her—not roughly, but in a sweep that caught Lia at the back of her waist and drew her to him in one motion. A man who could throw well could do that too. It was the same action and rhythm, and it brought her body to his in an arc and her mouth to the brink of his lips. There he stopped. ''I want very much to kiss you, Lia,'' Ronnie said properly.

''You may,'' she replied in kind, and they did, standing there at the water's edge, holding their shoes and themselves.

''That was very nice,'' Ronnie said, still holding her tight to him, looking into her eyes.

''Yes. But that must be all for now.''

''Why?''

''Because I know your heart is with another woman, and I don't ever want you to make love to me and think of someone else.'' He didn't argue, for she was right. ''Unfortunately, Ronnie''—a smile broke here—''you still wish to undress Felicity as much as I wish to dress her.''

♫

In her suite, after Ronnie had brought her home, Lia took out the report she had on him and studied it again. The picture first, for pleasant memories. The dossier, for more clues. Only then did she take out the tape recorder and speak into it: ''I had dinner again tonight with Ratajczak, and I will see him again in Manila, as well. Is he even a better actor than I am? He is so very different from the others you meet in this business. Can you be sure about him? He is not the type at all.''

But she could not resist. As soon, then, as she clicked off the machine, Lia said, ''But he is my type,'' right out loud, and, like a schoolgirl, cooed at his picture, and took her index finger, her trigger finger, and drew it across the lips that had kissed her under the stars on the beach.

LONDON
II

As planned, Gerry and Cynthia met each other the next morning at the Earl's Court underground station. Both carried the morning's newspapers and read them vigorously, for the news of Felicity's engagement was everywhere. The tabloids all played it as their lead story. The poor IRA: a distinguished old pub bombed, and not even front page. The *Star* had it: "TANTAMOUNT TO MARRIAGE." The *Sun*: "FABLE & FELICITY: THE POWER AND THE GLORY." And the *Express*: "LOVE MATCH SET."

"Well," Gerry piped up, scanning all the stories, "our friend Mr. Ratajczak was right on the money, wasn't he now?"

Their train on the District Line came in, and they boarded it together. Both Gerry and Cynthia were in business suits, with overcoats this raw day, and both carried briefcases. They looked exactly like the lawyer and real-estate broker they were supposed to be. "Yes indeed," Cynthia said as they took their seats, "I'm not so sure our new colleague wouldn't make a fine spy." The car wasn't crowded. This time of day, most of the traffic was commuters coming into the city, not spies going out.

"You mean for real, full-time," Gerry said.

"Quite," said Cynthia. "He has the right instincts."

They settled back to peruse their papers then. "I didn't

know this," Gerry squeaked after a bit, tapping a photograph of Prosper Hegginbosch pinning a diamond brooch on Felicity's shoulder. The pin was valued in excess of $100,000 and was, ostensibly, an engagement present from the Grenada War Memorial Invitational. In fact, Fable had had it written into the tournament's contract, as, in effect, his own engagement present to his affianced.

"Ah, just another bagatelle," Cynthia laughed. Everything's relative. After Felicity had won the Grand Slam two years running—and the million-dollar Lloyd's of London bonus that goes with such an achievement—the mere money had seemed so pedestrian that, the next year when she won the Slam again, the WTO had given Felicity a million-dollar diamond choker instead, and, the year following, when she won the Slam yet again, they presented her with a matching bracelet and ring of the same two-comma value. This year, should she make it her fifth straight Grand Slam, the rumor was that a million-dollar tiara would be the bonus. What was left?

Gerry and Cynthia chatted aimlessly the rest of the way, past Parsons Green and East Putney, past Southfields, which is the station that actually serves the All-England Club, and on to the end of the line and the Wimbledon stop. They alighted there and walked to the street, where a limousine was waiting for them. The driver rushed around to open the door. The driver was, in fact, Rudy, but he was decked out impeccably in a chauffeur's uniform, and not until they were safely ensconced in the back of the car did Gerry and Cynthia give any indication that the driver was, really, their colleague from the Chelsea CIA office.

Rudy drove them directly to the house in Merton that Cynthia had reserved for the Fortnight. The owner, a Mrs. Featherstone, was expecting them, and had tea and scones. It was lucky they had come today rather than later in the week, she said, because the family always gave up scones for Lent.

Politely but firmly Gerry explained: "Mrs. Featherstone, we must have a clear understanding. Miss Piper-Cross here has a check for the first week's rental, and the complete payment will be made on the day before the Fortnight begins, but should there be any publicity whatsoever regarding the fact that a player has rented these premises, then you will be obliged to forfeit all payments.''

''I quite understand, Mr. Whittelsley,'' she said.

''Good. I don't like to be pedantic, but I trust you appreciate that my client—who must go nameless—is an important tennis player and his or her whole purpose in renting this location is to be near the club, yet at enough of a remove to avoid the spotlight.''

''Yes, I'm aware of all that,'' Mrs. Featherstone said.

''And of course, as Miss Piper-Cross advised you on the phone, should my client enjoy the privacy he—or she—seeks throughout the Fortnight, an additional bonus payment of one hundred pounds will be remitted to you immediately.''

Mrs. Featherstone smiled broadly and assured Gerry that she fully understood the situation, so there was no need for her to run the contract past her solicitor, and she was, in fact, prepared to sign it right now. That done, she gave Gerry a full tour of the premises, even to the cellar and the odd closets.

''That will do perfectly,'' Gerry said to Rudy back in the limousine. ''And I must say, you make a very nice driver. Let's go straightaway to see that airfield Colin has found for us, but follow the path we have in mind, up past the club and then over by King George Park.''

It was not a pleasant day, with blustery winds and the first hint of a late winter's snowstorm circling in off the Atlantic from Iceland. They wanted to get down to Hampshire and back to London before the snow. Gerry looked out upon the fields, all brown and bare, as they moved along the M3. ''Hard to believe how it'll be so lush in just a few months' time, isn't it?'' he said idly.

''Yes, almost exactly four months to the Fortnight and strawberries and cream,'' Cynthia said.

NEW
ORLEANS

During the Crewe of Argus parade, Manda got a little chilly and left Ronnie to go back to their room and pick up a sweater. She came through the door and headed toward the bathroom, and just as she got there she heard the little bells. Even before she could react, it was too late, for his hand slid across her mouth and the knife flashed before her eyes. "Don't say anything," he said, although it was not necessary for him to say that, inasmuch as Manda's vocal cords were somewhere in her uterus.

He waited till she stopped shaking. "All right, get in the bathtub," he said, and she started shaking again. Manda had never been raped in a bathtub before. She wet her pants. He pushed her toward the tub, and when she climbed into it, for the first time she could see him. He had on a silly clown outfit, harlequin, complete with a mask and makeup and a little jester's cap. That was where the little bells were tinkling. "Not a sound," he said, menacing her one more time with the knife, shaking his little bells in the bargain.

Then he saw a pair of her panty hose. Manda had washed them out and hung them up to dry before she and Ronnie went out. The clown slashed them down the middle so he could use one leg to bind Manda's hands and the other for her feet. It was her last chance. She thought about screaming then, but he was liable to stab her in the heart if she did, and anyway, who would pay any attention if they heard some mere screaming during Mardi Gras?

$$\wp$$

Ronnie had a hard time getting the knots undone. The clown must have been a Boy Scout *emeritus* or a sailor or something. They were very good knots. "You know, Ronnie, I hate to bring this up," Manda said, "but it seems nowadays that whenever I get in your hotel room, somebody gets tied up."

"Yeah, I'm on a hot streak."

"I like the arrangement even less when it's me the one getting tied."

Still, if her wrists were sore, she was otherwise unhurt. "And he didn't do anything else to you?" Ronnie asked.

"No, just this." He got her feet undone and helped her out of the tub, and then he held her for a long, long time. Manda shook again.

"Oh, my God, I'm so sorry I did this to you, Manda."

"It's okay, hucklebuck. Since he had a mask on, he didn't even have to blindfold me."

"That would've been scary. I guess that's some consolation."

"Yeah, but if anything," Manda said, "I'd've requested earplugs."

"How's that?"

The whole time, he kept whistling country-and-western. And nobody can whistle country-and-western well."

"What was he whistling?"

"I told you. Country-and-western."

"No. I mean what exactly?"

"It was so awful it was hard to tell. I think it was 'The Orange Blossom Special' at some point. And then some truck-driving song, and a whole Tammy Wynette medley. I think."

Ronnie finished the job and looked on her sweetly. They were dressed as medieval royalty, he as a nondescript knight and she a lady of the court in a great flowing gown and (although it wasn't on now) one of those cone-type hats with a lace train flowing behind her head. "Well, you still look great," Ronnie said.

"As those fellows go, I'd have to say he was every bit the gentleman," Manda said.

"Spies are like that nowadays," Ronnie said.

"What do you mean: *spy*?"

He gave her a drink, and she tossed it down without even any ice. Ronnie said: "Yeah, well, I started to tell you this before, in New York and Grenada—"

"Tell me what?"

"Just something somebody should know about. In case anything ever happened to me. Somebody should know. Besides, now I feel guilty, because I'm responsible for this." And he wrapped Manda in his arms and held her again. "I'm so sorry I did this to you, honey."

Manda cocked her head. "What *are* you talking about?" she said. "What did you have to do with this? I'm a big girl. I can go back to my room alone. I do it enough."

"No, you don't understand."

"Yes, I do. Stop feeling guilty. There's nothing you can do. The guy was a pro, a second-story man. Sure, at first I thought I was in for a good old-fashioned rape—maybe a rape-and-murder combo, hold the mayo—but he never touched me, Ronnie. I mean even when he tied me up, not so much as a passing feel. He just got the job done, left me in the bathtub, and then came back out here and started going through your suitcase."

That was apparent. Ronnie's stuff was scattered all over. "Not yours?" he asked.

"No, you can see. And he left the bathroom door open so he could keep an eye on me. So I could see the whole time."

"And don't you think that's odd, Manda? If anything, the woman has more valuable stuff, jewelry. A thief is not going to pass up a woman's suitcase. I'm telling you, he's a spy."

"All right, whose spy?"

"I don't know that for sure. I don't really know what exactly he was looking for. Probably my code books, stuff like that."

"You have code books?"

"Well, no, I don't. But he obviously thought I did."

"Ronnie, why?"

"Because he thinks I'm a spy."

"Are you, Ronnie?" Manda said. "I mean, ever since I came on tour, the two rumors I heard about you were that you were a great lover and you had to be working for the CIA because you flew all over the world and dressed well and all that. Only I knew how you worked out your expenses and managed your life, and I knew you weren't the spy type. But then, here's Felicity passing you up for Dale Fable, so you must *not* be the great swordsman you're cracked up to be, so maybe you *are* a spy because I figured you weren't."

Ronnie said, "I hate to destroy all your illusions, but, Manda, I never even slept with Felicity."

Manda rapped her forehead with the heel of her hand in mock shock. "Is there nothing a girl can put her faith in anymore?"

"No," Ronnie said, "the only things left that you can still be sure of are airplane crashes and airplane food."

"And you're a spy?"

"No, Manda, I'm not a spy. But yes, I am working for the CIA. They're paying me not to be a spy."

"I need another drink," Manda said, so this time Ronnie fetched the ice and made them both a proper Scotch, and then he explained it all to her, about the contact in Punta, the deal, the money, Dana, everything.

"Only . . ." Manda said as soon as he was finished. "Only they promised you nobody would involve you, and right away there was Ludmilla defecting."

"That's right. Libor must have gotten the word right away that I was a spy now, and so he told her."

"Fine. And now you've got some whistling creep with a knife breaking into your hotel room, trying to steal your fucking nonexistent code books. I'd say it ain't worth it, hucklebuck."

"I'd say that too."

"So you're going to tell the CIA to keep their ten grand a month?"

"No, I'm not."

"Why?"

"Because I'm pretty sure I know who the real spy is, who Dana is, and if I can be a decoy and help, then I'm going to."

"The hero, huh?"

"No," said Ronnie. "A friend, that's all."

"You mean," Manda said carefully, "you know who the CIA spy is? You know who Dana is?"

"Well, I'm not positive. The way I figure it, there's two possibilities. And they're both my friends."

"Oh?" Manda said.

"Yeah, one of them's Felicity."

Manda immediately gagged on her drink, and some of it fell down the bodice of her costume. "Are you out of your gourd? Why in God's name would she do a thing like that?"

"Because, if you're the greatest woman athlete in the world, and you're the most beautiful woman in the world, after a while that gets old-hat, and if you're Felicity Tantamount, you look around for new worlds to conquer, don't you? Think about it, Manda. It'd be right in character for her to try to be Mata Hari on the side, wouldn't it? And maybe win the goddamn Medal of Honor and the Croix de Guerre and the Order of the British Empire and everything. I mean, how many Wimbledons can a girl win and not get jaded?"

"I still can't believe it," Manda said.

"And maybe you're right. I've got even more circumstantial evidence on someone else."

"Oh yeah? Who's that?"

"Remember in New York I told you not to mention anything about Young Zack Harvey appearing out of nowhere to help you?"

"Young? Young might be CIA?"

"He was the one who didn't want it to get out that he'd helped Ludmilla get away. Hell, I would have given him all the credit in the world."

"Young Zack? In the CIA?"

"It figures," Ronnie said, swirling the ice in his drink, like he was the detective about to declare that the butler did it. "First off, he went to Yale, where most kids practically major in the CIA. And he's always asking me questions about the places I've been, and about the Communists on the women's tour. And now, get this. He not only pops up in New York riding on strange freight elevators, the other day what does he do? He flies to Grenada on his way from California to Japan."

"Young was in Grenada?"

"You bet he was. Not only that—"

"Wait a minute," Manda said, grabbing the green vest-type thing Ronnie had on. "God, I'd forgotten all about this. Remember back in November we had the tournament in Bucharest."

"Sure. I was there. The first women's tournament behind the Iron Curtain, the President Ceausescu Round-Robin Classic."

"Right. And remember. We had everybody, players, press, officials, everybody staying at the same hotel. Only a couple of the British writers came in late, and we had to find space for them, and I had to take them over to another hotel, on the other side of the Dimbovita, and just as we're going into the lobby, I swear, across the way, over by the steps. It was Young."

"It was? In Bucharest?"

"Positive. Only as soon as he saw me, he ducked up the stairs. The next time I ran into him was a few weeks later, in Melbourne, and I asked him about it, and he said I was crazy, he'd never been to Bucharest in his life. So I figured what the hell, it was his double."

"Thanks," Ronnie said. "You can be sure it was Young. And not only that, but in Grenada he was hiding out, sneaking around, and he had a gun, Manda."

"A gun? Young?"

"A pistol, yeah. And I swear to you, if I hadn't been there, I think he would have blown away Libor the night he got the Mickey Finn."

"Slow down, Ratajczak. What's Libor got to do with the price of eggs."

"Well, obviously he's a spy too. You could tell in New

York how chummy he was with all those KGB pros. All right, sure, he's Rina's father and all that, but you know he can't coach worth a damn—not at this level. The Commies aren't dumb. If they wanted Rina to win—I mean, if that were priority—they'd say: Look, Papa Rodanya, you can come see her in Paris and Wimbledon, but for now, you stay home in the mountains, and we get a real coach for the tour.''

"Okay," Manda said.

"But what an opening for a spy. He's got carte blanche, traveling in the West. Athletics is brotherhood and all that crap Prosper likes to babble on about. What athletics is is the perfect invitation for the Russkies to send espionage agents all over the world. The perfect cover. And I'm sure it works both ways.

"I mean, this sort of thing has been going on for a long time. For years—I mean long before the CIA came into my life—I heard the story about this American player back in the fifties. He was only ranked about twenty, twenty-five in the country, but there wasn't a tournament he didn't play in in Europe. Back then, when Wimbledon was over, all the American players were forced to come back to the States by the U.S. Lawn Tennis Association. They had to come home and play in the American summer tournaments. Except for the one guy. He got to stay and play all over Europe all summer.''

"And he was a spy?"

"Yeah. For sure. And you can bet even more that the Commies have always had a spy on tour.''

"What's Young up to?" Manda asked. "I mean, if he really is Dana.''

"That I don't know. They won't tell me what the operation is. I don't think he's just supposed to tail Libor or rub him out or anything gross like that. I mean, if Libor was the whole point of interest, then they'd need someone besides Young—someone on the women's tour full-time.''

"Felicity," Manda said.

"You see? The interest she takes in Rina. Now you tell me about this new contract she's getting Fable to offer

Libor. Dale Fable's never in his life written a contract he knew he'd lose on.''

''But if it were to help save Western civilization and our democratic way of life—''

''Exactly,'' Ronnie said. ''So even if I don't know for sure which one is Dana, I'm going to stay on as their silent doubles partner and help out.''

''That's all very noble. Only your friends don't know you're Mr. Undercover, and maybe the next time, we don't just get tied up in a bathtub, we go down the drain.''

Ronnie shrugged, and moved closer to Manda and took her by the shoulders. ''I know. You're the best friend I've got, and I wasn't fair to you,'' he said.

''Oh, Ronnie,'' Manda said, and she fell against his chest. ''Please don't you get hurt.''

He held her tightly to him for a moment, and then stood back some. ''Want to go out to the parade again?''

''Not really,'' she said. ''Not anymore.''

''Me neither.'' Ronnie took his hands off her shoulders then and reached down to her breasts and untied her bodice.

''What are you doing, white man?'' Manda asked.

''I thought we ought to go to bed,'' he said, and she didn't stop him then, when he pulled the gown so fast that it fell at her feet, or next, when he reached around her and unfastened her brassiere, so that that tumbled to the floor too.

He had never looked at her this way before. ''You know, Mrs. Cross,'' he said at last, ''you could make some woman very happy.''

''Oh God, Ronnie, nobody ever spoke like that to me quite that way before.''

They rushed into bed then, and he switched off the lights, and soon, as she moved closer, he caressed her, and there were only the sounds of Manda's sighs. ''Oh, Ronnie,'' she cried, ''I'd forgotten how wonderful this could be. You do it so well.'' And moments later. ''Harder, harder! There, right there!''

Ronnie said: ''Do you want me to scratch you some too? I can scratch every bit as good as I can rub.''

"Yeah, do that for a couple minutes, and then it's my turn to rub your back," Manda cooed.

Ọ

The phone woke them the next morning. "Ronnie Ratajczak?" said the perfectly toneless male voice. "This is Colin's good friend."

"Yeah?"

"I've got something for you, from Colin."

"You weren't the son of a bitch in the clown outfit who already came here last night, were you?"

"What are you talking about?"

"You tell Colin that somebody broke into my room last night and went through my stuff," Ronnie said. "Now, this kind of crap wasn't supposed to happen."

"There's no such thing as a free lunch," said the voice.

"I don't need the cracker-barrel philosophy," Ronnie said.

"Well, all right, chief, can you use ten thousand dollars?"

"My March payment?"

"That's right. A couple days early."

Ronnie thought for a moment. He even glanced over at Manda, who was already asleep again. "Where do I go?"

"Houlihan's. It's in the Quarter—"

"You're not from around here, are you?" Ronnie said, interrupting.

"Maybe."

"Naw, don't bullshit me. You say 'Quarter,' not 'Quatuh.'"

"Okay, okay. Just meet me at Houlihan's at eleven o'clock sharp this morning."

"I'll be there," Ronnie said.

"Good. You stand by the jukebox and play 'Sweet Caroline,' by Neil Diamond. As soon as the song starts, I'll come by. I'll say: 'Hey, you got change for a dollar?' and you'll say yeah, and you'll fish into your pocket and give me the change. And I'll hand you the bill—only it'll be a five, not a single."

"Just to be sure?"

"Right. You're gonna make an extra four bucks outta this."

"Okay," Ronnie said.

"Now then, after I take the money, I'm going to be carrying a morning paper. The *Times-Picayune*. I'm going to lay that mother on the top of the jukebox there, and you say: 'Hey, you finished with that?' And I say, 'Yeah, you can have it.' And you take it, and when you open it up outside you'll find an envelope taped inside the paper, and your ten grand will be in it. Okay?"

So Ronnie got up and left Manda and went to Houlihan's. It was at the edge of the Quarter, away from the big hotels, more like a neighborhood bar. It was dark inside and most of the people seemed to know each other and the bartenders and waitresses. Except for a couple of tourists who were already in costume (or still in costume from the night before) who were snapping silly flashbulbs of themselves, there wasn't a whole lot of activity. Mardi Gras can be very wearing.

Ronnie went directly to the jukebox, found 'Sweet Caroline'—G7—met the contact, picked up the newspaper, and departed. It all went without a hitch, and outside, he crossed the street and discreetly opened the envelope and peeked in. It was all there, in hundred-dollar bills. But there were also a ten and a twenty, and with them a note, attached by a paper clip. It read: "Your share of the bet Colin cashed on Felicity's wedding plans. With thanks for tipping him."

Ronnie shook his head at that, and rather than hailing a cab, he walked back to the hotel through the Quarter, trying to figure out why Colin was continuing this charade about there being a betting line on Felicity's marriage. It didn't make much sense, unless, of course, the CIA had an especial professional interest in her life and loves, and Colin was merely applying a simple little ruse to try to extract more information from Ronnie about Felicity.

MANILA

The Philippines is one of those poor countries where airports are still arenas, where the people come out just to watch the planes land and take off. There were hundreds of spectators arrayed around the roof mezzanine, standing room only, when Manda and Ronnie got off the plane in Manila. Outside again, after going through customs and picking up their luggage, there were throngs more trying to sell them Pepsi-Colas and spare cigarettes and sticks of gum. The morning sun was blazing, it was already uncomfortably sultry, and Ronnie bought a soda for them to share, rubbing the cold bottle across his forehead as they steered behind the porter, trying to reach the cab rank.

Neither of them noticed the big Filipino watching them from across the throng. With the Spanish infusion, Filipinos tend to be somewhat taller than other Orientals, but this fellow positively towered over the others in the crowd. He was known as Bubbles; Filipinos all seem to have nicknames; the smaller guy beside him was Powder Blue. He was the one who spotted Ronnie and Manda. "There," he said. "There's the one they've named the Dahlia."

Bubbles started to go toward them. "Wait," Powder Blue said. "I wouldn't try to make contact now. Dahlia doesn't seem to be alone."

It was too late for Bubbles anyway, because suddenly a

stubby little Filipino driving a Chrysler left the car in the middle of the entrance driveway, jumped out, and ran over to Manda. "You Miss Cross, please?"

"Yes," she said.

"Then you come with me, please. You stay with Mr. Dale Fable."

"I do?" She and Ronnie both had reservations at the Peninsula.

"He has whole house. You guest."

Ronnie shrugged. "Come on, I'll ride with you," he said, and they piled into the big car, and Baby—for that was the driver's name—found his way through the mob. For that matter, he cut right by where Bubbles and Powder Blue stood, and for just an instant Ronnie's eyes met those of the huge Filipino standing on the curb looking in the window.

Baby drove them into town and took the turnoff where the sign said Makati. "I thought so," Ronnie said to Manda. "Makati's the best section of town, near here they're playing the matches." And soon enough, once Baby had eased the car past another brigade of cigarette and gum vendors, they found themselves almost immediately in a wealthy residential section with grand houses set back behind high walls. Some even had guardhouses, in that fashion of most countries where there are a few too many rich and far too many poor pressed close upon one another. Especially since the Communists—the New People's Army—had begun to show a more substantial presence, the wealthier Filipinos had begun to hedge their bets, with such traditional refuges for their capital as Swiss banks and Beverly Hills real estate. It had not been difficult for Fable to find a manor for a week's rental.

Baby pulled up to a guardhouse that was set in the middle of the road, with gates extending on either side. The guard, who was armed, recognized Baby and the Chrysler, though, and quickly raised the gate and waved them through. "Forbes Park," Baby announced proudly. In Makati, the best section, it was the best section. Baby pointed out the American ambassador's house as they drove past it, and then turned the car onto Pandan Street, and into the driveway of the estate Dale Fable had rented.

He was at the door, and he greeted Manda warmly, but when Ronnie pulled himself out of the car next, Fable did almost a stage double-take. "Don't worry, Dale," Ronnie said. "I'm just hitching a ride on my way to the Peninsula."

Fable was relieved by that report. "Listen, you're welcome to stay, Ronnie," he said with patent insincerity.

"No, thanks. I've got some jet lag, and I want to get settled at the hotel."

"Whatever you say. Manda got the last room, but we could find a sofa for you. We're just filled up with some of the sporting-goods folks."

"No, thanks, I'll be leaving . . ." Ooops. *Sporting-goods folks*. That's what Lia was, a sporting-goods folk. "You know, Dale, maybe a dip to take off the travel dust."

"Sure," Fable said. "Baby's going to run Rina and Libor back over to the Peninsula in a little while, and you can hitch a ride with them."

Then, as if on cue, the Bulgarian sort of rolled around the corner, his fat, hairy belly hanging out over a pair of bikini trunks. He had a large rum drink in his hand.

Fable forced a smile, and Libor managed a grunt, the scintilla of civility he was capable of. Fable somehow made himself approach Libor and actually laid a hand on his shoulder. "Now, of course, this is off the record right now, Ronnie," he said, "but Libor and I are very close to finalizing a contract for Rina to be managed by Fable Associates."

"Very much dollars," Libor said, and then he turned, walking out from under Fable's fraternal hand, and went back to the screen porch, where he plopped himself down there on the big couch with all the pillows, the papasan. "The Sultan of Sweat," Ronnie said to himself and to Fable, under his breath.

Then he changed into his trunks and made his entrance before the pool. Most of the houseguests were decorating themselves with the sun, around the pool—he saw Lia right away—and beyond, on the tennis court, Felicity and Young Zack were practicing against Tiffany Rogers and John McEnroe. It was another tribute to Fable that he had been able to bring so many of the biggest names in tennis together for (of all things) a mixed-doubles tournament, but then, Imelda Marcos had taken to the idea, and the government coffers had been opened wide; there was no telling how much guarantee money had been assured the biggest names—never mind the million dollars in prize money.

Fable had put the teams together himself, trying to handicap to a certain degree. Tiffany, for example, was as bad a doubles player as a professional could be, so he paired her with McEnroe, the nonpareil at the art of doubles. But also Fable had been sure to use the tournament and its worldwide television exposure to showcase his full stable of talent. He could have hooked Felicity up with any of his best male clients, but he picked Young Zack as her partner because his contracts for both racket and shoe endorsements were up soon. Fable put Rina and Ivan Lendl together as an Iron Curtain tandem.

But, Ronnie thought, to hell with the tennis.

Lia was there.

She was lying facedown on a chaise, chatting with Rina. They were over by the diving board, and so, casually ignoring her at first, Ronnie turned the other way and went around the shallow end, trooping the royalty of international sporting-goods fashions:

First there was Keiko Harimoto of Geisha, who smiled his usual smile and gave Ronnie one of the many pocket-size calendar/computer/currency-exchange calculators he always carried in his shoulder bag. Then, sipping a rum and calamansi and chatting in German with Prosper Hegginbosch, was Wilhelm Bunderhaas, the cut-throat business genius who had made Allmälich the largest sporting-goods company in the world. Bunderhaas barely acknowledged Ronnie, merely wagging his bushy eyebrows at him. René Lefèvre of Triomphe was more friendly. He waved from the pool, where he was lolling on an air mattress sipping rum out of a glass that he shared with Gigi, the former Belgian player who had become his mistress.

Ronnie turned to the players next. "Hello there, gladiators," he called out to the court. Tiffany said, "Hi, Ronnie." Felicity saluted him cheerily. Young Zack intoned, "Here comes the First Amendment." McEnroe hollered, "There goes the neighborhood." So Ronnie threw him the finger in a friendly way and turned back to discover, accidentally, of course, Lia.

He took further pains to clasp Rina's hand first. She snuck a look back toward the house to make sure her father wasn't watching, and then she squeezed Ronnie's hand warmly, and they exchanged a wink, as well.

Only then, at last, did he turn to Lia. She'd been sunning a bare back, but had fastened her top, and now she sat up. Casually then, precisely as he had planned it, Ronnie gave Lia his left hand (sort of an afterthought, you see) and said, *"Buon giorno, signorina."*

Lia did not miss a beat. She used the hand he extended to bring herself to her feet and trumped his Italian by using Tagalog, the native Philippine dialect. *"Hoy mama, kumusta ka?"* she said. "Hi, guy, how are you?" Put off for a second, pleasantly chagrined that Lia had bested him, he barely noticed that her eyes darted to the side, to where a practice point had just ended on the court. Suddenly, then, she took his shoulder with one hand and brought him to her so that she could kiss him.

Oh, it certainly wasn't passionate, but neither was it a casual peck on the cheek. It was square on the lips. And Ronnie was so surprised by the gesture that he didn't realize that Lia's kiss was meant mainly to send Felicity a message. And surely it did. She stood there on the court transfixed for so long, her breasts heaving under her T-shirt, that McEnroe, who was about to serve, at last felt obliged to call out sarcastically: "Whenever you're ready, Felice."

Ivan Lendl came out of the house then in his swim trunks. He and Rina had finished practicing, and he was going to take a dip. Rina went over to see him, and left

Ronnie and Lia standing there alone. "Well, that was nice," he said.

"Why not? I liked your kisses in Grenada."

"I only kissed you once."

"No, you forget—and even though you do it so well. Twice. Once on the hand. Once on the lips. Each was special."

"Mutual."

"Besides, in this bitchy little tennis world, I understand everybody already assumes that I'm sleeping with you, so I might as well give them what they want." And this time she gave Ronnie a playful little pinch on his cheek.

Felicity promptly dumped an easy backhand volley into the net.

"Sorry, love," she said to Young. "My boobs got in the way." But they hadn't. Just her curiosity.

Ronnie gestured toward the other end of the pool. "Well, does this mean that it's just down to a final four? Allmäh-lich, Triomphe, Geisha, and you?" He sat down on the chaise Rina had been using, Lia across from him, their knees touching.

"Hardly. As a matter of fact, now Von Reich has gotten into the running. They met with Dale last week in Chicago. And there's even an American company making some sound—"

"Making some noises."

"As you wish. And not to mention the Koreans. The president of Banner Day himself is flying down here later in the week, and he's bringing most of the '88 Olympic committee with him."

"What's that got to do with dressing Felicity?"

"Oh, just more prestige. More credentials. What chance does a poor little Italian girl have?"

"Good. Then let's you and me get the hell out of here. There's a resort just an hour and a half from here. Puerto Azul. As you said, we don't want to disappoint all those people who assume we're sleeping together."

"Oh, come on, Ronnie. You know what my mission is.

As long as Willie and Keiko and René are right here with Felicity and Dale, I can't budge.''

''All right, then''—and Ronnie put his hand on her knee—''at least dinner tonight.''

''Sorry. There's a reception at the palace.''

Ronnie started to petition her for tomorrow evening, but before he did, a male voice behind him said: ''You're invited tonight too.'' It was Fable. He plunked himself down in the chair next to Ronnie and Lia. Felicity blew an easy overhead. Too much was going on, off the court and in her heart.

$\wp$

Ronnie studied Fable as if he had just met him. Reluctantly he had to admit to himself that the man was actually attractive. He was in his forties, a bit older than Ronnie himself, but he was trim and bright-eyed, and the gray was arrested at his sideburns so that he looked like what airline pilots are supposed to look like, even if they rarely do. But beyond the simple appearance, Fable exuded a special presence. People would say this was his power. But no, that was too easy. Of course he held power. Fable was far and away the most powerful man in tennis. He not only had Felicity, but he also managed several other of the top players, male and female, as well as a dozen or more of the most promising young comers. Plus, he ran tournaments and exhibitions. As a consequence, his power was so complete in all phases of the sport that he was in a position to rule tennis—or even to ruin it—if ever he wanted. Perhaps, above all, that was the aura that clung to him: potential. Dale Fable was capable of so much.

There was a special jealousy directed at him, too, and it spurred him on. Fable was not *tennis*, not born into a sport that possessed an inherited hierarchy, even as it had expanded into a large and nearly real world. In fact, Dale Fable came this far from tennis: he came from french fries.

He had started out somewhere in the Sun Belt. (When Ronnie referred to Fable in print it was always as ''the Sun Belt millionaire,'' or, when he especially wanted to irritate him, "the erstwhile french fry magnate.") The way it came about was this: Fable had talked a banker he played poker with into loaning him enough to buy a little fast-food joint from a guy named Roger—hence the burger place's name, Roger and Out. It featured a scale menu for the time, which meant twelve-cent hamburgers and fifteen-cent french fries. But unfortunately for Roger and then for Fable, McDonald's had opened just down the street, and it was killing Roger and Out.

Fable couldn't undersell McDonald's (it was hard enough just matching them), so one day he erected a huge sign: "FRENCH FRIES 12¢," it read. At the same time, *sans* any sign, he also raised hamburger prices to fifteen cents, so that the combination package remained at twenty-seven cents—but the consumers thronged Roger and Out, sure they were getting a steal with twelve-cent french fries.

As Fable had divined, as people in the Sun Belt were first to illustrate, the most important thing in the modern world was to deal in items and ideas that *go with* something.

Soon Roger and Out was booming, featuring, of course, all manner of french fries: cheese-flavored, charcoal-tinted, yogurt-style, lowcal, caffeine-free. It became a franchise chain and was bought up by a pharmaceutical conglomerate that was diversifying. Thus, at a very young age Fable found himself a millionaire in double figures. At a loss what to do, he had some business cards printed up that identified him as a "consultant" . . . and he also took up tennis.

Fable went about playing tennis in a careful, well-planned way. He discerned that, up to the top ranks, success in amateur tennis was correlated with how few backhands a player had to hit. It's all very fine to talk about how Felicity Tantamount and John McEnroe disguise lobs and hit drop volleys and slice second serves to the ad court, but for 99 percent of players, it comes down to avoiding backhands—while trying to make the fellow at the other end hit backhands.

Divining this secret of the ages, when Fable built a court

and brought in a pro, he told him to work strictly on his backhand. He hit nothing else for weeks—not serves, volleys, overheads . . . and certainly not forehands. Fable just hit backhands. And soon he hit a pretty fair country backhand. More important, because of the way he'd gone about it, the backhand became his English, his mother tongue, and if he learned forehands and volleys and whatnot in the weeks that followed, he always thought in backhand. When he began to play competitively his opponents would instinctively hit everything to his backhand. Fable moved ahead as a weekend tennis player by leaps and bounds, and since he had little else to do but play weekend tennis all week long with other people who called themselves consultants, he slowly began to sniff around the tennis business.

Tennis, Fable decided, was an ideal enterprise. It was indisputably healthy, and it could be transacted in a convenient time frame, just like lunch, gin rummy, or illicit sex. There was modest financial commitment, unlike golf or yachts. Anybody could buy a shirt with an alligator or a muskrat on it, and, for just a bit more investment, a synthetic racket or an imagined tennis elbow could be obtained. Best of all, as Fable himself said to Ronnie one evening in Gstaad: "The fact of the matter is—although for Chrissakes, keep this off the record—tennis is a lot like french fries."

"It is? French fries?"

"Ronnie, tennis is a son of a bitch that goes with everything. That's the key. It goes with men, it goes with women, it goes with the two of them together, it goes with suburbs, with night or day, indoors or out, Sun Belt or Antique America. You might hear people criticize this or that about tennis, but I swear to you, you will never hear anyone say, 'Well, tennis just doesn't fit in.' It goes with everything. I'm telling you: it's french fries."

"So what's that make golf?" Ronnie asked.

"You mean if tennis is french fries?"

"Yeah."

"Well, then golf is curry," Fable said. "And skiing is

chili and jogging is unsweetened non-salt diet yogurt, and camping is cottage cheese.''

However much Ronnie disliked Fable—was jealous of Fable?—he knew enough never to sell him short. The guy was rich for a reason, and powerful for the same one—he was clever.

Lia got up from the chaise, excused herself, went to the board and dived in. Ronnie and Fable watched her without a word. When beautiful women do something athletic, men forbear (at least for the moment) making their usual salacious remarks. Ronnie and Fable watched only until she was away from them, swimming easily toward the shallow end.

Fable turned to Ronnie then and began addressing him softly, with that affectation that people who deal regularly with the press employ when they are trying to convince a journalist that they are letting them in on something. ''I just want you to know, Ronnie, as a human being—''

''*Moi?*'' Ronnie gasped in sham surprise, placing all ten fingers of both hands upon his breast.

''All right, don't be a newspaper wise-ass. I'm being serious. I don't like dealing with Libor. But Felicity convinced me that we can't let the sins of the father be visited on the daughter. So if we can work up some big-money deals for Rina, it might buy Libor out.''

''How?''

''Just greed. He likes Uncle Sam's green. He likes jewelry and baby dolls. Right now, you know how it is. Libor never lets the poor kid out of his sight. With enough cash on the barrel head, though, maybe he could be talked into taking a walk every now and then, letting a real competition coach come in and travel with her. You see?''

''Okay,'' Ronnie said, and he slapped Fable on the knee. ''It's not a bad investment on your part, whatever. Rina's a good player, getting better.''

Fable looked around conspiratorially and winked. ''Between you and me and the lamppost, Ronnie—and remember, you never heard this from me—I personally think

Rina's the only one around with enough talent ever to beat Felicity.''

"Gee, is that so?" Ronnie said. *Wonder where he got that notion?*

But to hell with the tennis . . .

. . . because just then Lia emerged from the pool, the droplets glimmering on her magnificent skin—morning dew on a garden statue. Lia knew that every man was watching her—and every woman, too—as she cut away from the pool toward the court, snatching up a towel as she went. Fable, for one, made no effort to pretend, even in Felicity's presence, that he wasn't ogling Lia. "The Italian Ice," he declared. "Look at that bikini." It was cut high up the sides and was held at the hips by shiny purple rings. Finally she reached the court, took a chair, and began to watch the practice.

Fable turned back to Ronnie. "Yes, that's some piece of work, friend," he cackled. Ronnie didn't say anything. "Yeah, that's the best thing to come around tennis since Felicity herself." Ronnie still didn't say anything, only nodded almost imperceptibly. "Heh, heh, you rascal," Fable said, and this time he slapped Ronnie on the knee.

"What's that?"

"Oh, don't be coy with me. I've heard that old Ronnie Ratajczak has latched onto that already."

"I think 'latched' is a word from your business. In journalism, we would prefer the more decorous 'item.' So maybe Lia and I are an item, but I'm afraid that I haven't latched onto the Italian Ice any more than she's latched onto Felicity's clothing contract."

Fable paused at that and stroked his chin. "I'm glad you brought that up. Let's go over here." And he led Ronnie away from the crowd, over to the far corner of the property, under the wall. Everybody watched them go. Felicity missed an easy forehand return.

"What is this?"

"I just want you to know that you're right—there's no way Lia can . . . uh, latch onto Felicity's contract. No way."

"No?"

"No. And neither can any of these other clowns." He jerked his head in the direction of Harimoto, Bunderhaas, and Lefèvre.

"Why?"

"Because I got a new idea. I thought to myself: why should it only be these piss-ant little sporting-goods companies in the hunt to dress the most famous woman in the world. Why?"

"You want *me* to tell *you*?"

"Yeah, go on."

"Well, Dale, you know, a sporting-goods company can justify it economically. They make tennis clothes. Put Felicity in their clothes, it advertises directly, and other women go out and buy their tennis clothes. A company that isn't in tennis wouldn't have the justification to pay millions of dollars to dress Felicity if they can't sell dresses."

"Okay, fine," Fable said. "So tell me. Does Goodyear sell blimps?"

"Very good," Ronnie laughed. "You set me up nicely."

"Well, forgive me, friend, but in Felicity Tantamount we have, in effect, a world form, something as identifiable as the goddamn pyramids or the Statue of Liberty or Big Ben."

"Only you can't dress them," Ronnie said "And you can dress Felicity."

"You're catching on. If I can convince one major company to consider the fact that every time the world sees Felicity in a dress she's advertising their product, we can go twenty steps beyond dealing with the little sporting-goods universe. And the dollars could be twenty times greater. If we announce that Felicity will henceforth be wearing the Toyota dress, the British Airways dress, the Pepsi-Cola dress, whatever, and that dress is distinct and we keep up the drumroll about it, there won't be a time she appears on the court that people won't think: Toyota or BA or Pepsi. We don't need to sell any other dresses to make Felicity pay. She's beyond that."

"That's a fascinating concept," Ronnie said. "She's like

french fries, isn't she?'' Fable nodded smugly. ''Can I use this, Dale? Is this on the record?''

''You bet. I *want* the word to get out. Only don't print this in some little nickel-dime tennis sheet. I want this where it belongs—*The Financial Times, Business Week, The Wall Street Journal*, something like that. Savvy?''

Ronnie nodded. ''Sure. Only why am I the one you're telling all this?''

''Because I want you to know: no hard feelings,'' Fable said.

''No hard feelings about what?''

''About Felicity.''

''What do you mean?'' Ronnie asked.

''Come on, friend. I wasn't born yesterday. The whole world knows you two were lovers.'' Ronnie bit his tongue. How interesting it was that Felicity had not set Fable free with the truth of that little matter.

''So?''

''So, like any red-blooded American man, I'm not crazy about the thought. And you're always around to remind me. But I just want you to know that professionally I'm not going to let that affect our relationship.''

Ronnie mulled this over for a moment. ''Don't you understand, Dale? I'm the one should have any hard feelings. You're the one who won, Dale. You won Felicity. I lost her.''

Fable nodded grudgingly at this technicality. ''You'll be at the reception that Ferdinand and Imelda are giving tonight, won't you?'' he asked.

''Which Ferdinand and Imelda is that?'' Ronnie replied.

Fable rapped him on his bicep. ''Now, now, Ronnie, you'e trying to make fun of me,'' he said pleasantly. As entirely dfferent as they were, at least Fable and Ronnie were able to understand each other, and maybe that at least began to explain how Felicity could love each one of them at one time or another.

$\wp$

When practice was finished, Felicty came over and welcomed Ronnie with a peck, and then went off to swim.

McEnroe ambled by then. He was sucking on a soda and munching on some potato chips, the two items that formed the heart of his diet. "Gee, I thought I actually saw you smiling out there once or twice," Ronnie said. It was sort of a running gag the two of them had, since most members of the press kept asking McEnroe why he never smiled.

"Well, mixed doubles really doesn't count," McEnroe replied. "I mean, you'd smile too if you were serving to Young and you had Tiffany's ass and Felicity's boobs staring you in the face."

Ronnie chuckled. "Yeah, and how's Young playing?"

"It's weird. Up to a few weeks ago, he was in the zone, out of his skull."

"Really?"

"Oh, Young was soaring. And then, just like that, as soon as he broke into the top ten, he began stinking up the joint. I mean, some clay-court dog from Peru actually bageled him a set on cement, and he's been lucky to beat anybody. It doesn't look like he's in any match. I mean, even today, Felicity was carrying him. If he'd been playing with any other girl but Felicity, he wouldn't have won a game."

"You heard anything about cocaine, Mac?"

"Young Zack into the nose candy? No, I haven't heard anything like that. But you know him. He's a private guy. Nobody ever really knows what he's up to. It's just weird that he's got so much talent and is going so lousy now."

"I know," Ronnie said. "It's a good story if I can find out what's up."

"Well, if you can't find out the story, just make one up like you assholes always do," McEnroe said.

"Keep smiling, Mac," Ronnie said. "Let a fucking smile be your umbrella."

Fable called to Ronnie from the patio. Libor was ready to go back to the hotel and had made Rina put her clothes on. "If you want a ride to the Peninsula now, Baby's going," Fable said.

"Yeah, I need a little shut-eye," Ronnie said. He said

good-bye to McEnroe and the others around the pool, waved to Young, who was on the phone over in the corner, and went out and got into the front seat. He wanted to make sure he didn't have to ride in the back with Libor. The Rodanyas got in back, Baby closed the doors, and they took off for the hotel.

Ω

The terrorists weren't even original about it. It was so pat. Unfortunately, Ronnie had jet lag, so he wasn't at his most alert. But there they were, around the bend on the first road past the guarded entrance to Forbes Park. ''Somebody broke down,'' Ronnie said to Baby.

The terrorists had parked their car, opened up the trunk, brought out some tools, and pretended that they had a flat tire.

The whole thing didn't take a minute. They were obviously ready for Baby. They knew he was coming. And as soon as he came around the corner, they flagged him down. He was moving slowly, and he had to stop. *''Kumusta ka?''* he greeted the terrorist who came over to the window.

"Come on, we no stop," Libor growled from the back seat. "We go to hotel."

He didn't have a chance to say anything else. *''Huwag kang maingay,''* the terrorist snapped at Libor—''Be quiet''—and he pulled out a pistol and laid it upside Baby's temple. With his free hand, then, the terrorist reached in and grabbed the keys.

Baby began to shake. "It's okay, Baby, it's okay," Ronnie said. "We got enough money to make them happy."

A second terrorist jumped up from where he was pretending to fool with the tire. He yanked open the back door and ordered Libor out. The third terrorist came over to the right side of the car, brandishing another gun.

Libor was gone, out the door, before Rina could even gasp. Ronnie breathed deeply. He figured he would be the next one they'd take out of the car. Instead, the first terrorist, the leader, Ronnie gathered, only leaned in the window a bit more and chucked an envelope into Ronnie's lap. He spoke in English then. "We know who you are. Read it, and make sure our demands are kept."

Ronnie nodded. The man to his right backed off then, and with his colleague, shoved Libor into the trunk of their car and slammed the door shut. The leader turned to go, then turned back for just an instant and saluted smartly. *"Taong bundok,"* he snapped off. And then he dashed to the car, and they roared away. A ways down the road, he tossed Baby's keys out. It was that short and that sweet.

Ronnie turned to Baby first. "What did he say there?"

"Taong bundok. NPA."

"Okay, go down and get the keys," Ronnie said, and when Baby went after them, Ronnie got out and went into the back seat and consoled Rina. Whether from fright for what had just happened to them all or fear for what might yet happen to her father, she was almost in shock, staring, wide-eyed, mouth open. "It's okay, Rina, it's okay," Ronnie said, and he wrapped his arms around her and drew her to him. With relief, she buried her head in his chest.

"I'm all right," she said at last, and he took his arms from her. He still had the envelope, and now he tore it open and read it out loud to Rina:

> Those who assist the devil Marcos must be punished. Dale Fable will be returned unhurt only if American tennis tournament is canceled and all U.S. troops leave Subic Bay. If not, the capitalist Fable will be killed. Death to Marcos. Freedom for Philippines.
>
> New People's Army
> 17 January Movement

"Baby," Ronnie said when the driver came back with the car keys, "the New People's Army—that's the Communists, right?"

"Oh yes. Mostly down in Mindanao and Negros. But up here more all the time, *taong bundok*."

Ronnie leaned forward to the front seat and showed him

the note. "What about this Seventeen January Movement?"

Baby shook his head. "I never hear that one. But many different Communists in NPA, and seventeen January is day in 1981 Marcos let up martial law. That's all I know, seventeen January."

Ronnie shook his head. "Yeah, I just wonder what these dumb bastards are gonna do when they find out they not only kidnapped the wrong guy, they kidnapped another Communist."

Even Rina had to crack a smile at that.

Ω

Imelda and Ferdinand personally welcomed their guests at the reception that evening at Malacañang, the white colonial palace that was downtown in the old part of Manila. It was the Marcoses' kind of crowd, rich and happy and apolitical. Many of the tennis people had come from abroad, and they were, in fact, fascinated to see the president and his famous first lady—perhaps especially since, the way the country was heading, this opportunity might not be available too much longer. An official palace photographer was there to snap souvenir pictures as the players and officials and guests came through the receiving line, shaking hands with the beaming Marcos, and with Imelda in her most glamorous pink-butterfly gown.

Ronnie watched as Felicity approached, accompanied by Fable, of course. Imelda caught the eye of the official who hovered near her, and then, almost imperceptibly, he signaled to the photographer. Just as Felicity reached Imelda, the photographer pretended to fumble with his camera and adjust it. Imelda was nobody's fool; no vain and beautiful woman wished to be photographed in the lee of Felicity Tantamount.

Ronnie drifted over to one of the many bars. There was no need for the usual rum and calamansi here, and with relief he ordered a Cutty and soda. He saw some of the players in a group across the way—McEnroe, Pat Cash from Australia, Boris Becker, a couple of the Swedes; Felipe Miranda, who had taken up with Tiffany Rogers; Diane Bishop, Polly Hutton; Manda was there too—and he started over there, but just then, out of the corner of his eye, he saw Lia alone on the other side of the room.

It was impossible to miss her, for the dress she wore was a dark purple, cut low with a white V trim, so this evening, in the tropics, she stood out all the more against the whites and pastels of the other women. Ronnie shook his head. Until he met Lia he had no idea how many shades of purple there were. This one, he decided, could properly be called a plum—or maybe an eggplant, the way the material shone.

He waved to her, but Lia was heading straight toward the large glass door that opened onto the porch. There she met a Filipino man, and they strolled even farther outside. The man was handsome and dapper; his embroidered barong tagalog was the match for any man's, even Marcos'. He was also obviously a match for Lia, and Ronnie didn't like it that they moved away, out of his sight, searching, the way people do, when they are anxious to find a place so they can share one thing or another: themselves or a confidence.

In fact, it was only the latter, but Ronnie had to turn back before he found out, lest Lia discover that he was spying on her. So he didn't see that when she drew the good-looking Filipino farther into the shadows, she only entreated him. "Now, Toots, are you sure?" Lia said— and sharply.

"I swear to you: no one has ever heard of them," he replied. "No one."

"But it is possible they're on the plain?"

"On the level?" Toots suggested.

"Yes, whatever."

"Certainly, it's possible they're legitimate. There're always splinter groups. You give yourself a name—and Seventeen January is very apt—and then you attach yourself to the New People's."

"Still, how dumb can they be? Fable doesn't look any more like Libor Rodanya than I do. You would have thought they would have checked in some way."

"Listen, Lia," Toots said, taking out a cigarette, offering her one, then lighting one for himself, "the terrorist business can be, as they say in America, a mom-and-pop organization. So these fellows—they find out who Fable is, where he's staying, who his driver is, what the car looks like, and they set the snatch. They're just not sophisticated enough to imagine that he wouldn't be in the car."

"All right. But it makes the New People's Army look like damn fools. These people ought to get Libor back safely and as quickly as possible . . . before anyone even knows."

"I agree with you. Only it is too late. The American journalist was in the car. The news is gone."

Lia shook her head. "Yes, of course. But could it be the CIA?"

"Here? In the Philippines?" Toots laughed out loud. "Never mind the American soldiers at Clark and Subic Bay. There are more CIA here than soldiers. Why?"

"Because maybe they took Libor."

"The CIA? Why would they do that?"

"Modern marketing, my friend, image-making," Lia said, looking down toward the gardens of Malacañang. "It's the 1980s and spies must use the same methods as everyone else. Suppose you're the CIA and you have an agent who works for you on the tennis circuit—"

"Ah, Dahlia?"

"Perhaps," said Lia. "So you pose as New People's Army, and then you do something very, very stupid that this agent sees—and if the agent happens to be a journalist, he lets the world know about it, and the NPA looks very stupid indeed."

"I see," Toots said.

"Good. If you find anything, let me know promptly. I want to know what has happened here. Very much." Then she turned sharply away, heading back into the ballroom, looking for Ronnie.

He found her first, snuck up behind her and rested his hand on her arm. "Didn't the charmer give you a drink?" he asked.

"Charmer?"

"Come on, Lia. The dapper home boy on the patio."

"You were watching me?" she snapped, secretly as delighted as she appeared to be irritated.

"I don't want to be with you, if your heart is with another," Ronnie said, straight-faced, echoing what she had said to him in Grenada.

"Don't worry. All business." She pecked him reassuringly on the cheek. But there wasn't time to say anything else, because suddenly a cymbal crashed, a horn blared, and the crowd hushed, parting to permit Marcos and the first lady to move to a dais at the far end of the room. Imelda appeared beatific, Ferdinand the kindly uncle, and flanking them, beaming, were Fable and Prosper Hegginbosch. Marcos stepped to the microphone:

"I can only say *mabuhay*, welcome, to you all, from all lands, near and far, welcome to our land, welcome to Malacañang, the palace of the Filipino people, as we greet you all in anticipation of this magnificent tennis championship." Then he introduced Felicity and McEnroe in the crowd, and Fable and Hegginbosch beside him before he resumed his remarks:

"This tournament is only one more evidence of the cooperation of the government of the Republic of the Philippines with the private capital of America, represented by my dear friend Mr. Dale Fable—thereby showing, as well, to fans of tennis the world over, the success of our nation, the brotherhood and the community of our people." He paused. Prosper grimaced, certain that he could have said it better. Lia set her face in anger, and she grasped Ronnie's hand and squeezed it.

Marcos resumed: "Unfortunately, there is a tiny minority of Communist bandits who would try to damage our country and hurt our people." A buzz began to skip about the room. While Ronnie had filed stories to the U.S. and Europe about the kidnapping, the incident was hardly so well known right here in Manila. "But our people are not fooled, and none of you visitors need fear," Marcos went on. "Because of an unfortunate incident in Makati this afternoon, which was witnessed by the famous international journalist Mr. Ratajczak of Canada, in which some imbecilic little Communists made an atrocious mistake, we will increase our security so that there cannot possibly be any more such episodes." The murmurs picked up more—questions from those who had no idea what he was talking about, grateful approbation from Marcos' friends and flunkies. "We assure you that our land is yours for so long as you are here with us, and from now on our hospitality will be matched only by our vigilance."

Marcos reached back to Imelda and took her hand. "And now, Mrs. Marcos, the governor of metro Manila and the minister of human settlements, joins with me in urging you to enjoy this evening with us, as we ourselves will enjoy your tennis."

"Welcome to you all," Imelda cooed. *"Mabuhay."*

Applause filled the room, except from Lia. Instead, she literally dug her fingers into Ronnie's hand—making damn sure he couldn't clap—and then suddenly she turned and yanked him out of the room, down the steps, past a covey of armed guards, and into the garden.

At last, by a beautiful bright pink flowering bush, she stopped, let go his hand, and breathed in deeply. "I'm sorry, Ronnie. I just can't abide that man. Talking that way."

"Well, he's not exactly my kind of guy either. But that's pretty standard, predictable propaganda. Not too stiff a price for some good drinks and a sumptuous buffet. I'll bet it was even going to be an A-one salad bar."

"Oh, the Globe's Guest," she cracked, turning away.

"Thanks. That was in my dossier too?"

Lia softened and turned back to him, even if she still wouldn't smile. "I'm sorry, Ronnie. I'm not mad at you. Couldn't we just go? I just can't stand even being in a place like this that's being taken from the people."

"Hey, keep it down. There's a goon behind every bush."

Lia walked away from him, down a little path that led

deeper into the garden. ''The bastard,'' she hissed. ''The poor Filipino people.''

From behind, Ronnie moved up to her and softly dropped his hands on her shoulders. ''You sound like that little college girl back in the Red Brigades,'' he said, and when she turned around to face him, he prepared to kiss her.

But then: ''*Tygil!*'' a guard shouted. ''Stop!'' It was from back toward the palace. Then more cries, in Tagalog and English alike. ''Catch him!'' ''*Tumigil ka!*'' ''Halt!'' ''*Dumating kana pala!*'' ''Watch out, he's got a gun!'' ''*Baril, baril!*'' Guards dashed up the path. Ronnie grabbed Lia and pulled her behind a bush.

It was a moment too late. A big man came dashing around the corner, brandishing a pistol. He saw Ronnie and Lia duck for cover, and he moved toward them, his pistol out, aiming it at them.

Ronnie pushed Lia to the ground and lay across her back. It took up just enough time. The big man started to come closer, but just then, from the other direction, down another path, came two palace guards toting carbines. They leveled them at the intruder, and he immediately dropped his pistol to the earth and threw up his hands.

''It is okay, people,'' one of the guards said, and Ronnie took himself off Lia and helped her up, brushing the dirt and twigs from her dress.

Other guards were starting to descend on the scene, surrounding the big man, but for just an instant then, Ronnie's eyes locked onto the intruder's, and Ronnie recognized him from the airport. It was the one known as Bubbles.

The guards came between them then, jostling Bubbles, roughly pushing him away. The leader of the detail hung back and saluted Ronnie and Lia. ''I am very sorry for this,'' he said. ''The man is a prowler. We spotted him, and he panicked. I hope he did not scare you too much.''

''He looked like he wanted to shoot us,'' Ronnie said.

''A cornered rat will shoot anyone. I am sorry. Can I get you anything? Can I escort you back to the party?''

''No, thank you. Just give us a few minutes by ourselves.''

"Of course," said the guard, saluting them again and moving away.

Ronnie put his arms around Lia and held her to him, but when at last she pulled away, her expression surprised him. It wasn't any fragile feminine fear she exhibited. Instead, there was concern on her face. "I wonder what they'll do to him?" she said.

"The guy with the gun?"

"Yes, of course."

"Well, I hope they hang him up by his thumbs."

"No, Ronnie. For all we know, he may be the good guy. Remember, the other ones, the guards, they are the ones who work for Marcos."

"My, my," Ronnie chuckled, "your politics are really showing tonight."

"I know. It's not very fashionable. But I guess there's a part of you that never changes—and Marcos has brought it all back to me. I can't deny all that once I believed."

Ronnie put his hands on her hips and looked far down into her face. "Look, I wouldn't want you to change, Lia. I wouldn't want you to stop caring . . . about good things."

The light of the lantern across the path cut a swath down her face, and he could see that her eyes softened as he spoke to her, and now she saw him only. So he leaned down to kiss her.

Only Lia raised a hand softly and laid her palm upon his chest. "No," she said.

"Why?"

"Because this starts more than a kiss this time."

"I sure hope so."

"Yes, so there is something you must know of me."

"All right, tell me."

"It's not to tell," Lia said, and she took the hand she held to his chest to her own, drawing her dress more open. She took the strap that was over her left shoulder and pulled it down, exposing her brassiere.

"Lavender," Ronnie said, by reflex. "Even your bra."

"Yes, of course." That brought a little smile from her. And then Lia pulled her bra aside, and turned, rather coolly, not so much immodestly as professionally, a model before her art class, or a patient before her doctor, moving just enough to catch the best light from the lantern across the path.

Ronnie was unsure how to react. She understood and helped him. "Yes, look. Look there," she said, and with her free hand she cupped her left breast and held it up, more toward Ronnie's eyes and toward the light, until, for sure, he could see, just beneath her nipple, the two words that were tattooed there: "Sempre Paolo."

"Sempre?"

"Always," Lia told him, and quickly then she pulled the bra back over the breast and hiked the dress strap back up. "I had that done the day after he was killed."

"It must have hurt there."

"It was very painful, yes, but not so much that I couldn't do it again and get it tattooed over skin-colored so that no one could see what was there."

"But you haven't done that?"

"No, as you saw."

"So, why do you keep it? In his memory?"

"No," Lia said. "In mine."

For a first time, their lovemaking was gentle and easy, fervent and sweaty, all of it so neat—so surprisingly so— in Ronnie's small hotel room, after clothes were fumbled and lights were dimmed and raised, eyes opened and closed at all the different times. At last, when they rested, Lia lay there with her head on Ronnie's chest, neither of them saying anything, because both knew they didn't have to tender any false compliments.

Finally it was Lia who spoke up. "I hate you," she said.

Given the circumstances and what had just transpired, Ronnie's instinct advised him that somehow this conversation was going to redound to his credit. "Oh, why?" he asked.

"I hate you, Ronnie Ratajczak, because bastards like you have ravaged women all over the world, and—"

"How can you be so sure of that?"

"Because I seldom let anybody ravage me, and you did it without hardly trying. Indeed, it was mostly my own effort, and so if I, a woman who almost never lets herself get ravaged, ravages *you*, then I can just imagine how you succeed with all those poor little things who have no defenses before your tricks."

"Charms," he protested.

"Tricks," she maintained.

"Okay, word-splitting aside, is that why you hate me?"

"No, I hate you because I know that, having ravaged all these women, scores of them, there is one somewhere that I remind you of—how I look, how I act, this whole evening, this room, something, the way I kiss you"—and she moved her head from his chest to kiss him, yet once more, upon the lips—"and you will think of her, damn you, think of her instead of me, and suddenly I'll be nothing more than the part of something else . . . and not the part of us."

Ronnie considered that for a long time, stroking her. "And I hate you," he said at last.

"Yes, and why?"

"Because for all these women I'm supposed to have ravaged, not one of them thought so much of me as to inscribe my name above her heart, upon her breast. And you, you loved a man enough to do that."

"So, you hate the man."

"Well, all right. But mostly I hate the woman, that any man could mean so much to her. And not me, ever."

She pecked him again. "Maybe you never tried hard enough," she said, and she got up, put his shirt on, wrapping it around her like a robe, and went into the bathroom. When she came out, she told him, "I'm getting dressed now. I'm going back to the house."

"Why?"

"Because I don't want to give them the satisfaction of knowing that I'm sleeping with you." Ronnie started to protest that rationale, but she turned away from him. Just at that moment Lia saw an envelope slide under the door.

She acted instinctively. Something told her that she could not wait even for a moment. If she paused at all—much less to pick up the note or read it—whoever had put it there would be gone. And so, in one motion, she yanked off the chain and threw open the door.

The little Filipino who had left the note barely had stood up, and he was dumbstruck at this beautiful woman before him clad in only an unbuttoned man's shirt. He was hypnotized stock-still, so it was easy for Lia to reach out, grab hold of him, pull him into Ronnie's room, and throw him onto the floor. She jammed one of his arms up behind his back, holding it there with her right hand.

Ronnie, no less flabbergasted than the Filipino that the lady possessed these martial talents, at last managed to throw the sheet off and rise up. "What the hell . . ." he said, and he began to search about for his underpants. The Filipino writhed beneath Lia's hold, but every time he moaned, she would yank his arm up some more and, for good measure, then slap the back of his head with her open left palm—and sometimes follow through, cracking him with her elbow, as well.

"For God's sake, Ronnie," she said, "will you spare me the modesty and close the door?" So, naked still, Ronnie stepped sheepishly over them and pulled the door shut. "Now, get my purse over there." He did. "Open it."

He did. The pistol Lia had worn strapped to her leg was in it. "God damn," Ronnie said. "Why is there a pistol here?"

"Because I was pretty sure I was going to go to bed with you tonight, and I didn't want you to find it strapped to my leg."

"Oh," he said.

"Point it at him," Lia said.

Ronnie did, and she let go of the guy—but he saw the pistol and clung to the floor. Ronnie managed to get his briefs on while Lia picked up the envelope.

"He was leaving this," Lia explained, and she opened the envelope and read the message:

Rodanya is all right. But do not look for him. We will release him on Thursday. We will notify you where.

17 January Movement
New People's Army

Lia made some sort of hissing noise and kicked at the man on the floor—not roughly, but rather like a horse pawing the ground. "This is nonsense," she said, and she gave the note to Ronnie in exchange for the pistol. "Who are you? . . . Come on, what's your name?"

"Apolonio."

"What do they call you?"

"Pebbles."

"All right, Pebbles, turn over." Lia helped flip him over with her foot. She kept the pistol aimed at him. "Now, what is this group, this Seventeen January Movement?"

Apolonio kind of shrugged and gestured his ignorance, so Lia turned to Ronnie. "Well," she said, "I guess we'll have to shoot him."

"What?" Ronnie screamed. The soft woman he had just made love to had left his bed, walked across the room, and turned into an assassin. "No, wait, Lia, wait, wait!"

She lowered the gun, shaking her head in disgust. "For God's sake, Ronnie, I was only kidding him."

"Kidding?"

"I was trying to get him to talk."

"Oh yeah."

Lia said, "You actually thought I'd shoot him?"

"I really don't know. I never had anything to do with guns until about a month ago, and now practically every time I make love, one pops up."

"What does that mean?"

"Oh, never mind. What do we do with him now?"

"Nothing, I guess. I don't think he knows anything." She turned to Pebbles. "You know anything about this note?"

"No, no, miss. They tell me: Take note to Peninsula, Pebbles, go to this room, put under door."

"*They?* Is they the Seventeen January Movement?"

"What say?"

"You a Communist? You New People's Army? *Taong bundok?*"

"Me? NPA? No, no, lady, no Communist me."

Lia put the gun up. "I don't think he knows anything."

Pebbles stirred a little on the floor. "So?" Ronnie asked.

"Well, we'll give him a note to carry back," Lia said, and she wrote one out:

> Who are you people?
> You are not New People's Army.
> We know that.
> Why did you take Libor Rodanya?
> Do not hurt him or you will pay.

"What are you writing?" Ronnie asked.

"I'm just telling them I know they're lying, and not to harm Libor." And then, just before she sealed the envelope, she added a signature: "CIA." And a postscript: "We will kill you if Rodanya is not returned safely!" She handed the envelope to Pebbles and sent him scurrying out the door.

Ronnie only stood there and considered Lia. "What do you know?" he finally said to her. "What . . . do . . . you . . . know?"

"I know that there is no Seventeen January Movement in the New People's Army."

"How do you know that? Who are you, Lia? The gun . . . the way you handled that guy."

"Don't worry, I'm not going to use it on you. I told you: the Red Brigades. I think I could still make a bomb if I had to, too. This business here—terrorism—is my territory. I remember. It all comes back. And I'll tell you, none of this makes any sense. How could any respectable terrorists mix up Libor with Fable? That's so dumb it's got to be somebody else trying to be very smart."

"Okay. Only, who in their right mind would want to kidnap Libor?" Ronnie asked.

"No one."

"So?"

"He just happened to be a convenient foil—someone who could *appear* to be confused with Fable. You see? And all the better that a journalist was along."

"Oh, so I'm part of this convoluted plot too?"

"In some way or another, yes."

Ronnie lowered his eyes at her. "And what does that mean?"

"It means that a lot of people think you work for the CIA, and if the CIA and Marcos were going to cooperate to make the Communists look bad, to make them look as if they're bumblers, it means that the obvious journalist to give the eyewitness scoop to would be the one already on the payroll. Wouldn't it?"

"You know, Lia, I've heard that crap about me being a spy for years now," Ronnie said. "And I'm not. I'm not a spy. Not for the CIA or anybody. Unlike you, lady, I don't even have any skeletons in my closet. I didn't even have to *reform*."

"So why do they leave go-between notes under your door?"

Ronnie put his hands on his hips, on the top of his underpants. That was still the only thing he had on. "So why? So why do you carry a gun? Because you're a gangster?"

"I've always carried one, since the Red Brigades. It's a habit."

"Yeah, well, it's a very bad habit. Don't ever do it again with me."

"All right. I won't," Lia said. "But don't change the conversation. Why did you get this note?"

"Oh, come on, Lia. I'm the logical one. I was in the car when they originally got Libor."

"All right," she said in that tone that suggested more patronization than agreement. She crossed in front of him to the other side of the bed, snatched up her bra and panties, and, very deliberately keeping her back to him, resumed talking as she took off his shirt. "But tell me one other thing. If these were real Communists, real terrorists, the New People's Army, and they set out to capture Dale Fable, and they botched it and they ended up with Libor Rodanya by mistake, what would they do when they found out that: number one''—she turned her head and raised an index finger over her shoulder—''they had the wrong man, and, number two, they had a colleague, another Communist? What would they do?''

She held her panties, ready to step into them but looking back over her shoulder to see how Ronnie would respond. ''They'd let him go. Pronto,'' is what he said.

''Absolutely. Of course. But look, this is Monday. The note says they're going to hold him till Thursday. Why?''

''I don't know that,'' Ronnie said softly.

''Yeah,'' said Lia, pulling on her panties. ''I'll tell you. It gives the government three more days to publicize how stupid the Communists are. Didn't you hear Marcos tonight? That was just the opening shot. This is the first public-relations kidnapping on record. And the ransom is the headlines.''

''Well, yes, that's certainly a possibility.''

''Yes,'' she shot back, jabbing her arm through one brassiere strap.

Ronnie came closer. ''Only I'm not involved, Lia. I swear to you. Yes, maybe they're using me. But no, I'm not a spy.'' He started to buttress that by telling her he was sure, in fact, that the spy must be Young Zack. Whatever circumstantial evidence pointed toward Felicity, Young must be the one. Why, this time he'd actually been on the telephone, calling, when they left the house. But Ronnie stopped short of saying this to Lia. If Young were indeed Dana, he wasn't going to put him under any unnecessary risk. Instead, he just said, ''I swear to you.''

Lia whirled around at that. Her bra hung down over one shoulder and her hair fell about her face. ''You swear to me. Or would you swear only so you could make love to me again?''

''Lia.'' He took her by the shoulders. ''I suppose I *would* tell you anything, if I had to, to make love to you again. That was the sweetest love I ever had, you and me—''

''You didn't say.''

''I didn't say because I've spent too many years telling women that when I didn't mean it, so when finally it was so, somehow I thought I didn't have to tell you, that you would know. Did you?''

''I only know for myself.''

''What?''

''How precious it was for me. I don't know you, Ronnie Ratajczak. I don't know what you think or what you would tell me.''

''I said, I would tell you things to make love to you again. But no. I swear to you, Lia: I am not a spy.''

Lia lowered her head and clasped her hands at her brow. ''Oh, please don't be,'' she said. And then she looked up. ''Please don't be, Ronnie. I want none of this sort of business. It's too much like the first time. I don't want your name written here.'' And she cupped her right breast, the one that was still a blank tablet.

''I'm not. I promise. Whatever you've heard. I couldn't be a spy and do that to you.''

''Oh God, Ronnie, I want to believe you,'' she said, and she fell into his waiting arms, and soon they were squeezing and kissing for all they could bear, until they fell upon the bed, and kissed again and again. Lia drew away from his lips only far enough to say, ''I'm staying with you.''

''But then everyone will know.''

''Let them,'' said Lia. And for just a moment she wondered whether Felicity would hold it against her—and Grazia—that she was Ronnie's lover now, or conversely, whether, maybe, Felicity would see her as a colleague . . . in arms. Maybe she would subconsciously favor the Grazia design because she and Lia shared this kinship. But then he touched her again, called her name softly, and all that Lia cared about clothes was that she wanted hers off. ''No, no, no more beforeplay,'' she whispered.

Lia and Ronnie were in bed on Wednesday evening when the phone rang. She reached for it, around him, over his curses. "Mr. Ratajczak, please."

"May I tell him who's calling?"

"It is about Libor Rodanya, and Ratajczak has ten seconds."

"Quick," Lia said, handing Ronnie the phone. "It's the kidnappers."

Ronnie grabbed it. "Ratajczak," he said.

"Where did Bobby Orr come from?" said the voice.

"Bobby Orr? The hockey player?"

"If you are Ratajczak, you will know."

"Parry Sound, Ontario."

"Good. This is Pinky. I am a captain in the Seventeen January Movement. We have Libor. He is safe. Tomorrow, at nine o'clock—"

"The morning?" Ronnie asked.

"Yes. You go to Chinese section of Manila. Stand in front of number seventy-two Grand Dragon Way. He will come."

"Do I bring anything?" Ronnie asked. "How—?"

But Pinky rang off. Ronnie turned to Lia and told her the details. "I guess it's on the high-and-high," she said.

"It's probably on the up-and-up, too," he said, and called Rina in her room and advised her of the situation, and she professed gratitude at the news; even though everybody knew that she had seemed happier since her father had been spirited away.

The next morning, Ronnie planted himself at 72 Grand Dragon. It was a children's clothing store. Lia positioned herself across the street, and she spotted Libor first when he came bouncing down the sidewalk. He waved gaily to Ronnie, and when everything seemed safe and in order, Lia rushed over, and they popped into the cab Ronnie had waiting. Libor was never better: washed and shaved, smelling of cologne. Except for the ride in the trunk, he said, he'd been treated courteously, spending the whole time in a shuttered basement room, where he was allowed plentiful amounts of food and drink, television and radio and other amenities. His captors had taught him hearts and crazy-eights. "Only a mistake," he explained. "They try to get Fable, get me instead. But, me a Communist, they good Communist too. Okay. Comrades."

Indeed, never did a kidnaping benefit more people. Libor felt a new and closer relationship with Fable, while Fable felt a certain guilt, and so they promptly signed the management contract they'd been haggling over, with terms even more beneficial to Rina. As for her, she had never played better, and the Iron Curtain team Fable had concocted of her and Ivan Lendl sailed to the semifinals before Young Zack and Felicity got by them in three spirited sets.

Ronnie not only had a first-rate story, but he was also a principal in the saga. He sold the inside story of Libor's return to the Los Angeles *Times*, which played it beginning at the bottom of the front page. Ronnie put in a lot of humorous stuff about the terrorists who couldn't kidnap straight—the *Times* ran pictures of the stylish Fable and the grubby Libor side by side, questioning how anybody could possibly mix them up—but Ronnie also included Lia's theory (which he attributed to "a seasoned European terrorism analyst"), which postulated that Marcos, possibly in cahoots with the CIA, had cooked up the whole scheme as a way to discredit the Communists. This made it a more substantive story of genuine international politics, and it also pleased Lia considerably.

But then, just about everything Ronnie did pleased Lia considerably, and with all the money he had made from the story, he and Lia decided to take the next week away from tennis matches and tennis clothes and go off together to a desert island.

Fable himself was ecstatic. The publicity about the kidnaping only increased the worldwide attention for his new mixed-doubles "classic," and Marcos, no less thrilled, signed an escalating three-year deal to return it to Manila in succeeding springs. Not only that, but the fans got their dream final: McEnroe and Felicity playing against each other on the same court.

It helped that Tiffany Rogers, McEnroe's partner, wasn't

really on the court with him. Accepting received wisdom, she moved over to the doubles alley and stayed rooted there unless a ball was hit directly at her. This allowed McEnroe, who was playing an outstanding game of singles, to carry them into the finals.

Tiffany didn't care anyway. Her mother was not making this brief Far Eastern swing with her, leaving her to the care of her manager, Fable, and the matronly Manda. Manda got Tiffany fitted with an IUD, and she immediately started sleeping with Felipe Miranda, who answered locker-room taunts by saying that there simply was no word for "jailbait" in Spanish.

Tiffany and McEnroe might well have won the whole tournament, in fact, but miraculously, overnight, Young Zack suddenly seemed to regain his lost form—he said it was due to recovery from jet lag, and of course everybody accepted that—and he and Felicity together were simply too much for McEnroe to deal with by himself.

And then, happily, everybody cleared out to the next stop. The men went back to the West, some to Richmond, Virginia, others to Munich and the start of the European circuit. The women headed for Taiwan, all except for Felicity, who was skipping that tournament to ponder her new contract. She had to decide soon. Now that she and Fable had met this week in Manila with the leading sporting-goods contenders, Fable was going to move on to the big companies—he was heading to Tokyo in a few days, when Felicity took off for her next tournament in Singapore—and so they had to make a few preliminary decisions, at least.

So the next night, when all the guests were gone from the house on Pandam Road, they got a little kinky, mixing business and pleasure to the optimum. One by one, Felicity would try on the latest originals that had been submitted by the sporting-goods companies—there was a little less frill now from Allmählich; not quite so much of the bathing-suit effect from Geisha; a stylish, modern version of the old pleated dress from Triomphe; the soft mixed reds with a bare midriff that Banner Day had suggested; and a complete redo that Grazia had come up with by a new designer that Lia had found—and then Fable would undress Felicity, kissing her and caressing her as he did, as they sought, scientifically, as Fable described it, to find the dress with the "highest turn-on factor."

Alas, for the purposes of marketing know-how, all the outfits were a draw. No matter what she put on and he took off her, he experienced the same excitement.

So finally Fable almost ripped the last dress off—it happened to be the one from Triomphe—and they made love relentlessly, right on it. The dress held up well under this stress; it proved Triomphe could go three long sets.

They lay there then, engaged. He played some with her hair, and she cooed. "If I can't work anything out with the big companies," Fable said, "if it just comes down to the sporting goods, to these . . ."

"Yes?"

"And you had to choose one—with modifications, of course. But still. Which one would it be?"

"If you put a gun to my head?"

"Yes." And he stuck his index finger at her temple, the thumb cocked up.

Felicity thought for a long while. "Well, I imagine the Grazia. I really like the new direction they're going in."

Fable nodded, but he didn't say anything—what he was thinking was that she had picked the outfit that belonged to Ronnie's new girlfriend. That's why Felicity would choose Grazia: a final favor to Ronnie.

Fable kept that to himself, though. He only reached across to bring her closer to him again, but when he did, his hand fell upon the cheap little bracelet Felicity so often wore. Here she was, naked, but she still had on that bracelet.

He was mad, too. The whole point of having power was that you could ask questions. But here he couldn't bring himself to do that, because he was afraid that Felicity would tell him, and he was sure he already knew who gave it to her.

FIJI

The Coral Coast of the island of Viti Levu is where Ronnie and Lia hid themselves from almost all of the world, a few hundred Australian tourists excepted. He did a little bit of work on a travel piece for a French magazine ("Fiji: Can It Become the Majorca of the South Pacific?"), but mostly they swam and sunned, danced, ate lovo pork and turtle meat, drank Fiji bitter, made love and strolled the beaches, and then did it all over again, doing one or two things more than the others.

Lia laughed more than she ever had before in her life, and Ronnie was more thoughtful than he'd ever been, and they both always said "bula," which is the all-purpose Fiji greeting. "Bula," said Ronnie. "Bula," said Lia.

When they talked, they never talked of tennis or tennis clothes, but they talked of themselves, of growing up in Ontario and Lombardy, and of their families, and all the other things they most cared about, save perhaps one another. It was easier and a great deal more fun to make love than to talk of it, especially because they both feared that if ever they did pause for analysis it might spoil everything, because she couldn't love him if she worried that he was a spy, and he couldn't love her unreservedly, he didn't think, because there was a piece of Lia that never seemed to fit with the rest, the piece that had something to do with the former terrorist who carried a gun and an assassin's name on her left breast. Then too, Lia didn't necessarily want him to stop wondering about that, because if another woman was still in Ronnie's mind, she preferred that he have Paolo there too, as company for Felicity.

But it was almost all wonderful, and the last two days they were there, they checked out of the Fijian, drove up the Queen's Road to Nandi, and then over to Lautoka, where they got a boat, and a captain, as it were. "Bula," the old salt said cheerfully. "Bula," said Lia. "Bula," said Ronnie.

And, like the owl and the pussycat, they sailed off to an atoll named Treasure Island, where they rented a cute little thatched-roof cottage (but with all the civilized amenities, of course). Hand in hand, then, they walked on the sands, alone, no one else for as far as they could see, to the end of the cove. She wore a purple sarong he had bought her, and nothing else but a flower in her hair. "Bula," said Ronnie. "Bula," said Lia, and she squeezed his hand and nestled in closer to him.

"You know," he said, "there's no word for 'violence' in the Fijian language."

"How in the world do you know that?"

"Oh, I just breezed through the entire Fijian dictionary when you were in the bathroom."

"Yes?"

"I told you, I know one thing about every place on the face of the earth."

"So there's no violence here?"

"I didn't say that. I said there was no word. You've got to remember that the Fijians are all descended from cannibals."

"So, what are you telling me?"

"Bula," said Ronnie.

That night and the next they slept in the little cottage, looking out at the stars, listening to the waves that curled into the cove and patted the beach there. They had to get back to work and other people the next day. When they fell asleep for the last time, Ronnie was smiling and Lia had tears in her eyes, and both of them were feeling exactly the same.

SINGAPORE

As soon as they got through immigration, Ronnie told Lia to wait, and went into the little shop there. He bought her a necklace and handed her the box. "What is it?"

"Go on, it's specially for you." She opened it up. From the gold chain hung a flower Pin, its petals several shades of purple. "You see," said Ronnie, "it goes with everything you wear."

"But how did you know it was here?"

"I told you: I know one thing about—"

"—every place on the face of the earth," Lia finished for him.

"It's called a vanda. It's the national flower of Singapore. All the purples."

"Oh, you darling," Lia said, and she threw her arms around his neck, kicked up a foot, and then kissed him full on the lips for all the world to see. "Does this ever end?"

It was not exactly an intellectual question. Probably it was rhetorical, and, whatever, it could best have been answered by a kiss back. Instead, Ronnie chose to say, "Well, if what we have can thrive in Singapore, it can anywhere."

"Oh, is something the matter with Singapore?" Lia asked.

"Not really. It's just that for romance it leaves something to be desired."

"It *sounds* romantic enough."

"Well, yes, but maybe Warsaw sounds romantic if you come from Singapore," Ronnie explained. "Actually, Singapore is sort of Atlanta taken to the fifth power. However indigenous they were once, both of them now are just neuter service centers. Singapore is so small, they actually ought to just put a roof over the whole country, air-condition it, and call it the Singapore Mall."

"You mean there's nothing to see here?"

"That's right," Ronnie said. "Until the tennis starts, we'll have to spend the entire time in our room."

"White slaver," Lia said.

"Hey, not so loud. They put you in jail for jaywalking in this place." Their luggage came then, they were waved along through customs, and a cab was waiting. Even if they had not been so involved with each other, they were so efficiently processed that they probably wouldn't have noticed the rather tall Oriental standing there pretending to read *The Straits Times*. "The Shangri-La," Ronnie said to the dispatcher, and the tall man rubbed one eye and walked away with this information. That was Bubbles, from Manila.

♌

Every hotel chain in creation now had a hotel in Singapore, but Ronnie had purposely chosen the Shangri-La. If only by a couple blocks, it was away from the concrete—all hanging gardens, the vandas everywhere. "Purple and green," Ronnie told her. "You never see that anywhere else except Wimbledon. Only here it's emerald and lavender shining, and there it's mauve and forest green, dusky and drab."

There were several messages waiting for both of them at the check-in. Lia flipped through hers and showed one to Ronnie. "Bite your heart out," she said. The message said to call Felicity, who was also at the Shangri-La, and when she did, Felicity told Lia to come right over to her suite.

She was alone, wearing the newest design from Grazia. ''I like this, Lia,'' Felicity said. ''I like it very much. You have the best taste of them all.'' And she twirled about like a model.

''What does that mean, then?'' Lia asked.

''Nothing yet,'' Felicity replied, and she explained that Dale had gone to Tokyo, soliciting additional offers to dress Felicity from other companies.

''Then, what chance do I have?''

''Every chance. I won't even necessarily take the highest bid. So long as you're competitive, if I like the Grazia dress the best, I'll make Dale take that.''

Lia wondered again, of course, whether the sustained affection for a certain mutual friend had anything to do with that acknowledgment, but she let it pass. Instead, all she asked was: ''Just tell me what you have in mind, and I'll get it off to our designers in Rome immediately.''

''Certainly,'' Felicity said, and she showed Lia all the improvements and changes she had in mind, shifting this way and that, as Lia took notes. ''Can you get all that done?''

''We'll certainly make every effort.''

''Good, I'll look at it again when I get to Europe in May,'' Felicity said, and she stepped out of the outfit. She had on bra and panties, but she took the bra off too, because it was a special one that went with the outfit, and she stood there then, before Lia, pointing out a couple more little changes that had only, she said, just now occurred to her. There was nothing improper about the gesture, and Lia knew that after a while on tour, many of the players grew less modest around a common changing room than women usually are and became known as ''paraders''; still, there was something brazen in the way that Felicity had acted, a certain flaunting that Lia had never before witnessed in the woman. It was as if she was purposely demonstrating to Lia exactly what it was that Ronnie couldn't quite forget.

Felicity picked up a hotel terry-cloth robe, and just before she put it on, she slipped out of her panties, revealing it all for Lia, even the legendary pubic hair. "Where have you been?" Felicity asked idly then, getting into the wrapper. "I've been trying to reach you ever since I got into Singapore two days ago."

"I took a week's holiday."

"Oh, good. Where?"

"Fiji."

"Yes, I was there once. How did you find it?"

"I don't know," Lia said. If Felicity was going to be transparent, she would be mysterious.

"Don't know?"

"No, I was with someone, and we have an expression in Italy, that if you go somewhere with someone who"— she paused, to draw it out—"who . . . is very special, then he *is* the place."

"Oh yes, I know. And so," Felicity persisted, "how was . . . the place?"

"Ronnie was wonderful," Lia replied, deadpan.

The name caught Felicity. She tried to take it in stride, but it showed on her face, and so she turned and looked out the window, past the gardens, over the Singapore skyline. At last she turned back and tried to regain the upper hand. "I just want you to know that for as long as I've known Ronnie, I've never seen him so . . . devoted . . . to another woman as he appears to be to you."

Lia winced at the clever rendering of "another woman." But, all right, she would play the assigned role for a moment more. "Yes, maybe he's just on the bounce from you, Felicity."

"The rebound? No. He couldn't be that, since he never *had* me to bounce off from. You needn't worry. We never . . . uh . . . We never."

"Oh, but he carried the flame for you."

"The torch. You carry the torch for an old flame."

"And Ronnie? Is he an old flame to you?"

Felicity stopped, and began tracing a finger across the desktop she stood next to. Finally she said, "I went out to dinner with Manda last night, and when she got a little pissed, she told me I was a damn fool.'' Lia didn't say anything. To respond would help let Felicity off the hook. ''Well? Manda's his best friend. You're something else altogether. Give me a second opinion. Was I a damn fool?''

''Probably,'' Lia said. ''Why didn't you want him?''

''Woman to woman, *donna a donna*?''

''*Si*. Sure.''

''Because it was never right.''

''Oh, please. Is it ever?''

''It should be. It doesn't have to be right if he doesn't matter. But Ronnie always mattered. He always mattered to me.''

Lia snatched up the tennis dress. ''All right. I suppose I am just not so demanding as you. I have never been the number-one in the world.''

Ronnie was typing out on their balcony when Lia came back. The Shangri-La is up on a hill, and the city is spread about below, crisp and clean. Like jaywalking and drug-dealing, littering is also totally forbidden, and everyone is required to wash behind the ears before going out to man the shops. Lia fell right into his lap and put on a pout. ''You never take me anywhere,'' she said.

''All right, name your shopping center. One of them has eight hundred shops.''

''Really?''

''Would I lie to you? Or we can just go up and down Orchard Road and make a smorgasbord of it, try to make *The Guinness Book of Records* for most shops in Singapore in one day. Then we can do some rooftop revolving restaurants.''

''Do they have revolving restaurants here?''

''Lia, my darling, the cutting edge of civilization now is rooftop revolving restaurants. I don't know if the world will truly end with a whimper, but I do know that on that last day all of mankind will be assembled in revolving restaurants, and all of it dressed the same, in T-shirts and sweatshirts and baseball caps, all signifying UCLA, the Dallas Cowboys, the Baltimore Orioles, and Ohio State.''

''Is there nothing quaint or historical left around here?''

''Oh, let's see: a little of old Chinatown, the Heavenly Happiness Temple, Little India, old Arab Street. Wait, I know. Ever had a Singapore sling?''

''A Singapore slim? What's that?''

''No, no. *Sling*. A Singapore sling. Come on, grab your coat and hat and let's go.''

Bubbles was hanging around in the front of the hotel when Ronnie told the driver: ''Raffles.''

Ω

Once, of course, the Raffles Hotel, named for Sir Stamford Raffles, who had actually founded the city for the British East India Company, was the most famous hostelry on the far side of the dateline, the Savoy of Singapore, the Ritz of the East. Now it was in some disrepair, with monstrous hotel towers looming high over its travelers' palms, so that most visitors came not to live there, but to relive, imagining that time when Rudyard Kipling, Somerset Maugham, and Noël Coward were sitting around in pith helmets, with Rikki Tikki Tavi and Gunga Din and Sadie Thompson and a cricket team or two, all of them sipping Singapore slings.

Slings were first concocted at Raffles, at the Long Bar, with gin and a variety of other killing ingredients. And, as the list on the wall of the Long Bar attested, everybody who was everybody had been there at one time or another. So it was this afternoon, as little birds flew in or out, as the ceiling fans played, as couples like Ronnie and Lia came in to have a Singapore sling and make off with the napkins and matches.

Lia fingered the vanda necklace that hung at her bosom, and then she reached across the table and took Ronnie's hands in hers. ''You said something today.''

''Astute or philosophical?''

''That's what I want to know.''

''All right, what did I say?''

''When we were standing there, right after you gave me

this''—she touched the necklace again—''you said that . . . well, it was something about Singapore, and how it was a hard place for anyone to be in love.''

''Yes?''

''Like that. In an airport. You have a week alone with me. In Fiji. You never say a word. In a stupid airport you say you love me.''

''Wait a minute. I said I was *in* love with you. I said we were *in* love.''

''Oh, sometimes my English—my American—fails me. You mean there's a difference between being in love and 'I love you'?''

''Absolutely.''

''How?''

This time he reached over and took her hands and looked long into her eyes. ''I'm in love with what I see. I'm in love with how beautiful you are, *signorina*, how lovely, how charming, how wonderful, how . . . sexy.'' Lia listened intently, as, indeed, we all do when anybody across from us is being so perceptive. ''Of course I'm in love with you. But love you, Lia? Love someone who carries a gun?''

''I told you I wouldn't carry it anymore with you.''

''*Did* carry a gun till I beseeched her not to. Someone who was a revolutionary—''

''Someone who loved a revolutionary so much she inscribed his name on her breast.''

''Yes. Fair enough.'' He shrugged.

''So, you can't love me because I was a Communist?''

''No. But because once you were a Communist and you carry a gun and all that, you are someone I don't yet understand, someone I don't quite comprehend. Not all of you. Not yet.''

''So, how convenient. To be *in* love with me, while you still love Felicity.''

Ronnie reached up from her hands and took the vanda necklace.

''Look, don't be cynical. It may be many things, but convenient it's not.''

It was a good answer, and Lia sort of grunted at it—at

least as much as someone so fine and feminine could grunt. Then she pushed Ronnie's hands aside, pushed the straw in her drink aside, and took a hefty swallow of her Singapore sling. "And I suppose you think it's easy for me, you being a spy," she snapped.

Ronnie snapped, "I told you, I'm not a spy."

They were both glaring so intently at one another that they didn't notice the tall Oriental. Bubbles glided into the room, kept his back to them at the bar, and ordered a Tiger beer.

"Of course you would tell me that," Lia said. "If you loved me, if you were not just this *in love* with me, then you would tell me the truth."

"All right, all right, shut up and I'll tell you." The fact was, it would be easier talking to Lia about the ambiguities of his spying than about the semantics of his affection.

"Tell me what?"

"Tell you all you want to know. Just shut up and let me talk. Unlike you, I don't have my past inscribed on me." And if she frowned at him, she listened, and Ronnie began to tell her: first, all about Punta (well, not the part about Luisa Isabel), about Colin and the money and how the CIA was going to pay him for just a few months. "But you see, I'm not a spy. I don't do anything. They don't even want me to do anything if I could do anything. I'm just sort of a decoy."

Lia appeared very skeptical. "I've never heard of this before. I mean, not even in the movies, in books."

"I know. I'm an original."

"So, who is the real spy?"

"I still don't know. I've got my suspicions, but I don't know. And I wouldn't tell you if I did."

"But you tell me this. About you. This is the truth?"

"Yeah. It's about me. I'll tell you the truth about me." Lia nodded, sort of. "Come on," Ronnie said, "drink up." It was good that he hurried her, too, for Bubbles was casing the joint by now, even fingering his gun, trying to decide if maybe this wouldn't be a good place to kill and run. Escape from the bar would be easy, and outside there were only a few old guys who drove the pedicars. It would be simple to melt away, then, into the old side streets. But before he could make up his mind, Ronnie and Lia were on their feet, and Bubbles had to turn back and hunch over his beer.

ℒ

Outside, Ronnie and Lia got into one of the pedicars. It was a vestige—old men in their coolie hats running a tourist concession that had otherwise long since left the streets. But it was fun to feel like a smug colonialist, and so they put up their feet and even necked a little, delicately, on the way.

It was a short ride. Ronnie had the old fellow stop and let them out at Queen Elizabeth Walk, the promenade which went alongside the Singapore River to where it flowed under Anderson Bridge and into the Marina Bay. This was the heart of the old town, not far from where Sir Stamford first stumbled upon the place. But then, people were always finding Singapore. A previous traveler had thought he spotted a lion there, and had renamed the place Singa Pura, which meant Lion City. And now, the present ruler, Lee Kuan Yew, had erected a large statue of what was called a Merlion—twenty-five feet high, the head of a beast, its mane shading into the scales of a fish, sea green and sea blue. It was situated on a pier, its back to Anderson Bridge, looking out to the harbor and the oceans beyond.

"See," said Ronnie. "Across the river. The Merlion." Water poured out of its mouth, spraying into the bay.

"It's beautiful," Lia said. "Can we go over there?"

"Sure." They only had to walk to Anderson Bridge, then across its pedestrian walkway, and down to the pier where the Merlion sat in all its splendor. "But you can really see it better from here, because it faces out."

"Well then, what's that little Merlion over there?" Lia asked.

In fact, it was a small replica erected a few feet from the original, but facing back toward the bridge, so that people could have their photographs taken in front of it.

"Very efficient," Ronnie explained. "It sort of reminds me of the little tennis trophies they hand out at tournaments, while the large original one stays in place."

Even now, out in the river, a sweeper boat breezed about among the junks and sampans, picking up the debris that any river mouth collects. Along the Walk, under the rain trees, Ronnie and Lia padded along a spotless pavement. Before them was a Japanese couple, the man fiddling with a tripod. Ronnie stopped, and half in sign language, half in Pidgin English, he inquired if the man would like him to take a photograph of him and his girl.

"No, no, thank you," the Japanese said proudly. "It okay. Time deray." And he pushed a button, ran over to where his sweetheart was, and posed happily for the shot.

"Well," Ronnie said to Lia. "There I go, being phased out of yet another function in life. I must have taken a thousand pictures of lovers around the world."

Lia tugged at his sleeve. "Come on, at least we're in-lovers, so let's go over and have our picture taken in front of the little Merlion."

As they were talking, Bubbles breezed by them, walking briskly ahead, going up the steps that led to the Anderson Bridge.

"But we haven't got a camera," Ronnie said.

"I know. You travel everywhere, and you haven't got one."

"They're for Japanese and amateurs," he sneered.

"Never mind. We'll find somebody nice over there, pay them for the whole film, so long as they'll mail us back the shot or two that we're in."

Ronnie shrugged, and Lia took his arm. It was toward the end of the day now, light enough for pictures, but late enough for the crowd to have thinned out. There were only a few people left fishing, their lines dangling down into the water, twenty feet below.

The ornate gray bridge went back to the time of Raffles. There were pedestrian walkways on either side, and at either end, large heavy arches, which, it turned out, made the most convenient place for a large Oriental to hide and lie in wait. Bubbles guessed that Lia and Ronnie would be coming across the bridge to see the Merlion, and so he positioned himself behind the arch on the far side and, almost casually, waited to commit murder.

Ronnie and Lia were almost skipping along the pathway when Bubbles jumped out into their path. He was only a few paces distant, and they wouldn't have had a chance even if Lia had been carrying her gun. The gunman was a blur for Ronnie, even as he steadied to shoot, and Ronnie couldn't have told any jury in the world what Bubbles looked like. All that registered were the words that the assailant bit off at him: "You die, spy."

Lia cried, "Oh my God, Ronnie." With that, Ronnie lunged forward, across her, toward Bubbles. It's amazing how quickly you can *learn* instinct. Only a couple of months before, another pistol aimed at him in Punta had frozen him. Now, though, Ronnie knew for sure that when people pointed pistols they really did intend to fire them. And this was point-blank, too. Better do something, anything, rather than just wait for death. And so he dived toward the assassin, hands extended, in the same instant that he heard the report and felt the pain as the bullet tore into his chest, smashing him gracelessly to the red tiles.

All Ronnie knew was that he hurt, but he wasn't quite dead yet, and as he gasped for breath he heard the gun go off again, and he looked up just in time to see Lia's foot land solidly in the man's groin—connect so squarely and with such force that Bubbles dropped the pistol. It fell clattering to the walkway.

But near as it was to Ronnie, he was too weak to reach out and get it.

Anyone else who had been in the vicinity had disappeared now, moving every bit as fast as Lia had—but away from the action. The few fishing lines fluttered, unattended, from the railings where they had been tied.

The assassin tried to reach for the gun himself, but the move had left him open for a repeat attack, and Lia caught him with even more force, full on the balls. As he fell back screaming, Lia stooped and snatched up the weapon, and, using it as a club, sent Bubbles reeling back.

For just an instant then she looked down at Ronnie's crumpled figure, and then she turned toward the man, pointing the gun at him, as he backed up, defenseless, against the railing.

In a haze, Ronnie saw it. *No, no, no,* he tried to say. It was coldblooded murder if she pulled the trigger now. Lia, his Lia, the woman he was in love with, Lia a murderer. *No, don't,* he tried again, but no words could form anymore, and instead, in another moment, it was Lia's snarl that he heard. "Go on, jump, you bastard," she said. "Jump, or I shoot you." The gun shook in her grasp. The gunman, still contorted with the pain in his genitals, tried earnestly to get a leg up on the balustrade, and when at last he succeeded, Lia rushed him, clubbed him upside the head again, and then helped push him over the brink. He plummeted without a sound, although he did make enough of a splash for Ronnie to hear it. But Ronnie was all but unconscious now.

Lia regarded the gun for an instant, and then tossed it, straightarmed, as far out into the river as she could. Then she knelt by Ronnie, picked up his head, and cradled it in her lap.

He was spilling blood from where the bullet had hit him in the chest.

"Are you all right, darling?"

Frankly, he didn't know. He had never been shot before. He could feel the blood and the air escaping from him together, and he hoped that it was only shock that was taking him away. But he didn't know. *You die, spy.* So he might. Not only would he die for not being a spy, but also he had nearly caused the woman he loved to be killed.

The woman he was in love with.

"Oh, damn you, Ronnie," that woman said, bringing his head closer to her breast. "Why did you get messed up in this?"

He thought he could hear the first sirens then, but he was weakening fast. The last thing he thought he heard was Lia saying "Bula," but he was too far gone now, and not even the excruciating pain in his chest could keep him conscious. The last his eyes made out was Lia's face, which made it all the more confusing and all the more like death, too, that, when they opened again, it was Felicity before him.

℘

"Hello, hero," Felicity said.

"I'm alive, huh?"

"And kicking." She leaned down and gave him a sweet kiss on his forehead.

"Where am I?" He could still feel the pain in his chest. There was a tube running out there. And another, the IV, pumping colorless liquid into the back of his left hand.

"Singapore General. About two miles from where the bloody robber shot you."

Robber. Ronnie let that sink in. Lia must have told the police that the assassin on a spy-hunt was merely a mugger with an itchy trigger finger. "Did he get away?" he asked. "The robber? You know, I passed out so fast."

"Apparently, after he shot you, he took off right down the road." She fussed with his bed, smoothing the sheets, fluffing the pillows and whatnot. "You know, really, love, when people hold you up, it's quite all right to hand over the lot of it."

"I lost my head."

"Or your heart—which you apparently had already lost to the lady, and which you almost lost for good." Felicity sat down next to him, and, notwithstanding her wisecracks, he could see there were tears filming her eyes. "Do you know the only reason you're alive at all?" He shook his head. "Because you were on that little walkway on the bridge instead of a regular sidewalk. I know you, Ronnie. There's a part of you that's very old-fashioned, almost chivalrous, really, and I've never walked down a sidewalk with you that you didn't take the outside, shielding me from the traffic. But on the bridge, with all the railings and wires and such separating the road from the footpath, I guess you didn't feel it was a proper sidewalk, and—''

"What's all this got to—?"

"The point is, if you'd been in a normal situation, you'd have been between the lady and the traffic, and when you leapt forward to defend m'lady from the brigand, the bullet would have gone into your left side"—she pointed to the spot on him—"and gone into your heart or the large aorta on that side. But as it is, you were on the other side, and that's why he only shot you in the right chest. Just a collapsed lung, loss of blood. Shock. They got the bullet out, and now they're blowing your lung up like a bloody balloon, and another two, three days you'll be out of here."

"No lasting damage?"

"None whatsoever."

"Thanks, Felice." He squeezed her hand.

"And you're going to Sydney as soon as they release you."

"Sydney? What?"

"No arguments from you, lad. You can't even begin to cover this tournament. It'll be the semis before you even get out of hospital. So, you pop down to Sydney-side, rest in the sun a few days. Doreen's already gone down there on business. She's got a house, and then Manda and I will stay there as well when we're through here. You'll have the three of us—your girls—as round-the-clock nurses. And by the time the tournament starts down there, you'll be as fit as a fiddle."

"All right," Ronnie said. "Only—"

"Yes, I know. What about Lia?"

"Yes. Is she all right?" He moved for the first time since he came to, and the pain jabbed into his chest.

"Oh, she's fine," Felicity said, and she got up from the bed and walked across the room to the dresser. Ronnie could see her pick up the vanda there, and she brought it back to him, with an envelope, Shangri-La stationery. "Only, unfortunately, she's gone." Felicity handed him the flower first. "What happened between you two on that bridge?"

"I got shot, remember?"

"Well, Lia's gone."

"What do you mean, gone? Where?"

"She went to the airport, and she told me she was just going to take the first east-west flight. It didn't matter what direction: Pan Am, BA, SQ, whatever. Just the first thing out of here, the fastest way back to Rome. And she asked me to be here when you came to, and she asked me to give you this." She handed Ronnie the envelope and turned to leave. "I'll tell the nurses you're awake."

He opened the letter as soon as Felicity left, and read:

Bula

My dearest Ronnie,

First of all, I told them it was a robber.

Second, you must forgive me for leaving you. The doctors said you will be boat-shape, but I cannot be with you again, ever. I lost Paolo this way, and I cannot risk it for myself that soon I will lose you too.

Someday I will remember that it was Fiji where we were. For now, I only remember you. Thank you for that. But now, I go from you.

Love and kisses for us, then
Lia

He finally reached her on the phone two days later at the Grazia office in Rome. He told her he was leaving the CIA, that he wouldn't even not be a spy for them anymore, but she said that she wouldn't listen, that men always said these things, and not to call her ever again for they were never to see each other for as long as they lived. She said that again, as a matter of fact, when he interrupted her and tried to argue with her. And then she said good-bye and hung up quickly, crying, he was sure . . . he thought . . . he hoped.

Then he called Colin to resign not being a spy.

Colin said it was most unusual indeed that he had been shot, that spies these days did not, as a normal rule, do that sort of thing to one another unless possibly they were in Beirut or Tehran or Colombia or uncivilized places like that, where drugs or religion got people all fired up—and spies most certainly weren't supposed to carry on that way in *Singapore*, where everybody was expected to be well-groomed and well-mannered, so there must be some explanation, and he would look into it personally and talk to Ronnie about it himself in San Francisco when he flew there after the Sydney tournament.

Ronnie said he didn't want to discuss it anymore, that he was getting out of this line of work, even if he wasn't quite in it. Colin said rubbish, he would personally deliver the April payment, hand-carry it to San Francisco. Ronnie said he didn't care if he brought it on a silver platter, he was quitting not being a spy.

So, here was the upshot: Colin wouldn't listen to Ronnie and said he'd meet him. Lia wouldn't listen to Ronnie and said she wouldn't meet him.

SYDNEY

For the first three days in Sydney Ronnie was alone with Doreen in the house she had borrowed from friends in Rose Bay. It was warm and peaceful for Ronnie, and he recuperated under the bright autumn sun, while Doreen went into town, scaring up new sponsors for the tour, meeting the press to hype the tournament the next week—or sometimes just seeing her old friends. Prosper Hegginbosch came through town one day to inspect the facilities or look at the contracts or talk about tennis and brotherhood, all the things he normally did, and Doreen threw a big cocktail party for him at the house, after which they all moved on to dinner at Prosper's hotel downtown. Ronnie was still too tired to accompany them, though, which was just as well, because it was past three in the morning when he heard Doreen come in.

The pain was subsiding in his chest, but he was still weak, and so, as Doreen put it, they had to simply stay "good mates," sharing the same house, but never the same bed. "Besides, you fit in this way, Blue," she told him. "The other girls will just think you're my handbag." That was the vernacular for a woman's homosexual escort. Sydney's gay population was burgeoning. Paddington, the section of town where White City, the main tennis venue, was located, had become known as Gay Gulch. "There're so many fairies Sydney-side now, they even have male whore-houses up in King's Cross to help the poor Sheilas who can't get anything," Doreen said, shaking her head sadly. "Who would've ever thought grand old male chauvinist Australia would've come to this, Blue?"

"And I go direct to San Francisco from here," Ronnie said.

"I reckon they'll be talking about you, Blue. Sydney to San Fran: You better get healed quickly so I can help maintain your proper image." And, indeed, on the last night they were to stay alone, Doreen came into his room as Ronnie was falling off to sleep. "Hey, Blue, want to go back to the smoking section for a bit?"

"I don't know," Ronnie said. "I'm still hurting a little. Will there be any turbulence?"

"I'll ask the captain to take it away from any choppy air," she replied. "For your safety and comfort." And gently, then, she seduced him. "That makes five continents for us," Doreen said, lighting up, and handing one to Ronnie too. "Antarctica's all that's left for us, Blue."

But that night in Rose Bay would be, in fact, the last time they would have a blue together. Things were moving faster now. The very next morning, not long after Doreen had gone off to a press conference at the Exhibition Centre, where the tournament would be held, the telephone rang. Ronnie was out on the patio drinking coffee and reading the *Herald*, and he still moved so slowly he barely made it inside in time enough to catch the last ring.

The voice on the other end was gruff and unmistakably American. It said: "I know what you and Doreen are up to, and it better stop. Pronto."

"Who is this?"

"Never mind, pal. Just tell her to knock off the little business on the side. Or you'll both be sorry." And the phone clicked off.

Ronnie wanted to call Doreen and tell her, but that was too risky, and then there was no chance when she came home that evening, either, because Manda and Felicity had just arrived from Singapore. Felicity had beaten Polly Hutton two and two in the final.

When the phone rang a few minutes after they all got to the house, Doreen was already in the bath. ''Get it for me, Blue,'' she called out, and although, after this morning, Ronnie was not exactly anxious to take a call in the house where Doreen was staying, better he than Felicity or Manda.

And, luckily, it wasn't any problem. It wasn't even for Doreen. It was the World Tennis Organization calling for Manda from Paris. Ronnie gave her the phone and wandered back to his own room to dress for the evening, but in a few minutes Manda came to his room and asked him to throw something on and come into Doreen's. Doreen had just put a robe on, but Felicity and Manda were dressed. ''I've just got some bad news,'' Manda said, ''and we might as well all hear it together.''

''Is this very bad, Blue?'' Doreen asked.

''Yes, it's very bad and it's very sad,'' Manda said, and it was clear to them all that she was trying very hard not to cry. ''They just called me from Paris. And they just got the word from Los Angeles.'' She reached for breath. ''Prosper—''

''Hegginbosch?'' Doreen whispered.

''Yes, of course. Right after his plane from here got into L.A. yesterday, he went to his hotel, and . . . he was murdered. In his room.''

Felicity grabbed at her throat. Ronnie gasped and he felt the pain shoot through his chest again. Doreen buckled, and so she just let herself fall the rest of the way, sprawling across the bed and sobbing into the sheets.

''Apparently,'' Manda went on, ''it was a burglary. Possibly he came back to his room when it was in progress, and . . .'' She tried to shrug the last details away.

''Go on,'' Felicity said. ''How?''

''Well, they choked him. It wasn't pretty.''

''God,'' Ronnie said. ''A thief choked him. Not a gun or a knife.'' Manda shot him a look, but he didn't notice because he had sat down next to Doreen and was consoling her, rubbing her neck. She was crying a lot.

"You know Prosper," Manda said. "He always wore lots of jewelry. Maybe the thief tried to literally rip him off, off his neck, and he fought back, and—"

"They don't have any idea who it was?" Felicity asked.

"No," Manda said. "You know Los Angeles. Probably some wetback or something."

"I've got to reach Dale," Felicity said. "He'll have to fly to Switzerland for the funeral."

"That'll probably be Friday," Manda said, and when Felicity left to make the call, she followed her out, to her own room. Ronnie stayed behind a moment more with Doreen, but by now she was heaving great gasps across her bed, so finally he just left her alone and went to his own room.

Manda came in a moment later and pulled the door shut behind her. Her face was even more drawn and white. "What else is up?" Ronnie said.

"There's one thing I didn't tell the others. The cops do have one clue to go on. Three people in the hotel saw a guy leave that floor right after the time when Prosper was presumably murdered."

"Yeah, what?"

"There was only one thing they all remembered. He was a whistler. And he was whistling country-and-western. Hank Snow and Marty Robbins, I think."

"Oh my God."

"Ronnie, there's no fucking way in hell two separate people could be going around America breaking into hotel rooms and trying to whistle 'A White Sport Coat and a Pink Carnation.' "

"No."

"Ronnie, what the fuck is happening?"

"I don't know," he said with great resignation.

That night there was supposed to be a press party downtown at a club named Rogues, but neither Ronnie nor his three housemates went. Later on, when Felicity and Doreen were asleep, Manda stole into Ronnie's room and slept there beside him like a little girl afraid of the bogeyman, because she was overwhelmed by the memories of New Orleans, and the dark of her room in Sydney suddenly illuminated them too much.

ℒ

Doreen left the next morning for the funeral in Lucerne. "I've got QF to the States, connecting with an AI and then an SR out of Heathrow," she said. Ronnie nodded as he walked her to the car. He was going to meet her the next week, because both had business in San Francisco, but he knew he had to tell her about the phone call before she left. Manda was driving, so he pulled Doreen aside and told her. "Jesus," she said, "it just can't be Herb."

"No, I'm sure it wasn't Herb. But then, it sure sounded like somebody who might tell Herb."

"But there wasn't any talk of blackmail, anything like that?"

"No, they just said we better knock it off." And he repeated what the man had said, word for word, the best he could remember.

Doreen considered that for a long time. Ronnie studied her closely. He had taken her away from the car so they could talk, and now they were standing above Rose Bay, the water shimmering under the morning sun, casting something of a halo about Doreen. It made her appear even chubbier, but, all the same, he had never seen her prettier; still, for the first time, there was an aspect of the fey and vulnerable, too. What he had told her had obviously unsettled her. "Blue," she said at last, "you're a good blue."

"You too, Blue," Ronnie said.

"And I want you to remember this: if anybody ever does ask you about us, ever, anyone, you tell—"

"Don't worry, I won't say anything. I don't kiss and tell, especially where irate husbands may be lurking."

Doreen put her palm on his cheek. "No, Blue, you *tell* 'em."

"Tell 'em?"

"Absolutely. You tell 'em every bloody thing they want

to know. You tell 'em we're just two real good mates who like to have some grog together and like to root a lot—but that's all there is between us. Nothing else. You tell 'em. All right?''

"All right, mate," Ronnie said.

And she reached up and pecked him on the cheek, patted him on the rear, and headed off to give a final farewell to Prosper. "See you next week in San Fran, Blue," she said.

Almost everyone in tennis was with Doreen in Lucerne four days later when Prosper was sent off. Most people said there had never been a funeral in the sport to match it. Some even said it constituted a more prestigious tennis gathering than that which had assembled for this year's annual WTO meeting in Monte Carlo—or even the one the year before in Acapulco, or the ones before that in Cozumel, Majorca, and Hawaii. All of the professional administrators and blazer-garbed volunteers alike came to pay their final respects to dear Prosper, but because it was Switzerland in March, nobody could play tennis—always a major agenda item at every annual meeting—so an inordinate amount of time was actually left over for business. Even while Prosper's body lay in his living room before a grieving widow and children, plans for two new tournaments and three new racket endorsements were finalized, not to mention a major long-term world TV cable deal for the Davis Cup; on the way to the services themselves Dale Fable was able to realign the entire men's autumn Oriental tour with the support of a new underwear sponsor. In death, Prosper Hegginbosch had accomplished more than ever he had in life.

His ashes would be spread about the show courts of all four of the Grand Slam tournaments, beginning in Paris in May.

That evening, before Dale Fable flew to Stockholm to see Volvo, he agreed to have a drink with Lia. He was very candid with her, too, and told her that even if Volvo wasn't interested, it appeared that Mitsubishi, Hertz, and

British Airways were all going to bid on Felicity's dress.
All three companies had even gone so far, he said, as to
hire designers, what he characterized as "world-class
names." It was most unlikely, he assumed, that any more
traditional sporting-goods company could possibly stay in
the running at the price level he saw developing. He had
to rush to the airport. "Felicity is more like french fries
than anyone else of our generation," he explained.

Lia thanked him for that analysis, even if she didn't
quite comprehend it. When she got back to her hotel room
that night, she called the Grazia designer at his home in
Rome and urged him on to new flights of genius. "We
have even stiffer competition," she said, "but we must
have this contract. We must."

She hung up the phone and saw herself in the mirror.
She took off her blouse then. And then she took off her
bra. And she stared at the tattoo. Why was she looking at
those words? She knew after a time. She understood that
nothing in her life—not even that which she saw upon her
left breast—had consumed her so as this quest now. Not
even that week with Paolo in the Red Brigades when they
had been planning to kill the NATO commander. Or Willy
Brandt. Or the American ambassador. Or King Carlos. Or
whoever it was they had been plotting to kill that particular
breathless week. But at that time she had had Paolo, so
even then she wasn't completely devoted to the endeavor.
No, no, no. Nothing had ever mattered so much as now,
trying to win Felicity Tantamount for Grazia, to dress the
greatest tennis player and the most beautiful woman in the
world, to make Grazia the leader in its field, ruler of its
world. How could some foolish little assassination match
a thing like that? Capitalism could be fun.

Lia turned on the bath, and she saw herself in the mirror
again. And this time she only saw her face, saw far beyond
those old words drawn on her breast, and she could admit,
for the first time, what was driving her so. If Lia D'Antonini could somehow convince Felicity Tantamount to sign
with Grazia, then Lia wouldn't just be getting the best of
the other companies who wanted Felicity's contract. No,

in some way, Lia could feel that she was getting the best of Felicity herself. It wouldn't be a fair fight, not really; Felicity wouldn't even know she was in the match. Still, for Lia, it was a battle, and the blood rushed through her.

Excited, she took off her skirt. Her hand flew naturally to her thigh, and she froze. Suddenly, only now, did Lia realize that she didn't have her pistol on her, hadn't even brought it with her from Rome. There had been times with Ronnie, when, to please him, she hadn't worn the weapon, but now, here she was, leaving it home in her bedroom—and not even realizing she had done such a thing. Or that Ronnie had done something to her.

It made her think of London. Not since she got back from Singapore had she called them to report on Ronnie. She knew she had to do it, but she put it off one more time, and got in her bath instead. As she lay there soaking, she thought about calling Ronnie himself, but finally she figured out that it was nine hours ahead in Sydney, early morning there, and if Ronnie wasn't at the house when she called, then Lia could only imagine that he was either with another woman or he had taken up jogging. And Ronnie had always told her that whatever he did with his life, even if he became an expert on wine, he would never take up jogging. He had told her he was going to write a how-not-to book, which would be called *Not To Be a Jogger*.

Lia didn't want to risk finding out that he wasn't out jogging.

♋

In the finals of the Sydney Indoor, Felicity played Tiffany Rogers. It was positively the best week anyone had ever seen Tiffany have, and she destroyed Polly Hutton in the semis. Tiffany had been sleeping with an Australian Rules football player all week, and absolutely glowed every time she stepped onto the court. He was an athletic lover, to say the least, featuring all sorts of positions that were analogous to Australian scrimmage procedures; also, he liked to screw in the bathtub. And so did Tiffany, she discovered. What a glorious learning process this had been. First pen-

etration, then oral antics, now variety. Tiffany simply had
had no idea there was so much out there in that field.

Her father, a pharmacist from Grand Rapids, had taught
Tiffany to play as a tyke, teaching her the same moves he
had seen Chris Evert employ on TV. Tiffany was able to
groove: she hit everything the same, exactly, every time;
went away to a tennis boarding school in Florida when she
was twelve, and was a regular on tour at fifteen, still hitting
every backhand, every forehand, with mindless repetition.
And now, here at last she was finding out, to her delight,
that there was actually something physical she could do
with originality and thought. Always before she had thought
that only neatness counted.

So Tiffany was beside herself, in the peak, playing her
best ever, and she went out against Felicity in the final at
Exhibition Centre and managed to win exactly three games:
2–6, 1–6. Ronnie had seen this so many times, but he
couldn't help but write "effortless" in big letters in his
notepad. In the first set, Felicity was at the net on every
point she served, knocking off volleys with disdain. When
Tiffany served, it would take an exchange or two before
she could work her way in, but soon enough she would be
there, looming over the net, daring Tiffany to try to pass
her, covering all but the most perfect pinpoint shots—or
backpedaling with anticipation and grace and crashing
overheads away whenever Tiffany tried to lob over her six
feet.

Then, when Felicity broke Tiffany to go up 2–0 in the
second set, she changed her whole game and stayed back
at the baseline, forcing Tiffany to compete against a mirror
image of herself. The soft red clay of Europe—"dirt,"
Felicity usually called it with disdain—would be coming
next on the tour, it was necessary for her to play more
from the back, and so she would start preparing herself for
that. Besides, as Ronnie knew, whenever she could, she
liked to display her mastery in even more emphatic terms
by destroying an opponent at her own game. There were
few enough challenges left.

The victory over Tiffany made the one hundred and

sixty-fourth for Felicity, and since everyone had grown
tired of evoking Suzanne Lenglen and Helen Wills (or Hel-
en of Troy, for that matter), some figure filbert at *World
Tennis* magazine had looked ahead, and he had calculated
that the Wimbledon final would not only be the last match
that Felicity would play as a single woman, but that it
would be, as well, based on her current schedule, her two
hundredth victory in a row.

The crush to interview Felicity once she left the Orient
and got back into the mainstream of America and Europe
was growing. Fable Associates was doling out tidbits of
time to the more important news outlets: Judy Elian had
been slotted an hour on April 27 for *L'Equipe*; Gianni Cler-
ici of *La Prascia* had been allotted a breakfast on May 18;
Barbara Walters an afternoon for ABC right before the
French Open; and Richard Evans the same thing for the
BBC right after it. When *Sports Illustrated* feared that its
usual tennis writers were not prepossessing enough to command Felicity's favor or attention sufficient to manage a
long profile that the magazine wanted to run just before
Wimbledon, the magazine called Ronnie in Sydney and
assigned him the piece.

So it was, like old times, a dinner interview together,
Ronnie and Felicity. He didn't ask; he just took her to
Doyle's, on the beach at Watson's Bay, with its glorious
view stretching all the way to the downtown, to the opera
house and the coat-hanger bridge. The first time they'd had
dinner there was a decade ago, that same trip after they'd
been in Hong Kong, when Ronnie gave Felicity the bracelet on the beach at Repulse Bay. He looked over; yes, she
had it on now, and she intercepted his glance. "I thought
this was tennis only," she said—and with some acerbity.
"An interview."

"No memories allowed?"

"Just one."

"Sure," Ronnie said. "The first time we were here, you
ordered the jewfish."

"No. I had the John Dory."

"Absolutely. I just wanted to make sure that you still remembered."

"Go on, you bastard, interview me." And she kicked him affectionately under the table.

"All right, you were devastating out there against Tiffany. You're also devastating here and now, but I understand I'm not allowed to say that to a woman betrothed."

"Correct."

"All right. But what amazed me is that Tiffany played so wonderfully. And still, you almost bageled her. Can she ever be any more of a challenge to you?"

"Tiffany? Not likely. Her father taught her to make shots, but nobody taught her to play the bloody game, and she'll never learn."

"Why not? A lot of players learn as they grow older. Young, for example."

"Fine, that's Young Zack Harvey, who went to college and learned to read and talk. And to adjust."

"Okay, but still, Tiffany's been playing so much better these past few weeks."

"Oh yes indeed," Felicity said, "but surely, Ronnie, you're privy to the information that it is exactly during this period of advanced tennis proficiency that various of the orifices in Tiffany's supple young body have been introduced to male genitalia."

"So it's been an exciting time for the perky little gal," Ronnie intoned.

"Yes, you only become a tramp once."

"Only in women's tennis could we find a silver lining in a display of hopeless nymphomania." The waitress came. "John Dory for me, the jewfish for the lady. Like always."

Felicity shrugged. "You know," she said, "I was talking to Manda the other day, and of course she's an authority on this subject."

"What subject is that?"

"Sexual preference."

"Oh, yes, of course she is."

"And Manda pointed out that with Tiffany's succession

to the top ten, straights now lead the gays five to three . . . with two undecideds. We thought it might be a good idea for my husband-to-be to promote a new competition, like the Davis Cup, the straights versus the gays.''

"But what do we do about the two undecideds in the middle?" Ronnie asked.

"Yes. Well, Donna always seems to have been a bi. Tough to put her in one camp or the other."

"We call that a free agent in the United States. Then the teams draft 'em. Who's the other bi?"

"Polly, it seems."

"Oh," Ronnie said. "I never knew that."

"Yes, Manda tells me she seems to be drifting now, too."

"Is that so? Polly?"

"Yeah. And she might very well be speeded into that, now that poor Prosper's dead. They had a little thing going, you know."

"Yeah, I'd heard that," Ronnie said.

"I don't want to speak unkindly of the departed, but Prosper wasn't just on the road to sightsee and look for doubles games, you know. He wasn't above dipping his wick. Always a bit handsy. We used to joke about it in the locker room . . . except when Polly was about. I was also pretty sure Prosper got it on with Doreen every now and again, too."

Ronnie perked up. "Doreen?"

"Didn't you see that display of grief the other day when we found out Prosper had been murdered? Rather a bit more than mourning for a dear colleague, wouldn't you say?"

"I just never knew," Ronnie said.

"Oh yes, the dutiful Mrs. Herbert Whitridge. I hate to have to tell you these things about married women, Ronnie. I know so how it destroys your illusions."

"Yeah," he said, taking a long swallow in order to help compose himself. After all, no man likes to be thought of as just another dick. No wonder he and Prosper got the identical luggage. And to divert Felicity, he pulled out his notepad.

"Ahh, you're finally going to ask a proper question," she said. "Let's see now: How does the incomparable Felicity Tantamount feel on the eve of her sixth straight Wimbledon, her twentieth straight Grand Slam, her two hundredth straight victory?"

"That's good enough," Ronnie said.

"Well, quite honestly, love, it can't go on too much longer. You Pit's best not to be great." Ronnie cocked an eye at her. "I'm sorry, but modesty be hanged."

"Okay."

"It's best to be very good. If you're only very good you're still a function of the world about you. When you're great, after a time you can't depend on anyone else to improve you. How in the world can I ever get any better by beating Polly . . . or Tiffany? At this point, I can only improve by drawing more from within, and I simply won't be able to dip into that well much longer."

Felicity leaned forward then and took Ronnie's hands—ball-point pen and all—in hers. "Let me tell you something. You can't write this, but I want you to know. I always want you to know me better."

"For history?" he asked.

"No, silly, just because," she said. "I *made* Dale sign up Rina. She's my only chance. There's no one else out there. And if Rina can concentrate and learn to enjoy this game, well, she can challenge me."

"Dale didn't want to buy her contract?"

"Not at all. He's the one who must work with Libor. Would you want that?" Ronnie shook his head ruefully. "Besides, it's a vicious circle. As long as Libor's in the picture, Rina isn't going to improve, so she's not going to make any more money, attract any new endorsements—"

"And so you can't pull in the money to pay Libor off and ease him out of the picture."

"Exactly," Felicity said. "Did you see her here?" Ronnie nodded. "That's the third week in a row she hasn't gotten past the second round—Taiwan, Singapore, and Sydney.''

"And she'd been so terrific in Manila, in the doubs.''

"Exactly. When her father was kidnapped, and she should have been beside herself with anxiety.''

"So what can you do?''

"Buy him off.''

"What does that mean?'' Ronnie asked.

"It means I'll pay. If we can get a clothing contract for, say, a hundred thousand dollars or so, we'll tell Libor it's for three hundred thousand—only he has to let someone else coach her.''

"And you'll pay the two hundred thousand? Have I got that straight?'' Felicity nodded. "You'll *pay* to make someone else capable of beating you?''

"That's right, love.''

"Felice, you're amazing. Excuse me, but you're fucking amazing.''

"It's lonely at the top.''

The waitress brought the fish. "Who gets the John Dory?'' she said.

"He does,'' said Felicity.

"You can have it,'' Ronnie said.

"I thought you ordered the jewfish for me.''

"Not really. I just wanted you to have a choice.''

Felicity caught on, and looked fondly into his eyes for a long time. "Thanks, love, but I had the choice.''

Ronnie shrugged.

"Hey, mate,'' the waitress said. "Who gets what?''

"It really doesn't matter. Whatever you feel like, Sheila.''

She dumped the fish down. Ronnie cut into his, whatever it was. But then he stopped before he put anything into his mouth. "Felice, it won't work,'' he said.

"What won't?''

"Paying off Libor.''

"Why?''

"Well, don't repeat any of this.''

"I get it. Now *you're* off the record.''

"That's right. But your problem is, I'm sure it's not Libor's choice whether or not he coaches Rina. I think he's a plant."

"What?"

"Listen to me. I know there's a CIA spy on the tour."

"Oh no, Ronnie, not—"

"No, not me, Felice. I'm not a spy. But I'm sure there is one. And if there's a spy for the CIA, you can be damn sure there's one for the KGB too. And who's the logical choice? Listen, don't you think the Bulgarians know that Libor's a rotten coach? The Communists are never sentimental. Here they've got a chance to have the second-best player in the world—maybe even the best someday—and they blow it. Why? Obviously because there's a higher reason. Libor is KGB, and Rina's probably being trained."

"Little Rina? A KGB spy?"

"Why not? If I were going to make a spy, I'd pick someone as unlikely as possible. Someone like Rina, someone even like you." He watched her expression. She just made a face at him. "Look, don't laugh at me. I'm pretty sure I know who the CIA guy is, and you'd never guess who."

"Tell me."

"You know I never tell anybody unless they sleep with me. And besides, I think maybe it's two people. Or was two people. I think maybe Prosper was one too."

"Prosper?"

"Yeah, the spy's code name is Dana, and that—"

"How do you know these things, Ronnie?"

"Never mind. I do. Only it took me a while before it occurred to me that Dana could just as well be two people. Even three. The one I really think is Dana isn't usually on the tour. But that Dana was in New York when Ludmilla defected. And so was Prosper. And then they were both in Grenada. And both in Manila. Where Libor was kidnapped. And then, after that, Prosper gets killed. By a hotel thief. And a few days before that, on the other side of the Pacific, I get shot."

"But that was just by a robber."

Ronnie ducked his head. Then he put his knife and fork aside and took another long drink. "No, Felice. He wasn't a robber. It took me a long time before I remembered, but it was a face I had seen. And finally it came back to me: I had seen that same guy in Manila, and when he jumped out . . . I can still see this so clearly"—Ronnie pantomimed pointing a pistol at Felicity—"he said to me: 'You die, spy,' and then he shot me."

"But you just told me you aren't a spy."

"And I'm not. But certain people think I am."

Felicity leaned toward him. "Ronnie, don't put yourself in any jeopardy," she said. "Please. For God's sake. Why? Do you need the money? I'll pay you what you need. If I'll pay Libor, whom I hate, I'll pay you, whom—"

"No, no, Felice. Don't worry. It's just been a bad mistake. And I'm taking care of it."

"Please, please," she said. "I don't have that many . . . friends in the world." And she reached across the table and touched his cheek, and when she did, the bracelet slid a little bit, down from her wrist to her forearm, and both their eyes turned to it, to what was still between them.

SAN
FRANCISCO

About the nicest thing that can happen to a man—especially to one whose chest still aches some from the bullet that pierced it ten days ago—is to land after a typical trans-Pacific flight and have a driver in complete limousine livery, right up to his little black cap, standing there with a sign that says "MR. RATAJAZCK"—even if it is misspelled.

"Who in the world gave me you?" Ronnie asked.

"Compliments of the International Women's Organization of Tennis Professionals."

"Thank you, darling Manda or darling Doreen," Ronnie said out loud.

"My name is Pierson, and may I help you with your luggage, sir?"

Ronnie said he could and Pierson did, and then Ronnie sat back in the town car for the trip into San Francisco. What had promised to be a nice sojourn in the States was starting out all the nicer. First, three days in San Francisco—including one licentious evening with Doreen. The rest of the time he would be working on a piece he was going to finish in Paris next month, entitled: "Not To Be a Gourmet." Then, down to Carmel for a few more days, where an old married friend from Philadelphia named Kathy, whom he'd met years ago in Philadelphia when he was covering the U.S. Pro Indoors, would keep him—while her own unsuspecting hubby was attending the Masters. It was the best and steadiest gigolo job he still had, for she was good company and aging tastefully, and she only wanted Ronnie in the evenings when she was through playing golf. He could write all day—doing the Felicity piece for *Sports Illustrated* on this occasion—and while it was against Ronnie's nature to sleep with golfers, joggers, and backgammon players, Kathy made for a fair exception.

It was April now. After Carmel, Ronnie would pick up the men's tour for a little refresher—Houston, perhaps; Dallas for the World Championship Tennis annual finale— and then back to the ladies and onto his favorite part of every year: Europe in the spring. Rome, Perugia maybe, Lugano, Berlin or Barcelona, and then Paris, and across the Channel to Eastbourne and Bristol, and Wimbledon itself. All the resorts and the cabanas and the palm trees and the places that only airplanes with painted tails went to— all that was mere foreplay for the time in Europe from Rome to Wimbledon. Maybe that was why he still had this silly life, why even Felicity had never been able to talk him into settling down somewhere.

Ronnie had told the driver to take him to the Stanford Court, and now, worn out and jet-lagged, he settled back as Pierson sped him up the Bayshore Freeway. "How's everything in this neck of the woods?" Ronnie asked.

"Oh, Frisco's the same as ever, sir," Pierson replied amiably, and if something jarred somewhere deep in Ronnie's brain, it was too muddled from the long trip to register. The car rolled north past San Bruno toward what everybody in the area always called, simply, "the City." San Jose, south of the Bay, beyond Silicon Valley, could grow to the size of Mexico City, to the size of Indonesia, and San Francisco, with only a corporal's guard of heterosexuals left to procreate, could shrink into becoming a real Disneyland, with nothing left but cable cars and hills and bridges and Carol Doda's tits, but San Francisco would always be the City to anyone west of the Rockies and north of San Luis Obispo.

To the right, as the limo moved up the Bayshore, Ronnie

could see Candlestick Point, where sits Candlestick Park. The Point, jutting out into the Bay, had never been good for much of anything, which is why, a quarter of a century ago, a city official who knew someone who owned real estate on useless old Candlestick Point had the baseball stadium for the San Francisco Giants built there. The winds howled and the temperature dipped, so that, even on a night in June that was everywhere else balmy, it was an arctic way station, and only the heartiest souls would venture out. Now, in April, there was nothing on Candlestick Point but an empty stadium and gulls swooping in the cold gusts.

And this made it all the more curious that Pierson suddenly swung the limo off the freeway onto the exit road that ran toward Candlestick Park. "Hey, Pierson," Ronnie said, "why are we turning off here?"

"Oh, I'm sorry, sir," Pierson replied casually. "I should have told you. There's some construction up ahead on the freeway, just as you get into Frisco, so we're going a back way."

And this time, when the driver said it, the word didn't filter through Ronnie's fatigued mind. It clung there: *Frisco*. Anybody who has ever stayed only a weekend in the City knows not to call it Frisco. Just isn't done. And for a limousine driver to use such a term . . . Besides, Ronnie had been to San Francisco enough to feel fairly confident that any alternative to construction on the freeway would go to the left, up the middle of the peninsula, not wandering up side roads out of Candlestick. He was going to inquire politely about this with Pierson, when, just then, the driver started whistling.

Ronnie was so at sea because of the jet lag and the detour that at first it didn't connect. He had to force himself to stop all his current thought processes and concentrate just to imagine what it might be. But it was not a very good job of whistling. So finally he asked. "What's that you're whistling, Pierson?" Ronnie said, as casually and stupidly as he could manage in the face of rising fear.

"Oh, I'm glad you asked, sir, because it's one of my oldest favorites, the Lefty Frizzell classic, 'If You've Got the Money, Honey, I've Got the Time.' " And Pierson then went back to butchering it, as any whistler must inevitably do to any country song. For good measure, then, he next launched into "I'm in the Jailhouse Now," doing it every bit as much injustice.

Ronnie's mind was spinning. It would appear, he concluded, that he was in a good bit of trouble. But there was still this: the car was moving on the frontage road, parallel to the Bayshore Freeway. If just once the car would stop—if he could but trick Pierson into stopping—Ronnie could open the door, jump out, and dash toward the warm headlights of the highway.

Unfortunately, exactly at the moment Ronnie figured all that out, the exit road swung right, away from the freeway, down around by the water, heading up toward the deserted parking lots that surrounded the deserted stadium. Ronnie couldn't jump out, and neither was there anything like a stop sign or cross traffic to oblige the car to slow down. For that matter, there was nothing at all there, so that even if Ronnie managed to get out of the car, where could he get to? It was like what Joe Louis said of Billy Conn: "He can run, but he can't hide."

"We just have to cut up past the stadium to pick up the way in on Third Street," Pierson explained, and then, at his maniacal best, he began whistling "I Fall to Pieces."

Instinctively Ronnie began to search about the seat. His luggage was all in the trunk, but maybe there was something lying about that he might use to overcome a clever professional murderer. A blackjack perhaps? A hand grenade? A direct line to Interpol? Alas, nothing of the sort. So next he started rifling his own pockets. There were: a few bills, his passport and wallet, his engraved gold cufflinks, a half-finished roll of Rolaids, a pair of royal-blue slipper socks, compliments of Pan Am, a travel toothbrush he'd been invited to take from the airplane lavatory, and a little bottle of Tia Maria that he'd taken off the drink cart and then decided to save. Precisely the sort of items a wounded man could use to subdue a crazed killer.

The car wound up toward the huge stadium, which was

dark except for the warning lights at the rim. Muddled and frightened, Ronnie knew only one thing. He had to surprise Pierson; he had to take advantage of his abductor before Pierson knew Ronnie suspected anything. *Well, here goes,* Ronnie said to himself, and quickly then he screwed off the top of the Tia Maria bottle with his teeth, tossed the contents down in a gulp for some instant bravery, and quickly, before he had time to think anymore, he grabbed the driver around the neck with his good left arm, and, with his right hand, laid the mouth of the little bottle up against the back of Pierson's neck.

Reflexively the man braced, his foot leaving the accelerator for the brake. Also, he stopped whistling; it had been either "Send Me the Pillow That You Dream On" or "Watching the Belles of Southern Bell Go By." Ronnie snarled as best he could: "Okay, motherfucker, stop this car and don't try a fucking thing, or I'll blow your fucking head off, you cocksucker. I got an M-78 Super Special with dumdum bullets ready to make a reservoir out of your fucking head."

Incredibly, Pierson did exactly as Ronnie bade him. He tensed in fear—Ronnie could feel that—and brought the car to a rolling stop. "Keep your hands on the fucking wheel," Ronnie said.

But then he paused. The reason he paused was that he hadn't thought much beyond this point. All he had was a Tia Maria bottle posing as an M-78 Super Special with dumdum bullets—whatever that was. Ideally, he would make Pierson get out of the car and put him in the trunk and drive him to the police station, but Ronnie knew that Pierson would too soon realize—or gamble—that Ronnie really didn't have a gun, and in any sort of fight, Ronnie was not going to win. He was not going to win it under the best of circumstances, and certainly not with a chest that had only recently accommodated a bullet.

He better bet on his legs.

"All right, motherfucker," Ronnie said. "Keep your left hand on the wheel, asshole, then reach out with your right hand and take the keys out"—oops, he was forgetting to say enough *fuckings*—"and just hold them up in the fucking air." Pierson did exactly that, and Ronnie snatched the keys from him.

"All right now, cocksucker, open your fucking mouth." Pierson did that, too. Ronnie shoved a royal-blue Pan Am slipper sock in there. It really didn't make much sense to do that, except nobody is very fond of having anything shoved into their mouth, and Ronnie figured it would irritate him and distract him for just a moment, when it counted most. "Ugghhh," Pierson said.

"Now, motherfucker, get down on the fucking floor." This was the tricky part. This was the moment when Pierson would actually lose contact with the Tia Maria gun barrel, and so there could be some kind of change in dynamics. So he made sure to keep the bottle to Pierson's neck for as long as he could, only slowly loosening his grip with his left forearm as he let him slide down.

Then, as soon as Pierson reached the floor, Ronnie took one deep breath, and, with all the power he could gain from the short backswing the space permitted, he flung the Tia Maria bottle at him as hard as he could. It was a good shot, and ricocheted off his skull. Ronnie heard Pierson issue a grunt—of surprise more than pain, perhaps, a gag into the slipper sock—and then he threw open the door and dashed off, hurtling himself down the road, down the hill, toward the lights of the highway.

After a while, Ronnie looked back over his shoulder. Pierson had gotten out of the car, but he was just standing there looking down toward where Ronnie had headed.

Exhausted, he staggered the rest of the way to the Bayshore, and, waving money, managed at last to flag down a cab deadheading back to the City from the airport.

⌀

Ronnie was lucky. The Clift had just received a cancellation, so he was able to get a room. He called up the Stanford Court, apologized, and told them that if anybody just happened to be looking for him, he had, unfortunately, had an urgent change of plans and could, in two days, be found at the Holiday Inn, Beirut.

But please, hold his messages.

The cops were quite agreeable, picked him up at the Clift, and drove him out to Candlestick. They couldn't find the car—Pierson must have hot-wired it—but just as they were heading out of the parking lot, one of the officers spotted Ronnie's luggage over by the side of the road. "I wonder why he didn't steal it?" the policeman said, and, indeed, the garment bag didn't even appear to have been opened.

The suitcase had been rifled, though. "Anything missing?"

Ronnie shrugged. "Can't really tell. There's nothing much valuable in there anyhow. The only jewelry I have worth anything is a pair of gold cufflinks, and I always carry them in my pocket when I'm flying." Ronnie didn't bother volunteering to the cops that, quite honestly, the driver didn't want to rob him; he only wanted to kill him because he thought he was a spy. But then, Ronnie wasn't a spy, and he didn't see any point in getting into all of that.

℘

The Stanford Court was holding messages for him. One was from Kathy, confirming her arrival in two more days at their hotel down in Carmel. One was from Colin, who was at the St. Francis, asking him to call immediately. The other was from Doreen, who had just arrived in town at the Mark Hopkins, and was requesting the same thing.

Ronnie thought about throwing Colin's message away, but at the last, he picked up the phone and called him and reluctantly agreed to meet him that evening. After all, the guy had come all the way from London. Then he called Doreen. She wanted to see him that evening too.

"Listen, Doreen," Ronnie said, "I'm really not myself. I mean emotionally, whatever."

"I don't want to root either," she said.

"Right. Somebody knows about us, and I just think it's time to put ourselves on hold."

"Listen, mate, I still have to talk to you. I have to tell you something." Ronnie drummed his fingers on the bed-side table. "Please," Doreen said.

"Okay. But I don't know exactly when. I've got to meet a guy at six, business, and I don't think it's going to take long, so I'll call you and come by, whenever."

"Fine, Blue. I'm staying in tonight: fourteen-thirty-six's the number. Knock three times and whistle 'Waltzing Matilda' through the keyhole."

♫

Ronnie had told Colin to meet him at the Washington Square Bar and Grill, but he was halfway through his beer before Colin called and told him to go to Fort Point, under where the Golden Gate Bridge ends on the San Francisco side.

"Colin, goddammit, I almost got killed last night. Again. Now you want me to play spy and go meet you in the middle of no-fucking-where."

"Please understand, Ronnie. This must be private. I have the money."

"But I told you: I don't want your money anymore. I won't take your money."

"Please, Ronnie, meet with me. I've come all the bloody way from London."

"All right, I'll meet. But that's all. And even that's against my better judgment—only, of course, I don't have any better judgment anymore."

Colin was at Fort Point when Ronnie arrived. Otherwise, there were only a few joggers, a few lovers strolling, a few old black guys fishing, a Japanese camera or two, the bridge soaring above them on its splendid way across to the Marin peninsula. "Hello, Colin," Ronnie said. "My, but you do pick pretty sites for us to conspire."

"It's all so lovely in Frisco," Colin said.

"Please, don't say 'Frisco.' The last person who said

'Frisco' to me I almost maimed. I stuck a slipper sock in his mouth.''

"What is all this talk, Ronnie?" Colin asked, and they leaned out over the fence, looking back toward the city, at dusk, before them.

"Well, just for the record, friend Colin. I sign on with you in Punta not to be a spy—right?" Colin nodded. "I'm assured that it's a showcase job, that modern espionage is as civilized as McDonald's, that every spy has been to Vatican II or some damn thing, and I am under no risk whatsoever."

"Now, now, Ronnie. I didn't say *whatsoever*. I mean, there are still some people in this bloody business with a wild hair or two."

"Wild hair? Well, let me just recap for our West Coast audience what's happened to me since I took this alleged no-risk assignment. First, I'm involved in a defection. Okay, fine, a public service. Later, I'm involved in a kidnapping. Not so nice, that one, Colin. Very scary. I end up the go-between—"

"Yes indeed, we read all about it. Saw you all over the telly.''

"Right, but that's not all. I've been knocked around by a crazy Bulgarian from the KGB, a lady friend of mine got tied up and dumped in the bathtub in my hotel room, and another one almost got shot, which I did for real, and last night I would have been either shot or stabbed or garroted or dispensed with in some more imaginative way if the guy wasn't so dumb he said 'Frisco' and whistled.''

"Well, we certainly had no idea that—"

"Yeah, I know. I'm a big boy. I appreciated I was taking a certain risk not to be a spy. But frankly, Colin, I think I might just as well be a spy, because you are a spy, and you don't catch anywhere near as much shit as I do.''

"So, I take it you don't want to continue?" Colin asked.

Ronnie strolled a few feet away before turning back with an answer for that. "Do I look like I have a death wish, Colin? I mean, really.''

"Look at it this way, Ronnie: I've got to believe the worst is behind you."

"Colin, look here. Look." Ronnie pointed up toward the bridge. "You see this, you see the Golden Gate?" Colin nodded. "I'll tell you an interesting thing. The people who jump—and they still jump here, they do it all the time. And something like eighty, eighty-five percent of them always jump this way."

"What way is that?"

"This side of the bridge. Looking back toward the city. By all odds, at random you'd expect it to be fifty-fifty, half of the poor bastards jumping the other way, out toward the Pacific Ocean. But they don't. Even a guy committing suicide, jumping off a fucking bridge, his last act is symbolic, a reaching back toward life, toward people, toward the city. Now, Colin, I'm not even suicidal. In fact, I'm antisuicidal. I'm not even on hold for suicide. I'm not even on the waiting list for suicide. And yet you keep asking me to jump out into the ocean."

Colin lit up a Players cigarette. "I just want you to know that the project, the one you're a decoy for, it'll definitely be concluded in July."

"That's what you said all along."

"Now, now, not with assurance. Stay with us, Ronnie. Ten thousand dollars for April, May, June, July—forty thousand. And I tell you what: I'll promise you another ten thousand when it's over."

"Oh, a balloon payment."

"What do you say?" Colin asked.

"I say, why did they kill Prosper Hegginbosch?"

"It's not germane."

"The hell you say. The same guy tried to kill me yesterday."

"He did?"

"Yeah, so it's very germane to me. Was Prosper a spy? Was he Dana?"

"I told you I can't tell you that. For your own good."

"Dammit, Colin, sometimes I think the whole women's tennis tour is spies. Prosper certainly was. Young Zack almost surely. Sometimes I think even Felicity. Libor on the other side. Rina probably, too. On-the-job training. And me—I'm a make-believe spy. So there's very few of us left on the tennis circuit still messing around with tennis. And I'm out. The only thing I want to do with this whole spy charade of mine anymore is write about it.''

Colin stepped up closer. "Never," is all he said. It was the first time Ronnie ever remembered the man being firm, much less disagreeable, and it took him aback.

"Wait a minute. You never said I couldn't write about it. That never even came up.'' But Ronnie spoke softly, and even, literally, backed off some.

"Really now, Ronnie, we can't have spies writing about the business. You can understand that, surely.''

"Yeah, but I'm not a spy.''

"Well, true enough, but this business of your helping out there in the deuce court obviously works very well indeed—''

"Obviously. Somebody regularly tries to kill me.''

"And so we might very much like to use this ploy again. You know, Ronnie, this is an old business, and there's not a helluva lot of new schemes left to try in the espionage field. As you say in your game, there's only so many plots. And I'd hate to see this one wasted in *The Reader's Digest*.''

"Fine for you, but for me that's—''

Colin assumed his soothing nature again, and laid an understanding hand on Ronnie's arm. "We'll pay you a settlement, of course.''

"We call that a kill fee in my business," Ronnie said, laughing. "Very appropriate.''

"Spare me the bloody gallows humor.''

"Okay. I'd rather be paid not to be a writer than not to be a spy.''

"Yes, fair enough," Colin said. "Five thousand?'' And he pulled out an envelope and peeled off the bills.

"Oh, you'd pay me right now?''

"I want to ensure your silence.''

"So you have. Now''—and Ronnie actually pointed a

finger at Colin's chest—"you go right out and beat the tom-toms and tell all those KGB boys and all the other interested parties that Mr. Ratajczak has retired from espionage and has returned to the safe haven of letters."

They shook hands then. Ronnie rather liked Colin. He really did. "Take care of Young Zack, Colin. I hope he knows what he's doing."

Colin only smiled a cute smile. "You know how to reach me should you change your mind," he said, and walked away.

Ⓠ

Back at the Clift, there was an envelope waiting for Ronnie, from Doreen. He opened it to find her room key for 1436 at the Mark Hopkins and this note:

> Dearest Blue,
> Have to pop out after all. Won't be long. Come on by at your leisure and enjoy the grog and the HBO.
>
>   Love,
>   D

Ronnie called her room, and since she was still out, he strolled down to Union Square and got a hamburger, and then, for the hell of it, he took a cable car up to the Mark. They'd been laid up for repairs the last few times he'd been in San Francisco. That also made him think how long it had been since he'd gone up to the Top of the Mark. Maybe if Doreen were still dressed they could go up there and have a proper drink, looking down over it all. But when he called her from the lobby she still wasn't back, so he decided to take her up on her invitation and wait for her with a drink in her own room.

The lights were on when he opened the door, which made it all the more grotesque in a brazen glare, Doreen sprawled across the bed, naked in the worst way, her head falling back, mouth grotesque, nothing but a cavity, eyes bugging out from the shirt that had been knotted tightly around her neck and then pulled and pulled and pulled.

It was a while before Ronnie even realized that it was his shirt, stolen from his suitcase. Somehow it made it even worse that his initials touched her—"RR," Doreen used to say. "Just you, Blue, Rolls-Royce, and Ronald Reagan"—and he made himself loose the shirt from around her. Then, although he was crying so, Ronnie was able to pull Doreen all the way onto the bed, prop her head on a pillow, and cover her body with a blanket he found in the closet. Hang the evidence. He wasn't going to let any strangers see Doreen that way. Then he called the cops, and while he waited, he took out a cigarette from a pack he found on her telephone table and smoked it for Doreen, for all it was worth, inhaling deeply, growing giddy.

Inspector Amico was, very politely but very sharply, grilling Ronnie. They were at police headquarters in the interrogation room, and if Amico was the only cop working Ronnie over, he regularly got assistance—officers and experts and doctors all coming in, one after another, whispering to Amico and leaving him folders. Just like the army is run with clipboards, the police is run by folders. And Amico knew how to be a cop; he knew how to use a folder. Every time he said anything to Ronnie, he held up a folder, waving it before him as if it contained the revealed truth of the ages. Sometimes, to make a point, he waved two folders. As the night wore on, as the dogged Amico persisted, the folders littered the table before him.

It was approaching dawn now. Ronnie did have counsel, though. He was a Mr. Tucker Traynor, who had been recommended to Ronnie by Barry McKay, the former American Davis Cup player who now promoted the TransAmerica Open tournament in San Francisco every fall. When they brought Ronnie in and advised him of his rights and told him he could make one telephone call, McKay was the person he thought of and called.

Unfortunately, while counselor Traynor might be a first-class lawyer, a most solicitous and thorough professional who quickly assumed all Ronnie's best interests, he was clearly of the opinion that his client was guilty as sin. This attitude was shared by Inspector Amico foremost, and by all others now familiar with the facts.

Traynor begged Ronnie to demand that he be left alone, but Ronnie only kept requesting a lie-detector test. Inspector Amico, delighted to continue a dialogue until the guilty man broke before his clever and relentless grilling, handed Ronnie another coffee, started up the videotape again, and began once more: "Now, Mr. Ratajczak, let me just recap. You're obviously a rational human being, a professional journalist used to looking at the facts objectively, and—"

"Really, Inspector, we've been all over this same ground," Traynor broke in.

"But I don't mind," said Ronnie. "Why can't I have a lie-detector test?"

"Do we need the videotape?" asked Traynor.

"It will make us all very secure if ever this case reaches the Supreme Court," said Amico. "Now, may I try to begin again?" Ronnie shrugged. "So, here are the facts, and you just correct me if I'm wrong. You've known the deceased for several years, and for about the last four years you've had an affair with her." He searched for the right folder before him and shook it at Ronnie.

"No. I told you," Ronnie said. "Not an affair. A series of one-night stands."

"All right, then: how many one-night stands does it take to equal an affair?"

" 'Affair' is not necessarily a cumulative definition," Ronnie explained. "A series of one-night stands is something else again, and no one would concur more in that judgment than Doreen." And he found he had to brush away a tear then. "If she could."

"Okay, okay," Amico went on. "Never mind the dictionary stuff. The point is, you two had a thing going, here and there. Your name is scrawled all over her daybook. Nights."

"All right."

"Now, last night, you arrive in San Francisco, and, very conveniently, your luggage is taken by a mysterious man who, very conveniently, leaves it in a place where you and a couple of officers can find it together. Of course, when you speak to the officers, you don't mention anything about how you think this man is a murderer, because it may involve the CIA and our national security. Instead, when Mrs. Whitridge arrives, you agree to meet her tonight, she leaves you a note—which you throw away—and the key, at your hotel, but, you say, before you can get to her room, someone else strangles her with your shirt—your *monogrammed* shirt—and you, very conveniently, show up to find the body." Amico paused and looked at Ronnie for some response.

"Innuendo aside, correct," Ronnie said.

"Well then, where might Mr. Ratajczak be while Mrs. Whitridge is getting killed? Well, after being very conspicuously on view at the Washington Square, you go off to Fort Point. Do you see anybody there? Well no, not really, just some fishermen and joggers and what-have-you, except for the one person you're meeting, whose name is Colin. That's all. But, of course, even that's not his real name. You don't know Colin's real name, only that he was in room 326 at the St. Francis, only when we check with the St. Francis, there's no Colin there, no one at all, as a matter of fact, since the last person registered in that room, a Mr., uh"—Amico checked his notes briefly—"Mr. Thomas Parker of Greensboro, North Carolina, checked out earlier in the day. And Colin, who may or may not be this Mr. Parker, might eventually be tracked down in London through a telephone number you refuse to supply right now, because even if we reached Colin he would almost surely deny ever having been with you anyway, since he is in the CIA and you have been involved with him in a project you still don't know anything about."

"That's all absolutely right," Ronnie said wearily. "You're a good listener, Amico."

The inspector smiled at Ronnie as if at a small child, picked up a folder for support, and then turned to look squarely in the camera. "Now, the suspect acknowledges all that, so let's proceed." Back to looking at Ronnie:

"You leave Colin, leave Fort Point, find your way to the Mark, enter Mrs. Whitridge's room with the key she left you, and discover, to your horror, that while you have been at Fort Point with a man unknown to the world, she has been strangled with a shirt of yours. Also, you have five thousand dollars cash on your person, which was given to you by the CIA. Why? To do nothing—not to write a story. All this is correct?"

"Absolutely."

"Fine. So, you being a rational man, Ratajczak, what would you think about someone who told me that story?"

"I would think a couple of things," Ronnie said. "First, I would wonder why, if he were the killer, he would telephone the cops from the dead woman's room and wait patiently there and then demand a lie-detector test, which he is still doing. And second, rather than asking him the same questions and getting the same truthful answers over and over again, I would, pronto, go to the telephone, as he has suggested, and call your confreres in the Los Angeles police department, and I would ask them what they know about the man who killed Prosper Hegginbosch, because he's the same man who killed Doreen Whitridge, as you will almost surely agree as soon as they tell you what— I believe you call it this—what M.O. was used to do in Hegginbosch, because it's the same one that killed Doreen, and then I would start looking for that guy, because right now, even as we continue this tête-à-tête, he's a murderer on the loose somewhere in Baghdad on the Bay. That's what I think. Now, what do you think?"

"I think you're a glib wise-ass," Inspector Amico said, "and I've had enough. Lock him up, Sergeant."

And so it was, while Traynor tried to arrange bail, Ronnie spent the first night of his life in jail, comforted only by the thought that this should have been the second night he spent dead.

PARIS

So you're free and clear?'' Manda said. She and Ronnie were having lunch together at a little café on the Left Bank. They hadn't seen much of each other in weeks, because Manda had been named acting director of IWOOTP, succeeding Doreen, and she'd spent much of her time in Tampa at the headquarters. Also, she'd taken up with Sarah Cardigan, the British left-hander, and they'd seldom been apart since Manda had arrived in Europe.

Ronnie said: ''I even got a call from Amico, apologizing, sort of.''

''Who?''

''Inspector Amico, SFPD. The gumshoe in charge of my case, the one who was convinced I was guilty. But now, he says, they have a good lead on the real killer.''

''My whistling clown from way down yonder in New Orleans?''

''One and the same, for sure. Of course, it certainly didn't hurt my cause that when the bastards finally let me take a lie detector, I passed with flying colors. And then they matched up Doreen's murder with Prosper's, and there were so many similarities it had to be the same guy. And I'd been in Sydney when Prosper was killed in Los Angeles.''

''Have you figured out yet—''

"Who would kill Doreen?" Manda nodded. "Well, I'd become pretty sure that Prosper was in the business, an agent."

"I thought you said Young Zack was."

"That's right. And he and Prosper kept popping up together. Then, the other day, when Amico called me from San Francisco, he said, 'I can't tell you anything more now, but your friend Mrs. Whitridge was more than meets the eye. She wasn't just running IWOOTP.' "

Manda shot up in her seat. "You mean Doreen was a spy too?"

"Apparently. So they got Prosper because he was a spy, and then they got Doreen because she was a spy, and they tried to get me because I was supposed to be one."

"But you're completely out now?" Manda said.

"I've been a civilian since San Francisco. I told Colin—he's my contact—I was finished, and he must have gotten the word out pretty quickly, because it's been more than a month now, and I haven't been involved in a defection or a kidnapping, I haven't had a woman with me shot or tied up, and I haven't even been shot myself. It's been a real change of pace. Just traveling and working—"

"And getting laid."

"No, Manda dearest, not even that. I've been celibate, virtually."

"Celibate or virtually?"

"Well, virtually."

Manda paid the bill—expense account—and they got up and strolled away. She took his arm. "I've got a favor to ask you, hucklebuck," she said.

"Shoot."

"I'm getting the kids for a couple weeks after their school, so they're coming over for the last part of Wimbledon, and then the first week back in the States, at Newport. Sarah's going to move out, get scarce, and I need—"

"A handbag!" Ronnie said. "You got it. Love to."

"Oh, Ronnie, you're a doll. Just be around. Maybe we can do the Tower of London—"

"—and the changing of the guard."

She hugged him around the waist, and he squeezed her back with his right arm. They were on a bridge now, looking over the Seine. Ronnie stopped walking. "You know, Manda, I'm thinking of getting off this ride. I don't know if I'll be at Newport."

"Getting out for good?"

"Yeah, I always knew I would, someday. I used to tell Felicity just to give me a little while. And now . . . maybe all this spy stuff hastened it. But I think it's time for me to . . ."

"What?"

"That's the problem," Ronnie said. He wished he had a stone to throw in the water. It was the kind of conversation that would have been helped by that. "When it was time for me to leave Canada, there was travel, and then, when it was time for me to get out of Africa, this sort of evolved. Now, I don't know exactly."

"Stay in Paris and write."

"Nah, I'm not good enough. I'm a damn good reporter, but I'll never make a damn good writer. I'm more inclined to try business of some sort. The more I deal with big shots in business, the more I see how stupid they are. Anyway, I'm almost forty, and it's time to move on. Or, in my case, it's time to stop moving on and stay still somewhere."

Manda jabbed him softly with her elbow. "Of course, none of this has anything to do with the fact that the most beautiful woman in the world has chosen to marry another man."

"Strictly coincidence," Ronnie shot back, smiling.

"I still think Felicity's an asshole when it comes to you," Manda said.

"I still think Felicity's wonderful when it comes to me."

He looped his thumbs in his pockets and started strolling again. Manda paused for a second and then hurried to catch up. "Say, whatever happened to the Italian Ice? I thought you two were a real item. She was a keeper."

"I thought so too," Ronnie said. "It really hasn't been an auspicious springtime for me. I mean, besides all the spy stuff. There were four women in my life. One I found dead, one's marrying another man, one eighty-sixed me, and . . .'' He stopped and looked down at Manda.

"Yeah, and I'm a dyke," she said.

"Yeah, but I think maybe you're the pick of the litter," he said, and he leaned down and pecked her. "Gotta go now. Gotta go play boy reporter. See ya." And he ran ahead to get a taxi he saw on the other side of the river.

"Where ya going?" Manda called after him.

"Believe it or not, I'm interviewing Bulgaria's favorite fun couple," he called back, and then he hopped in the cab and gave the driver an address out in Neuilly.

Ω

Dale Fable had set the interview up for Ronnie, and urged him, as a favor, to do it. It was all part, he hoped, of rehabilitating Libor's image and possibly expanding Rina's. Fable had also done something else for Rina. At Felicity's urging, he paid out a little extra money to Libor on the condition that, instead of hotel rooms, he take a little cottage for the French Open and a flat at Wimbledon. That way, Rina would have just a little more room, a little more privacy. Maybe, Felicity thought, if only the basic part of Rina's everyday existence with her father could be improved some, then she'd be happier all around, and she'd play better on the court. So it was that Fable was able to find a neat little cottage for father and daughter in Neuilly that was not too far away from the Roland Garros Courts in the Bois de Boulogne.

The taxi dropped Ronnie off there, and he started up the walk. Before he even got to the front steps he could hear the voices, loud and angry—the one somehow familiar, the other unmistakably Libor's, barking his harsh, heavy Bulgarian epithets, while, in counterpoint, Rina's high-pitched screams punctuated the argument.

"It's over, Libor. All of it," said the one voice. It was American.

"I kill you bastard focker."

Rina screamed again.

Ronnie dashed up the steps. For an instant he thought about opening the door, but instead he opted to peek into the window, and through the open curtains he could see clearly across the room. Libor was waving a menacing finger, while Rina, to the side of her father, was backed up against the wall, sobbing and cowering. Ronnie leaned over to the side of the window, straining to see whom the other voice belonged to.

It was Young Zack Harvey.

By God, Ronnie thought, the KGB and the CIA, tennis division, head to head, at last.

"I mean it, Libor," Young said, "it's over." He put his hands on his hips and waited.

Libor cursed him. Then suddenly he dashed to the side, out of Ronnie's view, and Rina screamed, "His gun! His gun!" and Young began to rush in that direction too, and quickly were all three gone from Ronnie's field of vision. So he jumped away from the window then, ran to the door, and yanked it open—just as a shot was fired. As Ronnie stepped across the threshold, Libor Rodanya's bulky form smashed against him, blood gushing from a hole in his head. Ronnie tried to slow the big Bulgar's fall, but Libor was reeling back from the shot, and he fell heavily through his arms and crashed to the floor.

Ronnie only had to glance at him. "He's dead," he said out loud. Then he looked up. Rina stood next to Young Zack, who held the smoking gun in his hand.

"It's his gun," Young said. "He tried to kill me."

Ronnie thought of Rina then, and he began to step around the body to go console her. Even if this was self-defense, even if Rina didn't love Libor—still, it was her father who had just been shot dead, and her father's murderer stood next to her. But even before Ronnie could reach Rina, the poor thing, distraught and sobbing, was so beside herself that she turned and fell into the arms of the murderer, the very man who had just killed her father. It was all Young could do to comfort her, what with the murder weapon still in his hand.

Ronnie took the gun from him, laid it down, and went

over to the closet. He found Libor's raincoat in there, brought it out, and threw it over the dead man. Then he remembered to close the front door. He looked out. The little street was still. No one else seemed to have heard the fracas or the shot.

And poor Rina. She just kept crying, clinging to Young, nestling into his chest. She had to get hold of herself. Ronnie had to figure out what the hell to do. "Young," he finally said. "Let's you and me step outside and talk."

"It's okay," Young said. "We can talk right here." Rina wouldn't let go. She kept crying all over his shirt.

"I'm not so sure," Ronnie said, and he nodded to Rina.

"It's okay," Young said. "You don't understand."

"No, I know a lot more than you think I do. For a while there, you see, I was your decoy."

Young cocked his head, puzzled, and for the first time Rina moved her head off his chest and stopped her crying. "Decoy? What do you mean?"

"Well, it was a new scheme. I guess they never let you in on it. The boys had me pretending to be a spy, to divert attention from you."

Young wrinkled his nose in confusion, and even stepped a little away from Rina. "Ronnie, what *are* you talking about?"

Irritated, Ronnie snapped back, "For Chrissake, Young, this is no time to playact. I know you're CIA. I know."

Rina put her hand to her mouth and gasped. Young screwed up his face. "I'm what? CIA? You mean, like intelligence? That CIA?"

Ronnie was getting mad now. A KGB star was dead. Some kind of international security was at stake. They had to make decisions about what to do with Libor—with Rina too, for that matter—and Young didn't have the luxury of continuing to play dumb. "Come on, knock it off," Ronnie said. "I know you're Dana. I've been working with Colin and the rest of the London office since the end of January. I wasn't supposed to know who Dana was, but I finally figured out why you kept popping up around the women's tour. You're CIA." Young shook his head, but

Ronnie gave him a comradely clap on the shoulder. "So you see, it's okay. You can trust me."

Young looked at Rina, and then he looked back at Ronnie, and he broke into a huge smile. Rina reached over and took his hand, and Young brought it up and held it at his heart. Something began to occur to Ronnie. There was a glimmer. "Ronnie," Young said, "I'm sorry, but I'm not CIA. I'm really sorry, but I'm not. I'm just here because I love Rina. Because we love each other."

Ronnie rapped his forehead with the heel of his palm. "Oh God, of course. You were just chasing her all over the place. Boy meets girl. Just plain old young love."

"Yeah," Young said. For her part, Rina leaned up and kissed him. It was an altogether sweet scene except for the fact that Libor's body was there because Young had shot him.

"Come on," Ronnie said, "let's get out of this room." The three of them went into the kitchen, and Ronnie hoisted himself up on the counter. "So, just for the record, your father isn't KGB?"

Rina shook her head, and then she glanced to Young. He had his arm around her shoulder, holding her next to him. "Go on, tell him, sweetie," he said. "We gotta figure how to get out of this."

Rina closed her eyes and gulped. Finally she opened them again. Still, it was a long time before she began, and Ronnie could tell she needed Young's closeness to give her the strength. "Ronnie . . ." She stopped. "Ronnie, Libor, he is—"

"Yes?"

"He is not my father."

Now Ronnie caught his breath. "He isn't?"

"No." She stopped.

"Go on," Young said.

"He was just the one who taught me. My father was dead when I was little girl. And Libor did teach me good, and when it was time for me to go to championships in Sofia, he got my mother to let him go with me. She knows no tennis, my mother. So he tells the people he is my father. And I became his . . . how you say it?''

''His meal ticket.''

''Yes. So he went along, and until Young come into my life, I know not what to do. It was nightmare, Ronnie.''

Ronnie nodded his head. Young walked over to the door and looked down at the body under the raincoat. ''What are we going to do now, Ronnie? I mean, what do we do with him?''

Ronnie said, ''First, tell me the whole thing. Then we'll see.''

''Okay,'' Young said. ''I met Rina at Wimbledon last year. In the players' tearoom during a rain delay one afternoon. I'd see her around, and I wanted to meet her''—Rina blushed happily this time—''and Libor had stepped away for a minute. But when he came back he got mad and wouldn't let me take her out, so I started following Rina— you know, whenever I could—and we would get a moment here, have a Coke or something. We got a lot of time like that at the U.S. Open. And then at Kooyong. It was driving me crazy. And of course I heard all the stories about how he beat her and everything.''

''Well, he did, didn't he?'' Ronnie asked, and Rina bowed her head in acknowledgment.

''All the time,'' Young said. ''I finally got her to admit that. So I couldn't stand it.''

''That's when your tennis game started going into the toilet?''

''Yeah. So I decided she had to defect. And I came to New York to have her run off with me. And wouldn't you know it . . . ?''

''That was the day Ludmilla defected?''

''Exactly.''

''But then Rina got even more scared. All those agents, all the threats.''

''He beat me much more after Ludmilla, too.''

''Yeah. So then I went down to Grenada to see her, and that's when I got the idea to put him out of commission so we could have a real evening together.''

"You mean you hired those guys to give him the Mickey Finn?"

"Yeah. That was my little scheme. Pretty good, huh? Remember when you saw me that night?"

"Sure, you looked like you were going to kill him."

"No way, Ronnie. I'd just borrowed his gun—in case he came to too soon and found us. When you saw me I was just going to plant the gun back on him. I was just clowning around. I didn't even hate him then. Because that was the first time Rina and I had ever really been alone." And he walked back over and hugged her again, and she blushed all the more. "Besides, I didn't know everything at that point."

"What do you mean, everything?"

"You know, like Rina hadn't told me he wasn't her father yet. I still assumed he was her father. Besides, you really saved my little red ass, Ronnie, because you mentioned that if someone had drugged him, they'd have robbed him. So I had to have Rina rob him after you left, so he wouldn't suspect."

"Well, I'm glad I could be of service."

"Then in Manila—"

"Don't tell me that little kidnapping was yours too?" Ronnie asked.

"Oh yeah. We got our first real holiday together there, didn't we, darling?" Rina shone through her blush. "I thought that was really clever of me. I knew there was no reason why anybody would kidnap some Bulgarian coach, but they would if they mixed him up with the richest man in sports. And then you happened along to be the perfect go-between."

"What would you do without me?" Ronnie asked.

"Well, after we had those few days alone, Ronnie, I knew it was just a matter of time. Rina and I loved each other, and it was only a question of figuring out how to get her away from Libor. We were sort of figuring to wait until we got back to the States after Wimbledon. But then today I learned the worst." His voice trailed off.

"Please, no," Rina said.

Young took her and held her again. "No, we must tell Ronnie, darling. Then he'll know exactly why this could happen."

"What are you talking about?"

"Okay, today, after practice out at Roland Garros, I saw Rina in the players' lounge," Young said. Rina covered her eyes and began to sniffle again. Young stopped to console her.

"No, you tell Ronnie. I just go out," she said, and she left the room, her hand trailing behind, touching Young's till their chain broke at the fingertips, so that it seemed as if she almost drifted away from him.

Young turned back to Ronnie. "This is the hardest of all for her to hear. Today, when I saw her out there she seemed especially upset, and Libor wasn't right there, he was out pinching bottoms or something, so Rina took my hand—she never did that in public before—and she led me outside, and when we were alone, she told me the truth, that Libor wasn't her father, that he had taken her over and posed, and . . ." Young stopped and looked away.

"Do you want to go on?" Ronnie asked.

"Yeah. Whatever happens because of this, Ronnie, I want someone to know."

"Okay."

"So then she told me the rest. I don't know how she managed. She was crying the whole time. She told me about how he beat her all the time, beat her whenever she lost, beat her whenever he was drunk or mad . . . or just for the hell of it. And there was something else, Ronnie."

"What's that?"

"He'd started raping her."

"Oh no. Poor Rina."

"Oh yeah. More and more. Whenever he felt like it. He raped her first thing this morning. He raped her all the time. And she was so scared, she never told anyone. So ashamed. All that time we had in Manila, she never told me. She was just so scared of him, Ronnie, so scared he'd kill her or make her go back to Bulgaria, so scared of everything."

"God, I'm sorry," Ronnie said, and he squeezed Young on the back of the neck.

"Yeah, but I think after Manila even Libor began to suspect. Something. Someone. I'm not sure he thought it was me. He started beating her more, making her . . . do—"

"Okay, I get the picture."

"And when he saw us talking this morning, I think he finally figured I was the one, and he came over and took Rina away and told me to fuck off, and I wanted to kill him right there, Ronnie, but instead, I told myself no, cool it, I'll go to their place and confront the son of a bitch, and if he doesn't let her go with me then, then I'm going to tell the world about what he's been doing to her. And I came here. He'd already beat her again, and just before I got here he was telling her to take her clothes off, and I came in, and I told him I knew everything, and we started arguing, and—"

"Young, was it your gun?"

"No. It's his. After Grenada, I swear, I never touched a gun till today. He went for his gun, Rina screamed, and I stepped in."

"And you got the gun?"

Young dropped his eyes and turned away. He took a deep breath, and only slowly then did he turn back to face Ronnie. "You must never tell anyone."

"I'm never telling anyone any of this."

"Okay. No, I didn't get the gun. I grabbed for the gun when he did. Only I didn't get it. It fell on the floor, and when Libor tried to get it again, Rina picked it up, and he grabbed for it again . . . and she shot him."

"But I saw you with the gun," Ronnie said.

"I saw the door open—I didn't even know who it was—and I grabbed it from her."

Ronnie took Young by the shoulders and turned him to him. "You'd have taken the rap for her?"

Young began to cry, and Ronnie drew him closer. "I'd do anything for her, Ronnie. She's had enough. She's had too much. All I want to do is marry her and take care of her. And now this.'' He collapsed the rest of the way onto Ronnie, who held him there until he saw Rina appear back in the doorway.

"Come here," Ronnie said to her, and when she moved closer, he sort of handed Young out of his arms into hers. "I think you're better at this." Then Ronnie left them alone and went back out into the living room and stared at the form under the raincoat and tried to figure out what they could do.

That was what Young said when he followed him back into the room. "All right, what can we do?"

"Well," Ronnie said, "first off I think you ought to get married."

"But Libor. The body."

Ronnie shrugged. "What are accessories to murder good for but getting rid of bodies?"

That stopped Young. "You can't do that, Ronnie."

"Yeah I can. As someone once said in this town: it's a far, far better thing I do." They both just looked at him. "Go on now, get the hell out of here."

"How will you do it?" Rina asked.

"As we say in the CIA, the less you know, the better off you are. You two just clear out of France. I'm going to call the Open office and tell 'em that Libor has taken sick and you've rushed your poor father home, Rina. Then . . . So what's the matter with you, Young?"

"What dya mean, the matter?"

"You know, knee? Tennis elbow?"

"Oh yeah. I think my back."

"Fine. I'll get Fable to tell them that your chronically bad back has acted up again, you must default immediately so that you can fly back to Johns Hopkins to be treated by that eminent specialist, Dr. Monkeyshines. And then, in a week or two the sad news will be revealed that Libor has succumbed to a mysterious illness back in darkest Bulgaria, and, following a decent interval of mourning, you two can be officially married—maybe as the semifinal windup nuptials on Centre Court before Fable and Felicity tie the knot. Okay, now, go on and get the hell out of here."

Rina and Young looked at each other, and then she hopped over and hugged Ronnie. "Manda always tell me Felicity was an asshole to let you go," she said.

"You know Manda. She has a way with words."

Young stepped up and shook his hand, and then he embraced Ronnie one more time, and quickly they were both packed and gone.

Ϙ

Ronnie called the contact number in London, and in five minutes Colin was back to him, "Are you still looking for a candidate not to be a spy?" Ronnie asked, and Colin said there certainly still was an opening in that line.

"Okay," Ronnie said, "but the terms of the deal have changed. Instead of cash, I'm yours for the next couple months if you'll just be so kind as to dispose of a body for me. . . . No, I just sort of inherited it, thanks." Ronnie gave him the address in Neuilly, and Colin said he knew the neighborhood well and was sure they could pop across the Channel and tidy up that little mess.

Ronnie told Colin he'd leave the key under the mat.

Ϙ

The concierge woke Ronnie the next morning and said that it was most urgent. Inspector deBeaufort of the Paris police was in the lobby and would like permission to come up immediately. Of course, if he did not grant permission for the inspector to . . . "No, no, tell him to come right up," Ronnie said. And then, out loud to himself, as soon as he hung up: "I guess I'm no better at not being a murderer than I am at not being a spy."

The inspector was a chubby little fellow who was very proper. "You work fast," Ronnie told him. He wondered whether they had found Libor's body before Colin got there, or afterward, while it was being relocated. He also wondered who squealed on him.

"Well, we just now receive ze information," deBeaufort said.

"Is there anything you want to check out while I'm getting dressed?"

"I only want to see your luggage."

"Sure," Ronnie said, and he pointed out his handsome matching IWOOTP suitcase and garment bag. "But save yourself the trouble. I don't have the gun."

"Oh?" said the inspector, "and what gun is that?"

Ronnie shrugged. "Okay, I'll play dumb too," he said, and went into the bathroom.

When he came out, toothbrush in his mouth, Inspector deBeaufort had cleared out the clothes still left in the suitcase and was fishing about the bottom of the bag. Suddenly, as Ronnie drew closer and watched with fascination, the inspector's hands caught on something, and with educated fingers he fooled around some more, found some button, pushed it, and then peeled back the whole bottom of the suitcase. It was absolutely amazing. The IWOOTP bag had a complete false bottom.

"Damn," said Ronnie, "where did that come from?"

Inspector deBeaufort giggled. "Detective Amico didn't think you had any knowledge of thees."

"Detective Amico?"

"But of course. Who else did you think had called us?"

"Oh, no one," Ronnie said.

"Now, hold on again," the inspector said, and with even more sensitive moves he worked around the inner side of the suitcase until he found some other lever and opened up yet another secret compartment. This time a much smaller space was revealed, but it bore some fruit, for a little green packet fell out. The inspector pulled out a clear plastic container, opened it, and put a touch of the white substance it contained on his fingers and smelled it. "Do you know what thees is?"

"I'm scared to guess," Ronnie said.

"Indeed. It's cocaine."

"How long has that been traveling with me?"

"We can't be sure. Probably since you were in Sydney."

"Are you going to arrest me?" Ronnie asked. "Nobody

will believe me, I guess, but I don't know anything about this."

"Do not worry, my friend. Detective Amico, he says: Ratajczak don't know nothing."

"Then maybe you can tell me where it came from," Ronnie said.

"You still don't know?"

"No. I don't."

"Well, it is courtesy of a lady friend."

"A lady friend. Of mine?" DeBeaufort nodded. Ronnie rubbed his eyes, wondering who, scared who.

"Of course, it is a lady friend who is no longer wiz us."

"Doreen?" Ronnie snapped. "Doreen?"

"Yes, ze late Mrs. Whitridge. You were fooled, my friend. She was leading ze double life. On ze one hand, yes, she was ze tennis executive. On ze ozer, she had become a drug dealer."

"Oh my God," Ronnie said, and he sank to the bed. "Doreen wasn't a spy?"

"A spy? Oh, no, no. Ze lady was very wicked. She was handling millions of dollars in cocaine and heroin a year, and you, you, my friend, you were paying a price for sharing her favors."

"Me and Prosper Hegginbosch?"

"Yes, you two gentlemen. Mrs. Whitridge would sleep wiz you, and zen, wiz access to your room, she would place ze drugs in ze bottom compartment of your luggage."

"Then I would transport it—"

"Exactly. You and Monsieur Hegginbosch would come back to ze States, or wherever, and once you were safely through customs, it was but a simple matter for ze confederate of Mrs. Whitridge to enter your room when you were out and relieve you of ze cargo."

"Sure," Ronnie said. "So the whistler in New Orleans—he was getting the stuff I brought back from Grenada, which Doreen had probably just picked up in South America—only Manda came back to the room and suprised him. And that's what he wanted in San Francisco. Tell me,

Inspector, did Hegginbosch catch him in the act in Los Angeles, going through his suitcase?''

"No, we don't theenk so. You see, there is not ze one but ze two compartments.''

"Why's that?'' Ronnie asked.

"Ah yes. It seems that your dear lady friend was not only doublecrossing you and Monsieur Hegginbosch, but, in time, she began to double-cross her partners. So: ze second compartment. For herself.''

"For herself? Look, whatever Doreen did, she didn't do cocaine.''

"No. Not ze drug itself. But ze profit. Wiz boz you and ze deceased gentleman—''

"Hegginbosch?''

"*Oui*. In your luggage, and in his, she had zis smaller second compartment sewn in. Ze drugs she put in zere, she has not to share wiz anyone. She would put zem zere when she slept wiz you somewhere in ze world, and zen, most conveniently, pick zem up ze next time she slept wiz you in ze States—or wherever she was selling.''

"But her partners found out?''

"Exactly. In San Francisco, zey have caught ze man you call ze Whistler. He says he found out what Madame Whitbridge was doing. Only he made ze meestake of thinking zat she had gone into business wiz you and Monsieur Hegginbosch.''

"Yes, of course,'' Ronnie said. He remembered the phone call in Sydney, when the caller told him he knew what he and Doreen were doing. Ronnie assumed that he meant screwing; in fact, he meant dealing. "So, the Whistler caught up with Hegginbosch in L.A. and tried to get him to talk and show him how he and Doreen were smuggling the stuff for themselves, but of course Hegginbosch didn't say anything because he didn't know anything more than I did. So the Whistler got mad and killed him, and then he came on up to San Francisco to get me to talk. And when I got away, he went after Doreen and killed her.''

"You are a very lucky man, Ratajczak.''

"I know,'' Ronnie said. "If anybody had ever found

this stuff''—he pointed to the cocaine deBeaufort had extracted from the second compartment—"I'd've been locked up for the rest of my natural life."

"Zat is so, *monsieur*. Like so many men, you zought you were fucking ze lady fair, but, instead, she was fucking wiz you unfair."

ℛ

Ronnie came out of the police station a few hours later, after he gave his statement, after he'd gone over everything he knew fifty times, after he'd talked to Detective Amico back in San Francisco.

It was midday now, a glorious warm afternoon in Paris late in May, and the first-round matches were starting out at Roland Garros, but he had no interest in going out there. He had no interest in going much of anywhere, as a matter of fact. He was in Montmartre, and he just walked, up this street, down that one, and all he knew for certain was that it was time for his life to change. "Ratajczak," he said out loud. "This phase is up. After Wimbledon: something else."

It was odd, too, for he never thought of himself by his last name. He always thought of himself as a Ronnie and called himself Ronnie. "Ratajczak" had become more a byline than a name. Or it was something on documents and hotel registers. Not that he didn't like his name. Of course, nobody ever spelled "Ratajczak" correctly. Everybody left out the J even if they got the rest right. But that was only a pain; it was still a nice name. "Ratajczak," he said, "let's stop here and get us a beer."

It was a little café where everyone else was drinking wine or Perrier, and talking about wine or Perrier. Ronnie only drank his beer and watched the girls go by. Involuntarily his thoughts turned to Doreen. He wasn't mad at her. Certainly, yes, she could have been responsible for his getting killed or jailed. But he knew she didn't *mean* him harm. Doreen just always needed to flirt around the edges; safety or victory was too easy. Besides, he remembered the last time he'd seen her, Sydney-side, and how she'd told him to make sure to let anybody know that there wasn't anything but sex between them. He was certain that the reason she was so anxious to meet with him in San Francisco was to set the record altogether straight.

Poor Blue.

Then he began to think about Colin. In these past two days in Paris, Ronnie had learned that he owed Colin an apology. He had kept complaining to Colin that his misadventures were all due to his not being a spy. But now Ronnie knew that that wasn't the case at all. Young Zack wasn't a spy, and Doreen hadn't been one, and Prosper hadn't been one, and so instead of all these things happening to him because he wasn't a spy, they had happened to him because Young loved Rina and Libor beat and raped Rina, and because Doreen was an international, double-dealing drug lord—drug lady—and he and Prosper were unwitting pushers. None of it had anything to do with his not being a spy.

But then Ronnie thought: Well, that's not *quite* true. There was one thing that did happen to me because I wasn't a spy, and that was when I got shot in Singapore. The other stuff might not be Colin's fault, but . . . Only:

Because suddenly Ronnie thought; Wait a minute. If all those other things didn't happen because I wasn't a spy, then maybe I didn't get shot at because I wasn't a spy either. Maybe. Let's see.

Now he saw it. He sat up in his seat. Ronnie could see the tall Filipino on the Anderson Bridge, see him jump out at him, and hear him say: "You die, spy!" There it was.

"Son of a bitch!" Ronnie cried out loud, springing to his feet, so that all the people around him drinking wine and Perrier looked over at him and were relieved to see that he was drinking a beer and was not one of them.

Of course. Where was it written that when the guy said, "You die, spy!" it meant Ratajczak? Just because it was Ratajczak who was the one who got shot and came the closest to dying—that didn't prove that the guy with the gun necessarily had him in mind when he originally said, "You die, spy!" Because there were two people there, and "spy" is genderless, and Ratajczak wasn't, in fact, a spy, so maybe the other person was, actually, every inch a spy.

Young Zack wasn't the spy and Doreen wasn't and Prosper wasn't and he wasn't. Of course! Lia was. Lia *was* the spy. Lia was Dana. And of course she didn't want anything to do with him anymore because here Ronnie was supposed to be her decoy and here they were almost getting killed together. They could have gotten killed on a bridge together. Hell, they could get killed in bed together. Some decoy he was. No wonder she had left him. She had to. They had told her who Ronnie was and made her leave him. The CIA had.

Ronnie was so excited, he threw some francs down to pay for his beer. He was so worked up, he had no idea how much he left. He jumped in a taxi—only then he realized he didn't know where he was going. He wanted to go to Lia's hotel and wait for her to come back from the matches, but he didn't know what hotel she was in. So he told the driver to go to the Sofitel, where all the players stay because they get rates, but she wasn't registered there. Ronnie called Manda out at Roland Garros then, and had her paged, and she told him where Lia was staying. So he got back in a cab and went to the Trémoïlle, which was on the Rue du Boccador, off the Avenue George Cinq.

Naturally, she wasn't in her room when he called from the lobby. Well, there wasn't any reason why she should be. It was the first day of the Open, and Felicity was scheduled after Noah in the second match on Court Central.

Ronnie could guess how long it would be, then, but he didn't really care. It had all come together. That was what mattered. He knew! So he was content just to wait for Lia. It wasn't much past one when he got to the Trémoïlle, and he sat there until four-thirty. That was when he looked up one more time, and there was Lia, coming through the revolving door. She was in a swishy lavender sundress, and she positively reeked of memories.

Since she had left him in Singapore, Ronnie had encountered her only once before, one day in Rome, at the Foro Italico, during the Italian Open. They were in a crowd, around the courts, and he saw her, in fuchsia, but as soon as he had stepped toward her, Lia had smiled and shaken her head, simultaneously yes and no, and melted away. After that, whenever they saw one another she steered the other way before he could even begin to approach her.

But now she was totally unprepared for Ronnie's appearance, especially since he leapt up from his chair and into her path. In fact, she had to stop so quickly that the lavender skirt whipped, as in a wind.

"I must see you," he declared. Lia stared back at him, glaring. "For five minutes."

She considered that for a moment. "I told you, Ronnie, we must never see each other again."

He gritted his teeth. The concierge was eyeing him as if he were ready to come to Lia's assistance. "You owe me five lousy minutes. I've been waiting here for four hours."

"Don't make a scene," Lia said. She turned away from him, a sharp right-face, and marched to the desk. The clerk handed her the key. When she passed him on the way back, as coldly as she could, she said, "All right, five minutes."

They rode up in the tiny elevator side by side, staring ahead, never saying a word. Ronnie followed her down the hall and into her room. As soon as the door had closed, Lia whirled to face him. "I never would have thought this of you, Ronnie. It's most adolescent and most unbecoming."

"Well, just to clear the air, I never thought you exhibited much style in the way you ran off from me in Singapore. Tit for tat."

Lia answered by turning and walking away, giving him her back on the pretense of looking out the window. "You have no more than five minutes, so I wouldn't waste it on little talk," she snapped, not looking back at him.

"All right. It won't take five. It'll hardly take one." He paused for breath, and then, slowly, each word by itself: "Lia, now I know who you are."

She still had her back to him, but even if he wasn't able to see any expression, Ronnie could tell well enough that she was startled. Her body stiffened perceptibly. "At last, today," he went on, "I know who you are—what you are."

Lia swung around to face him. "And what does that mean?"

"It means I know." He slapped his leg like a kid. "How did I miss it? I think it's Young, I think it's Doreen, I think it's Prosper, maybe even Felicity. I think it's everybody— and all the time, you. You're the one with a gun, you're the one with a past. In the Philippines, you're the one who figures it all out. But me—you're so beautiful, you're so, so . . . everything . . . I can't see it right before me." Ronnie shrugged at himself. "Bula," he said when he started again. "Even when the guy pops out with the gun in Singapore, naturally, I think it's me he's after. Me? It was you, Lia. Finally I know. You, you're the spy."

He stopped then, so proud of himself.

Lia herself was so quick and so practiced that Ronnie never saw it coming, but in that instant she reached up under the lavender and in the same motion had taken the pistol from its holster and leveled it at him. "Oh, Ronnie," she sighed. How strange her voice sounded, almost exasperated and so curiously at odds with her fierce stance.

It befuddled Ronnie. All he could say was, "Come on, Lia." *Come on.*

She kept the gun dead on him. "You damn fool," Lia said. "Why did you tell me you knew? Why did you do that? Why couldn't you just go? Wasn't my getting you shot once enough?"

"Hey, it's okay. I don't blame you," Ronnie said. "I understand. And it's really okay because I'm back working with you again."

Lia's head cocked with that, just a little, almost imperceptibly. But Ronnie saw it. "You know. I'm working with the CIA again. I signed back on. I'm *your* decoy."

He was so pleased with himself that it took just an instant more before he saw her sag, saw her face twist, and saw her then shake her head, gritting her teeth, sad, mad, and unbelieving all at once. Only then did it hit him. Only then did he finally see the light. "Oh my God," he said.

"You didn't know, did you? Not till right now?"

He shook his head helplessly. "No."

"You blundered into this. I can't believe it."

"I just didn't see. I finally figure out you're the spy, Lia, and I just never thought you wouldn't be *our* spy. But you're not. My God, you're *their* spy."

"How could you do this to me, Ronnie?"

"Not Libor. You. You're KGB."

"Bula," Lia said, even summoning up a bit of a smile to match the irony—even if the gun never wavered.

There was, though, such a bizarre, airy sense to the scene that Ronnie still could not believe that Lia had a gun even as he saw it pointing at him. He took a step toward her. "No closer," she said, her arm stiffening.

"Come on, Lia. Come on." She shook her head vigorously. "Put the gun away."

"Don't move."

"Then I'm going to take it away from you."

"And I will have to shoot you."

"No you won't," Ronnie said, and he leaned forward as if he was going to start moving toward her again. "But if you do, don't worry. If you can spend that week with me in Fiji . . . and all the rest . . . if you can do that with me and then turn around and kill me for some crazy political intrigue, then my whole life is so foolish—it's all so foolish, everything—then I don't care, Lia. If you *can* shoot me, Lia, then, you see, fine, because it doesn't matter if you do or not."

Ronnie looked up from the gun, directly into her eyes, and as he watched, they turned from confusion to hopelessness, and then her arm fell, and Ronnie moved up, without another word, and reached out and took the weapon and laid it gently on the bed.

"Of course," was all Lia said when it was over.

Then they stood there facing one another. "I'm sorry I found out," Ronnie said. "Not because it matters, really, but because it doesn't make any sense."

"You wouldn't understand."

"Well, you're not trying to assassinate Mrs. Thatcher or blow up NATO or Cape Canaveral or anything, are you?"

"No, really, it's very pedestrian business. Just minding the store."

"Yeah, trying to take over the world," Ronnie said.

"We will soon enough, you know," Lia snapped.

"Maybe you will." Ronnie shrugged.

Lia looked at him squarely. "I just want you to understand that you must never talk to me again. Ever. No exceptions. You must—" The phone rang. Lia answered it, and, after a moment: "Yes, that's fine. No problem. Dinner at eight-thirty. I'll be prompt. Good-bye." She hung up and breathed deeply. "That's them," she told Ronnie.

"That's who?"

"My associates. They know you're here. I told them, in our code, that everything was fine. But they know about you, Ronnie. They know about us, and they worry that maybe our time together was not only for the cause."

"Oh, was it? Was Fiji for the cause?"

Lia only stared back at him. She was in command now, and she would only hear what she chose to. "When you leave . . . *now* . . . you must go back through the lobby. If you try and leave any other way, they will suspect that something is up, and there will be one of them around the back, and he will kill you, I'm sure. So, you must go through the lobby and out the front door." She went over to the window and pointed down the Rue du Boccador. It sloped past the cross street, the Rue de la Trémoïlle. "Walk down that way."

"Okay," Ronnie said.

"You can't see it from here," Lia said, "but about a hundred meters down, there is a small side street that cuts to the left."

"All right."

"Just before you get there, look up here. Glance up here, casually. Don't look behind you. Just look up this way, toward the balconies. If I'm on the balcony, Ronnie, run. If you see me at all, run. Run for your life. They'll be after you."

"Oh great. Where do I go?"

"Well, take that little side street till it dead ends in a block. Cut right there, down the hill. When you get to the bottom—that's the Avenue Montaigne. Do you understand?"

"Yes, that's easy. Then what?"

"The Canadian embassy will be there, just a ways up on the left. I suggest you run in there. If you can."

"All right."

"Good. Then go. There is no more."

"Yes, there is. One thing. *If* I start to run, they'll know why. They'll know you signaled me. So then. What about you?"

"Oh, I'll try to get away. But it probably doesn't matter, because if they decide to follow you, then they don't believe me, and they'll get me too. That is the way it is in this business. So you see, it doesn't matter."

"All right, I get it."

"And you understand now. If they don't go after you, you must never talk to me again. Ever, Ronnie. Never call me, never even wave at me. If we pass at the tennis, you nod, I nod, we say hello, but we don't stop. Ever. You understand?" He nodded. "I appreciate that you can't comprehend how ideology can mean so much to people, but it does to them."

"Them?" he asked.

"Yes, and to me. Now you know. I've always been one of them."

"And me?"

"Of course you mean much to me, too. I have a heart like any woman. But there is much more of me, and I must foremost and first be that woman. Now go."

They looked at each other for a long moment, "It's all right with me if you kiss me good-bye," he said. Wistfully she shook her head, and he shrugged and started across the room to the door.

He had his hand on the knob when he heard her voice again. "Ronnie." He turned around and took a step back toward her. "No," Lia said. "Stay there. I only want you to see something. It is the last time I will ever be with you in my life, and I want you to see something.''

She intently raised her hand to the top of her dress and began to unbutton it. She pulled the top apart and then with both hands unfastened the brassiere from the clasp that held it in the front. She pulled the two cups to the side and with the palm of her hand held up her left breast for him to see.

On the underside, there was nothing; from his distance Ronnie could not even see the pale outline where "Sempre Paolo" had been tattooed over, skin-colored. "I see, it's gone," Ronnie said, and then Lia moved her other hand to cover herself, as you might salute the flag.

"Whatever, I wanted you to know you made it so I could forget that. Now I only must forget you. Now go . . . my love." And she brought her free hand to her lips and blew him the lightest of kisses.

Ԛ

There were several men in the lobby, all of them looking exactly like KGB assassins to Ronnie. He walked briskly up the steps to the revolving door, feeling positive that every one of the KGB had begun to follow him. But he did as Lia had bade him, he didn't look back, and outside, he casually turned left, crossed the Rue de la Trémoille, following the Rue du Boccador down the incline. As Lia had said, after a couple hundred yards or so there was a side street. The Rue Chambiges. He glanced back toward her hotel. He saw the balconies. She wasn't there. They had believed her. He sighed. He knew he could have run for safety and found the embassy. But now he knew that Lia was safe too.

LONDON
III

Ronnie met with Colin almost as soon as he came over from Paris. They sat downstairs, near the salad bar, at the Wendy's near Oxford Circus. "Finest American contribution since the airplane, the salad bar," Colin said, digging into the croutons and bacon bits and Thousand Island dressing. And, in due course, Colin assured him that the "business" in Neuilly had been taken care of. The business was Libor's dead body. Colin asked Ronnie if he wanted to know where and how and all that sort of thing, but Ronnie said: no, thank you very much.

It was mid-June now, with Wimbledon in the wings. The men were playing their preliminary on grass at Queens Club, the women down on the coast at Eastbourne. Felicity had triumphed in Paris with more ease than ever before, never so much as losing a set on clay, and only once losing as many as three games in any single set. That was to Ludmilla in the semis: 6–1, 6–3. Ludmilla was back on tour now, traveling in blue jeans with a green card and a coach from Texas she was sleeping with.

The final of the French Open was truly no contest, as Felicity destroyed Consuelo Contez love and love in thirty-six minutes, the first time anyone in modern times had been double-bageled in a Grand Slam final. That brought Felicity her fifth straight French title, which broke Suzanne

Lenglen's record, and, thus broke hearts all across France
that their *nonpareil* had been eclipsed . . . and by an Eng-
lishwoman at that. With that championship, too, Felicity
had now taken twenty Grand Slam titles in a row, and, in
recognition of another cycle, she had won yet another
World Tennis Organization one-million-dollar bonus—
which this year was presented to her in the form of a tiara,
to go with the matching bracelet and ring and the choker
from previous years.

And then, to Wimbledon next, where she would be up
against the ghost of Suzanne Lenglen again, seeking to become the first woman ever to win six Wimbledons in a row.
But then, everybody knew this by now. Variations on the
theme of Felicity's omnipotence were trotted out every day
in the British press, interspersed only with stories of her im-
pending nuptials, which would be held the Monday following
the Fortnight. Even Colin chattered on to Ronnie about what
sort of bridal dress Felicity would wear, who the bridesmaids
and groomsmen would be, and whether or not, as was rumored, the Archbishop of Canterbury would perform the
service himself. Since none of the bookmakers would take
so much as a pence on Felicity merely winning Wimbledon,
they had come up with all manner of other wagering tidbits
. . . on either the tennis or the marriage. Colin, for example,
said he was going to put down a quid or two on what hymns
he thought would be played. But then, you could also get
1:2 that Felicity wouldn't lose a set throughout the Fortnight,
12:5 that it would be a double-ring ceremony, and 100:1 that
Felicity would yet call off the wedding.

Ronnie meant to drop by Ladbroke's and put down a
couple bob on the latter.

Just for luck.

For now, though, he had to take leave of Colin and catch
the underground over to the Gloucester, which was the
players' hotel during Wimbledon. He was going to meet
Manda there and catch a ride with her and Sarah Cardigan
down to Eastbourne. He reached out formally across Colin's salad and shook his hand. "I trust this'll be the last

time I see you," Ronnie said. "You still expect this project to be wrapped up in another few weeks?"

"Yes, by about the end of the Fortnight, I should say."

"Well, then, we're square. I'm your decoy to the last, and you've paid me in full with your services in Paris."

"Indeed. Only there is one thing, Ronnie. If it's possible, could you find me a Centre Court ticket or two when Felicity's playing? A lot of the chaps at the office—we're not just agents, you know. We're tennis fans, as well."

"Sure thing, Colin. I'll get you a ticket for Felicity if you'll tell me who Dana is." And before Colin could recover, Ronnie slapped him on the shoulder and took off for the tube station.

♎

Felicity was all the more devastating at Eastbourne. Grass, after all, had always been her best surface—going back to learning in the graveyard. But at least for a time in Eastbourne Rina had been the center of attention, playing her first match as Mrs. Zack Harvey. The press loved it: the bittersweet tale of the little Communist lass who had lost her dear father and coach to a mysterious Balkan ailment, only to have her grief assuaged somewhat by eloping with her secret American boyfriend. "LOVE CRACKS THE IRON CURTAIN!" And: "STAR-SPANGLED BULGAR!"

Rina played marvelously at Eastbourne, too, adapting better than ever she had to the grass. She lost in the semis to Diane Bishop only because she suffered an incredible series of bad calls and because Diane played the match of her life—and even then Rina needed a dreadful bounce and a net cord to fall in the third-set tiebreaker.

Afterward, when Ronnie came back up to London, he settled into his flat at Dolphin Square, by the river, where he had stayed the Fortnight for years. The first night, he invited Young and Rina out to dinner. He wanted to give them some sort of wedding present—aside from having dispensed with the body. They went to Langan's, Michael Caine's restaurant, off Piccadilly, and raised a champagne toast—to the newlyweds, and to Ronnie for his services. "This is also a real special treat for us,'' Young said. "What an honor: to have dinner with Mr. Ratajczak alone.''

"We never know you have an evening without a lady,'' Rina added.

"I'm afraid this has not been a felicitous year for me and ladies,'' Ronnie said. "No pun intended.''

The place was packed, mostly with Americans. Of course, that made it convenient. If you heard a British accent, you could be sure that your waiter was nearby. What with the exchange rate and airfare from New York down to a dollar-ninety-five, London was now overrun by Americans, almost all of whom *had* to go to Wimbledon one day so that they could go back to the country club or the mall or the Nautilus and tell everybody that they had not only been to London, but that, unlike every other Tom, Dick, and Harry, they had actually been to Centre Court. It was only a few years ago that Wimbledon was an ideal place for Americans to go and hide. Johnny Carson could go over there every summer and pass unnoticed. Even a senator or a network weatherman could carry on an affair, safely, at Wimbledon. But now there were more Americans at Wimbledon than there were packing the best restaurants in Paris. A few years ago, Centre Court tickets for the finals might fetch two hundred dollars from the most respected touts. But now, with all the Americans throwing money at the scalpers along Somerset Road, the touts were getting three and four times that price for tickets in early rounds if Felicity was scheduled, and almost as much if McEnroe was up against someone he might likely lose his temper with.

"You know, I've decided to get out of tennis,'' Ronnie said.

"For good?''

"Yeah. This is my last tournament. It's time for me to find something else, and what I have in mind is that, with all these Americans over here every June, I'm going to bring some familiar attractions over here. I mean, these poor bored tourists can only do the Tower of London, a ride on a double-decker bus, and the Harrods summer sale so many times. Next year, if all goes well, during the Fortnight I'm bringing over the Rockettes, the Baltimore Orioles, a reconstructed Fisherman's Wharf, most of Orlando, Florida, and several pavilions from the Ohio State Fair, which I'm going to set up in Hyde Park. It'll be perfect. All the Americans can fly to London and still get the best of home.''

"Terrific idea," Young said. "American ingenuity rides again.''

"And you know how I'm going to finance it? I bet ten pounds on you today, Rina. At fifty to one. You can win, you know. That was too much of an overlay to pass up. You really are playing beautifully.''

"Come on, Ronnie, don't scare her," Young said. "Rina might get a Wimbledon someday. I know she's got the talent. But no woman in the world can even stay on the same court with Felicity now."

"Do not listen to him, Ronnie," Rina said. "Now that Libor's gone, and I have you, darling"—she turned back to Young and hugged his arm—"I think I can do anything.''

Ronnie had barely gotten back to his flat at Dolphin Square when the phone rang. The instant he heard the voice his heart fell. His stomach fell. His voice fell. "Hello, my old friend and mentor," Felicity said.

"Hello, Mrs. Fable, *née* Felicity Tantamount. To what do I owe this honor?''

"Will you be my date?"

"Monday week? I knew you'd come to your senses, child. I'll go out and rent the cutaway.''

"No, sorry, love, I'm still booked then. But how about this Saturday night at the LTA ball?''

"Sure, but where's your affianced?''

"I'll tell you then. My car will pick you up at eight that night. Black tie, ducky.''

There are several major social functions at Wimbledon, but perhaps most prominent of them all is the Lawn Tennis Association dinner dance. It's held Saturday, in the middle of the Fortnight, which takes advantage of the fact that there's no tennis scheduled the next day, Sunday, so every-body can stay up late (and even spoon some).

Ronnie was thinking about that, too, as Felicity's car brought him over to her house on Paultons Square, in Chel-sea—about how the very first time he, a lowly journalist, had ever been allowed in the LTA ball was when Felicity invited him. That was that first year, when the world dis-covered her shortly after Ronnie did. And now, here they were going together again, even as she prepared to marry another man.

At Paultons Square he had to use a bobby to help fight his way through the photographers and gossip writers in order to get in. "I hope they don't put my picture in the paper to-morrow as your mystery lover," he said to Felicity.

"Oh well, it might be good to give Dale a bit of a jab."

The butler, Randall, brought Felicity a beer and Ronnie a whiskey and then discreetly retired. "All right, Felice, where is the future Mr. Tantamount?"

"Really, we can do without that sort of rubbish, Ronnie. But the fact is, he had to fly over to the States yesterday and he won't be back till Tuesday earliest."

"Oh? It must be something pretty damn important to take him away from Wimbledon."

"It is," Felicity said, and she sat down across from Ronnie. She was so extraordinarily beautiful, so devastat-ing, that Ronnie had schooled himself through the years to carry on fairly normally in the glare of her loveliness, but suddenly, as she crossed her long legs, he was overcome again, and he gasped—literally. "Are you all right, love?" Felicity asked.

Her hair was swept up more than usual, her dress cut lower. It was a long gown, cream white with royal-blue piping revealing not only many of her personal assets but also the million-dollar choker she had just won in Paris.

"Oh, I'm fine," Ronnie said, composing himself. "Just tell me about Dale's trip."

"It's my tennis-clothes deal. We're about to sign the largest contract for anything like this—by far, ever."

"It's an American company?"

"Yes, but please don't even ask me, Ronnie. Only it's not sporting goods. I can tell you that. They simply wouldn't be able to compete with the figures here. It's bloody brilliant of Dale that he came up with this idea."

"Yeah. And do you like the dress?"

That rocked Felicity back a bit. "Well, yes, but I've only seen the rough designs. They're rushing round the clock to make one up, so Dale can bring it back Tuesday on the Concorde."

"After all this, and you haven't even seen the dress you're going to wear? *The* dress of all time?"

"Oh, Ronnie, don't be such an old woman. The designs I've seen I adore—and I promise you I won't sign a bloody thing until I've tried it on. Besides, I'll be paid millions to wear it, and Dale says once I start wearing it, I'll be as famous in it as the Eiffel Tower. It'll become the most famous article of clothing a woman has ever worn anywhere in the world."

Ronnie sipped his whiskey. "That's all fine. But why now? Why did Dale have to rush over and leave Wimbledon?"

"Oh, that's easy. We want to announce it Monday next."

"Your wedding day."

"Yes, of course."

"That's so terribly romantic," Ronnie said. "Something old, something new, something borrowed, and something endorsable."

Felicity shot him an angry eye. "Can't you ever stop?"

"All right, I'm sorry."

"No, Mr. Ratajczak, no, I will not walk down the aisle in my new tennis dress. But we will have the whole world press in our palms that day, and not to take advantage of that would be bloody balmy. You know that I can't have any privacy anyhow. Besides, Monday is really the first day we could legally announce such a deal, because my contract with Geisha is written to run out after next Saturday, when they play the ladies' finals."

"All right, but you do like the dress? The design?"

Felicity considered that, and then rose and went back

over to the bar and poured herself the rest of her beer. "Well, all right, I will tell you a little secret if you promise not ever to reveal it."

"I promise not ever to reveal it."

"And also promise not ever to say, 'just like a bloody woman.' "

"I also promise never to say, 'just like a bloody woman.' "

"All right." She appeared to switch the subject then. "Will your lady friend be at the ball this evening?"

"I have lots and lots of lady friends, thank you."

"Don't be evasive. The Italian Ice."

"Signorina D'Antonini is not included among my lots and lots of lady friends anymore."

"Oh, I'd heard through the grapevine that there was something of a falling-out after Singapore, but I didn't realize it was that extensive. Can I ask why?"

"Not really. But it never advanced our relationship that Lia knew I remained madly in love with another woman who is marrying another man."

"I'm sorry," Felicity said softly, and she bowed her head.

"So, I'm sorry, I can't help you anymore with Lia. What did you want?"

"I just wanted to tell her how much I loved the dress Grazia made for me. Of all the sporting-goods companies, it was much the most beautiful and right and simpatico. It was original and it was me. Simply smashing."

" 'Of all the sporting-goods companies,' huh? You're telling me you really like it better than the one you're signing with, aren't you?" Ronnie said, getting up and going to the bar for another couple of ice cubes. Even when the British know the drinker prefers ice, they can't bring themselves to put enough in.

"Yes, that's my little secret."

"Just like a bloody woman."

She slapped him gently across the face. "You cad."

Ronnie raised his glass. "Well, since I can never say it again: 'Here's to the dress you'll wear, and here's to the dress you love.' " They both drank. "And forgive me, Felice, and I'll never say a word of this again, either, but I'll always believe there is that same sort of analogy between you and your men as well as between you and your dresses.''

Since his tone was more bittersweet than snide, she let it pass. Instead, Felicity said, ''I know we've got to dash, but would you just like a peek at it first?''

''The Grazia?'' She nodded. ''Sure I would. Anything to prolong my final moments alone with *Miss* Tantamount.''

''Stay here. I'll be right back.'' Ronnie splashed some more Scotch in his glass and peered out front through the shades. There must have been twenty photographers jockeying out there, three or four television crews, another dozen or so reporters. Felicity's picture, with or without Ronnie in it, was going to be in every newspaper in the world the next morning. It was enough that the most beautiful woman in the world was poised to win her sixth straight Wimbledon, her two hundredth straight match, but after everyone else saw her as Ronnie had just seen her, there wasn't a front page in the world that could resist her. He wanted to call out the window, alert the poor devils to exactly what was coming. Ronnie was, after all, still a journalist, even if only for one more week. They were his brothers and sisters under the skin. But just then he heard Felicity come back into the room. ''Here it is,'' she said.

Ronnie turned around. He had expected that she was only going to hold up the Grazia dress for him. Instead, she had taken off her gown, even taken off the choker and her high heels, and she had picked up a racket, and now she stood there before him in her new Grazia. It was breathtaking, an even more stunning sight than Felicity had been in her front-page gown. Ronnie almost gagged on his whiskey.

It was a revolutionary body suit, original and distinctive, clinging to Felicity's lines, and yet, provocatively, covering them. The suit flowed with her as she moved the few steps into the room and whirled around before Ronnie.

The outfit began at the left shoulder, cutting down across Felicity's right breast, leaving her right, racket shoulder and arm bare, free for swinging. At the waist there was a belted fringe—just a dash of fun and femininity. Ronnie

could imagine it flying up as she glided about the court.
But otherwise, the outfit stayed close to her body lines, all
the way down to—and even including—her shoes, which
were not sneakers at all, but a light ballet-type footwear
that seemed to be hardly more than a natural extension of
her outfit. The color was a cream white, but Wimbledon
would never see it, for the outfit was colorfully striped,
vertically, contoured, the stripes broader where Felicity was
voluptuous, thinner where she was athletic—alternating
light pastels of orange and chartreuse and lavender that
picked up the highlights from her glorious red hair.

She whirled one more time, and then pantomimed hitting
a backhand volley, her right hand drifting off with the racket
as if she were a dancer finishing a move.

"What do you think?" Felicity said.

Ronnie thought it was not fair.

Ⓠ

The next day, Sunday, the Fortnight off day, Ronnie took
Manda and her kids, and they did the complete tourist Lon-
dontown. The following day started the second half of the
tournament, one that was going almost too close to form.
McEnroe and Becker were breezing along, and Felicity hadn't
so much as been threatened in a set in any of her first three
matches. She hadn't lost a single service game, and had
proved no less accomplished in the doubles, where she was
paired with Diane Bishop, or in the mixed, with Young Zack.
Could she be the first player ever to win all three titles without the loss of a set, without even the loss of a serve?

Monday certainly didn't change anything, either. In the
round of sixteen, Felicity beat a teenager named Cece
Toler, who hailed from someplace in California that began
with either a San or an El. The scores were 6–1, 6–0.
Then, on Wednesday, in the quarters, she took Sarah Cardigan, Manda's incumbent lover, 6–4, 6–3. For this defeat, Sarah was practically rushed into the Hall of Fame.
"CENTRE COURT SCARE!" screamed the *Standard*. "FELIC-
ITY TREMBLES," cried the *Mirror*. "Does this magnificent

performance give you renewed confidence in your career?"
the BBC asked Sarah afterward.

Manda was watching in the press room with Ronnie as
Sarah was being interviewed. "Jesus," she whispered, "I
love her and all that, but she only won seven fucking games
and never even got to deuce on Felicity's serve. If she'd
played this match against anybody else, the idiots would be
asking her when she was going to quit and have babies."

Nobody paid much attention to the bottom half of the
draw, especially the British, after Diane Bishop got upset
in the third round by Honey Bisker, a blond with a two-
handed backhand from someplace in Florida that began with
a Palm or a Belle, but for those pedants who kept an occasional eye on the proceedings, Rina Rodanya, now listed
as 'R. HARVEY" on the scoreboards of the All-England
Club, was rolling. She lost only one set, and that a tiebreaker against Honey Bisker in the round of sixteen, but
she steadied herself then and wiped Honey off the grass,
6–7, 6–0, 6–2. Then Wednesday, in the quarters, Rina
finally got on Centre Court, and there she annihilated Marissa de la Rey two and one.

Afterward, back at their flat, Rina told Young that it was
the first time in her life that she had felt totally comfortable
on the grass. "It was like when I am first learning to speak
English," she said, "and one day, suddenly, I am thinking
in English. Today, for first time, I am . . . What's the
word when you just do it?"

"Instinctively?"

"Yes. I am just instinctively playing the grass."

Still, Tiffany Rogers, seeded fifth, impressive upset con-
queror of the second-seeded Polly Hutton in the quarters,
was favored over Rina in their semifinal match on Thursday, a competition the newspapers bothered to address only
as a matter of determining the identity of who would be
"The 200th Victim" in Saturday's final.

Felicity's opponent in the semis was Ludmilla. They
came onto Centre Court at precisely two o'clock for the
opening match of the afternoon. At 2:42 Felicity and Ludmilla paused on their way out to bow to the Duchess of

Kent, the All-England Club's patroness, in the Royal Box. The score had been two and love, and, as everyone commented, Ludmilla had played bravely and wisely to take the two games she did. For the first time that anyone could remember in any match of consequence, anywhere (let alone the semis at Wimbledon), a player had not lost a single point on serve, Felicity outscoring Ludmilla 28-0.

A men's quarterfinal match between Becker and Tim Mayotte followed. By now the referee understood only too well how to schedule matches where Felicity was involved. She would win so quickly that there wasn't any need to rush the other women's semifinal on. The press could then comfortably interview Felicity (and her vanquished foe) and work on new ways to employ such words as "awesome," "devastating," "history-making," "transcendent," and what-have-you while the men's quarterfinalists had their knock-up. And then, after a bit of tea or a Pimm's Cup, the boys and girls of the Fourth Estate could leisurely return to watch Rina and Tiffany compete for the honor of being the slaughteree in Saturday's abattoir.

As for Felicity, promptly at four-thirty, having finished all her interviews, had a bath and a rubdown, she came out of the main clubhouse entrance. Wimbledon supplies cars for the competitors, little Leylands driven by young female volunteers, but of course Felicity always arranged to have a limousine meet her, and now a maroon Rolls nudged along through the crowd to reach her.

Fable had taken the Concorde back to London on Tuesday, once Felicity approved the dress. Now the contract needed only the deal settled, a few lawyers' jots and tittles before the formal signing the next morning. Fable came over to Felicity and pecked her cheek as the driver opened the door. "Now, tomorrow, sweetie, all you have is the doubles. Since they've got both the men's semis on Centre Court, you'll be on Court One," he said.

"Fine," Felicity replied. "When do I go on?"

"You're second match after a men's doubs. Count on five or so. Do you want me to arrange any sort of hit tomorrow morning?"

"Oh God no, darling, the doubles will be just right. Maybe a bit more afterward if they go quickly." And she squeezed his hand and climbed in.

"I'll see you at home in a couple hours," Fable said. "I just want to see Rina play Tiffany."

The driver closed the door, and the fans, held back behind ropes, screamed and cooed all the more that Felicity was so close and yet they couldn't see her. Many of them had come out to Wimbledon with no hope of getting into Centre Court and watching Felicity play; they were content to pay for the privilege of merely seeing her drive off.

Considerately, Felicity bade the driver put down the tinted window on her side, and as she departed the grounds, going out past the statue of Fred Perry, she smiled and waved at the people, just like Princess Di—who was, in fact, planning to come out and see Felicity's triumph on Saturday.

The Rolls inched the rest of the way, sharing the club roadway with the throng until it reached the gates at Somerset Road. The bobby halted traffic there, letting the limousine out, and as soon as the driver swung left toward London, Felicity asked him to put the window back up, kicked off her shoes, settled back, and began to peruse the final draft of the dress contract that Fable had given her. Even she had to shake her head, for the numbers appeared even more mindboggling when set in type.

The big maroon car sped toward Southfields, cutting over to Merton Road. Perhaps if Fable had paid more attention when he was putting his fiancée into the car, he would have noticed that the limousine had a different driver than the one who had picked up Felicity and him this morning at Paultons Square. In fact, the new driver was Rudy, Colin's colleague, and the reason he was behind the wheel now was that he and John had come up behind the real driver earlier in the day, when he was alone in the car park where the favored limousines are allowed to rest, and they had quietly shoved a gun in his face and then hustled him away to the house in Merton which they had rented for the Fortnight.

Where Merton Road split by King George Park, Rudy took the smaller fork onto Buckhold, and then he slowed the car. Felicity was reading carefully, and paid little attention. As soon as the car came to a halt on the shoulder, Rudy popped the lock, the doors opened, and from where they were casually standing idle by the side of the road, in hopped John from one side and Colin from the other. The car sped away again, only not at all where it had been going. Instead, Rudy took it onto Richmond Road, winding his way to the M3 highway, heading southwest then, away from London, away from Paultons Square.

*

At precisely six-thirty, one of the British enlisted men who gives up his vacation to serve as an usher at Wimbledon came up to Dale Fable. He had been given a seat in the royal enclosure this day, and was engrossed in the Rina-Tiffany battle. Presently they were engaged in the tiebreaker of what had been a terrific first set. Rina, charging the net, serving and volleying as if she had spent her whole life on the grass, was in perfect contrast to Tiffany, who was, as always, staying back, slugging ground strokes. They were both fighting every inch of the way.

The tiebreaker score was two-all when the sergeant from the Royal Air Force tapped Fable on the shoulder and whispered, "I'm sorry, sir, but there is a most urgent phone call for you."

In a frozen whisper Fable snapped back: "Are you crazy, man? This isn't even a crossover."

"It's most urgent, sir. Most."

"I'll come at the end of the tiebreaker. Tell 'em that."

"No, sir, I'm sorry," the sergeant said, and he actually turned Fable's head away from the court to look squarely into his face. "You must come, and you must come *now*."

At last Fable responded to the sergeant's urgency and leapt to his feet. He didn't even glance back at the roar, which came in response to a smash Rina made from well behind the service line, which put her up 3–2 and gave her a mini-break.

The sergeant escorted Fable to the office of the tournament chairman, Buzzer Hadingham, which was located directly below the royal enclosure. He handed him the telephone receiver. "Sir."

Gingerly Fable took it and put it to his ear. "This is Dale Fable."

"Yes, how do you do, Mr. Fable," said the crisp voice. "Listen to me carefully, and please keep in mind that this is not a hoax. We have kidnapped your fiancée. She is quite safe, though, and will remain so, for so long as you cooperate with us. I emphasize, you need not concern yourself with her person. We are not the IRA. We only seek a proper ransom."

"Who are you?" Fable managed.

"Please, sir, no questions. I would advise you, first, to contact your bankers in New York whilst they are still at their office and begin the necessary details of obtaining the proper cash that we will require."

"How much?"

"Excuse me, Mr. Fable, I said: no questions. You will shortly receive detailed instructions from a contact. I assure you, though, that, given your circumstances, it will not be oppressive. We would prefer that this transaction proceed expeditiously, and we believe we would suffer more risk were we greedy. Besides, I can assure you personally that we are all most devoted fans of Miss Tantamount's and only want her to enjoy Godspeed back to the finals . . . and then to your marriage bed. Good evening."

And the voice disappeared and the phone clicked off. "Get me Hadingham," Fable said to the sergeant, and then he collapsed into the chairman's own chair.

Momentarily, Hadingham arrived. He was in fine spirits. The weather had held remarkably well for the Fortnight, and there had been no controversy of any consequence; McEnroe hadn't so much as glared at an umpire. "Looks like you'll have two of your clients in the ladies' final," he said as he entered. "Rina won the tiebreaker seven to four."

Fable barely looked up. "Buzzer, Jesus," he said, "they've kidnapped Felicity."

"Oh my God."

Fable pushed the phone across the desk. "Call her home, please. I can't bring myself to do it."

"Of course." Hadingham dialed. Randall answered. No, he said, in fact Miss Tantamount had not yet arrived back at Paultons Square.

"Call the limousine company." Hadingham dialed. The dispatcher said, no, neither had the driver brought the car back nor had he reported in.

"Do you want me to call Scotland Yard now?" Hadingham said.

"I don't think so. But they didn't say not to. Let me think."

At that moment Ted Tinling, the dress designer, who serves as the liaison officer at Wimbledon for the press and players, knocked at the door. "I'm sorry, Ted, we're quite busy with something right now," the chairman said.

Tinling saw Fable at the desk, holding his head in his hands. He could see they knew. "I regret to inform you both that, within the past five minutes, both the press room and the BBC have received calls advising them that Felicity has been kidnapped and is being held for ransom."

"So I guess we can call the police and let them know too," Fable said, trying to force a smile.

Tinling got out the gin.

Ⓠ

Precisely as all this was taking place at the All-England Club, the object of all the concern was alighting from a small propeller plane that had just made an hour's trip. Briskly John took Felicity by the arm and escorted her to a waiting car. "Welcome to France," he said.

Cynthia helped Felicity into the back seat. "We have a private room ready for you," she said, and the car whisked away.

Ⓠ

Ronnie came back to his desk from the press briefing. The place was absolute bedlam. He had stopped at the press bar and bought two double whiskeys. He downed the second one now. The phone rang and numbly he reached for it—more to stop the damn thing from ringing than to converse with whoever it might be. It was, in fact, Colin.

Ronnie's first impulse was just to slam the damn thing down. He probably was looking for tickets again. "Dammit, Colin," he did say, "I can't talk. Don't you know that Felicity's been kidnapped?"

Colin said: "Only too well, Ronnie." It was the way he said it. The way he didn't say anything else.

Ronnie rose in his chair. "You mean . . . ?" He started to say, "You mean you know where she is?" but luckily he caught himself before he broadcast to the journalists milling about.

"I'm on the grounds," Colin went on. "Meet me straightaway at the Fred Perry statue. And don't tell a bloody soul."

Ronnie grabbed up his jacket, dashed out of the pressroom, down the steps, and through the crowd. The word about the kidnapping was everywhere by now, and even the people who held Centre Court tickets had deserted the Rina-Tiffany match—although it was a beauty: Tiffany had come back to win the second set, 6–3, and they were fighting tooth and nail in the third.

But no one could concentrate on that. It was one of those occasions when people had to gather, had to mumble and wonder and talk and confer, even if the questions were all the same and the speculations meaningless.

This drifting throng was all about the statue, and Colin wasn't in sight. Ronnie searched about madly—and suddenly Colin materialized, strolling, *ambling*, from over by the Pimm's Cup stand. He merely raised his glass to Ronnie and beckoned for him to follow through the crowd and out the gate to Somerset Road. Ronnie caught up with him on the sidewalk, where the touts were still trying to scalp weekend tickets. At least somebody was working as usual. "What the hell, Colin?"

"Please, Ronnie, no questions." He guided him across the street to the car park and pointed to a Ford. "Get in, my friend, and welcome to Operation Dana. It's in effect."

He roared out of the lot. It was easy. Nobody else was going anywhere.

"What the hell is happening?" Ronnie asked.

"You'll learn everything in five minutes at the house."

"What house?"

"Our house, the CIA house we rented for Dana."

"Well, just tell me this: is Felicity safe?"

"Of course she is. At this very instant she is safe and sound in the Operation Dana hideaway in France."

"France!" Ronnie cried. "Goddammit, I can't believe it." He pounded the dashboard. "Oh yes, I can believe it. I can. I had that hunch: Felicity! Felicity was the spy after all. Oh, Felice, you are something!"

Colin only smiled and took the corner toward Merton.

Ω

The house Gerry and Cynthia had rented in Merton was indistinguishable from the others around it, and perhaps the plainer inside, for Mrs. Featherstone had made sure to remove anything of value or sentiment before the invasion of the tennis crowd.

Gerry was waiting in the parlor, enjoying a bitter and relaxing in the manner of any suburbanite. He flicked off the television and welcomed Ronnie. "How do you do, Mr. Ratajczak. I've heard so much about you from Colin and the others."

"This is Gerry, Ronnie," Colin said. "He's the director of our office here."

"It's nice to meet you," Ronnie said, and he said he'd love to have something to drink himself, with ice. "Now, can one of you tell me what the hell is going on with Felicity?"

"Absolutely," Gerry squeaked. "That's why you're here now. That's why you've been working for us all these months."

"I must say, I'm just amazed," Ronnie said. "That Felicity would be the spy. I'm glad I didn't know for sure. I really would have worried about her."

"Well," Gerry said. "That's fine, because now you needn't ever worry about that again."

"Why?" Ronnie asked. Colin brought him a whiskey with one cube of ice in it. He took a sip. "Could you get me another couple ice cubes?"

"Certainly." He took the glass back.

"Why?' Ronnie said again.

"Because Felicity's not a spy."

Ronnie shook his head. "She isn't? I don't understand. Then what in the world is she doing with the CIA?"

"Nothing at all, old chap, nothing at all."

Colin handed Ronnie the drink back. There was one more ice cube in it. "What do you mean?"

"I mean, very simply, we're not CIA," Gerry said.

Ronnie dropped the drink, flat out, on the floor. "Oh my God, no."

Colin stepped forward to tidy up the mess. He looked up. "Yes, I'm sorry, Ronnie. I'm sorry I had to be somewhat deceptive with you."

"Well, then, who are you?"

Gerry took out a pistol. But nicely, for show, not in a menacing way. "I'm afraid we're just your everyday garden-variety international thieves," he said.

"I'll get you another whiskey," Colin said, leaving with the glass for the kitchen.

"And," Gerry went on, "in this instance we've branched out into kidnapping. There seemed to be an opening in the line, if properly managed. Everybody else is so dreadful about it these days. We not only do not wish to harm Miss Tantamount in any way, even emotionally, we'd like so very much to get her back for the finals. Come, let me show you something."

Gerry steered Ronnie down the steps into the basement. In the corner, sitting on a cot, one hand tied to a post, was Harold, the gentleman whose unfortunate lot it was to have been Felicity's driver. He was watching television.

"Now," said Gerry. "This is the driver. As you can see, he's not hurt. He's comfortable. He has his own loo and just has to call if he needs to go. And Felicity is receiving every bit as much courtesy. And so too will you, Ronnie. We simply want to take the money and run.'' Gerry turned to address Harold now. ''Turn that telly down a bit for a moment, Harold. We shall probably be leaving here with Mr. Ratajczak quite soon, and then you'll be free to work yourself clear and call the police. I assure you they'll retrieve you with alacrity once you contact them, and provide you proper transport home. All right?''

''Yes, thanks so much, Gerry. And did you call my missus?''

''Indeed. We assured her that you were just fine and to keep the bubble and squeak warm.''

''Thanks very much,'' Harold said.

''Yes, and don't worry if you can't free yourself. We'll call your wife ourselves and give her this address after a time.''

Gerry waved the gun then—nicely—and ushered Ronnie back upstairs. Colin gave Ronnie a new drink, with an ice cube in it, and he sat back down. ''All right, why me?''

''Oh, Ronnie, you were perfect for our purposes,'' Colin said. ''We had a little business we were attending to in Buenos Aires and your name came up at the time. A go-between in these matters is critical, and you seemed ideal. First of all, professionally you're a journalist. You know how to carry on properly with secrets and so forth. And then, personally, you're quite in love with Felicity Tantamount. The whole tennis world knows that. But it was also rumored—just tipped back then—that she was going to marry Mr. Fable. So, should we engage you, and then should anything go wrong, it would appear as if you had concocted the kidnapping yourself—acted out of jealousy.''

''As things have developed, too,'' Gerry said. ''You are incriminated by all sorts of circumstantial evidence.''

Colin laid out on the table before Ronnie a variety of snapshots. Ronnie taking money on the beach at Punta, in the bar in New Orleans, under the Golden Gate in San Francisco. There was even one of Ronnie and Colin together at the Wendy's salad bar off Oxford Circus. ''Of course, this is mostly redundant now,'' Colin said. ''Has been ever since you were so kind as to call us up and ask us to help you in the matter of a murder." And then he threw more snapshots on the table—these of the house in Neuilly, of Libor on the floor, Libor being buried somewhere. "And we have the gun itself that you left us."

"Of course."

"And," Gerry said, "should you cause us any difficulty, I regret to say that it would also force us to reveal the rather substantial part that your dear friends Mr. and Mrs. Harvey played in the demise of this gentleman." He tapped a photo of Libor.

Ronnie took a swallow. "You boys sure got me six ways to Sunday. But don't worry. I'm no hero. It's not my money, and I want Felicity safe. I'll do whatever you want."

"Good," Gerry said. "And if you do—as we were sure you would do—if so, all these photographs, and the negatives, everything will be returned to you as surely as Miss Tantamount will be returned to Mr. Fable. You needn't have to worry about any continuing blackmail. I'm not keen on that endeavor under any circumstances, and from a strictly business point of view, we would never risk any continued affiliation with you. It could too easily jeopardize our freedom. And after what we take with us in this venture, it would be pound wise and penny foolish indeed to try to squeeze a few bob out of a—"

"Ink-stained wretch," Ronnie suggested.

"Yes, something like that."

"Okay, so what are you asking for Felicity?"

"Ah, always the journalist. But, fair enough, since you will be the one transporting the demands to Fable, tomorrow, earliest."

"Tomorrow?"

"Tomorrow morning," Colin said. "And we're going to take you to France before that. We want you to see Felicity, see that she's well, and confirm that to Fable. And, frankly, we think it will be most reassuring for her to see you and know that her dear old friend is handling negotiations."

"You are the very soul of thoughtfulness," Ronnie said. "Also: could you give me some more ice?"

"Of course," Colin said, and he took the glass.

"Now, the ransom," Gerry went on. "You will be advising Mr. Fable, the following: that we want one million dollars in American cash, one million pounds in British cash, plus the diamond choker that she just won in Paris, and the other Grand Slam jewelry: diadem, bracelet, and watch. That's a total of somewhat in excess of four million dollars, perhaps four and a half."

"Not as much as I might have imagined you'd demand," Ronnie said.

"Quite so. But they'll have no excuses. Fable can easily lay his hands on that amount in a business day. If he was obliged to sell real estate, liquidate bonds, what have you, the matter could grow protracted, tempers flare. You're to remind him, as well, that the jewelry is all insured. He'll get some settlement there. This is every bit a ransom he can live with, and I will be disappointed if he doesn't respond favorably and quickly."

Colin brought Ronnie's drink back, with another ice cube in it. "Keep in mind, too," he said, "that there's a special urgency to get Felicity back now, for the Wimbledon final."

"Quite so," Gerry said. "That works in our favor too. There's really not a reason in the world why, at this very time tomorrow evening, we won't have our four or five million dollars in cash and jewels and be safely on our way, and you will be on the telephone, calling to say that all is well and that it's time to pop across the Channel with a little plane, to fetch Felicity. Why, she should be going for her sixth straight Wimbledon and her two hundredth straight match on Saturday at two o'clock, right on schedule."

"You can't seriously expect her to come out of a kidnapping and go directly to Centre Court."

"Oh, perhaps the club will grant her a special dispensation to play Sunday, after the men's final, or perhaps Monday, as a preliminary to her vows. But quite frankly, Ronnie, let's face it, the way she played today, she could return from this little adventure of ours at half-one Saturday, and be able to win with ease at the appointed hour."

♎

They got in the car and drove off, Ronnie in the back with Gerry, Colin driving. After a mile or so, when they came to a vacant area, Gerry took out a blindfold and put it on Ronnie, tied his hands behind his back, and obliged him to lie down on the floor. "I assume you would prefer this to the boot."

"Please, yes. I'm very claustrophobic."

"All right, then. Stay flat on the floor."

"I promise I will."

Gerry said, "Throughout the balance of our association, Ronnie, keep in mind that while all of us in this enterprise truly abhor violence, we cannot and will not let that squeamishness get in our way. It is absolutely necessary to maintain the mission. And also, don't delude yourself. You are not indispensable. Not unlike the CIA or anyone else, we have contingency plans. If you choose to be difficult, to be brave, to be foolish, we—"

"Don't worry," Ronnie said, and he lay peacefully, listening to the car radio, every station of which had little news except that of Felicity—and none of news, really, since Ronnie was really the only journalist in the world who did know what was going on, and he was tied up and blindfolded, compromised in every way.

"Hey, by the way," Ronnie said after a while, "can I ask you guys a question about something else?"

"Certainly."

"Who won the other semifinal?"

"Oh, it was a bloody shame you had to miss that," Gerry said. "I was watching it on the telly just before Colin brought you round. The little Bulgar won six to three in the third. Down three-two, and ran off four games in a row. Good show it was."

"Thanks," Ronnie said, and pretty soon he was lulled into drowsiness, as the car began to pick up speed, as if it had entered a major motorway, which it had. It buzzed along that way for another half-hour or so.

At last the car slowed and he could feel it turning off, and soon Gerry piped up again: "I'm sorry, it's going to be a bit bumpy for a time now, but we're almost there." It was, to be precise, about another fifteen minutes, half-past eight by the radio, when the car bumped to a halt.

The door opened and a pleasant voice said, "Hello there, Ronnie."

"You remember Rudy from Punta, don't you?" Colin asked. "He'll be your pilot now."

He helped Ronnie up off the floor and out onto the ground. Gerry came back over then, clapped Ronnie on the shoulder, said it had been nice to meet him, but he would be staying back in England to "handle things on this end." He drove off, while Colin and Rudy helped Ronnie into his seat on the plane and buckled him in. As soon as Rudy turned the engine over, Ronnie realized it was a propeller job, and when Rudy got the little thing up, it tossed along roughly in a warm summer's wind until he finally got enough altitude to find a bit of smooth space.

Still, it was too noisy for conversation, and no one talked for the next hour or so until Ronnie heard Rudy speaking in French, asking (the best he could make out) for landing instructions. Soon enough, then, Rudy swept down with the little plane, and it wasn't long after that before Ronnie felt it jostling along a runway of sorts.

The door opened and Colin said: "Just stay there, Ronnie. I'm getting the car. Rudy will stay with you." In another couple minutes Ronnie heard the automobile drive up; Rudy unbuckled his belt and helped him down the steps and into the back seat. "Same rules on this side of the Channel," Colin said. "Lie down flat and not a bloody peep out of you."

This car seemed a bit smaller, but Ronnie was able to scrunch down on the floor again for what turned out to be a short ride, first over some especially bumpy road, then down a paved street—going faster; he could hear other cars passing—and then, after a few miles of that, the car slowed and turned onto another, less improved roadway that Ronnie imagined might be a driveway. It was. "We're here," Colin said at the wheel, and he brought the car to a halt and helped Ronnie out and up some steps.

He heard a door open. "Ronnie!" chirped a friendly new voice.

"You remember John," Colin said, and since Ronnie still had his blindfold on, Colin guided the right hand out for him, and John clasped it and they both agreed how nice it was to see one another again, how it had been too long indeed since Punta.

"How's everything proceeding?" John asked Colin then.

"Spot on. Of course, you always forget some little thing. I told the limousine driver, Harold, that we'd call up his wife and let her know where he was tied up . . . just in case he wasn't able to work his way free. And wouldn't you know: I completely forgot that till now."

"It's always something slips your mind," John said.

John took Ronnie's arm then, escorted him into the house and down a hallway, where he opened a door. "Coming down, Cynthia," he called out.

"Righto. Come along," a pleasant woman's voice replied.

At the bottom of the stairs, in what Ronnie assumed to be the basement, John steered him to the left, around another corner. Then, at last, after hours, for the first time since Merton, Ronnie's blindfold was removed. He rubbed his eyes, blinking in the dim light. There was nothing to see but bare stone walls, exposed pipes, old crates, and boxes. Immediately in front of him there was a door. Cynthia rapped on it and called politely, "Open up, please."

After a moment the door pulled back, and there before Ronnie stood Felicity. She was still wearing the same jeans and blouse in which she had left Wimbledon several hours ago.

He blinked at the sight of her, but Felicity could only hold her mouth open. "Oh my God, Ronnie," she cried at last. "They brought me you." And then Felicity fell, sobbing happily, into his arms.

❧

"As you can see, she's quite well," Colin said. "And the accommodations . . ." He swung his arm about the room like a real-estate agent. "Not plush, but certainly not disagreeable—not for a day or two." The windows at the top of the room, peeking out at ground level, had been blacked out, but there were two lamps, a full bed, an easy chair, a table, and a private bathroom, as well.

"Are you all right, Felice?" Ronnie asked.

"Shaken, scared, but otherwise quite fine," she said,

stepping back from him but carefully keeping hold of one hand. "They haven't mistreated me in any way. They've been quite gentle, really."

Colin and Cynthia beamed as if they'd just received additional stars from Michelin. "I'll leave you alone now," he said. "Fill her in on how things are going, reassure her. When you're ready to leave, Ronnie, just rap on the door. We have a room for you down the hall."

Felicity stepped forward to Ronnie's side. "Oh no you're not. I'm not letting him out of my sight."

Colin shrugged. "As you wish. But you'll need your rest, Ronnie. It's almost ten now, and we're flying you back to England at four o'clock. We want you back in London by six, so you can contact Mr. Fable first thing in the morning and assure him that Miss Tantamount is well, so that then we can get on with this."

Ronnie nodded to the chair. "Okay, I can get forty winks there."

Colin gave them a little bow as he and Cynthia left the room, closing and locking the door behind.

Immediately Felicity called his name and fell into his arms again. He'd never seen her anything like this before, so scared and vulnerable—and now so happily relieved, too. He could imagine that she had even begun to cry, for she took an arm from around him and raised it to her cheek.

"Do you want a handkerchief?"

"No, no, it's all right. I just want you to hold me. Oh, I can't believe it's you, Ronnie. They told me someone was coming that I knew, but they didn't say who."

"It'll be okay, I promise. It's a long story, but I kinda know these guys."

"You *know* them?"

"Well, I do and I don't. I mean, I don't know who they are. We met in another context."

"Oh."

"And the point is, they're as nice as you'd ever want kidnappers to be. I mean: top of the line. Even their demands aren't unreasonable. Really, Dale could get up the ransom and have you out of here in a day, two at the most."

"Just tell him to pay it, whatever it is."

"Don't worry."

Then Felicity drew back, but still clinging to his hand. "Oh, Ronnie, I just want to look at you. I just can't believe you're the one here."

"Any port in a storm, eh?"

"Oh no, you damn fool, you. You. *You*." And as Felicity stepped back toward him, Ronnie could see that her lips were as moist as her eyes, and both had him in mind. "Kiss me please, Ronnie."

"Gee, I don't know, Felice." He backed away a little. An honorable man doesn't take advantage of a woman under the influence. Or one being held captive.

"You can't imagine, Ronnie. I was so scared. They had me in this plane, and then blindfolded, and it was so horribly frightening . . . and all I could think about was you. Not Dale. Not Wimbledon. But you."

"Me?"

"You bloody nincompoop. Haven't you known how much I've loved you? Always and always."

"Well, no, I—"

"Why couldn't you have just never let me go? Rushed me off my feet?"

"God, Felice, didn't I try enough?"

"No, you didn't, damn you. You kept *letting* me say no. You weren't supposed to let me say no. So each time, then, you'd just go on and get your quote from me, get your bloody story—take your *no* and move on to some other place and some other woman. Dammit, Ronnie, you should have known. I'm number-one in the world. Even if I loved you, I couldn't just let you have me. I'm number-one, darling. You had to win me. You had to beat me."

"How the hell was I supposed to know that?"

Felicity shook a finger at him. "Dale bloody well knew it."

"Well, I didn't. I simply loved you."

She came closer again. "And I loved you. And I thought surely I could back away from you, and when that didn't work, I thought I could escape from you with someone else, and I almost did it, too. And then this happened, and it took me being scared out of my wits to make me realize that I can't love anyone but you. So, Ronnie, kiss me. You must kiss me, darling."

And when he still paused in confusion, if only for another moment, Felicity took command, and she fell upon him, her arms around his neck, her mouth open and searching and full upon his.

There was such incredible fire in her. All the years Ronnie had waited for this, dreamed of this, how did he know she had been the same, and now all the furies of that frustration were released, and with one real kiss, she was beyond herself—in the zone, the way she played. In the bloody zone. She grabbed at her own clothes, twisting and pulling them off, then her underclothes in the same way, and suddenly, there she stood before him, all the glory he had ever envisioned, so that for a moment, in the half-light, he could only stare and gulp at the majesty before him, and think—if you can believe this—of cherry-vanilla ice cream (which had always been one of his favorites), for her light skin was flushed with the red bits; there was a ribbon of cherry that was her hair, tumbling down; her lips; the roseate of her nipples; the bud of her pubic hair—as magnificent a sundae as ever Ronnie had imagined. "Hurry now," she whispered.

He kicked off his shoes and tugged at his own clothes, but even before he had them off, Felicity was back upon him, hugging and kissing. "Don't worry, love. I don't care if it's right; I don't even care if it's good or sweet. We have a lifetime to gain all that. I only want it done . . . at last." And with that she held him tighter, and pulled him back with her until they reached the edge of the bed, and they fell back upon it, he on top of her, she never waiting, grabbing him and steering him inside her, crying now, laughing even, saying his name over and over, "Ronnie" and "Ratajczak" even, and "Ronnie Ratajczak," all of it, again and again, as they began to move together, rolling, tossing, thundering, waiting for nothing, saving nothing, holding nothing, not so much loving as celebrating the moment that at last they were one. And all Ronnie could think was that here, finally, incredibly he was making love to Felicity Tantamount, the most desirable, beautiful, magnificent woman there had ever been in all the world, the woman who had driven him mad for years, he was, at last, at this very moment, making love to her, and all he could think about was Lia D'Antonini. He called her name—"Oh, Felicity!"—and saw her face that he kissed, but when he fell back across the bed, it was mad, it was insane, it was Lia, he fantasized, who was the one drawing her hand across his brow, kissing him, and whispering that she loved him and always would.

℞

Ronnie awoke, Felicity snuggled in his arms, with Cynthia shaking his shoulder. "Come along with you, Ronnie," she said. "It's already half-three and John wants wheels-off at four sharp."

She left; he climbed over Felicity and out of bed and got dressed in the dark. Then he came back to the bed to say good-bye, but even before he reached Felicity, she grabbed him and drew him down to her and kissed him with all her might. "I must go," Ronnie finally said.

"All right, my wonderful darling."

"Don't worry, Felice. I'll see you very soon. Maybe even tonight. Tomorrow at the latest."

"And always after that," Felicity said, and she slipped off the little bracelet Ronnie had given her years ago in Hong Kong, and pressed it on him; then she lay back in bed and touched the place where he had just been.

Outside her room, John blindfolded Ronnie and took him upstairs, where Cynthia had toast and coffee waiting. "I'm afraid we won't have a stewardess to serve breakfast on this flight," she said. And then they were off, John and Colin taking him to the plane, Ronnie on the floor, retracing last night's trip.

"Well," Colin said as he strapped him into his seat, "aren't we the fellow?" Ronnie could almost feel the wink. "Got the bride practically on the way to the altar."

"I would hope that you would be discreet about that, Colin."

"Indeed, Ronnie. Just because we're involved in a kidnapping doesn't mean we also aren't ladies and gentlemen, as well. Rest assured, so long as Mr. Fable comes through with the ransom, he'll never have to read in the papers that he was cuckolded after the banns were posted."

The plane climbed quickly and rode smoothly in the air, still before dawn, before the sun came up to warm the currents and stir them. When they landed, Ronnie was moved back onto the floor of the first car, and again Rudy drove him off, first over the bumpy road, then over the smoother pavement, and then again picking up speed on what Ronnie took to be a highway. It was just before six, as he heard on the BBC, when Colin told him he could rise off the floor and take off his blindfold. "Where are we?"

"Back in London. On Cromwell Road, actually. Now, listen to me. We're going to drop you off in just a minute. You understand, you're to call Fable straightaway with our proposal."

"Yeah, I know. A million in pounds, a million in dollars, and the Grand Slam jewelry."

"Exactly. Then be in the bar at the Ritz at eleven this morning, sharp. If you don't hear from us then, come back at six."

"I got it."

"Fine," said Colin. "Let's get this business done, and done expeditiously and correctly, so that Felicity can get back to the Championships." And at that he pulled the car over to the curb and motioned Ronnie to get out. He found himself at Alexandra Gate, at the entrance to Hyde Park.

Ronnie watched the car drive swiftly off, and then he hurried across the street to the closest telephone booth and began to dial for Fable at Felicity's house on Paultons Square. He could be there in five minutes. Ronnie dialed the exchange: three-five-two. Then he paused. He turned the next number, a seven, but when he got to the next digit, a two, he stopped. *You aren't supposed to let me say no.* He dialed the two, but then he stopped again. *You had to win me, Ronnie. You had to beat me.* This time he replaced the receiver, and for a moment stood outside the booth and thought. When he stepped back in, he reached for the phone book, found the number for Claridge's, dropped in the ten P, and, instead of Felicity's house, he dialed that instead. "Miss Lia D'Antonini's room, please," he said to the operator.

Of course, he had woken her, and Lia issued a groggy hello.

"It's me, Ronnie. I must see you right away."

"What time is it? Are you mad?"

"It's six o'clock, and I'm not. And don't hang up!" He screamed that last part.

"Oh? Why not?" (But she didn't.) "This is not at all the behavior I expected of you, Ronnie. How plain did I have to be? We must never talk to each other again."

"Yes. But this is business I'm calling about. Strictly business."

"How's that?" Lia asked. It was a different tone.

"I know where Felicity is."

There was a long pause as Lia digested this information. She was awake now. "You do?"

"I've just come from her."

"Well, I must say, that's all very interesting, but what does it have to do with the price of chickens?"

"It has to do with tennis dresses, and I'll tell you everything if you'll meet me. Right now, I'm at Alexandra Gate. I'm going to try to get a cab. If not, I'm going to walk it. In half an hour, six-thirty or so, you meet me at Berkeley Square. No one will see us. All right?"

"I don't know."

"I know how to get Felicity to dress for Grazia. You have no other chance. Be there." And he hung up the phone without waiting for her reply.

He found a cab after walking to Hyde Park Corner, and it was still well before six-thirty when he arrived at Berkeley Square. It was a gray London morning, even a bit drizzly, and for a moment Ronnie even forgot all that was going on and wondered whether it would clear up enough so they could get in the men's semis this afternoon. McEnroe had Annacone in the first match, and then Becker was up against Lendl.

He paced then. By six-thirty he stopped pretending and moved toward the northwest corner of the little park, for Claridge's was only a couple blocks in that direction, down Davies Sreet. He told himself, okay, he'd give Lia some grace, until a quarter to seven. At a quarter to seven, he told himself he'd give her until ten of. A woman has to dress, after all. At ten of, he told himself he'd give her until seven sharp. But that was all. Except possibly five after. But that would absolutely be the limit. That, or a quarter past seven.

Luckily, it never came to that. Just then, at six-fifty, he heard the call. "Bula" is what it sounded like, softly. It came from behind him. He turned around, and there came Lia, cutting across the square from the far side. Like a beautiful ship, she emerged through the morning mist, wearing a London Fog, in a London fog, and looking, for all the world, like a spy. "I had almost given up," Ronnie said.

"Well, you needn't have. I've been here for twenty minutes."

"Where?"

"Silly. You really didn't expect me to come strolling down Davies Street like we were off to tea, did you? Really, Ronnie, I came around and tried to see as best I could if anyone was watching."

"Are they?"

"Not that I can tell. But let's be quick."

He steered her over to a bench, wiped off the dew and the drizzle with his handkerchief and a newspaper from the trash bin there, and sat down. "Look, Lia, it's a long story, and someday maybe I'll tell you all of it, but the end of it is that I've ended up as the go-between with Felicity's kidnappers."

"My, that's sort of a cottage industry of yours, isn't it?"

"Real funny. As soon as I leave you I'm going to contact Fable with their price."

"And she's safe? You saw her?"

"Oh yes. They wanted me to see the merchandise. They kept me blindfolded until I got to where Felicity was held. But I'm pretty certain I know where that is. And . . . Lia, we can get her out of there."

Lia shook her head. "Wait a minute, Ronnie. Back up. Where is she?"

"All right. They *want* me to believe she's hidden across the Channel, in France somewhere, but I'm damn certain it's really not far from London. Down in Hampshire, probably."

"Oh? Why?"

"Okay, listen. They pick me up at Wimbledon, blindfold me, we drive along, and pretty soon we're on a highway. Now, we've got to be driving *away* from London, not toward it, and so I figure it's the M3. We're going south on the M3. All right, after a half-hour or so, we turn off the highway—"

"Off the M3?"

"I think, yes. And in a little while we're at an airstrip. If that. Just a field, really. It's a tiny prop plane that can take off from anything. And it's got to be the middle of nowhere, because they can't have anyone see them with

Felicity, and they can't have anyone see them leading a blindfolded man.''

''Brilliant. It's not BA 10 out of Heathrow.''

''All right, Italian Ice, just listen to me. So we take off. And it was very bumpy last night. And, ostensibly, we're going to France. Now, I'm not an international pilot, Lia, but I do know damn well that if you fly into another country, there's only two ways you can do it. Number one, obviously, you identify yourself—and you can do that in English, that's the international pilots' language—or, number two, you can play games and stay down low, below the radar. Well, we didn't do either. That plane could have easily gone across the Channel at fifty or a hundred feet, under the French radar, but it didn't.''

''How do you know?''

''Because it never got bumpy again until we came back down and landed. Instead, Rudy, the pilot, went through this charade of requesting landing instructions in French—and you should hear his French—as if we were an AF or a TW coming into Charles de Gaulle from JFK.''

''All right,'' Lia said. ''So where did he land?''

''On a field every bit as bumpy as the one we took off from. There was obviously no tower there, no radio contact. In fact, I'm sure it was the same field.''

''You mean you think they took off from Hampshire, flew around, and then just came back down to the same field?''

''Exactly. But the clincher was, when we landed they put me in the back seat of another car again, down on the floor, still blindfolded, and I could tell it was a different car, but it was still a right-hand drive. I could hear the driver on the right side.''

''Ronnie, it's not impossible that these guys took one of their British cars to France sometime.''

''No. But I could hear the traffic. The traffic passing me was clearly on the left-hand side of the road.''

Lia patted him on the knee. ''All right. Not bad. You might yet make a spy. But why are you telling me this? Why aren't you telling Scotland Yard?''

''Oh, two little reasons, I suppose. First, I never spent the most wonderful week of my life in Fiji with Scotland Yard.'' Lia actually blushed at that and turned her head away. "And second, you happen to also be the only person I know, the only independent citizen of the world of my acquaintance, who has, at her command, a bunch of Communist thugs who could pull this off." She frowned—but more because she was expected to. "All right, 'revolutionary heroes.' You see, it would be easy with your 'people's insurgents.' All you have to do is watch me get in the car when they pick me up with the ransom. You have your guys posted down the M3. Radio ahead, they follow the car, and when it gets near the hideout where Felicity is, you make a move on them."

"It sounds so easy."

"It would be. Believe me. There's only five of them—and one of them, excuse me, is just a woman. These guys are slick, Lia, but they're not murderers. That's not their field. You'd really like them, I think. In fact, I'd prefer that you let them get away if you could—you know, accidentally on purpose. But anyway, you've got the pros. It'd be a piece of cake for you. Really."

"Fine, Ronnie. But why? Why would I do this?" She spoke a bit softer now. This gray Friday was dawning and the first few people were beginning to walk through the square on their way to work.

"Well, Lia, it's very simple. You want to dress Felicity, don't you?"

"Of course. But I know there's no chance now. Fable has come back from America with this extraordinary contract. I understand it's with Coca-Cola. It's their centennial, and she'll represent their new formula with an extraordinary new dress, the world over. They're paying more money than we can even begin to offer."

Ronnie nodded. So it was Coke. Fable never missed a trick. "That may be true," he said, "but take my word for it, the dress Felicity loves is yours. You won, Lia. And if you saved her from the kidnappers, saved her ransom, saved her jewels—and if you took that outfit down to Hampshire, I guarantee you she'd put it on, and when Felicity came back to London, every photographer in the world, every television camera would be there, and Felicity Tantamount would be wearing your outfit, her outfit, her new original Grazia. Even Fable would be for it. How can you get any better exposure than with a kidnapping? And after that she couldn't sign a contract with anyone else.''

Lia only stared at him, but with time her expression softened into a smile. "You know, Ronnie, you're absolutely brilliant.'' He beamed uncontrollably. "So may I be cynical?'' she asked.

"You never requested my permission for that before.''

"Might it also be true that if *we* save Felicity, if *we* bring her back, *you* will be on her arm, *you* will be the conquering hero—and maybe, just maybe that would be enough for dear Felicity to change her mind one more time, to call off her wedding with Dale, and to march off into the sunset with you?''

"Well, yes, I imagine that's possible,'' Ronnie said—and he had to admit to himself that Felicity would not be a bad consolation prize. For goodness' sake, he could swallow hard and learn to live with the most beautiful woman in the world—especially since Lia would be off spying for the KGB somewhere and wouldn't any longer be around to distract him. "But what's that to you? You've told me I'm never to see you again anyhow. And with Felicity in that dress, what does it matter to you who's on her arm?''

"Oh yes, of course that would be true,'' Lia said.

"Of course. What do you care? With Felicity coming back from her kidnapping in a Grazia, Grazia will instantly become the most valuable, the best-known sports-clothes company in all the world. And you, Lia, you'll personally make so much money for the cause that you'll single-handedly be able to finance the KGB. My God, they'll set aside tomb space for you in the Kremlin wall.''

He was surprised. She laughed at that. Well, smiled. And then again, maybe he wasn't surprised, for Ronnie had learned by now that, for a dyed-in-the-wool Communist, some of the most traditional capitalistic things sure could light Lia up. Did Marx ever have anything to say about purple?

"You're wicked,'' Lia said.

"Yes, but I'm dead right.''

"Uh-huh, you probably are.''

"Well then, let's do it.'' And Ronnie reached out to take her hand—albeit not so much for affection as for emphasis.

Instead, however, Lia turned away from him. Then she stood up and walked away. "When do the nightingales sing here?" she asked at last. "When do the nightingales sing in Berkeley Square? That's what the song says, but I've never even seen any."

"I don't know. Maybe they work odd hours—nights and weekends. I'm not sure if there's any bluebirds over the white cliffs of Dover, either. But if you're in love you can hear nightingales anywhere, I imagine. Don't change the subject."

"All right," Lia said, and she came back to where he sat, and sat right next to him and took his hands in hers. "All right, I haven't been fair to you."

"Oh hell, I know that," Ronnie said.

"No, not really. There've been only two men in my life, Ronnie, and"—she gulped for some air—"and one was killed for me and the other almost was."

"What does that mean exactly?"

"Paolo wasn't just killed in a . . . uh, caper. We were in it together, and he got away when the police came, but I was trapped, so he came back for me, he had no chance, and that's when he was shot. And I got away. He gave his life for me."

"I'm sorry."

"Why? You were no different in Singapore. That man was trying to kill me, and instead you jumped at him to save me, and—"

"Lia, I didn't know he was trying to kill you then."

"It doesn't matter. He would have if you hadn't gone at him. You did. I didn't. And you were almost killed. And after that, I said, no, no, Lia, never again. I'm sorry, Ronnie, I don't care how little you think of this risk, but I will never again do anything that might end up hurting the man I love."

Ronnie said: "You do love me, Lia. I love you too."

"Yes, I thought you probably did. I wasn't sure, but I thought so. I was only *sure* that you didn't love Felicity."

Ronnie shook his head in wonder at that. "You knew?"

"Oh, of course. It's just that she's the most beautiful woman in the world, and bright and charming and the greatest tennis player in history. And rich, too. No wonder you always thought you heard nightingales when you were with her.''

"Oh," Ronnie said.

"Besides, she's always been madly in love with you."

"You knew that too? Why didn't you tell me?"

"You think I'm crazy? You think I'm going to tell you that the most desirable woman in the world loves you . . . when I love you too?" Ronnie reached for her then, to hug her and kiss her, but suddenly she had jumped up again and was walking away.

"Hey," he said.

Lia just stopped to rub her chin. "You know," she said, "maybe there's more than one way to skin a dog."

CENTRE COURT

Two days later, that Sunday afternoon, at a quarter past five, Rina Rodanya Harvey and Felicity Tantamount came onto Centre Court, carrying their huge floral bouquets with their rackets. McEnroe had required only the minimum of three sets to beat Becker, which was just as well, for, as the champion himself observed afterward, it was apparent, even to him, that nobody cared much about the gentlemen's final this year, and it would be best for all just to get it out of the way. After Felicity had been returned, she had met with Buzzer Hadingham and they had agreed that it would be all right to play the ladies' final on Sunday, right after the men's.

The crowd was on its feet even before the two women came through the gates, under Kipling's inscription: "If you can meet with triumph and disaster and treat those two impostors just the same." And then there was a gigantic roar when Rina and Felicity appeared, and yet another gasp, swelling upon the roar, for, sure enough, there was Felicity wearing that Grazia dress she had been seen in the world over when she had come back to London from the kidnapping. Without even discussing the matter, the Committee of the All-England Club had unanimously accepted Felicity's request that the rules be waived on this one occasion so that a player would be allowed to appear on the hallowed greensward of Centre Court in colored attire. It seemed a small enough compensation for what Felicity had been forced to endure these past few days.

Naturally, in the spirit of fair play, Rina had been given the same option, but she chose instead to play in her favorite all-white dress. "It is," she declared, "the month of my wedding, and white is always for weddings and Wimbledon."

If only Rina had known how much that would stab Felicity when she read it in the *Sunday Times*.

The two finalists marched toward the waiting phalanx of photographers gathered at the umpire's chair. "All right," Felicity whispered. "Now. Stop." She and Rina came to a halt together. "Turn around, Rina." They did. "Now." They curtsied in perfect tandem to the Royal Box. Even Felicity, who had done this so many times, was overcome. Not only was the Duchess of Kent, the patroness, there, but so were Lady Di and Prince Charles, so were Princess Margaret and Prince Andrew, so was Princess Anne, and so were the Duke of Edinburgh, the Queen Mum, and Queen Elizabeth herself. They wanted to see Felicity—and her new dress—as much as any damn fool commoner. Never had so much royalty been assembled at one sporting event. No one could even recall Prince Charles or Princess Anne ever having attended a tennis match, and the last time that the queen—who much preferred the antics of thoroughbred horses to tennis players—had graced Centre Court was in 1977, for the Centenary final, when Virginia Wade won.

The two women turned back toward the photographers then. "My God," Felicity whispered to Rina. "The lot of them up there. They look like a whole bloody picture postcard." It might have been the first time she had smiled all day.

At the net, next, the photographers took a million pictures, all of them the same, until the umpire signaled that it was time to begin practice, and Felicity and Rina moved away from the cameras to the middle of the court. Rina glanced up into the Friends' Box, in the southeast corner of the stadium, where associates and loved ones of those playing on

Centre Court are seated. The guests of McEnroe and Becker
had vacated their seats, and now, on the bottom row of the
two, Young Zack Harvey sat there proudly, blowing a kiss
down to his bride. Ludmilla was there too, and so was Rina's
mother, who had just flown in from Bulgaria.

On the back row sat the Reverend Thomas Tantamount,
vicar, St. Andrews of the Stream, Staunton-on-Swale, and
Mrs. Tantamount; and with them sat Manda and her children. Dale Fable had given her his passes and urged her to
fill up the seats.

As for Fable, right at this moment he was handing his
boarding pass to the attendant and getting on the afternoon
Concorde to New York. Felicity had called off the wedding
the night before, because she told Fable that she loved
another man, she loved Ronnie Ratajczak and couldn't
marry him on Monday at Centre Court. And then she had
called Ronnie.

"Felicity. Felicity." She heard her name. She was in a
daze, looking up at the Friends' Box. But it was only Rina
calling her, from just across the net.

"Yes, I'm sorry," Felicity said.

"I just wanted to say—"

"Yes, Rina?"

"Only that, whatever happens, this is a real honor for
me, here, playing you. . . ." Felicity smiled sweetly down
at her, and Rina paused for an instant more, wondering
whether she should say more. Finally she decided she
would. "Felicity, I know I can beat you now. I am the one
who can."

"Yes, I know you can too," Felicity said. "I don't think
you will, but I know you can, and that'll make it better for
us all. I need something to divert me."

And then they moved away from one another, went to the
baselines, and began to hit up before what could be Felicity's
two hundredth straight victory, her sixth straight Wimbledon,
and her twenty-first Grand Slam tournament triumph—and
wearing a new design that not only made her more beautiful
than ever before but also covered her broken heart.

WASHINGTON

At that moment, as Felicity moved up to the net to practice her volleys, it was going on toward twelve-thirty in Washington, a typically dreadful, steamy July morning of the sort that used literally to drive Congress away—before air conditioning was invented and dialectic democracy was thus assured for a full twelvemonth every year. Lia was standing on the balcony of her room on the fourth floor of the Hays-Adams Hotel, looking across Lafayette Park toward the White House, and the corresponding balcony there. Her finger twitched, naturally. How easy it would be, she thought, to shoot and kill a president if ever he stood out there—but just as she began to file this observation away, Lia remembered that she had to stop thinking like this. It was, after all these years, only reflex; it wasn't even ill-intentioned any longer. Still, she must cut it out.

Lia came back into the room, closing the doors, cutting out the heat. She glanced over at the big television set and saw Rina serve the first point of the match, saw Felicity move in to clip a backhand crosscourt, saw her rush to the net then and knock off a forehand volley that thundered onto the ground and slid away; love–15. But, really, Lia didn't notice the action. She was only looking at her design, the Grazia design—or rather, as it was already known everywhere in the world (choose one): The Outfit or *the* outfit.

There was a knock on the door. It was expected. It was the messenger that had been sent. "Give him this," Ronnie said, and he held up a manila envelope addressed to George Solomon, the sports editor of the *Washington Post*, at his home in Potomac, Maryland. Ronnie had been paid a goodly sum, plus a couple of Clipper Class chairs, to fly over and provide the *Post* with a first-person insider's account of the kidnapping of the century.

Lia handed the envelope to the messenger and then turned back to Ronnie. He was still banging away at the typewriter. "All right, darling, you got the story in. Can't you leave this alone and pay attention to me and the match?"

"No, no. I'm almost finished, and then I want you to read it over. Then we can be done with it, forever."

"Are you really sure you want to write all this?" Lia said, picking up the sheets he had finished.

"It's important that I get it all done now while it's still absolutely fresh in my mind."

"But why do you want to write it all?"

"Oh, I'm not sure I really know. For myself. For us. For history. For posterity. For our grandchildren. For after the statute of limitations runs out."

"All right, I'll start reading it. Just to see if a journalist can actually get something right."

"And I'll finish the rest of it," Ronnie said, going back to the final page. The sound was off on the TV set, but when he glanced up, the graphics on the screen indicated that Felicity had won the first game. Up a break already.

Lia poured the last of the coffee from the pot on their breakfast tray and began to read Ronnie's account:

> It was my idea, of course, that if Felicity would only wear that Grazia design back from the kidnapping, it would be the most successful marketing device of all time. But it was Lia who, to our benefit, took that a step further. We were standing in Berkeley Square when

she said: "Maybe there's more than one way to skin a dog."

I don't know why I even bother to correct Lia's idioms anymore, but I went through the motions and said: "Cat. You skin a cat."

She just glared back at me and said: "Come along, let's go."

"Where?" I asked.

"My room. Back at Claridge's."

"But is it safe?"

"We'll take a chance. This is too good an idea."

And so we went back there, and this is what Lia told me: "The kidnappers are fools. They may be operating efficiently, in a modern way, but they're still out of touch. Sure, Felicity has money and jewels and Fable has money, but they're just scratching the surface with them."

"What do you mean?" I asked.

"Just think, Ronnie. This woman has endorsement contracts with some of the top companies in the world. There isn't a product she's not involved with. Just look at this." And she handed me a press release from the Fable Organization that had been made up to show all of Felicity's endorsements. Forget the simple basic tennis stuff—the shoes and rackets, socks, gut, wrist bands, the resort in Cozumel—but there were so many other things: an airline, a candy bar, her whole evening-wear line, a hotel chain, ladies' razors, tampons, hair spray, soup, deodorant, underwear, the country of Grenada, and on and on. "Now," Lia said, "if the kidnappers demanded that all of those companies had to pay ransom too, how could any one of them refuse? It would be the most disastrous publicity in the world to have the person who endorses your product, whom you support and identify with, get kidnapped, and you refuse to help. If you refused to pay a ransom for your endorser in her time of need, it would ruin any product. Who would ever believe in that company again? People would say: I'm not going to buy Midnight Murmur Lotion, because Midnight Murmur Lotion was endorsed by Felicity Tantamount, and when she got kidnapped, they wouldn't even help her."

"As a matter of fact," I said, "any company with any intelligence should be able to see that by paying a ransom they're enjoying a certain advantageous advertising."

"That's right," Lia said. "Think of the exposure that every company that pays a ransom will get."

"It'll be sort of an institutional advertising," I said.

"Yeah,"Lia said. "Kind of like: By Appointment to the Queen. Or: By Ransom to Felicity."

Lia put down the sheets Ronnie had typed. "Well, I have to give it to you. So far, you've gotten it right."

"More than right," Ronnie said. "Look at that. Turn the sound on." It was the second crossover, Felicity up 3–love, two breaks, and on the screen there was a crawl of product names, one after another slowly listed, and Bud Collins was saying: "Ladies and gentlemen, we just want to thank the real unsung heroes of this Wimbledon, the companies representing Felicity Tantamount, who so quickly and so nobly helped pay the ransom that made it possible for her to be here today."

"Dammit," Lia said.

"What's that?"

"We forgot NBC."

"You're right. I'll bet we could have squeezed a couple hundred thousand out of them too. And maybe something from the Beeb too."

"But this confirms my original point, darling."

"What's that?"

"That, really, by demanding ransom from these companies we were only taking proper fees for a new form of advertising. I mean, you simply can't beat the exposure."

"It's the right demographics, too," Ronnie said. "The companies that ransomed Felicity are getting favorable mention on all the front pages, on all the national news shows."

"You simply can't schedule that kind of publicity."

"Right. Sure, maybe we were illegal, but we certainly weren't immoral. And look at this." Ronnie had been scanning the *Post* sports section, and he came across a full-page ad for Target Tennis Rackets. It featured a huge picture of Felicity, wearing her new Grazia body suit, of course and with it, these headlines:

WE HELPED PAY A QUEEN'S RANSOM OF $7,000,000!
But now you can play
The Queen's own racket
for only $99.95!!

"I feel almost like I've performed a public service," Ronnie said.

Lia went back to reading the rest of his report:

We decided that $200,000 per endorsing company would be a fair price, going up a bit for some of the larger clients, like Target Rackets and Double Play Shoes, and not charging quite so much for the socks and nail files and posters and the like. I mean, it was important to be fair. But, all told, it came to about three million dollars extra.

Then I called Dale Fable, and I left Claridge's, and we met right away at Felicity's house on Paultons Square. I explained what the kidnappers wanted: the million pounds and the million dollars from him and Felicity, plus all her Grand Slam jewelry, plus the extra three million dollars from the various sponsors. Of course, I hastened to tell Dale that the kidnappers had warned me that all these details must be kept absolutely confidential until after Felicity was returned. I certainly didn't want Colin and the gang to read the figures in the newspapers and discover that I was double-billing.

Actually, too, Dale was most cooperative—especially when he learned that the package was being spread around, that he and Felicity didn't have to pay for it all. Why, after a while I had him agreeing that he and Felice were getting off dirt cheap on their end. And he concurred with me completely that the companies Felicity endorsed would be paying modestly for once-in-a-lifetime advertising. He promised to go right to work on things, and he sure did. There wasn't a company that wasn't delighted to help ransom dear Felicity.

It was about eight-thirty in the morning on Friday when I met with Fable, and by eleven, when Colin had me paged at the Ritz bar and then spoke to me on the phone, I could assure him that the package was coming together just magnificently.

By late that night, the last of the dollars had either arrived from America or had been released from British banks, and, in accord with Colin's instructions, I took all of the cash and jewels into my possession so that I could deliver it immediately whenever I was contacted. Fable was still the only person who knew I was the go-between, and I sure wanted to keep it that way.

I took the bundle back to my flat at Dolphin Square, where Lia was holed up, and we took our three million cash off the top and tucked it away, and then, at four the next morning—Saturday—when we got the word from Colin, I took what was left of the cash, plus all the jewels, plus the Grazia, of course, and off I went to exchange them for Felicity. She was, as I suspected, not the least bit in France, but was, instead, just down the M3 in Hampshire.

Colin and Gerry, John, Rudy, and Cynthia were absolutely thrilled with the professional way I had handled things, and since they were making off with nearly a million apiece, Colin asked me if I wouldn't take a bit of a tip, but I declined. Even if Lia and I hadn't been getting away with three million ourselves, I would have thought that that was pretty tacky.

Felicity, bless her, was ecstatic to be saved, and only too happy to wear her favorite outfit back. The instant she stepped out of the car at Paultons Square and the flashbulbs started going off, the Grazia body suit had become as much a living part of history as Felicity herself.

It was that afternoon, after she was rested, when she told Fable that the wedding was off, because she loved me. She called me then, and I came over. It was very hard for Felice, mostly, I think, because no one had ever turned her down before. I told her that. "It's been a long time since I was beat, either," she said.

"Felice," I said, "please don't say that. I didn't beat you."

"Oh, I know that. But Lia did."

And then she kissed me on the cheek, and she told me to tell Lia that she didn't care how much more Coca-Cola could offer, she was going to sign with her, sign with Grazia. It would be her wedding present to us. That was the last thing Felicity told me.

Lia finished and put the last sheet down. "That's lovely," she said. "But now we better put all this with the money," and she walked over to Ronnie's suitcase, which was sitting across the room on the luggage rack. It was his old IWOOTP suitcase that Doreen had given him, and Lia opened it up and went through the clothes until she found the catch that opened the secret bottom. There, arrayed in rows, were three million dollars. She put Ronnie's written report in with it, and started to zip it up again.

"Wait," Ronnie said. "One more thing goes in there." And he went over to his jacket and pulled out the bracelet he had given Felicity, which she had given him back. He tossed it onto the top of the bills. "Okay, zip it up."

Then he went over to the television and turned up the sound. It was just as Rina rocketed a forehand into the corner, and Ronnie and Lia heard Bud Collins exult: "What a shot! Another blazing beauty from The Bulgarian Bunny—and now she's only down three-two. You know, Dick Enberg, this is beginning to look like a real match now. First Felicity got two breaks, and now Rina will be trying for her second straight break and a three-all battle royal."

"That's right, Bud Collins, maybe we're not going to see the first Wimbledon champion wearing colored clothes, after all." The camera moved in on a closeup of Felicity as she sank into her chair. "We'll be back after this message from one of the companies that helped ransom Felicity Tantamount."

The camera hung on Felicity for another moment. Lia stared at her. "Oh God, Ronnie, she is so absolutely beautiful. I am glad you never slept with her."

Ronnie just watched the commercial for a while. Finally he said: "Well, I wouldn't necessarily say that."

He was lying on the bed now, pretending to concentrate on the commercial. So Lia placed herself in front of the set. "That's not what I understood," she said.

"If I were you," Ronnie said, "I think I'd rather believe that I actually did sleep with Felicity . . . and still chose you."

"You think I should rather believe that?"

"If I were you, I would, yes."

Lia sat down by his feet at the end of the bed to watch the TV and ponder that. Rina immediately went up 30–love on Felicity's serve, taking the net both times when Felicity missed with her first serve and hit a little short with her second. Ronnie chuckled. "What are you laughing at?" Lia asked.

"Oh, I don't know what made me think, but it just occurred to me: all this talk about spies on the tennis tour. And all along, you were the only one. It wasn't Young Zack and it wasn't Libor and it wasn't Doreen and it wasn't Felicity—and it wasn't even me. I didn't know it, but I wasn't even not a spy. You were the only one all along, and now you're gone, and there're no spies left."

Lia glanced back over her shoulder and shook her head. "I'm sorry, darling. You're wrong again."

Ronnie sat up more. "You mean there really is a spy on tour?"

"No. . . . There're two. There're two sides, you know. Just like tennis."

"There are? Two spies?"

"Oh, you're so naive. Of course there are."

"Well—who?"

"Hmmmm."

"That's not fair. Come on, tell me."

Rina broke at fifteen. Ronnie climbed down toward Lia, but she shooed him-away. "Wait, I want to hear this."

"We've got a real match on our hands, Bud Collins," Enberg said. "Felicity hadn't been broken once in the whole tournament, and now, before you can say strawber-

ries and cream, Rina's broken her twice in their first set—
and it's all tied at three.''

Ronnie rubbed Lia's neck. "Come on, who are the spies?"

"Well, if I were you," she said, "I think I'd believe
that despite all you did to help Ludmilla defect, it was all
a setup.''

"Ludmilla is KGB? Little Ludmilla?''

"They've trained her to be a spy since before she could
hit a crosscourt forehand. And now that she's defected, she
has carte blanche to the free world.''

Ronnie clapped the heel of his palm to his head. "But
wait a minute. When she defected the KGB was crawling
all over the hotel to try to get her back.

"You stupido," Lia said . . . Lia smirked . . . Lia chortled. "Of course they made a big fuss. They wanted a lot
of publicity so no one would ever suspect it was a setup.''

Ronnie shook his head. Rina made a perfect backhand
drop shot that caught Felicity flatfooted at the baseline, and
took a 15–love lead. "That's the first time the Defector
Dearest has been ahead in the match, Dick Enberg, and it
comes in the key seventh game,'' Bud Collins said.

"Well, I'll say one thing for the KGB," Ronnie said.
"They sure are good actors. When that guy started running
down Fifty-eighth Street after Manda, that sure didn't look
like any put-on job to me. That guy looked all business.''

"And he was," Lia said blithely. "He was really working then.''

Rina stretched at the net, just reaching Felicity's best
return. The volley found chalky dust on the side line.
Thirty-love.

"What do you mean, he was working then?''

"Because, dummox, as carefully as the KGB had set
everything up for Ludmilla to defect in the media capital
of the world, you threw them a hook—''

"A curve.''

"Yes. Because you brought Manda in. And when that
agent in the hotel cellar realized that it was Manda dressed
up like a maid, that's when he got scared, and he reacted

honestly, like a good KGB boy, and he started chasing her.''

"But I don't understand. Why?"

Rina aced Felicity to 40–love. "You know, it's truly rare when you see Felicity shaken," Bud Collins said. "But those last two points of Rina's—"

"The momentum in this match has very definitely shifted, Bud Collins," Dick Enberg said.

"Think about it, darling," Lia said.

"You don't mean . . . ?" Ronnie actually gaped. "Manda?"

"Sweetheart, Manda has been with the CIA so long that we even gave her a code name years ago. Manda's known from Moscow to Havana to Pyongyang to Prague as the Dahlia.''

"Manda?"

Felicity came back to 40–15 with a scorching service return off Rina's best and hardest.

"Why did you think I was so sure you were CIA? The rumors had been around for years, but when Ludmilla started reporting that you were seeing Manda all the time, we figured you had to be an agent too. You sure didn't usually pick women you couldn't sleep with to be your buddies.

"Oh, I don't know. Maybe I was able to show Manda the light. Maybe she did sleep with me.''

"Oh?"

"Listen, if I were you, I think I'd rather believe that I actually did sleep with another spy and still chose you." Then Ronnie took her by the shoulders. "Hey, will you marry me tomorrow?"

Felicity ran down an absolutely impossible backhand, reaching down and flicking it at the last instant, sending it at a perfect angle, dipping in front of Rina for 40—30. "Wait a second," Lia said. "I've got to see the slo-mo replay on that one." She watched intently. "Tomorrow?" she said then.

"Sure, we can drive up to Elkton, Maryland, and get married.''

"Where's Elkton, Maryland?"

"I don't know. A couple hours from here, I guess."

"Why get married there?"

"I really don't know. But when I was growing up, everybody in the movies was always getting married in Elkton, Maryland. So—"

"Maybe that's where the nightingales sing in America."

Rina hit out after a long rally, so Felicity saved her third straight game point and brought it to forty-all. But Lia and Ronnie didn't see that one because they had started kissing. They stopped for breath only as his hands found the bodice of her nightgown and untied it.

Felicity barely touched a terrific slice serve she never expected. Advantage, Rina Rodanya Harvey.

"Tell me something," Ronnie said. "Do spies ever have babies?"

"No," Lia said.

"They don't?"

"No. Only ex-spies have babies."

"What a shot!" Bud Collins screamed. "There was no way Felicity could possibly get that ball, but she not only got it, she turned it into a winner."

"The momentum seems to be going the other way, Bud Collins."

Lia pulled her nightgown over her head, and as they moved up onto the bed, she cuddled down next to Ronnie, pressing herself to him.

"An incredible match!" Bud Collins said.

"Yes indeed," said Ronnie. He meant himself and Lia, that match. He kissed her delicately, with fury.

"The highest level of play you'll ever see, Dick Enberg. It's simply amazing. Felicity has been kidnapped, and she called her engagement off barely a day before the wedding, and she's still playing the finest tennis of her life—and yet she's having to fight for every point. Deuce again!"

The camera moved in close on Felicity and studied her as the cheers rained down. She just stood there, in all her majesty, her bosom heaving, her stripes undulating, exertion and joy and a glint of glory upon her face. Rina had to wait a long time before the cheers for Felicity Tantamount began to subside. There was tumult. "Quiet, please," said the umpire.

"Yes indeed," said Lia, and she reached around Ronnie for the remote-control clicker and flicked off the television. Ronnie's mouth wandered away from Lia's lips and found its way to one of her lollipop breasts, which he kissed. His hand moved to one of her thighs, softly, rubbing, probing.

"Bula," said one of them.

ABOUT THE AUTHOR

Frank Deford is a senior editor at *Sports Illustrated* who has girdled the world several times covering the international tennis circuit. He co-authored the autobiography of Pam Shriver and currently appears as a TV commentator and in commericials. He lives in Connecticut with his wife and two children.